ROMANCING REMI

A SAN SOLOMAN NOVEL

DENISE WELLS

Copyright © 2021 by Denise Wells

All rights reserved.

No part of this book may be reproduced in any form or by any electronic or mechanical means, including information storage and retrieval systems, without written permission from the author, except for the use of brief quotations in a book review.

❦ Created with Vellum

For my Remi IRL

If you can't handle me at my worst, then you sure as hell don't deserve me at my best.

— MARILYN MONROE

ALSO BY DENISE WELLS

AGENTS AND ASSASSINS TRILOGY

Fearless - Book One, a steamy romantic thriller

Careless - Book Two, a steamy romantic thriller

Ruthless - Book Three, a steamy romantic thriller

SAN SOLOMAN

Keeping Kat, a steamy second-chance firefighter romance

Romancing Remi, a steamy enemies to lovers romance

Loving Lexie, a steamy cowboy enemies to lovers romance

Seducing Sadie, a steamy firefighter romance

Trusting Tenley, a dark second-chance romance

STANDALONES

Summer Shivers, a romantic thriller in the **Summers in Seaside Collection**

Overdrive, a steamy enemies to lovers romance **in KB WORLDS - DRIVEN COLLECTION**

Love Off The Rocks, a romantic comedy short

Pour Decisions, a romantic comedy novella in the **Girl Power Collection**

How to Ruin Your Ex's Wedding, a romantic comedy

I Heart Mason Cartwright, a romantic comedy

Rebel without a Claus, a M/M romance novella

Breaking Dylan, dark coming of age story

ANTHOLOGIES

GIRLS JUST WANNA HAVE FUNDAMENTAL RIGHTS - A Charity Anthology. Pre-order now. Releasing 9/8/22.

SEEDS OF LOVE A Romance Anthology to benefit Ukraine - Don't Break The Chain, a steamy romantic short

CAUGHT UNDER THE MISTLETOE - A Holiday Affair to Remember, a romantic comedy holiday short

STORYBOOK PUB CHRISTMAS WISHES - Mistle Oh-No, a romantic comedy holiday short

STORYBOOK PUB - Breezy Like Sunday Morning, a romantic comedy short

HOT AS F$#K SUMMER ROMANCE ANTHOLOGY - SULTRY SUMMER NIGHTS - Limited Release

LOCKED AND LOVED: An Isolated Romance Collection - Limited Release

SUMMER WITH YOU: Summer Shorts - Limited Release

JUST A LICK - Limited Release

LOVE LETTERS - Limited Release

STOCKING STUFFERS - Limited Release

PRAISE FOR ROMANCING REMI

Laughter, love, hot sex and fun made this story unforgettable and I was sad when it ended.

— GOODREADS

Denise Wells can really pull you in and get you turning those pages, and before you know it, The End!!!!!

— GOODREADS

I couldn't read this book quickly enough. A love story everyone can relate to. It is an engaging page-turner you won't want to put down.

— GOODREADS

INTRODUCTION

I don't gamble unless I know I can win. Simple as that. So, when my besties wagered I couldn't stay in a relationship for a month, I took the bet.

Because, really, how hard can it be? Four weeks is like four dates. I can do anything four times. Right?

But there was a flaw in my strategy. I didn't count on the relationship to be with HIM. The irresistible alpha-male from my past, Chance Bauer. The only man to ever make my insides quiver.

Or for my feelings from so long ago to be the same.

ROMANCING REMI

1

REMI

A drop of sweat falls from his forehead on to my face.

I reach up to wipe it away, trying not to be disgusted.

This isn't working for me.

I need to stop him before it goes too far.

He's going through the motions, all the right motions even. His angle is good, he's moving in and out at a nice pace, and he's throwing in a little bump and grind for good measure and clit pleasure.

Haha – that rhymes.

Focus, Remi.

Maybe if I touch myself.

I reach down but can't seem to wedge my hand between our bodies. He's at such an angle where his pelvis doesn't seem to be leaving mine. Yet still pumping away, I'm sure of it. I reach my hand around to feel. Yep, his ass is moving up and down.

His nicely rounded ass, I should say. I squeeze the hard, taut muscle. He groans in response.

Huh.

How is it that I can notice how great his ass is and still be getting nothing from this?

You know why, Remi. It's because you're a cold shell of a human—

I ignore that little voice in my head. The one that reminds me that I'm incapable of any real feeling or emotion. Just one more thing I can thank my parents for. The lack of any real feelings or love in the Vargas household growing up.

Don't think about that now.

I refocus my attention on the attractive man pumping away on top of me. He's trying hard. It makes me feel bad for wanting to stop him. But he's sweating. And I've got other stuff I could be doing right now.

I look at him, his eyes are closed, and his face has this dreamy quality about it. Like he's in a great headspace. Or, shit, like he's enjoying the sex.

What must that be like?

Get out of your head, Remi.

Stay in the moment.

Except, I haven't been in the moment this entire time. If I've not gotten into it yet, it's not like it's going to get any better.

It should be good though. I mean, we had two face-to-face dates that I enjoyed. And the six months of long-distance sexting and texting was good. Hot, even.

But this...

Is in person, not via text from hundreds of miles away where you can stay detached.

I never should have invited him to a champagne brunch this morning. I don't have the extra time in my schedule to waste a whole morning like this. I could be at work running lab trials like a good little scientist should. Or out with my besties, Kat and Lexie. And now I'll probably get a headache from the cheap champagne at brunch.

Fuck.

"Can you stop?" I ask him, my jaw clenched, as he grunts and thrusts above me. He doesn't seem to hear me, so I give his chest a shove.

"Yeah, baby, give it to me," he says.

"Hey, Alex," I say, tapping him on the shoulder instead. "Stop, this isn't working for me."

He stops and looks at me with his head slightly cocked, a confused look on his face.

"Off," I say gruffly, as I start to sit up, still pushing against him.

He rolls off me, pulling out as he goes, and turns to lay on his back beside me.

"What's the matter?" he asks, his chest rising and falling rapidly and his tone annoyed. He looks at the ceiling, forearm resting on his forehead, as he tries to catch his breath.

"This isn't working for me."

"What does that mean? What's not working for you?" He leans up, cocking his head, and squinting his eyes as he asks his questions.

"The sex isn't working for me. I'm just not feeling it," I say.

"Not feeling it? How can you not feel it? Am I doing something wrong?" He looks down at his dick.

"No. It's just me."

"Are you just not in the mood? Do you want to wait a bit? Maybe change positions? I can go faster. Or slower." His brown eyes wide with hope.

God, I'm an asshole.

"It won't make a difference, Alex."

"Well, how do you know unless we try?" A small smile lights his face. He really is cute. Handsome even. At one point I thought he was hot, but then we settled into a rhythm, got to know one another better. His humanity started to show and, well, I hate that part. When someone starts to let their walls down and you see things like weakness. I hate weakness.

"It's not going to happen. I don't know how to be any clearer. The sex *is not* working for me. I'm not going to get off. I don't see a reason to continue."

"How do you know you're not going to get off?"

Wow. He's so much more persistent than I thought. I need to shut this down. He needs to leave. I want to shower, change my sheets, and get on with my day.

"I just know, okay?"

"Okay," he says drawing out the word. "Maybe I could—" He reaches for me.

"I don't think so," I say, trying to be gentler.

"Okay, that's a little harsh—"

"I'm sorry." I guess he didn't get that I was being gentle. I get out of the bed and walk naked to the bathroom. "I don't mean to be harsh. I just… I think it's best if you leave now. If you'll excuse me, I'm going to take a shower and, uh, stuff."

I close the bathroom door behind me and turn on the shower. Then make the mistake of glancing in the mirror. My normally, carefully coiffed black hair looks like a back-comb teasing experiment gone bad. My makeup is still intact though, thank god. That's what hundreds of dollars at *Sephora* will get you. I pat at my face, trying to push down whatever moisture may have been there. I don't sweat, but I do gently perspire at times.

"Remi."

I hear him outside the bathroom door, still trying to talk to me.

"Alex, just go. Please. I'm sorry it didn't work out."

"If that's really what you want," he says, sounding petulant.

"It is." I keep my voice firm.

"Okay. I'll call you later," he sighs.

"You don't have to call me later."

"You don't even want me to call you?" he asks, sounding surprised.

I turn the shower off and open the bathroom door—at least put his boxers on. It's a start.

"I don't want you to call me. Not to be rude, I think it's best if we don't see each other anymore."

"Wow. Okay. I thought at least we'd be friends."

"We did have a good time." I gesture to the bed. "Before we had—"

"Okay, okay, I get it," he says. "You don't need to keep reminding me."

"Well, I hope you have a good rest of your day."

"Seriously, Remi? You stop me in the middle of sex to tell me it's bad, get out of bed, ask me to leave your house, and then tell me to have a good day? What is wrong with you?" His voice rising to a shrill at that last question.

So much.

I can't help it; his question makes me laugh.

After a brief pause, he laughs with me. His lightly muscled abdominal muscles contracting.

He really is good-looking.

I consider changing my mind about him, then shake my head, ridding it of such a thought. I grab a robe from the back of the bathroom door and put it on, then reach my hand out to him, "Friends?"

He takes my hand and shakes it. "Friends." He grabs his pants and puts them on, then looks at his watch. "I guess if I leave now, I can still make my game."

"Game?"

"Yeah, the law enforcement basketball league."

"You're in law enforcement? I thought you did IT consulting work." I try to rapidly think back to when he's talked about his job in past conversations. How had this not come up before?

"I do. But I specialize in IT for police departments."

"Oh. I had no idea."

"Does that make a difference?" he smirks and runs his hand through his sex-tousled hair.

Kinda.

I fight the urge to run my fingers through it after him. I've always found law enforcement sexy.

What is wrong with me?

"No." I laugh slightly. "I just have friends in the police department and the fire department."

"Why did you think I was traveling to two different regional police departments over the last six months?"

"Well, I wasn't really thinking about who you were working with. Or where you were working. Just that you were traveling for work."

"My base is out of San Soloman, but they lend me out to other divisions as a consultant. So, this last gig was two different locales, one in NoCal and one in the Central Coast. But both were PC refreshes," he says as he finishes dressing.

"Oh." I have no idea what a PC refresh is, but I don't want to ask him for fear that he'll try to explain it to me, and then he'll never leave.

"Anyway, the annual ball for San Soloman law enforcement is coming up. I was going to ask you to go with me."

"That's sweet, but I can't."

"Can't or won't?" His face hardens. I've made him mad. I try to soften the blow of rejection. "Can't. I'm actually already going."

"Weren't we still kind of dating, or at least talking, up until a few minutes ago? Or… is that why you stopped me earlier? Because there's someone else? Why did we even get together today then?"

"No. Believe me, that is not the reason. I wanted to get together with you today, I didn't realize it was going to go like it did." I don't blame him for being frustrated. If I were him, I would be too.

"Then how are you going to the ball?" he asks.

"I'm going as a favor to a friend."

He looks skeptical but doesn't question me further.

"Okay, well, maybe I'll see you there, then. If I go. I mean, I'm not going without a date." He kisses me on the cheek and turns to leave.

"I'll walk you out," I say.

"Don't bother," he says. "Take your shower. And enjoy your day."

"Thanks," I say. But I follow him to the door anyway so I can lock it.

"Hey," I say. He turns to look at me and I continue. "Not that it's a big deal, but if you had a basketball game you wanted to play in, then why agree to see me today?"

"Remi, we'd had two dates and then spent the next six months texting. Of course, I wanted to see you before anything else. I like you. It was important to me to see where this was going to go. I guess now I know."

"I'm sorry to disappoint you." And in that moment, I do feel bad for how this has played out. Even though a small part of me knew it couldn't have gone any other way.

He gives me a small, sad smile, then opens my front door and heads out.

2

CHANCE

"Hello?" I answer my phone as I'm getting out of the car, not checking to see who's calling first.

"Chance, dear, is that you?" my mom asks. She asks this every time she calls, as though I'm not going to be the one to answer my cell.

"Yeah, mom, it's me. You doing okay?"

"Oh yes, I'm good. Don't you worry about me."

"Dad okay?" I also ask, since she usually doesn't call me in the middle of the day without there being an important reason."

"Well, now your dad's good too, don't you worry about him. Are you doing okay?"

"I'm good, Ma, just heading to the Y for a basketball game."

"Well, I don't want to keep you, I just wanted to let you know that I'm making a roast for Sunday dinner, I know that's your favorite."

"It is my favorite, Ma, thanks. I look forward to it."

"Well, I do have to spoil my favorite son every now and then," she says.

"I'm your only son, Ma," I laugh.

"Well, if you weren't, you'd still be my favorite, I'm sure."

I chuckle at my mom's accent, it's very Midwest, betraying her Wisconsin roots.

"Well, I also wanted to remind you to bring my stamps," she says.

"I won't forget, Ma, I promise." She collects these little stamps from the grocery store. They give out several them after you purchase a certain dollar amount in items. She makes my sisters and I all shop at the same chain-store so we can collect the stamps for her. She's saving the stamps for a chance to win a European river cruise. She and my dad have never been anywhere they couldn't drive to in less than a day. The cruise is a big deal for them.

What she doesn't know is that my sisters and I have been saving money to send my parents on that same cruise for their fortieth wedding anniversary next year; no stamps needed. My mom has had her eye on it for years. It's two weeks and starts in Paris, and goes through Luxemburg, and then through Germany. We plan to have enough to send them on first class for their airfare, give them a couple of days of rest in the respective cities before and after the cruise, book them a suite on the ship, cover their onboard expenses, and send them with spending money.

"Well, you know I'm gonna win that cruise, Chancey," she says.

"I know you are, Ma. I'll bring the stamps, I promise. I gotta go, I'm walking into the Y and I'm running late. Love you. See you Sunday."

"I love you too, be safe."

I get in the Y with just enough time to change my clothes and get on the court. I don't see Alex, the guy who invited me, anywhere. But I do see a couple other guys from around the precinct, and one guy from the fire department. I think his name is Ethan.

I grab a ball and start doing some warm-up shots. I'm not a good ball player, but I'm not bad either.

"Hey, you made it." I turn and see Alex jogging across the court toward me. Sometimes I find it odd that he's really a computer nerd because he looks the part of a cop to a tee. Short hair, tall but stocky build, and he more lopes than runs. Limbs loose and at the ready for anything that might come at him.

"Yeah, thanks for the invite, man."

"We can always use another tall guy on our team."

The whistle blows and someone yells, "Play ball!"

We lose the game by five points but still head to *The Recovery Room* bar for beers afterward. I finish my first beer and am contemplating a second when the server sets a pint down in front of me.

"Well, thank you darlin', I was still undecided, so I guess you've made up my mind for me."

"Not me." She motions with her head over her right shoulder. "It's from the table over there." Both Alex and I peer around her to see a table of three women eye-fucking our table of two.

The other two guys that were at our table with us are in the back playing pool. But there's still another three tables of guys clustered around us, drinking beer and one-upping each other with stories and such. We're all still in our basketball clothes; the police department with shirts say SSPD on the front, and '*Cops = 'cause even firefighters need heroes*' on the back.

The firefighters with shirts that say SSFD on the front and '*How do you make a cop happy? Let him play firefighter*' on the back.

The two departments have been in a friendly (of sorts) rivalry for decades. And often meet for beers after the various games. Flag football in the fall, basketball in the winter, and softball in the spring. I'm looking forward to playing all three with them.

It's not surprising that a bunch of gym clothes clad police officers and firefighters would attract a table of women. And the one who sent me a drink? I've seen that look enough times to know that if I wanted to, I could tuck away in some supply closet or restroom stall and have my dick in her mouth in under fifteen minutes. Single guys in smallish towns, who work in law enforcement, are thrust into rock star status and with that status comes easy lays. It's only when it's too easy that it becomes boring and unwanted.

The woman who bought me the drink raises her glass at me and smiles. I raise mine in return and mouth a 'thank you,' then turn my attention back to Alex. It was a nice gesture, but there's no reason to encourage something I won't follow through on or take home.

Alex looks at me, one eyebrow raised.

"What can I say? It's good to be me," I tell him with a smile.

"The other one is trying to get your attention too." He motions back to the table. I pivot to look; the other girl is twirling her tongue around her straw in what I'm guessing she thinks is a seductive manner. I turn my head to laugh so they don't see me.

"I don't think that's for me, buddy," I hit Alex on the arm. "The straw licker has only got eyes for you."

"I've struck out enough for one day already. I need a break," he says.

"Already?" I ask him. "It's not even four o'clock in the afternoon."

"You have no idea, brother," he groans.

"Try me."

He takes a deep breath, letting it out while he talks. "I got with this chick I've been seeing—"

"Here or outta town?"

"Here. I started seeing her before I left."

"Wasn't that like a year ago?"

"Six months."

"So, long distance?" I confirm.

"Yeah."

"Sucks."

"We texted."

"Texted or sexted?" I smirk.

"Both." Alex sighs. "But I hadn't seen her in person since before I left."

I take a long draw of my beer. "Shit dude, how long you been back?"

"Couple weeks. Her schedule is insane."

"Insane cause she's seeing other guys?"

"I doubt it. We didn't talk about it, but I don't think so."

"Okay, so you hooked up?"

"We had breakfast—"

"Breakfast isn't a strikeout, my man."

"We started with breakfast."

"You had a date for breakfast?"

"Yeah."

"That wasn't a carry-over from the night before?"

"No. I'm telling you, this girl has a crazy schedule."

"Doing what? Saving the world?"

"Kind of, yeah. She does—"

"It doesn't matter," I say. "Chicks aren't that busy unless they just aren't interested."

"Oh, she's interested," Alex huffs. "Trust me. The texts she would send me... Dude, let's just say she was hot for it. Smokin' hot for it."

"Then what's the problem?" I ask.

"I'll tell you the problem," Alex says. "She says 'hey, meet me at this champagne brunch.' We meet, we have a good time, she invites me back to her place, and I know where this is going. This chick is hot. And she wants it, man. Wants it bad."

"Not seeing a problem."

"Quit interrupting, dickhead."

"My bad." I hold my hands up, surrender style. He seems satisfied with that and gives me a nod.

"Okay, so we go back to her place, have some more champagne, one thing leads to another, things get seriously hot, and then she fuckin' taps out," he pauses to take a drink, so I assume it's okay to interject a question.

"Taps out? As in, like, taps out?"

"Taps. The. Fuck. Out."

"No shit? Before you slip it in?"

"After. A while after. Like right in the middle."

I choke on my beer. Alex pounds me on the back to make sure I'm okay.

I catch my breath and look at him. "She tapped out in the middle of sex?" I say a little too loudly as the music is fading.

"Can you say it any louder, dude? I don't think the guys at the fucking pool table in the back heard you."

The girls at the next table turn to look at us, giggling. A new song starts on the jukebox. Some pop song and the same girls start squealing and bouncing in their seats. I turn away from them and back toward Alex, then scoot my stool in closer.

"Sorry, man." I motion for him to continue.

"She literally tapped me on the fucking shoulder, while I'm going at it, and says, and I quote, 'this isn't working for me,' end quote."

"Dude," I say. "I've never even heard of that before."

"Yeah, well, me neither until today. No complaints. Not ever. It's just this girl, man. She's cold as fucking ice." He hangs his head and twirls his pint glass in the condensation on the tabletop.

"It's not like you're a bad looking guy," I say.

"Thanks, dude," he says smiling.

"You got a real purty mouth."

"Okay," he says, dragging the word out.

I get the feeling he doesn't get the reference. I don't want him thinking I'm complimenting his mouth.

"It's a quote, man."

He looks at me blankly.

"From *Deliverance*. The movie. Ring a bell?"

Still nothing.

"Fuck, never mind," I say.

We sit in silence. For some reason I feel the need to cheer the guy up.

"You gotta get back on that fucking horse, brother. No pun intended."

He smirks.

"Go ask the straw licker for her number," I say.

"No. No way. I'm out. This morning was like the worst experience, ever." His face scrunches in a blend of horror and fear. I feel bad for the guy.

"That's why you've got to move on now. Don't think about it. Just do it."

"Eh, maybe in a bit," he says, shrugging his shoulders.

The girls with the straw licker are packing up their things, getting ready to go.

"Do it now," I tell him. "Before they leave."

"She's not that hot," Alex says.

"It doesn't matter. This is just to keep you prime. Plus, you're better looking as a guy than she is as a girl. She'll be flattered. Believe me. Do it."

"Fine."

He heads over to the table with the girls. I look around the bar. It's not the first time I've been here. I like it, there's a good vibe, the seats are comfortable, and you can always find a game on.

I hear giggling and look back to see him charming the girls at the table. I'm glad to see he's got his balls back.

Some women are just completely fucked in the head, like the one he was with this morning, obviously. What kind of heartless bitch do you have to be to tap out in the middle and tell him it's not working for you? I mean, fuck. Give him something to go on. If he needs to change it up, then say something. Take some goddamn responsibility for your own pleasure. It takes two to tango, baby. I mean, I'll put you on the train to pleasure land, but you gotta walk to the station with me.

Alex comes back to our table, a huge grin on his face.

"Score?" I ask.

"Oh yeah," he says. "Her friend said to give you this." He hands me a bar napkin with a phone number and *'Call me anytime. I'm waiting. And I'm always ready'* written on the back of it.

I wad it up and toss it in the middle of the table. It lands in the condiment basket between the ketchup and the hot sauce. Not to sound ungrateful for the attention, but I'm over the easiness of getting laid.

"Dude, you're not even going to call her?"

"Nope."

"You kidding? That's a sure fucking easy lay right there, man."

"It's too easy, brother. Don't get me wrong, I don't want something that's so easy, it could've been anyone. I wanna know it's about me."

"I wouldn't kick her out of bed."

"Yeah, 'cause she would have kicked you out first."

"Fuck off, asshole." His face reddening slightly.

"Dude, you fuckin' walked into that one."

"Yeah, well, that has not happened to me before. And it's not happening again. That girl has issues, man."

"Yeah, okay."

"You don't just run hot and cold like that without something being seriously wrong with you."

"Someone is feeling better about himself."

"Yeah, well, there's plenty of fish in the sea, my man."

"That there is," I say. "How'd you even meet her?"

"Online."

"One of those girls."

That just can't handle reality.

"What do you mean?"

"You know, one of those girls who think there's no way to meet a guy in real life, so she turns to meeting them online. She puts all her hopes on one guy, so of course he's going to be a disappointment. No one could possibly live up," I say.

"She's not like that." Alex shakes his head.

"All girls are like that," I say dryly.

"No," he says. "It was hot in the beginning. Then she just flipped a switch. Hot to cold, just like that." He snaps his fingers.

"No offense, bud, but she tapped out. It was never hot."

"It was, I swear."

"I'll believe it when I see it."

"You should see it then."

"Bring it on."

"Bitch turned cold. Like an ice queen. You can't melt that shit."

I laugh when he says ice queen, thinking of Remi. A girl from college who rocked my world in one night. She's my one who got away. And who I've never forgotten. Even though I never really had her. But I saw her again recently, she's my friend Kat's best friend, and it brought all the memories of that one night with her back.

"Brother, you have no idea my experience with a cold, frigid bitch. You bring her to me; I'll melt her for sure."

"Okay, you're on," he smirks.

"I'm on?"

What did I just agree to?

"I'm going to set you up."

Aw, shit.

"No way, dude, I am not going out with some holier than thou, stuck-up, bitch who can't pull the stick out of her ass long enough to have a good time." I lean back in my chair and cross my arms over my chest.

"Yeah, 'cause she'll tap out on you too," Alex says.

I snort out a half laugh of disbelief. "Brother, she will not tap out on me."

"Prove it."

"What's in it for me?"

"Outside of fucking a near centerfold? Shit, care to wager?"

"Name your terms, asshole."

"Pretty sure of yourself for someone who's never even met this girl, aren't you?" he sneers.

I smirk back at him. I don't fucking care who this girl is. If I want her, I'll get her.

"A grand," he says.

"As in a thousand dollars?" I ask, thinking about what I could do with that money. My share of the expenses for my parents' cruise is only another twenty-five hundred dollars, and then I'll have my entire part covered.

I look him in the eye trying to gauge how serious he is. His gaze is level and direct.

"Care to up the wager?" I ask.

"To what?" His eyebrows raise.

"Let's say twenty-five hundred."

"Dude, for that much money, you're going to have to do a hell of a lot more than just get her to fuck you," he half laughs.

"Such as?" I ask.

"For that much money you're going to have to get her to date you and fuck you."

"Consider it done."

"More than once." He narrows his eyes at me.

"More than one date? More than one fuck?" I clarify.

"Both," he says. "Four dates, two fucks."

"No problem."

"In a month," he clarifies.

"A month?" I scoff. "You kidding? You can't make it any easier for me."

"I had more time than that and couldn't do it."

"Well, I'm not you, chump."

"She doesn't have a lot of time," he says.

"Okay."

"She hangs out with her girlfriends a lot."

"Of course she does." I totally know the type.

"She works crazy long hours."

"Still not seeing the issue." I feel completely self-assured.

"Consider yourself forewarned then. Shake?" Alex reaches his hand out to me. I take it and give it a solid shake.

"Tell me when to show up and where, fucker," I say.

3

REMI

Alex is barely out the door before I've showered and thrown on a t-shirt and boy shorts. I need an immediate video chat with my girls, Kat and Lexie. Between the two of them, they'll figure out exactly what went wrong. Kat because she used to be a little slutty and Lexie because she's always been a little bit awkward.

I pace while I wait for each of them to pick-up.

And pace some more.

What the fuck? It's not even two o'clock in the afternoon, what could they possibly be doing?

Finally, Lexie picks up, and Kat is not far behind her.

"Hey, hey hot mama!" Lexie's face pops into view. "Why are you online? Didn't you have a date this morning?"

"I did." I sigh, sounding melancholier than I really mean to.

"Oh, that doesn't sound good," Kat says.

"Guys, it was weird. Really weird."

"Weird good? Or weird bad?" Lexie asks.

"Weird… Bad."

Kat gasps. "What happened?"

"Well, everything was going great. We went to brunch, we had mimosas, we came back to my place, had more champagne."

"And?" Lexie and Kat say at the same time.

"And, we had sex."

"Woot! Woot!" Lexie pumps her fists in the air.

"It was so awful," I groan.

"Wait, awful, like awful?" Lexie asks.

"Yeah, awful, like awful, like bad."

"The sex was bad?" Kat asks. "With Alex the hot IT guy?"

"Right!?" I say. "It's almost too ridiculous to believe. Everything else was so good. The kissing, the flirting, the texting."

"Wow. I didn't think that could really happen," Kat bemoans.

"Neither did I. Until it did."

"Okay, I hate to be that person," Lexie says. "But how does it even happen if it's bad? Do you finish? Or whatever? I mean, did you, you know, come?"

"Not even close. I had to stop him in the middle."

"You stopped?" Kat's voice rises to a near shriek. "In the middle?" She sounds incredulous. As if the idea of stopping sex would never occur to her.

"Yes!" I groan. "I mean, I didn't really know what else to do. It wasn't working for me. At all. Like, I think I almost came in the beginning, but it would have been one of those lackluster orgasms where you can't really tell if it happened or not. And you end up feeling more unsatisfied than if nothing had ever happened."

"I hate those," Kat says.

"Do you still have those?" Lexie asks.

"Pfft. Not even remotely." Kat rolls her eyes. She recently got back together with the love of her life. Their sex life is amazing.

"Bragger," Lexie mumbles.

"Ladies, can we get back on topic, please? We are talking about me," I say.

"Sorry, okay, so lackluster sex that you stopped in the middle . . ." Kat motions with her hands for me to continue.

"That so sucks by the way," Lexie says.

"Tell me about it," I say. "I had really high hopes for this." My shoulders slump and I let out a huge breath of air.

"What about Alex?" Kat asks.

"Like I said, I had really high hopes for this."

"No, I mean what about Alex?" Kat repeats.

"Well, then what do you mean what about him?"

"Did he enjoy it?" Kat asks.

"I don't know. I think so. I mean, with all the thrusting and grunting and sweating, it was hard to concentrate on anything else. He was still going strong when I stopped him, and he definitely didn't want to stop."

"Well, of course he didn't want to stop," Lexie says. "It's easy for guys. A little pushing, a little pulling, a couple grunts, release, and they're good 'til morning."

"Wow, Lex, who shit in your cheerios?" Kat asks.

"I just call it like it is," Lexie says.

"Well, alright then," I say.

"How did you stop him?" Kat asks.

"I tapped him on the shoulder."

"You tapped him on the shoulder?" Lexie asks, sounding confused.

"That was the only way to get his attention," I say.

"It's so MMA of you," Kat says.

"So, *what* of me?" I ask.

"MMA. Mixed martial arts. A tap out. When one guy... never mind, I'm obviously around Brad way too much. What did you do after you tapped out?" Kat asks.

"Tapped out," Lexie laughs. "That's funny."

"I know, right," Kat says.

"Anyway, after I *tapped out*, I asked him to leave, and then I went into the bathroom to take a shower."

"What did he do?" Lexie asks.

"I was hoping he would just leave. But he stayed and talked to me through the bathroom door. I eventually opened it, we agreed to be friends, and then he left."

"Wow," Kat says.

"What she said," Lexie agrees.

"I know. He's a great guy, he just really didn't do it for me. It almost makes me wish I knew someone I could set him up with."

"Don't look at me," Lexie says.

"No, not you, Lex," I tell her.

"Well, you should set him up since you blue-balled him and cut him off," Kat admonishes.

"I wasn't being serious."

"I am. You kinda suck for doing that. At least as far as he's concerned. What's the harm in setting him up? Who do you know?" Kat asks.

"I don't know, probably nobody. Or maybe the girl who teaches my Yoga class. She's nice, and single, and she seems to be more, I don't know, maybe simpler than I am?"

"Pfft. Well, that doesn't take much," Kat says.

"Shut up." I roll my eyes at her.

"Rem, have you ever noticed that you do this a lot? Find something wrong with every guy you date and then break it off?" Kat asks.

"Well, duh," I say. "If I didn't find something wrong, I wouldn't break it off, and then I'd still be seeing them and wouldn't have gone on this date to begin with."

"Right." Kat nods her head. "But you don't think you're a little hard on them?"

"No, I don't. You know just as well as I do, most guys are boring as fuck. I get tired of them easily, they can't carry a conversation, there's no banter, and I just don't want to waste my time spending time with them. I want someone who challenges me, not someone who is—"

"The tar to your bulldozer?" Lexie suggests.

"Good one, Lex," Kat says.

"Haha," I say. "Note the lack of humor in my tone."

"Well, it's a good metaphor for you where relationships are concerned," Kat says.

"Kat, the sex sucked."

"I get that," Kat agrees. "And I know it's going to seem like I'm trying to sprinkle my happy relationship dust all over everyone else, but when are you going to give a guy a decent shot?"

"What do you mean? I always give them a shot," I say, not quite believing what they're saying.

"Really? What happened with Alex?" Lexie asks, joining in.

"It just wasn't there. We're much better off as friends," I say.

"If I think back, I'm fairly sure that it's always 'not there' for you, with a guy, usually right after you have sex with them for the first time. This is just the first time you tapped out in the middle," Kat says.

"Wow, make me sound like a slut why don't you?" I say. Even though I can totally acknowledge that what she says is true.

"No, not a slut. But definitely someone who never goes back for seconds, shit, sometimes not even firsts. No matter what.

I think you just have a problem with sticktuitiveness," Kat says.

"Is that even a word?" I stand up and start to pace.

"Kat's right," Lexie says. "You never go back for seconds."

"Rem, you go through guys faster than babies go through diapers," Kat says.

Lexie snorts a laugh. "That's a good one, Kat."

"Thanks, Lex," Kat smiles.

"You guys are exaggerating," I say, trying to recall if there's any truth in that part of what they are saying.

"I don't think we are," Kat says.

"Me neither," Lexie seconds.

"But, if we are, then you won't mind making a little wager," Kat says.

"What do you mean little wager?" I ask.

"You know, a wager, a challenge, a bet," Kat says.

"Ooooh, I like it!" Lexie claps her hands.

"Come on." I drag out the words and roll my eyes.

"I'm going to bet," Kat says. "That you can't stick with the same guy for more than two weeks."

"Of course I can do that, don't be ridiculous. I was with Alex for longer than that."

"Only because he was gone the entire time and it was long-distance," Lexie says.

"That doesn't matter, I could still do it."

"Okay, that's too easy then. What about a month?"

"Piece of cake," I say.

"Right, except that you have to go out on a date with them at least once a week for the whole month," Kat clarifies.

"Oh, that's good, Kat," Lexie says.

"I can't do that," I protest. "Not with my work schedule, you know that. My lab trials take precedence."

Lexie begins to cluck like a chicken in response. I glare at the computer screen in return, hoping she realizes I'm giving her a dirty look.

Kat just stays silent. I hate it when she does that. She's good with those uncomfortable silences that most people want to rush and fill with talking and noise. She's the only one who can get me to start talking during them.

"Fine," I cave. "I will find a guy to date for one month."

"I have a better idea," Kat continues. "Since Alex is such a great guy, and you want to set him up with your Yoga instructor, why don't you tell him you want to set him up, and then ask him to set you up with someone at the same time."

"You're the devil." I narrow my eyes at her.

Kat stays silent and Lexie pretends to look at her nails.

"You want me to set Alex up with my Yoga instructor? Nobody likes blind dates," I say.

"I love blind dates." Lexie dances about in her seat as she says it.

"You also love presents and surprises," I glare at Lexie's image on the screen.

"Exactly!" Lexie says.

"Well?" Kat asks.

"So, just to confirm, you want me to set Alex up on a blind date? And then ask him to set me up on a blind date in return?" I ask.

"Yes!" Kat is clearly getting excited at the idea. "You guys can double."

"A double-blind date sounds like a bad Rom-Com," I moan.

"It sounds like an awesome Rom-Com!" Lexie gushes, clearly a lot happier about it than I am.

"You're just agreeing with everything Kat says," I say to Lexie.

She shrugs her shoulders in return.

"Fine. I will call Alex and tell him I want him to set me up in return for my setting him up. Happy?"

"Very," Kat sighs.

Lexie just claps her hands, a huge grin overtaking her face.

"So, what do I get if I do this?"

"We'll never bug you about it again," Kat says.

"And if I don't go through with it?"

"You've got to donate your Louboutin's to a homeless woman on the street," Lexie declares.

"That's perfect!" Kat says.

"Jeez. Harsh. When did you get such brass balls?" I ask Lexie. She just smirks.

"It's perfect!" Kat cries.

"And you've got to set it up this week." Lexie pounds the final nail in my coffin.

Fuck me.

"Fine," I say. "I'll reach out to Alex and have a date set up before the weekend."

I log off the chat session without saying goodbye. I know it's petty. But I feel bested by Kat and that pisses me off. Just because she's all happy in a relationship, doesn't mean everyone else has to be.

4

REMI

Lexie and I get ready together for the Law Enforcement Annual Ball. It's not an event either of us would ordinarily attend, but tonight is special. Kat is getting engaged to her boyfriend, Brad.

Again.

Only she doesn't know it.

Brad has arranged dates for both Lexie and I so we can attend and surprise her. We'll be the first surprise, and Brad's proposal will be the second. Even though I have no desire to go anywhere near the institution of marriage, I'm excited for Kat. Brad is a good guy and such an amazing partner for her.

It's only because Brad is proposing that I let him talk me in to attending the ball with Kat's sometimes law enforcement partner, Chance Bauer. And she's only a sometimes partner because she's on an indefinite leave of absence from all work. Chance and I knew one another briefly in college, and I've had an intense dislike for him since. But, because of his connection to Kat, I run into him from time to time.

I'll admit that he's good-looking, but he knows it. And once upon a time, I found him attractive enough to almost fuck him. I saved myself by vomiting on him instead. That's a story for another time.

Tonight, I need to focus on being civil to him, for Kat's sake and making sure she has the perfect night. She deserves it.

Even though tonight is for Kat, I still feel the need to make sure I look amazing at the ball. Better than amazing.

Drop. Fucking. Dead. Gorgeous.

I want Chance Bauer's little head to explode when he sees me.

I see no need to examine my rationale behind that feeling too much, however.

The event is semi-formal, so I got a new dress. One that can fit with a variety of dress codes. I like styles from the 1950s, if I had to pick a fashion icon, Dita Von Teese would fit the bill. In true Dita fashion, my hair is pinned back in victory rolls, eyes are lined like a cat, and my lips are red to match my dress.

A gathered, red wiggle dress with a crossover neck, three-quarter sleeves, and a slit up the back. My legs are bare, as are my ass and tits, this dress can't afford any lines under it. Black peep-toe stilettos complete the look.

"Wow," Lexie exclaims when she sees me, her eyes wide. "All I can say is wow."

I look at myself in the full-length mirror, trying to be both objective and critical at the same time.

I agree.

I look good.

I may detest Chance, but that doesn't mean I don't want him to eat his heart out. So to speak.

Lexie, on the other hand, is my polar opposite. While my look screams Hollywood siren, hers screams sexy punk-rock pixie. Her black strapless baby doll dress fits her personality to a tee with the full tulle skirt, large glitter belt, patterned tights, and stiletto ankle boots, she is ready to rock. She's petite so she can easily pull off a mini with tulle. We styled her pink hair in little spikey knots on either side of her head, gave her a black smoky eye, and a nude lip. She's perfection personified.

"Back at you, Lex. You look positively edible." I wink. "I'd do you." And I would too, if Lexie were into it and I could guarantee it wouldn't completely fuck up our friendship. I'm not bisexual, I would consider myself to be more fluid with my sexuality. Basing it on attraction to the person more than anything else. And I find Lexie attractive. But, not only is Lexie not into chicks, she's a relationship girl. And if there's one thing I do not do, it's relationships.

My doorbell rings.

"That's either Ethan or Chance," I say.

While Brad arranged for me to attend with Chance, he arranged for Lexie to attend with his SSFD partner, Ethan. There was a time I thought Ethan and Lexie would make a cute pair, but Lex is slow to get involved. Even more so than me. I suspect Ethan would have her in a heartbeat, he makes no secret that he's had a crush on her for a while.

I open the door to find Ethan on the front stoop. I eye him up and down appreciatively—he was once the cover model for the annual firefighter calendar. Brad was as well. Both men are worthy of appreciative stares. Tonight, Ethan has his blonde hair slicked back, making it look a shade darker, giving his all-American boy look an edge. Between that, and his perpetual surfer boy tan, his green eyes pop.

"Hello, handsome." I smile.

"Hey gorgeous." He leans in to kiss my cheek.

Lexie comes bounding up behind us. "Hey, date!"

Ethan looks up at her, his eyes lighting up when he sees her. "Lexie, you take my breath away." He grabs her hand and kisses the back of it, bowing slightly at her. "How about we go right now? Ride into the sunset, rescue dogs, have babies, drink wine, and live happily ever after. What do you say?" The look on his face hopeful.

She giggles at him and pats his chest. "I'm not the girl for you, E."

"You could be," he says.

She leans in to give him a hug, and I catch him taking a quick whiff of her hair. Man, he's got it bad.

"Ready?" Lexie asks him.

"Your chariot awaits, my love." Ethan motions toward the open door.

"Rem, you want us to wait for you?" Lexie turns back to face me.

"No, Chance will be here any minute."

They leave and I close the door after them. Then check the time and see that Ethan was a few minutes early to pick up

Lexie. Probably couldn't stand the wait. Poor guy. My luck, Chance will be late.

I smooth my hands over my hips and glance quickly in the mirror again.

You look fine. Better than fine.

I hear the motorcycle before I see it.

He wouldn't dare.

I open the front door and watch as Chance pulls up in front of my house. He takes his helmet off and shakes his head. With the sun setting behind him, he reminds me of the cover of a romance novel. A little scruffy, a bit broody, and a lot beautiful. Kat thinks he looks like Bradley Cooper from the *A-Team* movie. I don't see it. But then again, I still picture him as the cocky college kid I met first. He'd reminded me of a young Paul Walker, from the first *Fast and Furious* movie. Complete with the twinkling eyes and cocky, confident smile. It was why I'd been attracted to him back then. His confidence and sense of self had been almost intoxicating. And then there was his kiss.

Gah!

I can't think about that right now.

I study him as he comes up the front walk. He looks like he shaved this morning, 'cause there's a bit of beard shadowing his face. But his tuxedo fits him like a glove. A really nice glove. Maybe satin. Like sheets that you can slide all over and bury yourself in. He smiles when he sees me. I cock a hip and lean against the doorjamb.

"Fuck, Ice Q. You sure know how to dress for the occasion." He uses the nickname that I hate.

"Is that a compliment?" I ask.

"It is," he says, looking me down, and then up again. Slowing his gaze at my hips and stopping at my chest.

"Eyes up here, big boy." I point at my eyes.

"Nuh uh," he says, still staring at my chest with a smile.

"Neanderthal."

"That's me, ice baby."

"Stop calling me that," I snap.

"Can't stop saying what I know to be true." He finally looks me in the eye.

Have his eyes always been that beautiful?

I stare at him a little longer than is necessary.

Fuck, get it together, Remi!

"Are we leaving, or are you going to stare at me all day?" I ask.

"I'm happy with either."

"I vote for leaving. Please tell me you don't expect me to ride on that thing?" I point to the motorcycle on the street.

"I don't expect you to ride on that thing."

"Thank God," I breathe.

"Of course, we're riding on that thing."

"Um, have you seen me? No thank you. I'll drive."

"I have seen you, you look positively edible," he says, using my same line from earlier. "And you can't drive."

"Why?"

"Well, one because I'm being a gentleman and picking you up. And two because your best friend is getting engaged tonight and you want to be able to celebrate with her. And if you're driving, you won't be able to do that."

"If that happens, you can just drive my car home."

"Are you afraid of my beast, Ice Q?"

"Pfft. No."

"Well then." He gestures to the motorcycle.

"It's going to mess up my hair." I pat my head lightly, knowing by touch that all the hairs are in exactly the right place.

"I never took you for the high maintenance type."

"I'm not high maintenance," I say. But I can hear a bit of a whine in my voice that disgusts me.

"I'm not high maintenance," he mimics in a high-pitched voice that is definitely a whine.

"Fine." I grab my clutch, lock the door, and walk ahead of him toward the motorcycle. "Let's go."

"I gotta say, Icy, the view is just as good from the back." He lets out a wolf whistle. I can't help but smile, glad that he can't see my face.

We get to the bike; he pulls a leather jacket and a helmet out of the saddlebag and hands them to me. "Here, put these on."

I put on the jacket and carefully arrange the helmet around my hair. If I look like shit after this, I'm going to kill him. He gets on the bike, then puts out his hand to help me get on behind him.

"How did you expect this to work, exactly?" I motion to the seat and then to my dress.

"Hmmm." He looks me up and down thoughtfully. "Well, I think you're just going to have to hitch it up and straddle me tight."

"Excuse me?"

"Hitch up the dress and climb on."

"I'm not wearing anything underneath," I hiss.

His eyes darken, and he looks to where my underwear would have been, had I been wearing them. He licks his lips, and I can't tell if it's intentional or not. A little shiver goes through me.

Rein it the fuck in, Remi. You are not attracted to this guy. You just had a tap out situation and you're feeling a little desperate.

Knowing that he's watching, I take my time hitching up my dress to a length that is close to illegal. His eyes never leave the edge of my gown, following it all the way up my thighs. I flick him in the head to get his attention.

"Ow! That was unnecessary."

"But effective."

He tells me how to hold onto his shoulders, put my heel on the peg and swing a leg over. I swear he tries to sneak a peek when I do.

Unzipped, his leather jacket hangs low enough on my sides that it covers the bulk of my thighs from anyone driving by. But I know, and Chance knows, that there is not a lot separating my bare skin from his. He starts the bike and I feel it vibrating beneath me.

"A girl could get used to this between her legs," I whisper in Chance's ear. He responds by reaching behind him and running his left hand up my calf.

"Hands off." I slap him on the arm.

"Then don't give a guy ideas, especially not when you're commando on my ride."

And with that, we are off.

I admit, the ride is thrilling. And it's not just the bike. It's more the combination of everything: we are both dressed up, I'm straddling a beast of a machine, and I've got a tight hold on a nicely built guy. I may find him to be distasteful on the inside, but that doesn't mean I can't appreciate what he's got on the outside.

It doesn't take us long to arrive at the venue. He parks instead of using the valet.

"Can't you valet a motorcycle?" I ask as he helps me off the bike.

"Not really, and you can usually park close enough that it doesn't matter. But more importantly, I didn't need all the valet boys seeing the goods of the girl on the back of my ride."

"Good point." I open my clutch to check my hair and makeup in the little built-in mirror, surprised to see that everything is still intact.

"Satisfied *Ms. I'm-Not-High-Maintenance*?"

I glare at him in response.

"Relax Ice Q, you look beautiful," he says. I smile at him, grateful for the compliment.

"I'm going to get whiplash watching your moods flit back and forth. Make up your mind. Mad? Not mad?"

I roll my eyes at him and walk ahead into the hotel.

"I guess you're going with mad at me," he mutters from behind me.

We find Ethan and Lexie in line at one of the bars.

"Have you seen them yet?" I ask Lexie.

"More like have they seen us." She shakes her head. "And the answer is no."

"Good to know."

Ethan is at the front of the line to the bar, when he turns to Lexie and says, "The happy couple is in that far corner there." He points out their location. "Why don't you ladies go surprise Kat-alicious and the man. Bauer and I'll be right behind you with the drinks."

"Ok!" Lexie bounces in place with excitement. "I want—"

"Champagne," Ethan affirms.

"How'd you know?" Lexie smiles.

"It's my job to know what the apple of my eye desires," he says.

I touch Chance on the arm. "Can you get me a martini? Dirty. Please."

"Coming right up, Ice Q."

"Why do you call her that?" Ethan asks him.

"And that's our cue to leave," Lexie says, pulling me alongside her.

Brad sees us approaching before Kat does and turns her to face him. When we reach them, he turns her back around just in time for us to yell surprise.

She looks good. I tell her so. Her dress is sexy as hell and she's wearing a wig that makes her look dangerous yet alluring. We exchange hugs and tell her that we are here to support her on her first big night out since going back into treatment. Because she doesn't need to know yet that we are here because Brad plans to propose.

Chance and Ethan arrive with our drinks, one of the first times I'm happy to see Chance. Not that I'm not happy and excited for Kat, because I am. But marriage makes me uneasy. That whole idea of being with one person, the same person, for the rest of your life. Or the rest of theirs. I can't think of anything more monotonous or tedious than that. And since engagements usually lead to marriage, they make me uneasy as well. So, this martini is going to go a long way in helping with that uneasiness.

"I can't believe you did this." Kat turns to Brad a huge smile on her face. He shrugs in return as if to say it's no big deal.

"And I really can't believe you did this," she turns to me and motions to Bauer.

"I'm offended, Cookie," Bauer says. "Icy and I have become friends."

"I wouldn't go so far as to say *friends*," I assert.

"How about tolerating one another for an evening for the sake of a friend," Lexie suggests.

"I'll drink to that," I say with a grin.

"Hear, hear," Ethan says raising his beer bottle. Chance shakes his head at the idea but drinks to it anyway. Brad excuses himself from the group, and everyone except Kat knows why.

The Chief calls everyone to their tables and we find our seats. I take the one farthest from Chance, so I can avoid him for the bulk of the evening.

The Chief announces a special presentation that's about to take place, it's cute to watch Kat look around for Brad, not realizing she is that presentation.

Brad gets up on the stage and starts talking about Kat, it takes her a minute to realize what's going on. The mood at the table is giddy, and the rest of the proposal is nothing short of magical. This from the girl who doesn't even like them. If I were the emotional type, it may have made me cry. It certainly made enough other women in attendance go all weepy in the eyes.

After dinner, Kat begs us all to stay for the dancing. There's a live band and they are really good. The lead singer is a woman with a very sultry and bluesy Etta James/Stevie Nicks kind of voice that is well suited to a lot of slow dancing. Which is why, I'm surprised when Chance grabs my hand and drags me to the floor.

The band is playing the song *"Somebody Stand by Me"* by Stevie Nicks, and the singer is doing it some serious justice. I expect Chance to pull me in for the grope and sway, but he surprises me with a standard slow dance stance.

My breath catches as he pulls me tight against him. I hate that my body responds to him. It's been ten years. And in those years, still the only one to ever get a physical reaction from me. At all.

He starts to guide me around the floor. And the man can move. I take a deep breath and let it out slowly.

"Problem, Ice Queen?" he asks, one eyebrow arched.

"No. Why would you ask that?"

"You seem a little tense."

"I'm not tense. Maybe you're tense." My voice is way too shrill for my liking.

"I would say there are parts of me that are very tense right now," he murmurs into my ear. His breath hot on my neck.

Breath I can feel down to my very core.

I try to stay and dance with him for the entire song. But the longer I'm in his arms, the more palpable the sexual tension gets, which makes my desire for him that much stronger.

"If you'll excuse me," I say. "I need to visit the ladies room." I retreat on shaky legs, feeling like a coward, looking for the restroom and then the bar, in that order.

5

CHANCE

I watch her ass as she walks away, leaving me on the dance floor. It is a fantastic ass. It's too bad I'm going to be tied up for a while with Alex's snooty bitch of an ex, or I might try something with Remi. There's always time, I'm not going anywhere. Not that I'm looking for a relationship, just a good time.

I turn to head back and see a stacked blonde standing in front of me.

"Did your date abandon you?" she asks, her lips pursing into a small pout, as if she's feeling sad for me.

"She did indeed. Care to keep me company until she returns?" I ask, gesturing to the dance floor. We finish out the song with me keeping a demure distance and classic stance, and her trying to rub up against me in a way that is most definitely not lacking in suggestion or intent.

When the song ends, I make my way to the table. Ethan is there, looking a little forlorn.

"You okay, man?" I grab my bourbon and take a seat next to him.

"Yeah, I'm good. Hey - you played a good game the other day, sucks you guys lost."

"Thanks, man," I say. "We're not very good, but all we can do is try, right?"

"I hear you."

"Does Matthews play too?" I ask of Kat's new fiancé not sure if I want him to or not.

"Not anymore. He spends most of his free time with Kat now, but he'll come back to it, I'm sure."

I nod in response, satisfied with that answer. I take a drink of my bourbon and look out over the dance floor. I see Kat and Matthews dancing, her with eyes closed and head leaning against his shoulder, content smile on her face; him looking down at her like he's got all the riches in the world right there in his arms.

I've gotten over my general dislike of the guy. It helps to see Kat so happy with him. I had the hots for her for a while the first time we worked together. Hard not to, she's the whole package: smart, funny, gorgeous, determined, self-assured.

Like Remi.

It also helps to see that he appreciates what he's got. I may not be the right guy when it comes to relationships, been there done that, got the hell away from it. But I can recognize the value that they bring to some people's lives.

Just like I can recognize that Ethan has the hots for Lexie. He wants to shackle her to his bedpost, pump her full of baby gravy, and sign life away as he knows it. Right on the dotted line. I'm watching him keep an eagle eye on her as she twirls around the dance floor with the Chief. And just like with Alex before, I feel the need to say something to make this guy feel better. What is it with all this sentimental bullshit going on in my head?

"He's not competition."

"What?" Ethan turns to me, the expression on his face one of confusion.

"The Chief, he's not your competition with Pinky."

"Pfft. I know that," Ethan says. "I mean not that it matters. Lexie and I are just friends."

"But you want more?"

"More what?" Remi asks as she approaches the table with a fresh martini in her hands. I try to remember how many that makes for her. Two? Three? I stand and pull her chair out for her.

"Why thank you, how very chivalrous of you." She plants her ass on the seat. I feel a little jealous of the cushion as I help her scoot in. Acknowledging, and not for the first time tonight, it's just that dress that's between it and what I'm sure is sweet and creamy goodness between her legs.

I grunt, trying to get the thought back out of my head.

"And, the Neanderthal returns," Remi scoffs, rolling her eyes.

Wonderful, my favorite reaction from her. Didn't her mother ever tell her that her eyes will get stuck like that if she keeps rolling them?

"I wasn't... never mind."

"So, E." Remi turns to face Ethan. "What is it that you want more of? Or do I already know?" She smiles, winks, and gestures toward the dance floor where Pinky is still dancing with the Chief. A fast song now, where both are twisting and twirling to the beat.

"It's nothing," Ethan says at the same time that I say, "He's got the hots for Pinky."

Ethan glares at me.

"We already knew that simpleton. Try to keep up." She pats my hand in a condescending manner.

"Does she know?" Ethan asks.

"I don't think so," Remi answers. "Not the extent of it at least. She thinks you're just being cute."

"God." Ethan bangs his forehead on the table. "I hate cute!"

"Cute can be good," I say with a smirk.

Ethan glares at me. "Really, Bauer. When have you ever been called cute?"

I think on that for a minute. Even though I'm certain the answer is never.

"That's what I thought." Ethan doesn't even wait for me to say anything in response.

"Don't try to help," Remi says to me.

"Go cut in on the Chief," I tell Ethan.

"Did you not hear what I just said?" Remi asks.

"Go," I give Ethan a little push in the direction of the dance floor.

He gets up and heads for Lexie.

"Why are you encouraging him?" Remi asks.

"What's the harm, Ice Q?"

"She's not the girl for him, Chance."

"How do you know? 'Cause you are?" I ignore the twinge of jealousy that runs through me.

"Good God, no," she laughs. I ignore the relief that I feel as well.

"What's wrong with him?"

"There's nothing wrong with him. Lexie is still hung up on her college sweetheart. She has been for a while. I don't think that's changing any time soon."

"You never know," I say. Mostly just to keep arguing with her.

"When did you become the relationship guru?"

"I'm not. I'm just saying you can't predict what draws people together when it does. And you never know, something could draw them together. I mean, look at them." I gesture to the dance floor. Ethan has cut in on the Chief and is attempting a tango type move with Lexie to a particularly rousing version of *The Lady Is A Tramp*. Her head is thrown back and all you can see of her face is her smile. It's that big.

"She's having a blast."

"Lexie always has a blast. That's just her personality."

"Too bad that hasn't rubbed off on you," I say, before I can stop myself.

"Excuse me?" she asks, her tone cold.

"I'm just saying, you could loosen up a bit. Maybe pull that stick out of your ass occasionally."

Her eyes narrow as she glares at me. I can almost feel the anger radiating off her. She's practically vibrating with it.

"I do not have a stick up my ass."

"Prove it."

"I don't have to prove anything to you. You can go to hell."

"And score one for me." I tick off an imaginary mark in the air.

"Score one? Score shit. There's no score. And if there were, you wouldn't have that one. I would."

"How'd you score, gorgeous?"

She sits there, her chest rising and falling rapidly. Her tits look fabulous like this. Twin mounds of white, creamy flesh just waiting to bust free from the confines of that oh-so-sinful dress; begging to fill my hands and mouth with their deliciousness.

"Eyes up here, asshole." She tilts my chin up.

God, she's stunning when she's pissed. Gaze piercing, cheeks slightly pink, red lips pursed. I don't even care that she caught me eyeing her rack. It was worth it.

"You're exquisite when you're mad," I tell her.

"Flattery will get you nowhere."

"That's not what I heard," I smirk.

"Oh, funny. Haha," she says dryly. "Does this attitude actually work for you?"

"I've had no complaints, Icy Q."

"That's because women are idiots."

"Do you count yourself in that classification?"

She rolls her eyes at me, then pushes her chair back and stands. "I'm going to the bar."

"Again? I'll come with you," I say.

"You don't need any more to drink. You're driving, remember?"

"I've had two bourbons over four hours, I think I'm fine." I stand.

She stares at me, her face impassive, and her eyes hard.

"Fine. I'll get water," I say.

"I'll bring you back a glass." Her voice is cold. "I could do for some time without your company."

I sit back down and, once again, watch her ass sway as she walks away. I don't care how cold she is, that view will ever get old.

6

REMI

I can feel him watching my ass as I walk away. I can't tell if I like it or not. He infuriates me to no end. I can't stand his cockiness or his attitude, and he's rude too. How the man has ever been laid is beyond me.

Except that most women really are idiots.

I turn back to look at our table as I stand in line at the bar, relieved to see that both couples have returned from dancing, Brad and Kat, and Ethan and Lexie. Kat is on Brad's lap and he's nuzzling her neck, making her squirm ever so slightly.

I admire what they have. It would never work for me, but I'm happy they have it. I can't imagine having to deal with the same man every day. Having him know your schedule, your habits, how you spend your down time, what you're like on your period, what you look like first thing in the morning, and how you smell after working out. All of it just sounds nauseating and exhausting. When do you get a break?

But Brad and Kat are all in. Like all the fucking way in. And it doesn't seem to bother Kat at all. He's seen her at her best and her absolute worst, I mean, he's held her hair back when she's vomited. A shiver of disgust runs through me.

Chance looks up from talking to Lexie and catches my eye from across the room. I turn away quickly and face the front of the line. Trying to ignore the memory of when he held my hair back as I vomited.

God, I can't think of anything worse than that night. Anything more demeaning. But I'll give him credit, he'd handled it well.

It was ten years ago now. And still the most humiliating thing I've ever experienced.

My roommate had convinced me to go to a party with her, considering my normal Friday night consisted of books or movies, a party was completely out of my norm. Our college's rugby team was all the rage, and they'd won some sort of championship, so the celebration was huge. And, in a house filled with girls wearing tiny denim short-shorts, and cut-off U of C Rugby shirts and jerseys, my outfit stood out.

I was used to standing out, my style has never conformed to the fashion of the time I'm in. But this night was a little different. It made me feel almost self-conscious about how I looked.

My roommate assured me I looked great, but black cigarette pants, white/black polka dot halter, and peep-toe heels don't exactly blend in a room filled with shirtless, sweaty men playing beer pong and passing around scantily clad co-eds like they were candy.

I noticed Chance right away. He stood inches above everyone else and was more filled out than all of the other guys. In fact, compared to a lot of them, he looked downright huge, towering over them in height and with the shoulder width of a linebacker, not a college student. He was tan, with a light smattering of hair in the middle of his chest and across his pecs. And a happy trail leading all the way down his chiseled abs into his low hanging shorts. His hair was a little curly and obviously damp, slicked back from his forehead by his hands. I wondered if it was wet from a shower, sweat, or beer.

He was holding on to the legs of some guy doing a keg stand with one arm, the other arm was around a little blonde girl who was preening from the attention. The group around the keg made room for me as I approached. I knew the moment that Chance saw me, even though I didn't know who he was at the time.

He left the blonde and dropped the keg stander's legs on to stagger back dramatically clutching at his heart. I looked around to see if anyone else thought it was weird.

Apparently not.

"And she," he pointed at me, "shall be crowned my Queen!" He approached only to kneel before me and kiss my feet.

What the fuck?

Is he talking to me? Why is he kissing my feet?

"Queen! Queen! Queen!" The room started chanting as I giggled nervously, wondering if I was about to be a human sacrifice.

Chance looked up at me, his hands running up and down my calves and thighs. He hugged my hips and pressed a kiss to abdomen before bouncing back to his feet, surprisingly spry for such a big, and probably inebriated, guy. The crowd roared with approval.

I looked around for my roommate, but she seemed to have disappeared into the throngs of people.

Is this normal for parties?

"Yens, a beer for My Queen!" he yelled to the guy staffing the keg, his eyes never leaving mine.

"Aye, aye Captain," Yens yelled back.

"I've been waiting all night for you," he said cupping my cheek with his palm.

Not knowing what else to say, I responded with, "I just got here."

"Then let's not waste any time." And with that, he grabbed me by the waist, as though I weighed nothing, and perched me atop his broad left shoulder.

"What the fuck!?!" I yelled. "Put me down!" I tried to jostle myself off him, he only held on tighter.

"Hold still My Queen, or you'll fall," he said.

"I won't fall if you put me down," I said grasping at his forehead with both arms for balance at the same time as trying to move off it. Noticing that he smelled good, not sweaty or like stale beer.

"Your shoe, Milady," another guy said as he slipped my right shoe off my foot.

"Hey, bring that back!" I yelled.

"The Queen's shoe is but a chalice for the nectar from the gods that is our reward," Chance said as the other guy headed towards the keg.

"Those are my *Badgley Mischkas!*" I cried to no one in particular, since apparently no one cared. Then watched in part horror and part fascination as the guy began to pour beer into my beautiful shoe.

"They're open-toed," my voice softening as I realized it wasn't going to matter. He was pouring beer into my shoe, and then trying to drink out of it. Too drunk—or stupid—to realize it was all pouring out the toe of the shoe before he could get it to his mouth.

I couldn't help but scoff at the lunacy.

"You're paying for those shoes." I knock on Chance's head with my knuckles to get his attention.

"My Queen has a second chalice for the next brave man to partake from it," he yelled.

"Do you ever speak at a normal volume?"

He ignored me.

Yens handed me a trophy shaped mug, filled to the brim with beer. I had to grip it with both hands, making it difficult to hang on to Chance and not fall.

"Fuck it," I said to no one in particular. Then lifted my right leg to straddle his head, my weight now evenly proportioned, making me feel ten times more stable. I took a long pull from my beer. It had already been a stressful week with a huge paper I'd had due for my lab practicum, which I'd barely completed on time. And now, clearly, I'd entered the collegiate twilight zone.

My left shoe disappeared.

I knocked the trophy cup on Chance's head to get his attention. He looked up at me.

"You wanna tell me what the fuck is going on? And how you're going to pay for my shoes?" I asked, making my tone as snotty as possible.

"Pay for your shoes?" He sounded confused.

"Your idiot friends took my *open-toed* shoes and tried to fill them with beer. They're ruined."

"It's an honor to have them drink from your shoes. You're the Queen," he yelled, as though that explained everything.

"Why am I the Queen?"

He stopped and tilted his head back to look at me. "Do I have to explain everything to you?"

"Yes!"

"Fuck." He walked us into the kitchen, lifted me up over his head, and set me down on a counter in the corner.

"Okay. What part don't you understand?"

"Why am I the Queen? Where are my shoes? Why did those assholes try to drink out of them? And why the fuck did you put me on your shoulder?"

"Sweetheart, it's the rugby championship celebration," he said. I waited for him to continue, but he seemed to think it was an adequate amount of information to explain things.

"And?" I asked.

"You're my Queen."

"Are you simple?" I asked, once again knocking on his forehead.

"Quit hitting me on the head! Am *I* simple? Haven't you ever been to a rugby party before?"

"Nooo." I drew the word out, thinking this should have been obvious all along. He throws his head back and laughs.

"Fan-fucking-tastic! My Queen is a virgin."

"I'm not a virgin."

"You're a rugby virgin, darlin'," he said with a grin.

I took another deep drink from the trophy mug and waited for my explanation.

He grabbed my trophy mug and took a drink himself. Though his drink equated to over half the glass.

"Let me get us both another beer and I'll answer all your other questions."

I looked around the room while he was gone. There weren't many people at this end of the kitchen, but a huge group gathered around the keg at the other end. The living room, which I could see through the pass-thru window over the sink, was packed with people. And the air held the faint stench of old, spilled beer already.

Chance returned and handed me my beer. I took a big drink, then asked, "How'd you get through that crowd so quick?"

"I'm the rugby captain," he said as though the answer was obvious. "Which also makes me your King."

I took another drink and motioned for him to continue with his explanation.

"Ok, we won the Division One All Collegiate Championship, which is a huge fucking deal. So, we have a huge fucking party." He paused for a beer break, and I downed a quarter of my mug in the time it took him to drain over half of his.

Then he continued, "At the party the King is always the captain of the team, which this year is me. Again. And, not to brag, but I'm also Collegiate All-American two years running now."

He puffed out his chest slightly. It's obvious that he's proud of this even though I have no idea what it is. I widened my eyes. "Cool." And then drank more of my beer.

"The Queen is always the hottest chick at the party. I knew as soon as I saw you, you were the hottest chick here. So, you're my Queen."

I had to smile at that.

"Thank you for the compliment, but that doesn't explain my shoes."

"Oh, well the guys drink beer from your shoes as a sign of your royal status. You are the Queen, and they are your willing servants."

"I like that." My anger about my shoes dulled a bit by my beer consumption.

"So special is our Queen, her feet mustn't touch the ground, it's too ordinary. Which is why we carry her around all night. And she gets to order people around and they must do what she says, no matter what. The best part being she picks who gets nectar, and who gets swill."

"That doesn't sound good," I said, taking another drink.

"That's a rugby party, baby doll. You ready?"

"Why? What happens next?"

"Well, I sure as fuck don't carry you around all night. We've got guys for that. Two will put you on their shoulders, not the same two all night, there are three sets of guys. At the end of the night we have a little ritual. Up until then you just hang out, order people around, and have a great time. Sound good?"

"Sounds good!" I moved to take another drink and was surprised to find that the trophy mug was already empty, and I felt good. Really good.

Chance transferred me from the countertop to the shoulders of two other guys. I had one butt cheek on each shoulder. But instead of feeling precariously perched, I felt stable. And invincible. Each guy had a stronghold on my thigh, I was going nowhere.

Chance bent to one knee in front of us.

"Your wish is my command, My Queen. Pray tell, which poor peasant in your realm should be forced to drink swill and which should be honored to fill your cup with nectar?"

I giggled at his word choices.

I never giggled.

Not sure why, it was fun.

I found the blonde who was hanging off Chance's arm earlier and pointed to her, "You, fair maiden, will drink swill!" Her mouth dropped open and she gave me a dirty look.

I pointed to Chance. "And you, My King, please fill me with your nectar," I said, feeling a little loose, not really knowing what I was saying, but enjoying it nonetheless.

Chance winked at me, then stood, looked up toward the ceiling, and bellowed, "The Queen has spoken!" Then he banged on his chest like an ape. The rest of the team followed suit, and I swear they shook the windows with the noise.

My feet never touched the floor again. Except when I had to use the restroom. But even then, some poor sap would throw his shirt or shorts on the ground so my feet didn't touch the actual floor. Which made me happy since my shoes were gone and I had no idea what had been on that floor.

Everything that night made me giddy, the guys carrying me, the people bowing to me, Chase coming to kiss my hand periodically, being able to force swill upon people I decided not to like on sight, and copious quantities of beer.

The rest of the night passed quickly, and I soon lost count of the number of beers I drank, as well as the number of partygoers I forced swill upon, and who I let drink nectar. Swill, I learned, was beer that the guys had swished in their mouths and then spit back out into a pitcher.

It wasn't good to drink swill.

I almost felt bad for the blonde.

Almost.

My head was starting to spin.

I looked around for my roommate, hoping that we could sneak out and go home. I feared that if I had any more to drink, I would be sick.

I heard a chant starting, but I couldn't tell what they were saying.

I looked around and saw Chance approaching. But he was so much taller than normal. I squinted my eyes trying to get my bearings, and realized he too was on top of two guys' shoulders.

"My Queen," he said as he reached me.

"King!" I reached out and fell into him. He pulled me onto his lap so I was straddling him, albeit awkwardly. The guys holding us stumbled a bit at the additional weight but recovered quickly. Chance grabbed me around the waist to steady me, and then he kissed me.

I resisted at first, trying to push at his chest. Until I realized I liked it.

A lot.

So, I kissed him back.

And kissed him.

And kissed him.

It was the best kiss I'd ever had. Lazy, like he had all the time in the world and just wanted to spend it getting to know my tongue and my lips. But, still hurried and desperate, like he couldn't get enough of me, like he could never get enough. And if he didn't get me then, he'd miss his chance.

I was fairly sure at least one of my thighs was wrapped around some guy's head at the side of Chance's waist, and I had no idea how they were even holding us up, but I didn't care. I needed at this guy. Right away.

"I think I love you," I told him.

I could feel his dick harden, the material from his shorts and my pants too thin to conceal anything. I moaned, not caring who heard.

"You're perfect, don't ever leave me," I said.

"So. Fucking. Hot," he said. I rocked against him, feeling the pressure building. The chanting was getting louder. I finally realized what they were saying.

Heaven! Heaven! Heaven!

I pulled away from Chance. "What's heaven?"

"God, baby, you're heaven," he groaned.

I giggled at that. Then the guys carrying us made a quick turn to walk down a hallway, causing my head to fall to the side. And just like that, I couldn't hold it up any longer. When I tried to straighten it on my neck, everything started spinning. I leaned into Chance.

"I don't feel very well," I whimpered into his ear.

He pulled my head back and looked at me. "I know that look," he said. "Boys—"

That's when I threw up.

All over him, all over me, all over the guys carrying us.

And then again, with more projection this time. When I opened my eyes again, I saw in horror as Chance spit to the side.

I'd vomited in his mouth.

OH MY GOD!

I covered my face with my hands and started crying. Chance hopped off the shoulders with me in his arms, somehow not dropping me, and brought me upstairs to a private room with a bathroom.

Which is when he held my hair back as I vomited repeatedly. He flushed after each time, wiped my mouth and face with a cold rag, and rubbed my back; whispering things like, "it's okay" and "get it all out" in my ear as I cried and vomited.

I know at some point he put me in the shower with him and washed me off and brushed my teeth. Because I vaguely remembered most of it the next morning. And when I woke up next to him in bed, I was clean, and I didn't smell like, or taste, vomit.

I took in my surroundings cautiously, noting that he kept his room remarkably clean for a college boy. I glanced at my body under the covers, relieved to see that I still had my bra and panty set on. Then I looked over at Chance and saw that he had boxers, and nothing else, on. Giving me full visual access to all his goods.

His body was nothing short of amazing. Not in a gym-rat sort of way. More in an athletic ability and great genetics sort of way. His dick bulged from the boxers and the tip peeked out from the waist band. I wanted to see more but didn't want to risk waking him up. There is nothing worse than an awkward morning after.

Especially if the night before was you projectile vomiting in someone else's mouth. Then falling down repeatedly while they tried to keep you positioned over the toilet for further expulsions. And let's not forget passing out completely after which he apparently attempted to clean me up and then put me to bed.

Oh God. The shame. I didn't want to look at myself, let alone let anyone else see me.

I carefully extricated myself from his grip and eased my way to the side of the bed. I made it all the way out and into the bathroom without waking him up.

He must have rinsed my clothes in the shower as well because they were damp when I tried to put them on. They did still smell like vomit though. There was no way I could wear them. In fact, I never wanted to see them again.

I shoved them in his bathroom trash can, and then quietly went through his drawers, trying to find something I could wear. I ended up with a white sports jersey that went to my knees in one direction, and socks that went past my knees to my thighs in the other. It would have to do.

I snuck out of his room and down the stairs. People were passed out around the living room in varying stages of undress, continued inebriation, and cleanliness. I winced as I opened the front door and it creaked loudly. But no one seemed to be disturbed. So, with that, I ran back to my dorm. Vowing never to speak to any of those people again.

And I didn't. To me, they ceased to exist.

Until I ran into Chance again about six months ago when Kat brought him to a girl's dinner.

I shake my head, to clear it. Realizing it's my turn at the bar. I get my martini, a sparkling water for Chance, and head back toward our table. Thinking about that night still affects me in ways that I don't care to think about. Mostly because I've still not had a man kiss me like that, since.

I remember most everything about that night, about him, and about our kiss. And how I publicly humiliated myself with massive amounts of projectile vomit. But more than that, I remember how Chance was afterwards. How caring and gentle he was, and how he took care of me and made sure I was okay. Even my roommate had left the party without checking on how I was or who I was with.

Rehashing it all in my mind leaves me feeling tense and a little worked up. Not even realizing until I sit down that I've drank half the martini already between the bar and the table.

My head spins just a little bit.

Oh dear. I cannot have history repeating itself with Chance Bauer. I just can't.

7

CHANCE

Remi teeters back to the table. I can tell that she's had too many martinis and not enough dinner. I think all she ate was her salad. I hate when women don't eat on a date. When they pretend that all they ever eat is salad, and then go home afterward and gorge on half a leftover pizza and a pint of Ben & Jerry's once they're alone. I wouldn't have brought you to a restaurant if I didn't want you to eat.

Knowing Remi has done that, I just want to shake her and tell her I know she eats for real. No one can have an ass like hers and not eat like a normal human. And I mean that in the best way possible, her ass is luscious. I want to sink my teeth into it and leave a mark. I want to spank it until she quivers and then slowly caress my handprint away.

Not that she and I are on a date, because we aren't. I'm here for Kat, and even then, only because her little Romeo, Brad Matthews, asked me to be. And it must have killed him to have to ask me for anything.

Escorting Remi here was just a side bonus. I'm her companion for the evening. Which means I get to pull her close when we dance, fantasize about what she looks like under her dress, and—

"Here," she slams a glass of sparkling water down on the table in front of me.

"Thanks, darlin'." I meet her eyes as I say it, she looks pissed.

"Uh-oh, what'd I do?"

"You're just you," she says, as though the answer is obvious.

"Glad to see I'm me, baby doll, I'd hate to be showin' up as someone else."

"Must you?"

"Must I...what?

"With the nicknames. Always with the nicknames. Is it that you can't remember a woman's name after she tells you? Do they all just blend due to the mass numbers that flock to you? Is it laziness? Or a lack of respect? Have you ever called a woman by her name?"

"No ma'am, not that I recall."

"You're such an ass." She turns away from me.

"Hey, Remi," I say softly. She does nothing. I touch her shoulder and wait for her to turn back to me.

"Remi." I stretch the word out with a singsong voice.

Still nothing.

"Come on, gorgeous, turn around."

"See what I mean?" She turns back and points at me.

"I said your name! Twice in fact. You didn't even pay attention until I resorted to nicknames."

"That's not the point."

"That's exactly the point." I take her half full martini glass away from her. "I think you've had enough for one night."

"Oh no." Her eyes narrow at me. "You don't get to tell me when I've had enough to drink. You don't get to tell me anything, actually."

"I can't have you falling off the back of my ride because you're too drunk to hang on."

"All the more reason why you never should have brought it." The slur to her words is a further sign that she's had too much to drink.

"It's what I drive, hot stuff."

"You don't have a car?"

"Nope."

"What do you do when it rains?" she asks.

"I drive slower."

"No, I mean, how do you avoid getting wet?"

"I don't. I usually have a spare pair of jeans or pants in my saddlebag in case mine are too wet. But my boots are waterproof, and my jacket and helmet take care of the rest."

"That's a lot of hassle just to ride a motorcycle," she says.

"Depends on your perspective, I suppose." I shrug my shoulders. I don't tell her that I can borrow an unmarked sedan from the stations when I need to.

"What are you guys whispering about over there?" Lexie asks from across the table.

"Nothing," she says at the same time I say, "Driving in the rain."

Lexie laughs and then yawns, stretching her arms high above her head. Ethan's eyes about bug out as the top of her strapless dress lowers more as her arms go higher.

Kat whispers in Brad's ear, he smiles big.

"Okay, well it looks like we are going to head out," Brad announces to the table. "My girl is tired, and I'd like to get her home."

He comes over to me and shakes my hand, and then leans in to give Remi a kiss, saying loud enough for me to hear, "Thank you for doing this. It meant a lot to Kat to have you here. I know it probably wasn't much fun given the circumstances." He nods his head in my direction.

"I'm right here."

"I know," Brad smirks.

I'll be honest, Matthews and I aren't ever going to be friends, and it's because I wanted to have sex with his woman, and he knows it. But I still work with her periodically, and she's wearing his fucking ring, so it would be nice if once in a while he could let that shit go. I glare at him in return.

Kat moves in from behind him, gives me a hug and a kiss on the cheek, and says,

"Thank you so much for bringing Remi. I know it couldn't have been that enjoyable, given that she was your date and all," she says. The last part a loud whisper. Then she tries to wink at me, which contorts her face in such a way she looks like she's having a spasm. But it breaks the tension between Matthews and I, which I appreciate. Remi, however, does not like Kat's comment and says as much.

"Thanks, bitch," she says to Kat.

Kat blows her a kiss in return. Remi flips her off.

The couple's departure spurns the rest of us to leave as well. Remi and I say goodbye to Ethan and Lexie at the valet station. I walk over to my bike and pull my leather jacket from the saddlebag, then wrap Remi in it. If her nipples are any sign, she's cold in that dress.

I have the valet signal for a cab and sit back to wait with her.

"You're putting me in a cab?" Remi asks.

"I am."

"Why?"

"Because it's late and you're cold. Plus, you've been drinking, and I don't want to risk your safety if you can't hang on."

"That might just be the sweetest thing you've ever done for me, Chance Bauer," she says slurring her words just a bit.

"More so than holding your hair back when you puked in college?" I ask.

"Oh, why'd you have to bring that up?" She slaps me on the chest. I grab her wrist and pull her toward me. She stumbles into me, then relaxes her body.

"You're warm," she sighs. I wrap the edges of my suit coat around her as well and envelop her in my arms. She snuggles in closer. I start to feel warm inside. A weird warm, like when I've just received a compliment, or my mom tells me she's proud of me.

I like it.

The cab comes just in time to save me from thinking too hard on how much I like the way Remi feels in my arms. I put her in the backseat, swipe my credit card to pay in advance, then follow the cab to her house anyway to make sure she gets there safely.

8

REMI

I get a text message just as I'm walking into my lab to run trials. I check it before going inside. The last thing I need are my 'mean-girl' male co-workers commenting on my taking personal calls and/or text messages during business hours. Not that it matters that they do the same. Working with them and their prima-donna attitudes every day is exhausting.

They don't respect my work because I didn't go to an Ivy League school, and they don't believe I can produce the same quality results from my trials because I'm a woman. My job as a chemical engineer is demanding enough without taking shit from them. I'm on the cusp of a breakthrough in developing an environmentally friendly way to repurpose non-biodegradable materials. And I am not letting anything get in my way until I do.

I look down at my phone screen and see that it's Alex, asking me to call him when I get a chance. Which reminds me that I forgot to call him about setting each other up.

I hit the button to dial his number. He answers on the second ring,

"Hey, that was quick."

"Yeah, you caught me as I was walking into the lab so I figured I'd call you now rather than in another six to eight hours. I was going to call you today or tomorrow anyway."

Obviously, I didn't meet my challenge of talking to Alex before this last weekend, so I swore to the girls it would be early this week with a date set up for this weekend.

"Before you tell me why you were going to call me, let me tell you why I'm calling you."

"Okay."

This better be good, because I'm already annoyed with this whole game that Kat has forced me into with the double-blind date.

"I've got a guy I want you to meet," he says.

"Excuse me?"

"I know, it's weird, since we dated and all, but we're friends now, and I think you're a really great girl. And there's this guy I think you would hit it off with."

How is it that he is stealing my exact speech from me before I have a chance to give it?

"Uh, okay, sure," I say. This will be easier than I thought if I let him think the whole thing was his idea. "So, do I get to introduce you to someone in return?"

"Oh, uh, sure. I guess turnabout is fair play."

"Great," I say. "How's this weekend?"

"This weekend? Wow, you're way more into this than I thought you would be."

Dial it back Remi, you're too eager.

"Oh, well, I just happen to have some free time available, so I figure, what the hell."

"Okay, let me double check with my buddy and I'll get back to you with a time and place to meet."

"You got it," I say. "Hey, Alex, thanks for thinking of me. After everything that happened with you and I, this is really nice of you." Thinking that was nice of him to do. Especially after I did a tap out in the middle of sex. Some people might consider that to be rude and never speak to me again.

In fact, some have.

"Yeah, same to you Remi, thanks. I'm looking forward to it."

"Okay, see you Saturday."

"See you Saturday."

I send off a quick text to my Yoga instructor, Harley, asking her if she's free on Saturday and why. Then walk into the lab, fully prepared to immerse myself in six hours of running trials on elemental breakdown analysis.

I meet my girls that night for dinner at our favorite place, The Crazy Burro, which has salty chips, spicy salsa, and the best margaritas in town. We meet here at least once a week, except when Kat is too sick, from cancer or treatment, to get together. But when that happens either Lexie or I, or both, are at her house with her. Brad too since the two have been back together.

I arrive first, which doesn't happen often, and order drinks from Maureen, our favorite server, then sit back to wait for them.

Lexie sends a text saying she's running a few minutes late, just as Kat arrives at the table. She looks good, healthy even, with a dark burgundy loosely curled wig that goes past her shoulders, and wearing skinny jeans tucked into black stiletto boots, paired with a black dolman top.

"Hey, sexy," I tell her as she walks up.

"What's up beautiful girl?"

"I'm good, just waiting for you."

The server brings our drinks and some chips and salsa. Kat and I both dig in. Lexie arrives looking adorable, as always, in her jeans and sneakers, with a *Lovestone* (her winery) branded hoodie and her hair in twin braids on either side of her head.

"Oh look, all my favorite things at one table!" she says as she sits at the table.

I ask about her day and she fills us in on everything going on at the winery.

"And I'm planning another movie night. But I can't decide if I should do a romance or a comedy. And if I do a romance, do I make it a contemporary Rom-Com or one of my classic oldie-but-goodies?"

"Rom-Com," Kat says at the same time that I say, "Oldie-but-goodie." We all look at each other and start laughing. It does amaze me how close our friendships are when our personalities, likes, and dislikes are so vastly different.

"I like the oldie-but-goodie idea too," Lexie says pointing her drink filled hand in my direction. "What about *Casablanca?*"

"That's a good one," Kat says. I nod my head in agreement, as my mouth is filled with chips.

We don't ask Kat about her day because it's not always a happy topic for her, depending on how she feels, what her doctors are saying, and how much of her hair she has left. Of course, that doesn't stop Kat from asking *me* about things that aren't happy topics.

"So, Rem," she says, her tone snide. "How's the date planning going?"

"It's actually fine, Kat. We are going out this Saturday. I just need to decide on a place and time and get back to Alex." I'm feeling smug as I say this. Because I know that after I missed my earlier deadline for setting the date, they both thought I was going to crash and burn with this whole thing and lose the bet.

And, therefore, lose my beloved Louboutins.

Which is SO not happening. I worked hard to save the money to buy those shoes and I am not going to watch some homeless woman take them for herself. Will she love them like I do? No, she won't. She'll sell them, or worse. Maybe I could secretly buy them back from her? Though there's no telling what condition they'll be in by the time I find her again.

I tune back into the table when I realize Kat is talking.

"I'm shocked. I kind of can't believe you actually did it."

It makes me happy Kat is shocked. I hope Lexie is too. That'll teach them to doubt me in the future. I don't tell them that Alex approached me first with the same idea. There's no need for them to know that. And I don't want them coming up with some reason why it now doesn't count. All that matters is that a date has been scheduled and I will be going. Well, and making sure the guy likes me enough to want to see me once a week four separate times.

"Should we have brunch on Sunday morning so we can hear all about it?" Lexie asks.

"I can't," I say. "I'm already taking time off tonight and Saturday, so I'll need to be in the lab on Sunday."

"FaceTime?" Kat asks.

"Definitely," I say.

"When does this schedule of yours end, Remi? This is brutal. It's like me at harvest time, only you've been at it for months." Lexie reaches out to touch my arm.

"It won't last forever. And I know that I'm so close. There's something I'm missing. I just have to find it." Something I'm presenting on at a conference soon. Hence the rush to figure out the hole in my theorems.

"Hey, I'm meeting Bauer at the precinct tomorrow," Kat says. That surprises me because she hasn't done any consulting work for the San Soloman Police Department since she was re-diagnosed six months ago. But it's also why she calls Chance by his last name, Bauer. It's a law enforcement thing. Except that Chance calls her Cookie, further proving my point that no matter who you are to him, if you're female he can't be bothered to learn your name.

"Are you working on a new case?" Lexie asks.

"I don't think so. He has a couple of things he wants to run past me. Pick my lawyer brain and all that. Otherwise, I think we're just going to grab lunch."

"Is it just the two of you going to lunch?" I ask.

"Probably," she says.

"How does sexy-not-ex feel about that?" Lexie asks. Our new nickname for Kat's fiancé, Brad since they got back together.

"You know, I think he's okay with it. He doesn't like it, but he trusts me. And oddly, I think he trusts Bauer. We're friends, Bauer and me. Even if Brad didn't like it, he'd have to suck it up," Kat says.

I feel a little pinch in my chest when she says she's meeting him for lunch.

It's not jealousy.

I don't get jealous.

It's just a pinch.

"Where are you going to go for lunch?" Lexie asks.

"Probably the food truck in the precinct parking lot," Kat laughs.

"Kat, that food isn't healthy, you shouldn't eat there." Lexie is, always trying to be the voice of reason where Kat's health is concerned.

"It's one meal, Lex, it'll be okay." Kat pats the top of Lexie's hand. "More importantly, what are you going to wear on Saturday, Remi?" She turns toward me as she says it.

"I hadn't thought about it," I say. "Alex just called me today about it."

Fuck.

As soon as the words leave my mouth, I realize my mistake.

"Alex called you?" Kat asks. Honing right in on what I would have loved for her to ignore.

I shrug my shoulders in a noncommittal sort of way.

"Was he calling you back?" Lexie asks.

When did she get so attune to our conversations?

Usually she's got her head in the clouds and not paying such close attention.

"No," I say.

"So, Alex called you about a blind date?" Kat confirms.

"Yes."

"Wow, what are the chances?" Lexie asks.

"Apparently pretty good," I say.

"So, at the same time that you were going to call Alex to set him up, he calls you to set you up?" Kat confirms again.

"Weird, right?" I pick at my napkin.

"Very," Kat says.

"You don't believe me?" I ask.

"I totally believe you," Kat says. "I was just thinking it's a little odd. You even said it was weird. Don't be so defensive."

"Well, it doesn't matter anyway." I sit up straighter in my chair. "The bet wasn't that I had to call him, just that we had to double blind date and I had to stick with the guy for a month."

"And see him once a week, don't forget," Lexie says, then turns in Kat's direction. "Technically, she's right. Her calling him wasn't in the bet, it was the way to the bet." Kat grumbles about it, but we finish our meal in relative peace.

We leave the restaurant a short time later and say our goodbyes in the parking lot. I sit in my car until they both drive off. Then I start my car and slowly head toward home.

It used to be that my house was my sanctuary. But lately it's more like a reminder that it's just me in my life outside of Kat, Lexie, and work.

All by myself.

And sometimes I just don't want to be reminded of that.

9

CHANCE

Kat is on her way into the precinct to help me on a case. She hasn't been around for a while, so I'm grateful to get her help again. Don't get me wrong, she's a real pain in the ass, but she's smart and not remotely hard on the eyes.

I've called her a few times over the past few months, sometimes because I have a question or something I want to run past her about a case, and sometimes just because I miss her. We became good friends in a short amount of time after we met, and I care about her. In fact, she's one of my only friends in this smallish town outside of my other buddy, Alex.

I came to San Soloman a little less than a year ago as a favor to the mayor, an old family friend, and then just stayed. It's actually a great place to live. I've got an apartment a block from the beach, I can run on the sand in the morning with my dog, Hudson, and anything else I need is within walking distance mere blocks away. And my parents are nearby.

"What's on the docket today, boss-man?" Kat asks as she breezes in.

"I do like it when you address me appropriately and with reverence," I say with a grin.

"Pfft, in your dreams." She rolls her eyes.

"You have no idea what you do in my dreams, Cookie." I wink back at her.

She blushes slightly. "Uh, down boy, I'm engaged now. All-a-dis is spoken for." She gestures to her body as she says it, and I laugh.

My phone rings, and it's my buddy Alex.

"One sec," I say to Kat.

"Hey, dude," I say into the phone.

"Chance, you ready to lose our bet?"

"No way in hell that's gonna happen, brother."

"How's Saturday work for you?"

"This Saturday? That works."

"Cool, I'll let you know as soon as we decide on a place and time."

"Sounds good. Oh, and get your checkbook ready, cause if I . . ."

I look over at Kat to see if she's paying attention, but I can't tell. I tone down what I was going to say just in case. "If I tag it and bag it, man, you are payin' up."

"Nobody uses a checkbook anymore, bro." Alex laughs.

"I use a checkbook."

"You might be the only person."

"How else do you write a check if you don't use a checkbook?"

"Bank check."

"Okay, cash then."

"Why don't we just wait and see if she's even willing to go out with you again after Saturday."

"She'll want to."

"We'll see."

"See you Saturday, man," I say back at a normal volume and hang up.

"What's happening Saturday?" Kat asks.

"Not that it's any of your business, but I have a date."

"Really?" Her eyes widen. "With whom?"

"I refer back to my earlier comment about what is and what is not your business."

"Come on, Bauer. We're friends. Friends talk. Tell me!"

"I don't know."

"Yes, you do! Come on. You can tell me," she says.

"No," I say. "I mean I don't know who I'm going on the date with."

"How do you not know?" she asks.

"I know you've been out of the dating pool for a while, Cookie. But traditionally when one has a date with someone they don't know, it's called a blind date."

"Oh!" she gasps. "You have a blind date on Saturday?"

"Yes."

"A blind date?" she asks, repeating herself.

"Uh, we've covered this," I say.

She gets this weird look on her face. One that's like a combination of wonderment and cunning.

"Why do you look like that?"

"Who's setting you up?" she asks back.

"My buddy, Alex."

She bursts out laughing. Like laughing so hard she's doubled over and snorting like a pig.

I start laughing just because she's laughing. But I truly don't know why we're laughing.

She finally calms down, but she's laughed so hard that tears are streaming down her face, her eye makeup smudging on her cheeks. I'll never understand why girls wear all that shit on their face.

"Uh, you got a, uh . . ." I gesture toward her face, point to my eyes, and then back to her face. She swipes under her eyes with her finger and looks at the black that has streaked along the side.

"Oh my God, that's just amazingly delicious," she says. "Oh my God."

"What?" I ask.

"I'll be right back," she says. "I need to use the restroom and text Lexie."

"Okay."

She's much more composed when she returns.

"What was that all about?" I ask.

"Nothing."

"Oh, I get it, I have to tell you mine, but you don't have to tell me yours?" I ask.

"You wouldn't understand, Bauer," she says. "It just made me think of something, and the something that it made me think of was funny."

She's right, I don't get it.

"Chicks," I mutter under my breath, but still loud enough for her to hear.

"I know." She shrugs her shoulders. "What are you gonna do?"

"Well, I'm not going to have one in my life, I can tell you that."

"I guess we'll see about that," she says laughing once more.

"Are we going to lunch or not? I'm hungry," I grumble.

"Yes, let's go."

We head out to the parking lot where the lunch truck typically parks. And it's not until we are halfway to the lunch spot that I realize I didn't even check out her ass as I was walking behind her.

10

REMI

Saturday comes way too soon. I work for a little bit in the morning but am home by early afternoon. Lexie texts me to ask what I'm going to wear.

Me: I'm not sure yet. I'm not too worried about it though.

Lexie: Why not?

Me: I have hours to decide. And if Alex's friend is anything like him, I'll have no problem getting him to date me.

Lexie: You realize this is not just about the bet, right? Like this is to help you try and realize that dating someone is an okay thing to do.

Me: Says you.

Lexie: Says most of the world.

Me: I can't help that most of the world are idiots.

Lexie: You're impossible.

Me: Thank you.

Lexie: Well, I think it's great that you are going and I think you'll be surprised. In a good way.

Me: Uh, huh.

Lexie: Okay, well text a pic when you decide on an outfit. Have fun!

Me: Will do.

I hate Kat for making me do this. I text her to tell her so. She texts me back, quickly.

Kat: Look, you can either go into this with an open mind and have a good time or remain determined that it sucks and is a waste of time.

Kat: Your choice as to how you want your night to be. And your attitude is going to make or break your night. So decide if you want to be the amazing woman that I know you are and have a good time. Or do you want to stick with this whole 'I hate people and relationships' bullshit and make everyone suffer?

Me: I hate it when you get all sensible on me. You used to agree with me about this shit.

Kat: I can't help it now. I'm ridiculously happy with Brad and I want everyone else to be happy too. I think relationships are awesome. And you don't hate it when I get 'sensible' you hate it when I'm right.

She's right.

I hate that too.

Me: Fine.

Kat: That's my girl.

Kat: What are you going to wear?

Me: I don't know.

Kat: I recommend something sinfully sexy that makes you feel good.

Me: That I can do.

Kat: Text me pics.

Me: Will do.

I decide on a black tea length dress with a sweetheart neckline, quarter length sleeves, and a cinch waist. Then accessorize with a large red flower in my hair, Celtic cross on a velvet chain around my neck, and black platform pumps with matching red flowers on the toe. Bright red lips and cat-lined eyes complete the look. I snap a selfie in my full-length mirror and send it to Lexie and Kat. Both respond with compliments, which makes me happy.

I do feel good in this outfit, and I am determined to make it a great night. If for no other reason, then to save my Louboutins. But also for Kat. It seems like it's important to her that I be 'happy' in a 'relationship.' And I would do anything for Kat that she wants. I love that girl more than anything else. I mean, I won't get into a relationship for her, but I will go through the motions and pretend to if it puts a smile on her face.

I'd told Harley that I would help her with her hair and makeup, and that I'd drive her to dinner so we could arrive together. Alex picked a place called The Chesterfield, which is technically a supper club. It's a throwback to the supper clubs from the 1930s and 1940s with a live jazz orchestra. Tables for two and four surround the dance floor and are lit primarily by candles. I've been there before and loved it, but I'm not sure if that's why Alex picked it or not.

I get to Harley's house in plenty of time to help her get ready. She's a super cute redhead with a long, lithe body honed by years of Yoga. She's also a bit of a computer geek, like Alex. And she loves online gaming, specifically X-box Live, like Alex. I know that they're totally going to hit it off. Plus, I think they will look good together physically. I mean, Alex is a good-looking guy. He's tall, built, a good dresser. Just not the guy for me.

We outfit her in a fitted black maxi dress with spaghetti straps and a long slit up one side. Which by itself appears casual, but I'd brought an assortment of shoes and accessories with me. So, we fancy it up with some strappy heels, metallic belt, and a sheer wrap. Then style her hair in a partial up-do with loose waves cascading down her back. Her makeup is light and natural; she looks like a bohemian goddess.

"He's going to love you," I tell her with a sincere smile.

She blushes prettily. It's interesting because in yoga class, she's a ball buster. But outside of class, she's shy and a little timid. I'm hoping that side of her personality will appeal most to Alex. Of course, in comparison to me, most women appear shy and timid.

"You don't know who you're getting set up with either?" Harley asks me.

"Not a clue," I say. "But I plan to make the most of it."

"Me too." She smiles.

I put up a good front, but inside I'm nervous as hell. I have no idea how I'm going to pull this off. Not only tonight but then having to date this guy for a month? What if I hate him? What if he's a total prick? How am I going to stop myself from saying anything? And what if he doesn't even like me? Or find me attractive? Then how do I get him to even see me again? Why oh why didn't I think this through more before I agreed? Kat always brings out the competitive side in me. I mean, I hate losing anyway, but I especially hate losing to Kat, even if she is the most important person in the world to me.

We get to The Chesterfield a few minutes before seven o'clock. I valet park my car and we head inside. I send Alex a text to let him know we've arrived, then ask Harley if she wants to wait at the bar.

"I could use a little courage in a glass." Her smile is nervous, backing up her claim to need courage.

We find two empty stools and sit down. The bartender tends to us at once.

"I'll take a Grey Goose martini, extra dirty," I tell him.

"Uh, white wine," Harley says.

"House okay?" the bartender asks.

She looks to me, I answer for her, "House is fine, thank you."

"Buck up, Harley, you look amazing, he's going to trip over his tongue when he sees you."

"Thanks, Remi."

The bartender serves us our drinks, I take a sip of my martini, and it's perfect. I tell him so.

"I thought I recognized that ass." I hear from behind me.

It sounds like... no, it can't be... there's no way.

I turn around cautiously.

Chance Bauer stands before me.

I look him up and down, he's dressed up in a charcoal gray suit, white dress shirt, a Robert Talbott tie, and shiny shoes.

I'm impressed.

"Icy, you look edible as always," he says licking his lips.

"What are you doing here?" I ask, purposefully not returning the compliment.

"I'm on a date."

"Figures you'd scope out other women while on a date."

"She's not here yet."

"Uh huh."

He clears his throat and nods toward Harley. "Who's your friend?"

"Sorry," I say. "That's rude of me. Harley Reynolds, this is Chance Bauer. Chance, Harley. Chance is a police officer—"

"Detective," he says.

"And Harley owns a yoga studio where she teaches," I say.

Chance looks her up and down as well, the smile on his face is, dare I say it, downright charming. Harley blushes prettily. She wears a blush well; it looks good on her.

"What are you lovely ladies doing here this evening?" Chance asks.

"We're on a date," I say.

"With each other?" he asks. "I like it. Care to make it a threesome?" He waggles his eyebrows at us.

"I doubt your date would approve," I say dryly.

"Not with each other," Harley says awkwardly. "We are waiting for our dates. We aren't, well, you know."

"I *don't* know, actually," Bauer says. "Care to enlighten me?" A devilish smile on his face. I turn my back to him and take another drink of my martini. He takes the seat next to me.

"Really?" I ask. "Must you sit here?"

"Seat is open, and you ladies are enjoyable to look at. I'll be the envy of every man here," he says.

I roll my eyes at him. He's so annoying.

My phone buzzes. I look down, it's a text from Alex.

I lean over to Harley. "Alex just texted me, he was just in the restaurant restroom and will be here in a sec. His friend is already in the bar. Look for a guy with blondish brown hair in a gray suit."

I peruse everyone whose reflection I can see in the mirror on the back wall of the bar, seeing no one that fits the description. I wish I could swallow the lump of nerves that is lodged in my throat. Harley turns slowly in her stool, looking around, then elbows me lightly in the side. I turn to her. She gestures toward Bauer, who is sipping his bourbon and watching the room.

"What?" I ask.

"He's in a gray suit," she whispers. "And he's got blondish-brown hair."

I look Chance up and down. She's right, his suit is gray.

"I wouldn't go so far as to say his hair is blondish-brown," I whisper back, hoping, beyond hope, that I'm right. "Maybe more light brown with blondish highlights?"

"Which is pretty much what blondish-brown is though, right?"

There is no way Chance Bauer is my date.

I look at him again.

In the bar? Check.

Gray suit? Check.

Blondish-brown hair? Check.

Fuck my life.

Any other gray suits around? Negative.

I close my eyes and try to rein the sudden surge of emotions in. Because this can't be happening. I feel my stomach hit the ground as the bar around me starts to spin. I want to throw up. It seems Chance Bauer always brings out that reaction in me.

Okay Remi, just calm down a minute. Maybe it's not what you think.

Alex is in IT for the Police Department. Chance is a Detective. Chance is waiting for a date. We are waiting for a date.

Fuck. Fuck. Fuck.

It's totally what I think.

"Hey that's funny," I hear from behind me. "You guys are sitting next to each other and probably didn't even know it."

Chance and I both turn around. Alex is there behind us.

"Come again?" Chance says while I say, "Excuse me?" I look at Chance, he looks at me, we both look at Alex.

It's confirmed. My life is fucked.

"Oh no," I say. "Oh no, no, no, no, no, no." I stand up and grab Alex by the tie and pull him away from the bar towards the waiting area.

"Harley, talk to Chance," I say over my shoulder as we walk away.

"How did you know it was him?" Alex asks once we stop walking.

"I did *not* know it was him."

"But you know his name."

"Yes," I hiss. "I know his name. Because I hate the man. Despise really. He can't be my date. There's no way. You be my date and we'll set Harley up with Chance. Please, Alex. Please."

"No way," he says. "I got a glimpse of Harley and she's hot. Plus, you don't like me."

"Of course, I like you. We practically dated for six months. I mean, look at you," I gesture up and down his body. "What's not to like? You're funny, you're good-looking, we get along great. That whole sex thing was just a fluke. In fact, I shouldn't even bring it up, it was so insignificant. We can just forget about it. Poof. Gone," I say, my voice rising crazily.

He looks at me, one eyebrow lifted.

I wouldn't believe me either.

"Well, I like you way more than I like Chance," I say.

He just stands there.

"Fine. Fuck, let's get this over with," I say through gritted teeth.

"Do you, um, want to cancel?" Alex clears his throat.

"No." I think of my Louboutins. "It's fine. Let's go." I drag him by the tie back to the bar.

"I'm right behind you, you don't have to pull me."

"You figured out what I figured out and you aren't very happy about it, isn't that right, Ice Queen?" Chance smirks as I get to the bar.

"That is right, simpleton. But I plan to make the best of it, even if it is you that I have to spend my evening with." I pat him on the chest in what I hope is a patronizing manner.

"I'm Alex Fields," Alex introduces himself to Harley and her back to him. Since, clearly, I've lost sight of my manners when faced with Chance Bauer as my date.

Before I have a chance to apologize to Harley for not making the introductions, the host approaches. "Mr. Fields, your table is ready if you'd like to follow me."

Alex motions to Harley to go before him. He walks beside her with a light hand on the small of her back. I like that he's in his alpha protective mode already.

Bauer holds out his forearm for me to grab. "Shall we?" With no other choice, I wrap my hand around his arm and let him lead me toward the table. Because a bet is a bet, and I am not giving up my Louboutins for anyone.

"That's the spirit, cupcake," he says. "I can practically feel my little Ice Queen melting already."

11

CHANCE

I lead Remi toward the table. I'm absolutely floored the evening has turned out this way. I can, and at the same time can't, believe that Remi is Alex's ex-bitch. And suddenly I'm not as certain about my victory with this bet as I was before.

I know Remi and I had chemistry at one point, ten years ago. But do we still have it? No doubt about it, the woman is gorgeous. I mean like cartoon-guy's-eyes-popping-out-of-his-head gorgeous. A dark-haired Jessica Rabbit in human form. And Remi is a spitfire so I can see her tapping out on Alex during sex. But Alex doesn't seem to be lacking in lady skills.

What if she just doesn't like sex? What if she's frigid? The thought makes me shiver as we're walking. And not in a good way.

"Cold, simpleton?" she asks, eyebrows arched.

"Just a little draft, I think. You okay?"

"Oh, I'm good." The way she says it, the huskiness in her voice, makes me hope that this won't be such a bad night after all.

We take our seats at the table, boy-girl-boy-girl, and peruse the menus while waiting for the staff to take our order.

"So, you guys know each other?" Alex asks Remi and me.

"He worked a case with my friend, Kat, earlier this yea—" she says at the same time that I say, "We hooked up in college."

"Which is it?" Alex asks with an uneasy laugh.

"Both," I say at the same time Remi says, "We never hooked up."

"Huh. Okay. So, Harley…" Alex turns toward Harley and begins talking to her.

I face Remi. "What's it gonna take to thaw you, Icy?"

"Thaw me?" she scoffs. "That's a good one. Did you think of that all on your own?"

"I did," I say, then add, "And I went potty all by myself today too." Only I say the second part in a baby voice.

She starts laughing, which is what I want. She's stunning when she laughs. It warms her face, which is usually so stoic; and her laugh is full. You can tell that she's enjoying herself and isn't afraid to feel it or show it. It's one of the few times she shows any emotion at all, outside of anger or disdain. A man could get addicted to it.

The server checks in and Alex orders a bottle of wine for him and Harley. I order a martini for Remi, extra dirty, and a bourbon, neat, for myself.

"What if I didn't want a martini?"

"You always order a martini," I say. "And you always order it extra dirty. It's like you think the olives are the appetizer course."

"Oh, I'm sorry." Her voice drips with sarcasm. "I didn't realize you were an expert on my life and how I take my cocktails. Please continue while I take notes."

"Would you prefer something else?"

"No, it's what I would have ordered," she sighs. "But there might be a time when I don't want a martini, so stop being presumptuous."

"You're implying there will be a next time," I say. "So now who's being presumptuous?"

"Touché," she says, and raises her glass toward me. I tap mine to hers lightly.

Time to step it up a notch.

I set my drink down; take hers and set it down. Then lead her by the hand towards the dance floor.

"I wasn't finished with that."

"I know."

"It's going to get warm," she protests, pulling me back toward the table. She's surprisingly strong.

"I'll get you a new one," I say, trying to get her to move in the general vicinity of the dance floor once again.

She plants her feet and leans in the opposite direction of where I'm trying to get her to go. I think about letting go of her hand and watching her fall, but that's not going to get her to dance with me.

So, I try something else. I look her in the eyes. "Please dance with me?"

That does the trick.

Her face softens. "Don't think I'm not immune to your puppy dog eyes. I'm choosing to dance with you."

"Understood," I grin.

We reach the floor and I pull her into my arms. Loving the feeling just as much as ten years ago at the party, and two weeks ago at the law enforcement ball. The song is sultry and bluesy, and the woman singing has a deep, beautiful voice.

"I love this song," she sighs.

"What song is it?"

"It's called 'Misty Blue.' The singer is doing a bluesier version, like Etta James. But my favorite is the version by Dorothy Moore. Nothing against Etta James, she's a God as far as I'm concerned."

"Is it bad form for our date that I don't know who any of those people are?"

She laughs. "Not at all." I'm glad we're dancing to a song she likes. She's humming and singing it softly; it's like her entire demeanor has changed with this one song. Her body practically melts into mine. She seems almost relaxed.

I don't know what the next song is either, but I do know that it changes her entire body language. The change is subtle, but it's there.

"I'm hungry. We should head back to the table and order."

I offer her my forearm once again and lead her back to our seats. Harley is laughing at something Alex has said, and he's leaned into her. Suffice it to say, I think their date is going very well.

"Have you guys decided on dinner?" I ask Alex.

"No," he says. "We've been talking. I'll look now."

I open my menu and try to figure out what I'd like to order.

"Hey," I say to Remi. "Look, they've got meals for two. Want to share?"

"No," she says flatly.

"Why not?"

"Because I'm sure I won't like what you like."

"Do you know what I like?" I can't help it, I wiggle my eyebrows at her.

A move I do a lot around her. She rolls her eyes at me. A reaction she has a lot around me. But I'll take it. At least it's a reaction, which is better than none.

If I'm going to get her to agree to go out with me beyond tonight, I'm going to need a reaction from her. This must be the easiest way to make twenty-five hundred dollars outside of gambling or prostitution. I can't fuck it up. I picture Mom and Dad on that cruise, and Mom is beside herself with happiness. I want to give that to her.

My mom has given to me and my sisters for our entire lives. Not only raising us while my dad worked long hours at the precinct. But also taking in sewing and alterations at night after we were asleep, for extra money.

This is our opportunity to give back. In a way that we know she will love. I turn back toward Remi in time to hear her say, "No, but I'm sure it's rare beef of some sort combined with a fat slathered starch."

Oh, right, we're talking about dinner. And what I would order from the menu. Well, shit, she's right. There's not much that I like more in this world than a medium rare cowboy steak and a loaded baked potato.

"Well, what were you thinking of ordering?" I ask her.

"Fish."

"At least it's not salad," I mutter.

"What?"

"Nothing,"

"No, tell me what you said."

"I said at least it's not a salad," I say.

"What's wrong with a salad?"

"For a meal? Everything."

"Well, not all of us have to feed that much body." She gestures at me.

"I'll take that as a compliment."

"It wasn't."

I wish someone was keeping score here, because I should get bonus points for being so fucking patient with her.

And nice.

I'm so fucking nice.

"How about the surf and turf for two?"

"Why do we have to get anything for two?" she shoots back.

"Because we're on a date."

Harley interjects, "Are you guys getting a meal for two?"

"No," Remi says at the same time that I say, "Yes." I swear this woman and I will never be on the same page.

"Oh," Harley says. "Well, we're getting the chicken parmigiana and pasta for two. Alex says we're going to reenact the spaghetti scene from Lady and the Tramp, but only if I plan to let him kiss me on the first date." Harley giggles. Alex preens.

I give Alex a look. Because, really dude, where'd your balls go?

Even Remi is giving him a look. He just shrugs his shoulders. Harley looks positively enchanted. I guess if nothing else, he's totally got her number. Figuratively speaking.

"Gross," Remi says quietly.

"So gross," I agree.

Remi starts to giggle. It's a lovely, light tinkling sound.

Since when did I start using words like 'tinkling?' And 'lovely?'

Oh, for fuck's sake, Bauer, where'd your balls go?

But I laugh with her anyway. I've already admitted I'm addicted to the sound; I can't go too much farther down the proverbial rabbit hole now. Can I?

She looks devious.

"Would you like to share the surf and turf for two? I can't guarantee it will lead to a kiss, but there is something delicious in it for us both."

I like that way she says that.

A lot.

"Why, yes, I would, Ms. Vargas. Thank you for the concession."

"Concession?" she asks. "Are we in a debate? A contest? Who's winning?"

"Isn't life just one big contest, beautiful?"

"And Mr. Bauer for the lead," she says.

I smile.

"But not quite the win."

Oh.

12

REMI

He's acting different tonight, but I can't quite put my finger on what it is that's not the same. Regardless, I've got to step up my game, otherwise I'll never get four weeks of dates, and I can kiss my Louboutins goodbye. And watch them walk down the street away from me.

He places our order with the waiter and orders us both another round of drinks. There's a small part of me that likes this 'take charge' side of him. Like I know that I can sit back and relax, he's going to handle everything. I don't have to worry at all. I'm safe and cared for. It's a feeling that completely freaks me the fuck out and that I crave intensely at the same time.

My parents had me late in life. I was an accident. There's fifteen years between my next closest sibling and me. So, not only am I not close to my brother or sister, but my parents didn't appreciate the disruption that a baby caused to their lives'. They'd built a successful business together and once they sent my older brother, their youngest, off to college it was supposed to be time to travel and take time for themselves. Not raise a three-year-old.

So, they put off the travel until it was acceptable to send me to boarding school. And that was it. I rarely saw them after that. And I never saw my brother or sister. They took their cue from my parents. If I wasn't worth my parents' time, then they weren't going to take the time to get to know me.

Which makes the idea of someone taking care of things for me completely foreign. The same with being cared for or loved, outside of Kat and Lexie. The three of us met in grade school before my parents sent me away, and we connected immediately. After I left, we all stayed in touch via letters, and shortly after that, email. Kat and Lexie were my only connections to the outside world and I valued that so completely even if I didn't admit it. I craved it like one craves oxygen after being under water a few seconds too long for comfort.

My parents were extremely generous in that I never had to worry about getting a job in high school, college, or grad school. My tuition and living expenses were paid for, and I was given a liberal allowance. What I didn't get from them were birthday celebrations, holidays at home, or any kind of emotional connection whatsoever.

I don't blame them, not anymore. But it took me a long time to get to that kind of acceptance where they are concerned. I wasn't in the plan, plain and simple. Though why my mother didn't just abort me or put me up for adoption, I'll never know. I'm grateful for life, don't get me wrong. But even I'm self-aware enough to know how fucked up it's made me.

Which is why Chance makes me uncomfortable when he's nice. When he cares. The bickering I can handle, that's easy.

In fact, the worse we get along, the better it is as far as I'm concerned. But even in the face of such dissension between us, there's still something that intrigues me. I'm not bored with Chance Bauer yet. And I don't know why.

I bring my attention back to the table when the server brings our cocktails.

"Where'd you go, gorgeous?" Chance asks.

"I was just thinking."

"About?"

"Nothing even remotely important," I say. "Hey, how about a toast?" I direct that at the whole table. Harley and Alex stop talking and look at me.

"You know, a toast? To blind dates clearly working out," I say as I gesture toward the two of them with my glass.

"Well, and back to the two of you clearly working out," Harley says. She's so cute in her naiveté that I snort just a little bit when I laugh.

"What? I saw you two on the dance floor. There's a connection there. You may not see it yet, but I do." She smiles sincerely.

I scoff at that and look at Chance to see his reaction, but he's a little more thoughtful than I'd anticipated. I backhand him in the stomach to get his attention. "That's funny, simpleton, this is where you laugh at the absurdity."

He looks at me. "I'm not so sure it is absurd," he says softly.

I look at him skeptically. "What do you mean?"

He hunkers down closer to me. So close that I can smell him, he smells woodsy and clean.

"I don't think the idea of the two of us together is a bad one."

"Shut up!" I laugh and backhand him in the stomach again.

He doesn't move.

Doesn't change his expression.

"Are you serious?" My eyes widen.

He nods. "I am."

I swallow what I'm sure is my heart in my throat as I try to digest what he's saying. I mean, I know this was the plan all along, at least for me. I get him to date me for a month, I save my shoes, and I'm done. But that plan involves me convincing him to date me, not the other way around.

I mean logically I know he, or any guy for that matter, has to want to date me to go out with me. But that's me pursuing him. And this, well this feels like he's pursuing me. And I don't like that feeling. I'm the one in control here. I'm the one who is deciding our fate. I'm the one who is saving my shoes.

Fuck.

This feels like he's changing the game.

Yeah, that's not going to happen.

"If you're serious, then where do you see this going?" I ask, stalling for time while I try to come up with a counter plan to this new development.

"Do you mean like white picket fences and babies? Sure, if that's what you want? I'm open."

I choke on my martini.

"I'm kidding, Icy. Jeez. Relax, would you? I'm just saying that despite everything, I kind of have a good time with you, all things considered. And it might not be so bad if we go out again, you know?"

I calm down.

Okay, we are still on the same page. For the most part. At least the page where I end it in a month.

Jesus.

"Don't scare me like that again."

"Sorry babe didn't mean to," he says with a wink.

He called me babe.

I hate that.

He called Kat babe.

I hate that too.

"Don't call me babe," I say a little too harshly.

He holds his hands up as if in surrender. "Okay, no babe, sorry. In fact, forget I even said it just then. It is gone from my vocabulary."

"Thank you," I say.

"So, about that second date?" he asks.

"Why don't we see if we make it through this one first," I say. But then I remember the stakes. This isn't real life. This is saving my shoe's life.

"Actually, let's do it," I say. I can tell he's a little surprised by my change of heart. "Let's set a date now. My schedule can get kind of busy with work, so if I get something on the calendar now, I'll have to honor it."

"Did I just hear you say you were planning a date in advance?" Alex interjects into our conversation. I can see the shock on his face.

"Yes," I say. "We're having a wonderful time. You did a great job with this set up. And we plan to see each other again."

"Great," Alex says weakly.

"Right?" Harley says clapping her hands, clearly oblivious to Alex's seeming distress. She reminds me of Lexie that way. Though I hope Alex's response doesn't mean he's still hung up on me.

"It is great, Alex," Chance says, a smug look on his face.

I don't have the time to try and figure out what that little exchange between the boys means, because our food arrives. I'd opted for scallops as my surf part of the shared meal, and they smell divine. I start eating at once. Not having realized how hungry I was.

The scallops taste just as wonderful as they smell, practically melting in my mouth.

"Good?" Chance asks.

"So good," I moan.

"I like seeing you eat," he says.

"Because you like to see things go in my mouth?" I smirk.

He laughs lightly "You got me there, Icy. But also, because anything you put in your mouth, lends itself to that luscious ass."

I want to take offense at that, but it's hard when he's looking at me with desire in his eyes.

13

CHANCE

I've confused myself a bit tonight with some of the things I've said and done. Especially the comment about having babies with her. That was not something I'd expected to say. But oddly, once it came out of my mouth, it didn't seem so bad.

Maybe I would like to see Remi with my baby inside of her.

Except this is just for a month. And only so that I can help send Mom and Dad on their cruise. I need to get all those other ideas out of my head immediately. 'Cause that long-term relationship shit just won't fly. Been there, done that. Not going to do it again.

I was almost married once, and it wrecked me. The story that I tell people was that she got too caught up in the planning part of the wedding, that she lost sight of the marriage part and of the two of us together. But that's only part of the reason I called it off. The only people who know the truth outside of me, are my parents and my sisters.

And of course, my ex, Helen.

I tell that story because in some ways she did lose sight of the marriage part, but I'm also not sure she ever had it. At first, it was just her acting out in odd ways and getting upset over things that shouldn't matter. Like whether the napkins at the reception should be cloth or paper. Or what size the font in the program should be. I explained it away as her being a little Bridezilla-esque. But then came the day that she threw a plate at the baker during our cake tasting because the chocolate wasn't *chocolate enough*. The baker needed twelve stitches in her forehead as a result.

When I tried to talk to Helen about it, she turned it back on me and said that I didn't care because I wasn't upset enough. It escalated from there. She went from calm to chaotic in a matter of seconds over tiny things. A car did a rolling stop at a corner near our house before turning. Helen threw a rock at the rear window and broke it, almost hitting a child in the back seat. The cable repair person was thirty minutes late to fix our cable, when he arrived, she refused to let him in. Then she called his supervisor and reported the repair person as inexcusably rude and sexually inappropriate; that she didn't feel safe in his presence.

I tried to get her medical help, but she refused to see anyone. I had her locked away for a seventy-two-hour psychiatric hold, but they claimed to not find anything *wrong* with her. Helen's parents ignored the problem and wouldn't help me. It wasn't until I came home one night, after a two-day sting operation, and saw that she had locked Hudson in a small closet, that I finally left. He'd been locked in there so long he had not only defecated on himself multiple times but was severely dehydrated and stressed. You don't just do that kind of shit. It's not normal.

I called off the wedding and moved out, leaving her the house. I wanted to help her, but not to my detriment, or at the risk of my dog's safety. That was when she started breaking into my new place. At first, she would just move things around. Not enough for me to really notice, just enough to make me feel forgetful. Then she started leaving some of her things at my house: lipstick, a scarf, perfume, shampoo, underwear, which is how I knew it was her.

I didn't get a restraining order because I didn't want to be that guy. The cop who can't handle his own shit. So, I tried to control it. But I couldn't. Each time she went on the attack, it was worse than before. She cut holes in my clothes, slashed the tires on my motorcycle, pulled the stuffing out of my couch, and unplugged my refrigerator. All of that I let go and tried to ignore. But when she tried to poison both me and Hudson, I finally pressed charges and got a restraining order.

I took Hudson to my parents' house and transferred to the undercover division shortly after, then spent the next two years buried in work and another identity. And now, I'm here.

Our food arrives, which breaks me out of my hellish memories. I must admit my steak looks good. Before I even have a chance to pick up my fork, Remi has started eating. I like it when she eats, so I tell her so. She says something again about putting things in her mouth, which makes me think about my dick and those red lips.

I feel myself harden.

I want to kiss her. I want to see if I can smudge that lipstick all over her face. I want to pull that flower out of her hair and mess it the fuck up. I want to take her to the bathroom, lock us in a stall, and—

"How's your steak?" she asks.

"Good," I say, my voice gruff.

"You've barely touched it," she says, sounding suspicious.

"I'm savoring," I say.

"Let me have a bite." She pulls my plate toward her and cuts a piece off before I can blink.

She closes her eyes and moans. "Oh my God, that is so good. I've not had meat in so long."

"I can fix that for you, Ice Q," I leer.

She laughs. I expect a caustic remark or shut down. But she just laughs. So I do too.

"How is everything?" Alex asks us from across the table.

"Great," I say. "You?"

"Really good," Harley says. She nudges Alex with her elbow. He nudges her back. They obviously already developed a secret language between the two of them. I'm amazed at how quickly they've connected. No games, no pretense.

The band is on a break, and there's regular music playing. This song I recognize. "Maybe, I'm Amazed."

"Oh, I love this song," Harley says.

"It's anti-American not to love Paul McCartney," I say.

"Wasn't he with the Beatles?" Harley asks.

I laugh. I was never a Beatles fan, but I love Paul McCartney and the Wings. And to me, they far eclipsed anything the Beatles ever did.

"Yes," I say. "But don't let that turn you off his music."

"What's wrong with the Beatles?" Remi asks.

"Everything," I say.

"What if I tell you they're my favorite?"

"Then we are going to have a problem, darlin'," I say.

"They're not," she says. "I just wanted to see what you would say."

"What music do you like?" I ask. "Besides the song 'Misty Blue?'"

"You remembered," she says.

"It was barely twenty minutes ago, sweetheart," I say.

"I know, but it was a little thing, easily forgotten." She looks touched that I remembered. Sometimes it's so easy with women I wonder what kind of idiots they had in their past who didn't remember what they liked or tended to their needs. Those guys just pave the way for the rest of us. Then I remember Alex was the last guy she dated and laugh.

"What's so funny?" she asks.

"Nothing," I say.

"Did I say something to amuse you?" Her tone quickly going back to frosty.

I lean over and whisper into her ear, "It's important for a man to listen to his woman." She stiffens when I say, 'his woman,' but I continue anyway. "And to remember what she says. So, I wondered what kind of idiots you dated before who didn't remember those things. And then I remembered one is sitting across the table from us." I let my lips brush against her ear lightly as I talk, feeling gratified when she shivers.

"Oh."

I give my attention back to my steak and finish it quickly, feeling borderline uncomfortable after.

Remi finishes her scallops and dabs at her mouth primly. "I'm going to use the restroom if you don't mind." I stand and pull her chair out for her, clearly surprising her, if the wide-eyed look she gives me is any indication.

"I'll go with you," Harley says. Alex tries to stand and do the same, but she's too fast for him and ends up just bumping into his thighs with the back of her chair.

I wait until they are out of earshot before I start talking. "Date two is on the books, brother. You scared?"

"Nope," he says. But the look on his face doesn't match the confidence in his voice.

"Do you know what I'm going to use the money for?" I ask.

"What?"

"I'm going to hire one of those billboard trucks that drive around town and it's going to say *Alex Fields is a chump*."

He laughs. "Fuck off, dude."

"So, hey, in all seriousness, it seems like it's going good with Harley. You good?" I ask him.

"Dude, she's amazing. She plays X-Box Live, she's hot, she can talk about anything."

Except for the brilliance that is Paul McCartney and the Wings.

"Have you *Lady and the Tramp*'d her yet?" I smirk.

"Nah that was a joke."

"You should ask her to dance, man. Get her out on the floor, pull her up close," I say.

"I can't dance," he says.

"What, like you're bad at it?" I ask.

"Probably. I've never done it," he says.

"How is that possible?" I ask. "What about high school dances and shit?"

"Didn't go," he says.

"Weddings? Bar Mitzvahs?"

He shrugs.

I think for a minute. Who doesn't go to high school dances? There's no easier way to score, as a teenage guy, than at the prom or homecoming dance.

"Okay, you air drum, right?" I ask.

"You mean like?" he pantomimes drumming on the table.

"Exactly. That's beat, right?"

"Okay."

"I have three sisters, man, I was forced to dance with them all the fucking time. If I can do it, anyone can. Okay, so, this is how they got me to understand beat and timing. Take this song, right?"

The song is "I Never Loved a Man" by Aretha Franklin. I'm impressed that I know that. Or else I should hand in my man-card. I'm not sure.

Alex nods in response to my question.

"Okay, so it's easy to pick out the drums. But alongside the drums is the underlying beat. The part that makes you want to move your head back and forth or tap your toes, right?" I start swaying back and forth and encourage him to do the same. Then I start tapping my fingers on the table. He follows suit.

"You got it, man," I say.

"How does this teach me to dance?" he asks.

"Well, that sway, that's what you're going to do with her, only slower."

He slows a bit.

"Slower," I say.

He slows more. But it's still not enough.

"Watch me," I say, and I slow my back-and-forth way down. "You don't want to be swinging her around. You just want to do a gentle move. Like slow fucking."

We are still weaving side to side when the song changes. "Tender Years" by Marc Cohn.

But it continues to work. My hand is undulating in the air, conducting the beat for us.

Which is when the girls return.

"If you boys care to do a partner swap, that's fine by me," Remi says with a smirk. Alex stops at once, but I continue moving. Not knowing how else to get out of this, I stand, grab Remi's hand, and pull her toward me, forcing her to step in time.

"We can't help it, when the music moves us, we must obey, right Alex?" I ask. I twirl Remi a bit, narrowly missing a waiter who looks at us with a scowl on his face.

"Okay, okay," she says. "You're going to get us in trouble."

I pull her chair out for her, get her situated, and then seat myself.

"I don't know what his problem was," I say. "It is a dinner AND dancing club."

"On the dance floor," Remi says, laughing.

"Well," I say.

"My dinner was so good," Harley says. "But I'm so full now I can hardly move."

"Maybe dancing would help," I say, looking pointedly at Alex.

"This is a good song," Remi says.

"Van Morrison?" I ask.

She nods. "Someone Like You."

"Shall we?" I ask. She nods again, and we move toward the floor. I swing her out gently then pull her into my arms. My moves have advanced since high school. Plus, I enjoy dancing, it's like an acceptable form of public fucking.

14

REMI

God, this song. It kills me every time I hear it. It was Kat and Brad's wedding song the first time around. I don't know if they will use it again. But it's also the song in the movie *Someone Like You* with Ashley Judd and Hugh Jackman. I freaking love that movie. It was based on a book *Animal Husbandry* by Laura Zigman, and I absolutely love that book. I'll be honest though; I think I'd love pretty much anything Hugh Jackman was in.

"I like the way you move," Chance says softly.

"It's because of how my partner leads."

"Well, would you look at us," Chance says. "Being all civil and complimentary. You better watch out, beautiful, or I'm going to think you like me."

"Everyone is capable of a momentary lapse of reasoning," I say looking up at him with a smile. He falters in his dance step, but recovers nicely, and holds my gaze until I look away. The moment being a little too intense for my comfort level.

I look over his shoulder and see that Alex and Harley have joined us on the dance floor. I chuckle lightly, grateful for something else to focus on other than Chance.

"What?" His breath tickles my ear.

"Alex, he does the clutch and sway," I whisper back.

Chance turns us slowly in the dance so he can see where Alex and Harley are.

"He doesn't know how to dance," Chance says softly. "That's what we were doing at the table. Swaying to the music so he could get the hang of it before asking Harley to dance."

"Really?" I lean back and look at him, not believing that he would be so nice.

"Surprised?" he looks me in the eye. "See, I'm not a total asshole."

I'll give him that. He's not a *total* asshole.

"This is nice," I say, a sigh escaping from my chest.

"Dancing?" he asks.

"Dinner, dancing, the whole thing. I haven't done something like this in a long time. And I'm enjoying myself. Even though I'm with you."

"That was almost a compliment, Ice Q. Watch out," he says.

"We've Got Tonight" by Bob Seger plays next.

Jesus, I feel like I'm dancing to Kat's 'sudden death' playlist. The music she plays whenever she wants to feel sorry for herself and sink into a total depression about life and love.

When is the band coming back?

Chance is singing softly.

"You know this song?" I ask.

"It's Bob Seger, of course I know this song."

Surprisingly, he has a good voice. A voice that sends a tingle down my spine and warms up my insides.

"Why 'of course'?" I ask.

"Kat didn't tell you?"

"Tell me what?"

"I used to sing in a Bob Seger cover band. We called ourselves the 'Night Moves'."

"Shut up," I say, my eyes wide.

"No joke."

"I want to see you sing." The words come out before I can stop myself.

"I said I *used* to sing in a cover band."

"So, you've lost your voice? You can't ever sing again? The band broke up and you aren't friends anymore?" I ask.

"The band still plays," he says. "And we're still friends." He pauses for a moment, then continues. "I'll tell you what, go on a second date with me, I'll take you to see the band sometime, and maybe I'll sing a song for you."

"Really?" I cringe inside because I sound like a squeaky girl when I say it. But I'm excited to hear him sing. "What song will you sing?"

"I said maybe. You're just going to have to be surprised," he says.

And I realize, I'm really looking forward to a second date with Chance. Too much.

Louboutins. Louboutins. Louboutins.

Stay focused, Rem. It's all about the shoes.

The band returns. Finally. I recognize the opening strands of the song.

"I Hope That I Don't Fall In Love With You."

Kat is a huge Tom Waits fan and she loves this song. Hearing it sung by a woman almost puts an even more desperate edge to the piece. I feel like it could be the one-song soundtrack to my life. As far as I'm concerned, falling in love is the equivalent to emotional quicksand. You get sucked in slowly until the day you realize you've suffocated and you're dead.

"I think I'd like to sit down," I tell Chance, trying to pull away.

"Finish the song," he says.

"My feet hurt," I lie.

He grabs me tighter around the waist and hoists me slightly, so my feet hardly touch the floor. But now my core is aligned with his. I can feel he's slightly hard. He feels good.

"Am I feeling the real reason why you don't want to go sit down, Mr. Bauer?" I ask coyly.

"In that dress? You've had me half hard all night, beautiful," he says, his voice slightly husky.

"Only half?" I ask. "I must be doing something wrong." But I'm a little surprised by how deep my voice is when I say it.

"Tell me something really unsexy so I can get rid of this hard-on and walk back to the table without being embarrassed."

"Baseball."

"I like baseball."

"I thought all men recited baseball stats to get rid of a hard-on."

"Not all," he says.

"What about grandma?"

"Mine or yours?" he asks. "Because if it's yours, and she looks anything like you, it's not going to work."

"Yours."

He closes his eyes for a minute, and I feel his dick deflate.

"That's kind of cool," I say.

"There is nothing cool about a limp dick, Icy."

"I'm kind of surprised I've never been in this position before," I say.

"What position?"

"Where I've said something and felt a dick go down," I say.

"You, Icy? I'm surprised, I'd think that would be old hat for you by now. I mean, didn't it just happen when you tapped out on Alex?" He sucks a breath in between his teeth, his mouth moves to a grimace. He mumbles something close to, *I can't believe I just said that.*

That would make two of us.

"He told you that?" I ask, my cheeks reddening.

"Guys talk," he says with a shrug.

I push him away and turn to walk back to the table. He grabs my arm and pulls me toward him.

"I'm sorry," he says. "That was a shitty thing to say."

I just pull my arm from his grasp and keep walking. He's right, it was an incredibly shitty thing to say. I walk away, leaving him along on the dance floor.

"Hey Alex," I say when I get to the table. "Do you think you could take Harley home? I'm not feeling well, and I don't want to cut your evening short."

"No, I'll go with you," Harley says. "Especially if you aren't feeling well. We came together, we leave together."

"I'm going now," I say. "Sorry."

Harley stands and grabs her wrap and clutch.

"Uh, I'll call you," Alex says to Harley. She gives him a hug; he glares at me over her shoulder. I don't care. I just want out of here.

I head for the door with Harley close behind me, happy to leave here and get home. Where I can put on my pajamas, eat some ice cream, and watch reruns of *Project Runway*.

15

CHANCE

I head to the restroom after Remi leaves me on the dance floor, mentally kicking myself the entire time. Fucking idiot. Why did I say that? It was stupid. I wanted to get a rise out of her. It was going too good, we were getting along, so I wanted to get more sass out of her.

I splash water on my face, give myself a little pep talk in the mirror, and head back to the table. Alex is there signing the bill.

"You owe me $170."

"Where are the girls?" I ask.

"They left, so thanks."

"Thanks?"

"You pissed Remi off, she took Harley and left."

"How long ago?" I ask, thinking I can catch her.

"They're gone, dude. What the fuck did you do?"

"I said something stupid to Remi," I say.

"What?" he asks.

"You don't want to know."

"Well, now I do."

"It was something stupid, and it didn't make her feel particularly good about herself. And I regret it." We start walking toward the front door of the restaurant.

He puts his arm around my shoulders "Well, as long as you regret it, buddy. That's all that counts, right? Makes ruining both our nights a-okay," he says dryly, patting one shoulder, hard.

"I apologized; she just didn't want to hear it."

"I didn't call her an ice queen for nothing," he says.

If only he knew the half of it.

"Well, on a positive note," he says. "I'm that much closer to twenty-five hundred buckaroos. So, thank you for that."

Fuck.

I'd lost sight of the bet at some point toward the end of the night. What was wrong with me? I cannot afford to lose focus. Literally. Because I don't have an extra two thousand five hundred dollars. If I did, I wouldn't have needed to get into this bet in the first place.

We say goodbye, and I order an Uber to get home. I didn't ride my bike because, if I'm honest, I wasn't quite sure how the night was going to play out. I had no idea who I'd be meeting or if I'd feel the need to drink excessively to get through the evening. I like to leave my options open.

I go to text Remi from the car on the way home and realize I don't have her number. I go to text Kat and realize it's too late to text her. Then remember that of course Alex has Remi's number. But I'm not sure he's going to be willing to help me out like that. Especially since he now thinks he's that much closer to winning.

I make a mental note to text Kat in the morning for it. Then sit back and close my eyes for the remainder of my trip home.

I go for a run in the morning with Hudson. He loves it when we run on the beach, biting at the waves as they come in. Not understanding the ebb and flow of the water, thinking it's chasing and then running from him somehow.

We run extra-long today, punishing myself for being an ass to Remi. When we get back to the apartment, it's all I can do to collapse on my couch with a beer. I turn on football and settle in but get called in to the precinct a few minutes later. I jump in the shower and am out the door, having forgotten my mental note to get Remi's number.

It takes me longer at the crime scene I'm called into than it should have, so I barely have time to grab Hudson and get to my parents' house in time for Sunday dinner. We do this every other Sunday, get together as a family for dinner. Two of my sisters, Audrey and Eliza, are married, Audrey is pregnant, and Eliza has a kid. My other sister, Charlotte (Charlie for short) is single, like me, and happy about it, also like me. But when everyone is in attendance, dinner can get crazy. Especially when I drive the work sedan and bring Hudson with me.

This week Mom made pasta, a favorite of Audrey's. Last time it was roast, my favorite. She switches off making the favorites of her kids and my pops, Brian. Eventually, she'll have to add grandkids' choices to that schedule, and pretty soon my favorite will only be in rotation a few times a year. That thought makes me sad.

My pops, a detective like me until he retired last year, loves hearing about whatever case I'm working on. So, we sit on the back porch and discuss today's crime scene as we wait for dinner. My sisters are in the kitchen helping my mom, and she sent Audrey's husband, Mike, to the store for cream. Eliza's husband, Nate, has the baby in the living room, so it's just the two of us. I like both my brothers-in-law. I never would have let my sisters marry them if I hadn't. But I like the time alone with my pops more.

I'm just finishing telling my dad what happened when Mom calls us in to dinner. We sit at the table and dish up. I've hardly taken a bite when Audrey starts in on me.

"So, Chancey," she says with a grin, knowing I hate it when she calls me that. Only my ma can call me that. "One of my girlfriends saw you at The Chesterfield last night. She said you were pretty cozy with a gorgeous brunette. Do you have a girlfriend you haven't told us about?"

"You have a girlfriend?" my mom asks, clapping her hands, her smile wide.

"Gafend, gafend!" my niece, Hailey, chants. Hudson barks his appreciation for Hailey's chant.

"Busted," Charlotte says, drawing out the word.

"That's right," Eliza coos to the baby. "Girlfriend. Good girl."

"Well, that's good news, son," Dad says. "It's about time you start thinking about settling down."

"I don't have a girlfriend."

"Oh," Mom says, her tone forlorn.

"I had a date."

"A date is a good start," Mom says. "What's her name?"

"It was just one date, Ma," I say.

"Hey, Audrey and I started with one date," Mike says. "And now look at us."

"Not helping, dude," I say to Mike, and then to my mom, "Her name is Remi."

"Remi," my mom says. "That's a pretty name. Is she ethnic?"

I look at my mom. "What do you mean, is she ethnic?"

"I'm just trying to guess at what my grandkids are going to look like," she says.

"Ma!" I exclaim.

"She has dark hair," Audrey says. I glare at her. Which eggs her on. "And she's really pretty. Kinda pin-up-ey."

"What's pin-up-ey?" Dad asks.

"You know," Audrey says. "Like a pin-up girl. Those calendar girls from the fifties that guys would hang up in mechanic shops."

"Nice," Nate says, elongating the word. Eliza backhands him in the stomach.

"Ice, ice, da da," Hailey chants.

"No, Hailey-girl," Charlotte says. "It's *ice ice, baby*."

"Ice, ice, baby, ice, ice, baby," Hailey yells. And Hudson joins in once again, running in circles behind her highchair. He's a smart dog, learning early on that anything that drops to the floor is fair game. And that most of the food that drops will come from Hailey. So you can usually find him camped out under her highchair.

"Dun dun dun du du du dun dun dun dun dun du du du dun. Stop, collaborate and listen," Mike starts.

"Word to your mutha," Charlotte joins in, with arms crossed over her chest and a chin nod, rapper style.

And on goes family dinner. It's always total and complete chaos. And I love every minute of it.

The boys clean up after dinner. We always do if Mom and the girls cook and vice versa. My dad has always done it that way, so the rest of us do too.

My sisters all leave soon after, but I stick around with my parents. It's my favorite time of Sunday dinner. Dad and I have a bourbon, Mom has a glass of wine, and we sit on the back porch. After the chaos of dinner, it's the perfect counterpoint.

Until Mom starts talking that is. "So, Chancey, tell me about Remi."

"There's nothing to tell, Mom," I say.

"But you brought her to The Chesterfield," she says.

"That's a nice place, son," Dad says.

"A friend of mine set me up on a blind date, he picked the place. Sorry to disappoint."

"Audrey said you were cozy," Mom says.

"We were dancin', Ma."

"You always were such a good dancer, Chancey," Mom says, patting me on the shoulder. "Did you have fun?"

I think about it for a minute. Contemplating what to tell her. I could never tell her the truth about the bet, she'd be disappointed in me. Which begs the question, why am I doing this? Should I be disappointed in me? It's certainly not right to be doing this to Remi, she doesn't really deserve the deception, even if she does freeze me out most of the time.

But the other part of me thinks, it's for the twenty-five hundred, man. So you can reward these two amazing people right here. And it's only a month. It's not like you're marrying the girl. Four dates, give or take a few, some quality time between the sheets, everyone has a good time, no muss, no fuss.

"I did have fun," I say. "She's a great girl. Smart, pretty, challenging, but in a good way, you know?"

"It's good to be challenged, son," Dad says. "Keeps you sharp."

My phone buzzes with a new text. I pull it from my pocket. It's not a number I recognize so I silence it and make a mental note to read it later.

"I'd love to meet her," Mom says.

"Mom, it was one date, don't get ahead of yourself."

"Well, you know, Chancey, usually you just, what? Hook up with these girls? You don't date them. And I certainly never meet them."

I choke on my bourbon. She pats me on the back.

"What makes you say that Mom?" I ask, my voice suddenly raspy.

"Well, I know things Chancey, word gets around, you know. And your sisters tell me things," she says.

"I'm never telling any of them anything again," I mutter.

"I love how close you are to your sisters. It makes me prouder than you'll know. Knowing that I raised children who love and care for one another." She starts sniffling a little bit.

"Oh, Ma, don't cry."

"Are you alright, baby?" my dad asks. "Annalise?"

"I'm fine, Brian." She pats him on the knee. "I just get a little emotional over my kids."

Dad hugs her around the shoulders and gives her a long kiss on the temple. After all these years, they still have so much love for one another. I like knowing that it's possible for some people.

Shit, maybe relationships aren't such a bad thing after all.

16

REMI

I spend the day at work running trials and don't get home until dusk. I open the door to an empty house. I should really get a dog or a cat or something. But I can't handle having something rely on me so completely for something as simple as nourishment and life. I wash my face, change into yoga pants and a cami, and head to the kitchen. Trying to decide between a frozen meal or ice cream for dinner. Everything I eat comes from the Crazy Burro, a take-out menu, or the freezer.

Which is part of why last night's dinner was so freaking good. I haven't had food like that in a long time. Not since Kat, Lexie, and I spent Kat's first honeymoon in Europe after she called off her wedding. I gained eight pounds on that trip; it was totally worth it. I decide on ice cream, vanilla bean, then I pour some Bailey's Irish Cream over it. It's like dessert and a cocktail at the same time.

I sit on the couch and channel surf the TV trying to find something to sink myself into. I hear my phone chirp signaling a text message. I grab it, seeing the message is from Kat.

Kat: I've been patient all day waiting for you to reach out to me. You disappoint me, woman. How was the date? Did you like the guy?

I so don't want to get into this. Kat is going to laugh her ass off when she finds out my date was Chance Bauer. I've hated him forever. And I gave her a really hard time when she thought she had a crush on him for a short time before she and Brad got back together.

Me: The date was . . . nice.

Kat: Nice? Like in the guy was nice? The restaurant was nice? What???

Me: It was all nice.

Kat: What was he like? Did you like him? What does he look like? Is he hot?

Me: He is good-looking, yes.

Kat: Sigh.

Kat: What else?

Kat: Wait - before you get into details, let's switch to the group text. Lexie will be devastated if she misses out on this first-hand.

We add Lexie into the text and continue.

Kat: Okay, Rem, now tell us.

Lexie: I'm so excited to hear about it!

Me: It was good.

Lexie: Good?

Me: Yeah.

Lexie: Good, like, good? Or good, like, bad?

Me: Good, like, good.

Kat: Was there chemistry? Did he kiss you? How was the food? Isn't The Chesterfield great?

Me: Maybe. No. Great. Yes.

Lexie: Kat, do you get the impression that maybe Rem doesn't want to talk about it?

Kat: I do Lex. But too fucking bad for her. SPILL IT REMI!

Me: Don't laugh.

Kat: LOL!

Me: I mean it.

Lexie: Okay.

Kat: OK

Me: Alex set me up with Chance Bauer.

And both girls go radio silent. I can see the three dots, but no text appears.

Me: Hello?

Kat: Uh, Chance Bauer, like the guy I work with? That Chance Bauer?

Me: Yes.

Lexie: Oh that's so sweet. You were college sweethearts and now you can be grown up sweethearts.

Me: We were NOT college sweethearts.

Lexie: Well, you know what I mean.

Kat: So, how'd it go? Did you enjoy it? Can you see yourself dating him for a month? Or are we taking a trip downtown to donate some shoes?

Me: I can handle it for a month. No problem.

Kat: Yeah, but can he handle you?

Me: Funny...

Kat: Well, alright then. When's the next date?

Me: We don't have one yet.

Lexie: That's gonna make it hard to get to a month. :-)

Me: He pissed me off last night, so I left.

Kat: You okay? What happened?

Me: I am now. But he brought up the whole tap out with Alex and it made me mad.

Lexie: Alex told him about the tap out?

Me: Apparently.

Kat: You didn't do anything wrong, Rem. In fact, you are an inspiration for women everywhere who don't stick up for themselves and their needs during sex.

Me: Thanks, Kat.

Lexie: I'm gonna tap out.

Kat: You have to have sex with something that isn't battery operated to do that.

Lexie: Rude!

Me: LOL

Lexie: Just wait, Kat. I'm going to tap out on my raunchy rabbit vibrator.

Kat: And that would serve your needs how?

Lexie: Okay, I see your point and I concede.

Lexie using the word concede reminds me of Chance. And I realize there is a teeny tiny part of me that might miss him just a little bit. Possibly.

Kat: Well, you'd better get back on that horse, lady. Why don't you text him and apologize for walking out.

Me: I don't have his number.

Kat's next text is her sending me his contact e-card.

Kat: Text him now, let us know what happens.

Louboutins. Louboutins. Louboutins.

I save his contact info in my phone and then pull up his info to text him. Eight o'clock on a Sunday night. What if he's not alone? What if he's on a date? What if he's chasing bad guys and I blow his cover?

None of that matters Remi. This isn't real. It's a bet. Suck it up.

Me: Hey. It's Remi. I just wanted to apologize for leaving last night without saying goodbye. That was rude of me to do.

I wait to see if the three dots pop up, but they don't. Then I wait for another five minutes and get nothing.

So, I binge watch *The Big Bang Theory* and eat another bowl of ice cream with Baileys. I'm already in bed when my phone chirps with a text at nine-thirty pm. I look down and see Chance's name on the screen. Do I ignore it? Pretend I'm already asleep? I open the message instead.

Chance: Are you still awake? If not, and this wakes you up, I'm really sorry, go back to sleep.

Me: I'm awake.

Chance: Hey.

Me: Hey back.

Chance: Sorry for the delay in responding, I was at my parents' house for dinner. I like to stay after to hang with them once my sisters leave.

Me: I didn't ask.

Chance: I know.

Me: Ok.

Chance: I should be the one apologizing for what I said.

Me: It's not like it wasn't true.

Chance: That's not really the point. It was a crappy thing to say.

Me: Apology accepted.

Me: On one condition.

Chance: Anything.

Me: Oh, you better watch it, you have no idea what I'm about to say.

Chance: I can handle it. I'm not afraid.

Me: What if the condition was something awful? Like, you have to direct traffic, in only a thong, at rush hour, in the middle of town square.

Chance: LOL. No problem.

Me: Wait, wouldn't you be arrested for that?

Chance: Most definitely.

Me: Haha!

Chance: :-)

Chance: Is that the condition?

Me: No.

Chance: ?

Me: You accept my apology as well.

Chance: Already done, beautiful.

Me: And, we go on that second date.

I hesitate hitting send. Yes, this isn't reality, it's a bet. But somehow it still feels like there is so much at stake here.

Fuck it.

I press send.

And wait.

Almost a full minute goes by before he responds.

Chance: When are you free this week?

Me: This week? Like during the week?

Chance: Yes.

Me: Never. During the week is terrible for me. I have to work.

Chance: Every night?

Me: Yeah.

Chance: So, you won't be doing girls night with Kat and Lexie?

Me: No, I'll still be doing that.

Chance: So, not every night.

Me: Well, that's different.

Chance: How is that different?

Me: It's a standing date, every week.

Chance: So, make me a standing date every week.

Me: Every week??

Chance: Every week. But I want a weekend night too.

Me: We don't even know if we like each other.

Chance: We don't?

Me: And we don't know if we're sexually compatible.

Chance: I can fix that tonight. Send me your address.

Me: Ha!

Chance: I'm serious.

Me: One day at a time, big guy.

Chance: That's not a no.

Me: Uh, it's NOT a yes.

Chance: I'll still take it.

Chance: How about Tuesday night?

Me: As in two nights from now?

Chance: Yeah, we can do Tuesday and then maybe Saturday.

Me: Aren't you getting a little ahead of yourself there, simpleton?

Chance: I don't understand. Can you explain what you mean?

Me: You aren't as funny as you think you are.

Chance: So, you think I'm funny?

Me: I can do lunch or after-work coffee on Tuesday, only an hour regardless. Then a 'date' on Saturday. How's that?

Chance: I'll take what I can get.

Me: Desperation is unbecoming.

Chance: Don't be a hater.

Me: That made me laugh.

Chance: Then I will end this on a high note. Good night, beautiful.

Me: Good night.

I turn out the light, get re-situated in my bed, and try to ignore the smile on my face.

And the fact that I'm looking forward to seeing him on Tuesday.

17

CHANCE

Remi and I agreed that I would meet her at her office, and we would walk down the street for lunch. When I get there, I'm surprised to see that it's a controlled access building with some serious security. Technically, I don't know exactly what she does for a living, but I didn't expect it to require such safeguards.

They buzz me into the lobby after mentioning I'm there for Remi. The receptionist waits until I'm standing in front of her before looking up from the pad of paper she is doodling on.

"Oh! Um, well, hello," she says, perking up when she sees me.

"Hi, Chance Bauer here for Remi Vargas," I say giving her a big smile.

"For, Remi?" Her head snaps up and her eyes widen.

"Yes, for Remi," I confirm.

"Huh, ok. I'll let her know you are here," she says. "May I tell her what it's regarding."

"She knows," I say. The receptionist continues to look at me, expectantly. She looks vaguely familiar. But I'm not sure if it's because she's checking me out and sorry to say I'm used to that look. Or because we've met before.

"I'm picking her up for our lunch date," I say. She looks a little disappointed at that but calls Remi anyway to let her know.

"Can I get you anything while you wait?" she asks.

"No, thank you."

I look around the lobby, it's nice. Lots of large green plants, dark tile floors, and large tinted windows. After a few minutes, I sit on one of the plush couches they have scattered about. The receptionist keeps stealing glances at me, so the next time I see her from my peripheral, I turn and wink.

The look she gives me in return stuns me for a minute. But also clues me in as to why she looks familiar. She has the same face shape and mannerisms as my ex, Helen, with different hair. I'm still staring at her, mouth hanging slightly open when Remi approaches.

"Same tricks, same dog," she says, her eyes narrow and her mouth pinched.

"Icy, nice to see you too," I say, turning to take her in, ignoring the comment. She looks stunning, not that today is an exception to any other day. She's wearing a full skirt with flowers on it, a black cap sleeve tee with crisscrossing across the V-neck, and little ballet slippers. Yes, I know what cap sleeves and ballet slippers are, I have three sisters.

"Connie, can you mark me as out for the next hour, please? Thank you," she tells the receptionist. I take Remi by the hand and lead her out the doors.

"Sure thing. Have a nice lunch, Rem," Connie calls after us.

"Is there a woman that you won't flirt with?" she asks as we walk toward the end of the block. "She's my friend. You're shameless."

"I wasn't flirting with her," I say. "I just winked at her. And I'm not even sure why I did that. There is no reason to be jealous. Plus, it's not her I'm taking to lunch."

"Oh, I'm not jealous."

"Then why the comment?"

"Why the wink?"

"You look very nice today," I say, changing the subject. I wonder if there is anything in her closet that she doesn't rock the hell out of.

"Thank you." She looks me over. "So do you."

"This old thing?" I say gesturing to jeans, t-shirt, and biker boots, my typical off-work outfit. And sometimes my typical at work outfit as well.

She laughs. And, I notice, still hasn't let go of my hand.

"So, where are we going for lunch?" I ask.

"Greek," she says. "That okay?"

"Absolutely. How's your day going so far?"

"It's good," she says in a way that almost belies what she's saying. I give her hand a little squeeze.

"Yeah?" I confirm.

"Better now." She smiles and squeezes my hand back. But I'm not sure if she thinks it's better because of me or because we are about to have lunch.

"Here we are." She points toward a carved wood door connected to a small building that looks slightly out of place amongst the other modern glass structures on the block.

I open the front door for her and follow her inside the restaurant.

The man behind the counter greets Remi as we walk in, as though they're long-lost friends.

"*Bellisima*, you return to me. Lovely, lovely, please sit." The older gentleman motions to the seating area. His eyes crinkle as he smiles at us and nods his head, covered in salt and pepper hair, thinner on the top, and too full around his ears. He's taller than I'd expected but still portly. And his mannerisms make you feel at home.

We pick a table and get situated, the place is small but most of the tables are full, and it looks as though the guy is the only one working here.

"He doesn't sound Greek," I say to Remi.

"He's Italian. But he makes the best *dolmathes* and *avgolemono* you've ever had."

"Then I'll try both," I say.

The man comes to our table. "I choose for you, *bellisima*?" He looks at Remi.

"Yes please, Adamo. Thank you."

"He's picking our food?" I don't think I've ever not picked my own food. It makes me a little nervous.

"Yes, are you okay with that?"

"If you are, then I am." I clear my throat and feel my pocket for the list of questions I brought with me, unsure how to bring it up. "So, I was thinking… I mean… I have this list of questions."

"A list of questions," she laughs. "For what? Where'd you get it?"

"Questions for us to get to know each other better. But they're for both of us to answer. And I got them from one of my sisters."

"Where'd she get it?"

"From some girly magazine. Cosmo, I think. Hey, see how well we are already asking and answering questions? It's working." I grin.

She giggles. That's a sound I've not heard from her often. I like it.

"You game?" I ask. She nods, a small smile on her face. One that makes me feel warm on the inside.

A feeling I'm going to ignore for now.

I pull the paper out of my pocket. It's on a regular sized sheet of paper, but the picture of the questions my sister, Audrey, scanned and sent, only covers a part of it. I smooth it out on the side of the table, only a little bit nervous about doing this.

"Is that your cheat sheet?" she laughs.

"Yeah, I can't remember all these questions on my own."

"How many are there?"

"Total? Fifteen."

"Okay. Let's do this.

"Are you a morning person or a night person?"

"Neither," she says.

"How can you be neither?"

"Well, I hate mornings, so I'm clearly not a morning person," she says. "But I also don't stay up late at night. So, neither. I'd say I'm more of a sleep person. What about you?"

"I'm a morning person. I love getting up before the sun, dragging Hudson down to the beach, and running 'til we're pumped. Then coming home and getting a jump start on my day."

"That sounds awful." She shudders. "Who is Hudson?"

"Hudson is my dog."

"I love dogs. What kind?"

"Siberian Husky."

"Oh, Lexie has huskies too. Like seven of them, I think."

"That's a lot of fur."

"Totally. She loves them though."

"If you hate mornings, what are your thoughts on morning sex?" I ask, going off script.

"It's great, as long as it ends up being worth waking up for," she says. "But then let me go back to sleep after."

"Sex makes you tired?" I ask, trying not to appear as though I'm already imagining us having sex.

"If it's good sex, yeah. Really it's orgasms that make me tired."

"Would you like to be tired now?" I ask.

She throws her head back; a full belly laugh resonates in our little corner of the restaurant.

Laughing is good.

"Sex amps me the fuck up," I say as she quiets.

"How annoying."

"Not really, not if you're expecting it."

"Okay," she says. "So, it's morning, and we've had sex."

I attempt to subtly readjust when I feel myself getting a little hard at the idea of sex with Remi. Especially morning sex with Remi because that means I've already spent the night with her.

I clear my throat a bit. "Yeah?"

"And you're pumped, and I'm tired. What do you do?"

"Well, clearly, I let you sleep. Because you can be a real bitch when you don't get enough sleep—"

She scoffs.

I continue, "And so I go on my run with Hudson, come back home, shower, make you coffee, then wake you up. Gently."

"What if I don't like coffee?"

"Who doesn't like coffee? That's like saying you don't like sex. But, ironically, that's a question on the list, coffee or tea? So, which is it?"

"Coffee," she says.

"Phew," I say. "Crisis averted. For now."

"What about you?"

"Was I not clear? Coffee, all the way. The grittier, the better."

"What makes coffee gritty?" she asks.

"You know, when it's been sitting on the burner all day, and the bottom of the pot is slightly scalded, and the coffee gets that bitter taste?"

"No."

"Or when it's a fresh pot and you've put twice as many required grounds to the ratio of water?"

"Can't say I know that either."

"Well, that's gritty coffee. Puts hair on your chest." I punch my chest to accentuate my point. "What kind of coffee do you drink, anyway?"

"Organic Blue Mountain in a French press," she says. "You?"

"At home? Instant. At the precinct? Whatever they've got that's hot."

"You can never make me instant coffee."

"So, I get to make you coffee?" I wink. She blushes slightly.

Adamo brings our food, it's enough to feed twice as many people.

"*Bellisima*, I make your favorite, no? And the rest to feed your man. You got a big boy, eh? Big appetite, no?"

"Thank you, Adamo," I say. "I do have a big appetite." He winks at me. Which I laugh at. Remi thanks him as well and we dig in.

For Remi, he has prepared the *dolmathes* and *avgolemono* that she loves so much, along with an array of hummus, pita, olives, and cheese.

For me, he has a generous portion of gyro, pita, tzatziki sauce, rice, and spanakopita. And it looks amazing.

"So, do you think we're actually going to go through all fifteen questions while we're at lunch?" she asks.

"No, but over the next few dates we will."

"We're going on other dates?"

"At least one more, remember? Saturday?"

"I do, actually."

"And, if I have my way, more after that."

"You're very persistent," she says. "Why is that?"

"Isn't everyone persistent when they see something they want?"

"Are you saying you want me?"

"I thought that was obvious, Icy." Her eyes widen, and she holds my gaze for a few seconds. Then goes back to eating and not meeting my eye for the next few minutes.

I ask another question from the list. "How often do you visit your family?"

"Is that another question from the list?" Her body stiffens.

"Yep. Our third question. See how great this is going? Just like a normal cordial conversation." I smile to show I'm joking, but she has yet to look back at me. I'm hoping this makes her uncomfortable because we are connecting and not because there's something weird with her family. "So, what is it, once a week? Once a month?"

"I don't really visit with my family." Her face goes completely impassive when she says this, her eyes showing no emotion.

"Not at all?"

"No."

"I'm sorry. Did something happen?"

"That's another question, and I've already answered the first. So, what about you, how often do you visit with your family?"

"We talk a lot, more on the phone than in person. But we get together at least every other week for Sunday dinner. And sometimes more often than that if it's a holiday or someone's birthday."

"Every other week? As in twice a month?" she asks.

"Yeah, and sometimes that doesn't seem like enough. My niece is growing so fast I feel like I'm missing everything. And I have another niece or nephew on the way, and I want to see that one grow. And my parents aren't getting any younger. So, yeah, at least twice a month."

"Wow, I would have no idea what that's like. I'm not sure if I'm jealous over it or relieved I don't have to do that myself."

I wonder what happened in her past to make her say that. I always assume people have a good relationship with their families and visit them. That's just what you do. I forget that not everyone is like me.

"Why don't you visit your family?" I try again.

"What's the next question?" The stony look on her face clearly tells me the conversation about her family is over.

"Ok," I mutter. "Tabling the family discussion."

I pause to eat some more of my gyro. Which, I have to admit, is the best one I've ever had.

"What's something you've never tried, but are dying to do?" I ask.

I like the way she scrunches her mouth when she's thinking. I doubt she realizes she does it.

"I don't think I have one. Whenever I want to do something, I do it."

"That's such a bullshit answer," I laugh.

"No, it's not," she says. I look her in the eye and wait. Because we both know it's a cop-out.

"Fine," she says. "I have issues with heights." I stay silent, there's got to be more to the answer since she hasn't really answered the question. She takes a deep breath, and then apparently decides to share something about herself with me, because she adds, "I'd like to get over it. So, maybe do something that helps with that."

"What kind of heights are we talking about? Empire State Building? Seattle Space Needle? Skydiving?"

"Among other things."

"What other things?" I ask.

She shrugs her shoulders a bit, then says, "Ladders, balconies, bridges, glass elevators."

That's a new one.

"Ladders? Like how tall?" I ask.

"Honestly? I don't even like my step ladder at home. Anything more than two steps and I'm having a tough time."

"What about stairs?" I ask.

"Enclosed stairs don't bother me. But I don't like open stairs, especially exterior open stairs."

"So, it's the feeling of having nothing around you that you don't like?"

She takes another bite of her lunch before answering. "I think so. If there's nothing around me, I'm always tempted to jump." She covers her face in her hands as though embarrassed.

"From exterior stairs?" I try to get a gauge on what we are really talking about here.

"From anywhere high and exposed: ladders, bridges, rooftops. It all has to do with the height," she says.

"So, heights make you want to jump?"

"Well, *want* is a strong word. I would say it's more like an inkling. Not so strong as an urge, but not just a fleeting thought either."

I reach over the table and take her hand in mine. "Are you . . . okay? I mean, is it because you want to . . ." I'm a trained law enforcement official and I can't bring myself to ask this girl if she wants to off herself with some kind of suicide jump.

"It's not about suicide, if that's what you're asking," she says.

"Asking poorly, apparently. But that makes me feel better."

"It's more like a fucked-up curiosity thing. An impulse that I would never give in to. I just wonder what that sensation would be like. Not with something like a ladder. That's just a flat-out fear of falling and cracking my head open. But with bridges or balconies, and rooftops, it's more about the jump itself."

"Okay, I'm trying to understand here, so killing or hurting yourself is not something you feel compelled to do?"

"No. Not at all."

"That's a relief," I say, running a hand over my face. This got deep in a small amount of time, but I still want more information. "Then why the jump?"

"Clearly I'm not explaining it right. It's like the epitome of total control. Knowing that there is always a choice and that a split decision can cause such lasting results. Let's say you decide to jump, once you make that decision you're done, right? You don't get a chance to do it again. The consequences are what they are."

I nod, still not seeing how this isn't about suicide somehow.

She leans forward, a little more excited about what she's trying to explain. "And then you have the action of what you've decided. To jump. And then you get to fall. And what must that feel like? And not just the weightlessness of falling, but that consciousness right beforehand. And then, of course, right after. I wonder if it'd be empowering to jump? Like would I feel invincible in that moment?

"Or would I regret it immediately after? And then what if I died? Or worse, ended up a comatose vegetable? It's not about creating a result, like death, it's about making a decision with lasting consequences. I'm not explaining it right.

It's just. . . it's silly. They're just thoughts, nothing I'd ever act on or anything like that."

She's put some thought into this for sure. And it's deep. A little too deep for a Cosmo questionnaire. But I'm going to roll with it as best I can. "I don't know what to do with that."

She laughs. "I don't expect you to do anything with it. It's just how I feel. No big deal."

I smile at her. "Everything you feel is a big deal."

She looks down at the table and fusses with her napkin in her lap. I like that I can fluster her like this. But I also can't stop myself from thinking about how I might be able to help her. Because even if this is a bet, there's still a small part of me that is starting to care about her, more than I should. And that part doesn't want to see her afraid of anything or thinking about jumping from anywhere just to see how it ends up.

Either way, I don't like the morbid ideas that are running around in her pretty head.

18

REMI

I take a few more bites of my lunch, completely regretting that I've shared so much with him about myself. I should have made something up. He's going to think I'm a fucking nut case. Who thinks about shit like that without being crazy? It makes me feel anxious to admit my thoughts on jumping and falling to people. The only people I've ever talked about it with are Kat and Lexie. And even Kat said I was a nut job for thinking that.

So, no more confiding in Chance Bauer.

This is a bet. Nothing more.

Something I keep forgetting when I'm face to face with him. The man must have the patience of a saint to put up with me. Because I know I've been a bitch. Part of me thinks he likes it because he keeps coming back for more.

Just don't push your luck, Remi.

"Did you like the food?" I ask, noticing he's already finished.

"It was fantastic."

"I'm glad," I grin. "So, hey, what about you? What's something you've been dying to try but have never done?" He gets a huge smile on his face, and I feel the need to remind him. "Not something sexual."

The smile dies, but the twinkle in his eyes is still there. He does have the most beautiful eyes, so expressive and clear.

"Hockey," he says.

"Hockey? Like the game?"

"The *sport*, yes. I've always wanted to play hockey. But I don't know how to ice skate."

"I can ice skate," I say.

"You grew up in California, how can you ice skate?"

"There are ice rinks here, you know."

"Is that how you learned?" he asks.

"Well, no. I learned by spending the winters in Philadelphia."

"Why were you in Philadelphia for the winter?" he asks. I'm already regretting opening this topic of conversation.

"Winters. Plural. It's where I went to school."

"You went to college here, same as me. First time we met, remember?"

"Grade school."

"Your parents moved to Philly so you could go to grade school?"

"They didn't move. And high school."

"Okay, you're going to have to explain this one, I know I'm the simpleton and all, but there's something that's not connecting here for me."

I don't want to tell him the whole story. Not now. And not ever. But he's right, what I'm telling him now doesn't make sense.

"Shall we start walking back and I'll explain?"

"Sure." He throws forty dollars on the table, which I know is way too much, grabs my hand and we are out the door. Saying thank you and goodbye to Adamo on the way.

"So, Philly, huh? You an Eagles fan?"

"No."

"Flyers?"

"Who? No. It's doubtful," I say.

"So," he says. "Tell me how you went to school in Philadelphia while your family was here?"

"Boarding school."

He stops us in the middle of the sidewalk and turns me to face him, one hand on each of my shoulders. His face is soft, and his eyes look concerned.

"You went to boarding school all the way across the country for grade school AND high school?"

I take a deep breath and let it out slowly, then turn to continue walking back to my office. I can feel the tension building in my shoulders. From unresolved anger and bitterness, longing for love from the ones who chose to bring me into this world to begin with.

"Yes."

"Were you a bad girl?" he asks with a pretend gasp, which lightens the angst growing inside me. I don't like talking about my childhood. Hell, I don't even like thinking about my childhood.

"I don't think so," I say.

"Then why?"

"That's a topic best left for another time. Besides, if we don't pick up the pace, I'm going to be late back, and I hate it when I'm late." I turn and start walking again, now only a few buildings away from my office.

"Why didn't you say so?" He picks me up in a fireman's hold and starts running down the street.

"Chance! Put me down!"

"You said we had to hurry,"

"Put me down!" I bang on his back with my fists. It feels futile even as I do it. "I swear to god I will kill you if I'm flashing anyone right now."

"I got you," he says. I know he does, since one of his arms is at the base of my ass, holding my skirt down. He slows to a jog, and then walk, as we get to the front of my office building, stopping in view of the lobby.

"You'd better hope no one can see us!"

"Relax, Icy. No one is even paying attention." He slides me down the front of his body. My skirt bunches between us and I move to smooth it down. He smooths the back for me, taking extra time with the part of the skirt over my ass.

I laugh at him.

"You're incorrigible," I say, trying to give him a stern look while I poke my index finger at his chest.

"I can't even spell incorrigible," he says, bringing his hands up and placing them on either side of my face. "I can spell kiss though. Which is what I'm about to do unless you say no."

I really want to say no.

I think.

No, that's not true, I really want to say yes.

God, it's hard to think when he's this close to me.

With those eyes, and those lips. I nod. He lowers his head slowly to mine. I close my eyes and open my mouth slightly. I feel his breath before I feel his lips, so soft is his touch that I might have missed it were I not expecting it. His lips linger on mine, and long before I've had my fill, he pulls away.

"I'll see you Saturday, beautiful," he whispers. Then he turns and walks toward his parked bike on the street. He puts on his helmet and his leather jacket and takes off without looking back. I stand there for a minute, hands still on my lips, not believing what just happened and how much I enjoyed it.

He has such an effect on me. Still. I don't get it.

I barely take two steps before I swipe my badge to get into the building. The coolness of the air feels good against my heated skin. Connie is sitting at the front desk fanning herself with a piece of paper.

"That. Was. Hot. Remi," she says.

"That guy is trouble, Connie," I tell her as I board the elevator.

"That only makes it hotter," she says as the doors close.

I meet the girls for dinner Wednesday, anxious to fill them in on Tuesday's date. For no other reason than to prove that I'm holding up my end of the bargain. They're both already there when I arrive. My favorite thing about being the last one to arrive is that my margarita is already there.

"Ladies," I say in greeting as I sit down. "Kat, you look fantastic." She's wearing a longer scarf around her head, with the ends pulled down over her one shoulder and twisted, like a side ponytail. She's got a black floppy hat on over that, accessorizing an outfit of cuffed boyfriend jeans, black ankle boots, a loose white tee, black belt with a killer silver buckle, and a long tan cardigan.

"Thank you," she says. "As do you. I love that blouse!"

"I'm doing casual Friday, just on Wednesday," I say gesturing to my slim fitting blue plaid capris and white cap sleeve button-down, and white tennis shoes.

"If that's casual Friday, then what do I wear every day?" Lexie asks.

"Wine-making clothes," Kat says of Lexie's jeans and *Lovestone* branded t-shirt and ball cap.

"Hmmm," Lexie says, not sounding totally convinced.

"You always look good, Lex," I say. "You have that natural effervescence that shines from within no matter what you wear."

"Thanks!" She blows me a kiss.

"So, how was lunch yesterday?" Kat asks.

"It was good, I introduced him to Adamo's."

"Oh, I love that place," Lexie says.

"And?" Kat asks.

"And I'm seeing him again on Saturday, which will make three times. So start getting ready to eat your words."

"Come on, Remi, this isn't all about the bet. Isn't it nice getting to know someone?" Lexie asks.

I really want to tell them about the kiss. At the same time, I don't want to tell them about the kiss. Just like I do and don't want to tell them about how he periodically texts me just to say something nice that always makes me smile. And how much I'm looking forward to our date Saturday night.

I'm so fucked.

"When you have a pair of Louboutins on the line, we'll talk about whether it's all about a bet," I say.

"You can act all hard-ass if you want to," Kat says. "But we know you, and there's something you aren't telling us."

"You're right," I say. "There is something I'm not telling you. He had this ridiculous list of questions for us to ask one another."

"That's so cute," Lexie says.

"What kind of questions?" Kat asks.

"You know. Like do you like coffee or tea? How often do you visit your family? Stuff like that."

"What did you tell him?" Lexie asks.

"Coffee, of course," I say. "You know that."

"No," Kat says. "What did you tell him about your family?"

"That I didn't talk to them."

"Did you tell him why?" Kat asks.

"No," I say. "That's none of his business."

"What else did you talk about?"

"Let's see." I tap my finger to my lips as I pretend to think. "We talked about my fear of heights combined with my jumping obsession. I emo-vomited all over him and now he thinks I'm crazy."

"You are crazy," Kat says.

"But good crazy," Lexie says, laughing.

"There's no such thing as good crazy." I shut my eyes and shake my head. As though ridding the memory from my mind will erase it from having happened.

"Ohmigod. You like him," Kat says.

"No, I don't. Why would you say that? Take that back!"

"I will not take it back. You told him two things about yourself that are personal and true," she says.

"About drinking coffee? Please," I scoff.

"Kat's right," Lexie says. "You told him you don't talk to your family and your whole issue with heights and jumping thing. You never admit things like that to people. You always make up a story about your parents and why you don't see them."

"Didn't you even start telling people your parents were dead? Which was so not cool to Lex," Kat says.

"It was okay, I get why she doesn't want to go into it with strangers," Lexie says. "But you didn't tell him a lie. You just didn't include the whole story, but what you said was true."

"That doesn't mean I like him." I'm tempted to roll my eyes. But I'm trying to tamper that habit. I know I do it *excessively*, I hate the idea of something so rote defining me.

They both just look at me. Kat does that to me all the time to get me to talk.

But Lexie surprises me, usually she's jumping right in to fill a gap in conversation or uncomfortable silence. Kat must have taught her the trick to doing it or something.

"None of this is as big a deal as you both are making it," I say.

Silence.

Lexie is squirming slightly in her chair though, like she's about to crack; that is if I don't crack first.

"Fine. I'm looking forward to seeing him on Saturday. Happy?"

Kat grins big and swipes at her eyes, I don't know if she's got real tears or not. "Lexie, our girl is growing up." She fake sniffles.

Lexie claps her hands, bouncing in her seat.

"Shut up," I say.

"I won't," Kat says. "Do you know how nice it is to see you have real emotions about something that doesn't involve work, fashion, or us?"

"I'm not having emotions about this."

"Remi," Lexie says in a singsong voice. "Anticipation is an emotion."

"You guys are blowing this way out of proportion," I say.

"No, we're not," Kat says. "We've known forever that you guys like each other."

I can feel my cheeks heat slightly.

Fuck it.

"He kissed me yesterday," I say.

"How was it?" Lexie asks.

"Soft. Fleeting. But it rocked my fucking world." I feel a little relieved at being able to talk to them about it. "Even Connie, the receptionist, was fanning herself when I walked back in the building."

"He kissed you in front of your office building?" Kat asks.

"Yes. And he held my hand the whole way to Adamo's and the whole way back."

"And you let him?" Lexie asks.

"I did. But, guys, this is kind of freaking me out."

"I get it," Kat says. "But don't think on it too much. Just one day at a time. Relationships are only scary when you try to look at them in their entirety. And that's too big, too uncertain. All you can do is day by day. And trust me, Remi, you give good relationship. And good day-to-day."

"We have nothing in common."

"Opposites attract," Lexie says.

"He rides a motorcycle, and my wardrobe consists of ninety percent skirts and dresses."

"You'll get some jeans," Kat says.

"He was in a *Bob Seger* cover band," I say.

"Cool!" Lexie says.

"I forgot about that," Kat says. "But that is pretty fucking cool. I do love me some Bob Seger. Can you imagine if you get to hear him sing? If he sings to you? Swoon!"

"I guess." I shrug, trying to stay non-committal.

"What are you going to wear on Saturday?" Kat asks.

"I don't know. I guess I'm going shopping for jeans."

"Did you thank him for lunch?" Lexie asks.

"Of course," I say. "At least I think I did."

"You think you did?" Kat asks.

"Text him," Lexie says.

"No," I say. "Why?"

"She's right," Kat says. "You should totally text him and thank him for lunch."

"And tell him you're shopping for jeans," Lexie says.

"Why would I tell him that?" I ask.

"It shows him that you're thinking about the next date," Lexie says. "It's a nice thing."

"It's a relationship thing," I say. "I may be looking forward to seeing him on Saturday, but make no mistake, this is not a relationship."

"Whatever you say, babe," Kat says, patting my shoulder in a super condescending way. "But make sure you're flirty when you text him."

So, despite this not being a relationship, I pick up my phone and text him.

And I make sure it's flirty.

19

CHANCE

I get a text from Alex on my way home.

Alex: B-ball tonight. You in?

Me: Hell yeah, what time?

Alex: 4:30

Me: See ya.

We win the game against the firefighters, which puts both Alex and I on a bit of a high. Kat's Romeo, Brad Matthews, played this game, so I'm not surprised to see him and his buddy Ethan Shane at the bar for beers after.

Alex and I grab a table and order a pitcher and some wings from the server. I notice Matthews and Shane taking seats at the bar.

"I had lunch with Remi today," I tell Alex.

"Really?" he sounds surprised.

"And we are going out Saturday night. That makes three dates, my losing friend."

"Three? I only count two?"

"Dinner, lunch, and Saturday."

"Dinner doesn't count," Alex says. "You can't count a date I set up. You gotta do it on your own, man."

"That's fucked up, dude."

He shrugs in return.

"Fuck. Fine. Two then."

"Dude, I can't just give you a free pass, a bet is a bet. And with two, you are barely halfway to the end zone." He pats me on the shoulder.

"I like bets, two what?"

I look up and see Matthews and Shane standing there.

Fuck. I thought they were at the bar.

I say, "Nothing important," at the same time that Alex says, "Two dates toward thawing the ice queen."

Fuck again.

"Sounds interesting," Brad says, then he takes a long pull of his draft beer. "What's the wager?"

"Twenty-five hundred," Alex says.

"Hey Alex," I say. "We don't need to drag these guys into it." Hoping he'll get the hint and shut the fuck up.

"Oh come on now, Bauer," Brad says patting me on the back, unnecessarily hard. "We're all friends here. Right?"

"Bauer here thinks he's gonna thaw my ex," Alex starts, clearly preening a bit for the other guys' sakes. It's all I can do not to cover his mouth with my hand and drag him out of the bar. "But he only has a month to do it."

"Eskimo Brothers," Ethan says raising his glass.

"It's not exactly like how it sounds," I say.

"No?" Alex says. "You've got a month to fuck her twice and take her on four dates. Have you even kissed her?"

"No," I say, lying. Not sure why I don't want to share that with Alex. Or Brad and Ethan for that matter. That kiss was between Remi and me, and that's where I'm going to leave it.

"Who is this chick?" Ethan asks.

"No one," I say.

"Remi," Alex says, throwing me under a bus I didn't even see coming.

Brad chokes on his beer and glares at me.

"It's not what it looks like, man," I tell him.

"How would you know how it looks, *man*," he says. Then turns to Alex, "You're making a bet about my Remi? Kat's Remi?"

"She was my Remi too," Alex mumbles.

"She's Kat's best friend," Ethan says. "Not cool man."

"Hey, blame him," Alex says, backing up the bus and throwing me under it a second time for good measure. "He's the one who said he could thaw her. He practically begged me to set up a bet."

"That's not exactly how it went. And I didn't know it was her when we were talking."

"Pretty sure they were dating for months, dude," Ethan says.

"Texting, not dating," I say.

Alex scoffs.

"Don't even, dude," I point at him. "You said you'd barely seen her before the tap out."

Brad and Ethan both laugh-choke on their beers.

"Dude," Alex says, sounding accusatory. Sure, now he wants to cover up part of the story.

"Tap out?" Brad asks, his voice hoarse from laughing and choking.

Alex hangs his head, not looking at any of us.

"She tapped out in the middle of sex," I say, softly.

Both Brad and Ethan burst out laughing.

"It's not fucking funny," Alex says, his face reddening and his voice rising.

I can't help it, I start laughing then too. I feel bad for Alex, I do. But it's pretty fucking funny. And not something I think any of us had ever heard of happening before. Even Alex.

It doesn't take Alex long before he's laughing with us though.

"It ain't right, man," he says. "That shit just ain't right."

"You were robbed," Ethan says. "Remi's smokin'."

"I swear it's never happened to me before; I mean what in the actual fuck?" Alex says.

"Sure, it's never happened," Brad says sounding doubtful. Alex flips him off in return.

"Why don't you flip him off back, B?" Ethan asks Brad.

"Fuck off," Brad says.

"Alex, you think you got it bad," Ethan says laughing.

"Shut the fuck up, E," Brad says.

"Ask Matthews to flip you off," Ethan says to Alex.

Alex gives Brad a head nod. Brad hesitates, then flips him off. Only it's unlike any flip off I've ever seen.

"What the fuck's wrong with your hand?" I ask, trying not to laugh.

Ethan's laughs dissolve into coughs he's laughing so hard.

"My fingers won't do it, man," Brad says. "I don't know why. I just can't get around looking like a jackass when I try to give the finger."

I'm glad, for Alex's sake that the focus is now on a shortcoming of someone else's and not his.

"Back to the bet," Brad says.

I spoke too soon.

"Tell me how a tap out leads to a fuck bet?"

"It's not just a fuck bet," I say.

"Bauer said he could get any girl in bed," Alex says.

I bury my face in my hands. I'm not sure this conversation could be going any worse at this point.

"That's not quite what I said. And I didn't know it was Remi when I made the bet," I say.

"Did finding out it was Remi change the bet?" Brad asks.

"No," I say. I'm mad that I'm feeling ashamed. But I know why, it's because I'm starting to care about her and it's not just a bet to me anymore.

"Remi is like a sister to me," Brad says, his voice warning.

"I'm sorry, man," Alex says.

"This is on him, man, not you," Brad says to Alex, nodding his head in my direction.

"I'm not going to force her to do anything she doesn't want to do," I assure him.

"That goes without saying," Brad says. I nod and take a large drink of my beer, then refill my glass from the pitcher.

Brad rolls his head on his shoulders, cracking his neck. Then flexes his hands to do the same with his knuckles. "If you hurt her, I will end you," he says.

"I would do the same in your situation," I say.

Alex points out something on the TV to Ethan and they are off talking about the game that's on.

"I'm not going to hurt her," I say. My phone beeps as I say that. I pull it from my pocket and see it's a text from Remi. I can't stop the smile that brings to my face.

Remi: I meant to thank you for lunch earlier, but this guy kissed me right before I went back to work, and it kind of rattled my brain enough to make me forget my manners.

Matthews leans over my shoulder and reads who it's from before I can pull it away.

"She texted you," he says, his voice has a tinge of surprise to it.

I like that he's surprised.

He leans back in his chair and drinks more of his beer, giving me a little space to respond.

Me: A similar thing happened to me.

Remi: You had a guy kiss you too?

Me: I forgot to thank a beautiful woman for joining me at lunch, because a kiss left me rattled.

Remi: Aren't you a charmer. Wait, I am texting Chance Bauer, right?

Me: Funny.

Remi: I thought so.

Remi: So, about Saturday...

Me: Yes.

Remi: If you are picking me up again, I was thinking I'd get a pair of jeans for the ride. Any recommendations?

Me: The tighter the better.

Remi: And there's the Chance I know.

Me: I'll pick you up at 7pm. We'll have dinner and then see where the night takes us.

Even though I already know what we are going to do. The Night Moves, the cover band I used to sing for, is in town. It's been forever since I've seen any of those guys and I'm going to take her to watch them play.

Remi: Looking forward to it.

Me: Me too, beautiful.

I set my phone down on the table. Matthews is staring at me.

"You like her." His eyes widen.

"Of course I like her."

"No, I mean you LIKE her."

I shrug my shoulders, not really knowing what to say to that.

"I don't really know her."

"I thought you guys dated in college or something."

"No - we just hooked up at a party, sort of."

"How do you sort of hook up?" he asks.

I tell him a brief version of the rugby championship party, ending with Remi's projectile vomiting and the resulting freeze out.

"Dude," he says gagging slightly. "She threw up and it got in your mouth? Shit. How did you not hurl right then?"

Part of me wants to point out that I'm made of tougher shit than he is obviously, but this doesn't really seem the time to throw our dicks on the table and compare size. Especially when he's got me by the short and curlies with this whole Remi thing. So instead, I shrug my shoulders and hope he leaves it at that.

"Dude, did you see that catch?" Ethan backhands Brad in the chest to get his attention. So I turn mine toward the game as well. Happy that, at least for now, the conversation seems to be over. We order another pitcher, more wings, and finish out the game.

It isn't until I'm on my way home later that I realize that I kind of liked Matthews tonight. Not like I'd be his friend per se, but he's a decent guy. I can see why Kat fell for him.

Kind of.

20

REMI

I end up getting a pair of cuffed boyfriend jeans with a skinny cut, which I pair with a tight, white cap sleeve V-neck t-shirt, and black platform stilettos. I pull my hair partway back with a red bandana and leave my bangs straight. My hair is ready for a helmet, and my outfit is ready for the bike. I grab my own leather jacket and set it by the door. It's still ten minutes before he's due to be here.

I check my makeup one more time, then my outfit.

Calm the fuck down, Remi.

My phone buzzes, it's a text from Kat.

Kat: I know you're ready, and probably fretting. Grab a shot of tequila and sit the fuck down and relax. It's just one night. No big deal.

Me: It's creepy how well you know me sometimes. I love you for that. Thank you!

Kat: Love you more. Have a great time! Try to get laid!

I laugh at that, then head to the kitchen to grab a shot of tequila. I've just started to feel the effects of the alcohol when the doorbell rings. I look through the peephole, even though I know it's him. Then giggle slightly when I see we are wearing near identical outfits, with him in his trademark jeans, white tee, and leather jacket.

I open the door.

He looks me up and down. "Wow. Icy, you dress down well. I mean really fucking well." He pauses at my tits.

"Eyes up here, big boy." I push his chin up with my finger.

"I feel like we've had this conversation before," he says with a wink.

I laugh. "I'm ready to go if you are."

"Let's go." He grabs my hand and pulls me out the door. I feel more prepared this time getting on his bike. I scoot right up against his back and wrap my arms around his waist. He taps my hand. "You good?"

"I'm good."

He starts the bike, and I lay my head against his back to enjoy the ride.

We pull up to a curb a brief time later, behind what appears to be a food truck.

"A food truck?" I ask.

"A culinary delight disguised as a food truck," he says.

I take a big whiff of the air around us. "Oh my God, it smells amazing," I say.

We round to the side of the truck and I see the name painted on the side, *Motion of the Ocean*. "Is it seafood?" I ask, excited and hungry.

"Yes," he says. "These guys go out and catch it in the morning, then come back and grill it up at night. They're only open a couple days a week. And they switch out the location all the time, but it's worth tracking them down. The food is that good. And right now it's lobster season."

"You're speaking my language," I say.

We order and get our food, me a curried lobster wrap, and Chance the lobster tacos. He finds a bench for us to sit on to eat. He's right, the food is that good. I moan as I take another bite.

"I'm glad you like it," he says.

"Oh God, I love it," I say. "Can I try some of yours?"

He feeds me a bit of taco. It's divine.

"You have a—" he starts, then reaches up with his thumb and wipes something from the side of my mouth. I dab at my face with the napkin.

"Did I get it?" I ask. He nods. We finish eating quietly. He gets up to throw the trash away, then comes back to sit with me.

"Do I have food in my teeth?" I ask, showing him.

"No, do I?" he asks, doing the same.

"Nope," I say, feeling lighthearted and free at the same time. Both unusual emotions for me to experience. I lean my head against his shoulder, and he puts his arm around me. I close my eyes and enjoy being this close to him, something about it feels comfortable and right.

He turns his head toward mine and nudges my nose with his. I open my eyes.

"Hi," I say softly.

"Hey," he says.

He's going to kiss me.

I want it.

I'm ready.

Instead, he pulls back slightly. "We need to be where we're going soon. Ready?"

"Sounds good," I say, trying not to be disappointed. He stands and pulls me up after him and we walk back to the bike holding hands.

He helps me with my jacket, then turns me to face him, his hands on my hips, and my back against the bike.

"I wanted to kiss you back there," he says.

"I wanted you to kiss me back there," I say.

He picks me up and sets me on the bike seat, then nudges my legs apart and steps between them. One hand is still at my hip, but the other moves up to my neck, his fingers wrapping around toward the back, and his thumb caressing my cheek.

"How about now?" he asks.

"Now?"

"Do you want me to kiss you now?" he asks, his face now inches from mine.

I nod my head, not sure if I can speak.

This time the kiss is not soft and fleeting. It's hard and possessive, with tongue and teeth. He growls as he pulls me tight against him with the one hand and holds my head in place with the other. I wrap my legs and arms around him. I can't get close enough. If I could crawl inside him, I would.

We stay like that, in our own world of kisses, mixed with breaths and feels. So many feels. He slows the kiss after another minute or so, and pulls his head away slightly, resting his forehead to mine. I slowly lower my legs as I try to catch my breath.

"So," he says, still out of breath. "I guess we've still got chemistry, huh?"

I laugh. "Was there any doubt?"

"I think you were a little worried."

"If I was, I'm not anymore," I laugh.

"I need a minute." He looks down. "Riding with a hard-on is not fun."

"I'd say he likes me." I point to the bulge in his pants.

"He likes you a lot," Chance says.

"Think about your grandma," I say, remembering the similar moment at The Chesterfield.

He closes his eyes, waits a moment, I feel him start to go down. He opens his eyes and says, "So, you're smart and beautiful." A question that he makes a statement.

He fastens my helmet on my head, climbs on the bike, and starts it. Then he helps me on behind him, I wrap my arms around his waist loving the feel of him against me.

I don't know how it is that I'm having fun with Chance Bauer, but I am. And, putting my life in his hands when on this motorcycle, but that too is okay. I trust him.

Whoa.

I do.

I trust him.

Holy shit.

Even thinking about my Louboutins right now isn't piercing the little bubble I'm in.

Time to rein it in.

Just not now.

Later.

After tonight.

Because tonight I'm going to enjoy the wind on my face, the vibrations under my ass, and my arms around this delicious man.

We pull up to this little place on the side of the road. It looks small and unassuming from the front. The kind of place that you would pass by without a second thought. Except that the dirt lot surrounding it is already packed with a mix of cars and motorcycles, and there's a line at the door. I peek around the side of the building and see that it's long. Like football field long.

Chance helps me off the bike and takes my helmet off. Then, and fuck me for enjoying this, he fixes the bandana in my hair. I reach up to touch it when he finishes, it feels perfect. I look at him questioningly.

"Three sisters," he says with a smile as he gets off the bike.

"Thank you," I say. He puts our helmets and jackets away. "Where are we? Is this a bar?"

"This is a live music venue. And . . . a bar." He grins.

"Are we going to see a band?" And then it occurs to me. "Ohmigod, are we seeing your band?" I'm excited by the prospect.

"What if I say, yes?"

"Then I say, hell yes. Lead the way."

We head toward the building. The line to get in is out the door and wrapped around the far side. I lean up, closer to his ear. "What do you think the chances are we can cut through the line since you know the band and all?"

"I'm gonna do you one better, beautiful." He pulls out his phone and sends a quick text. Then we go stand by the side door near the rear of the building, which opens quickly, and in we go. He grabs my hand, and we walk down a long hallway toward a room at the end. The noise from the bar is dimmed back here, but I can tell it's loud, and a little rowdy.

We walk into the room, and four guys stand, surround us, and start talking at once.

"There he is."

"Took you long enough, fucker."

"Dibs on the babe."

"You still owe me twenty bucks, asshole."

Chance man-hugs them all individually, and then introduces me.

"Remi Vargas, meet the Night Moves. This is Chad on the drums, Taylor on guitar, Carter on keyboards, and Trace is the singer and also plays guitar."

"Gentlemen, I've heard a lot about you. It's nice to meet you."

Chad looks around the room. "Who's she talking to? There ain't no gentlemen here, sweetheart." We all laugh.

Trace hands a beer to both Chance and me, and we sit back into couches too deep and worn to be comfortable. The guys take turns sharing stories about when Chance was with the band.

They make it easy to join in the conversation, or sit back and listen, so I do both. Chance has his arm around my shoulders and is lightly caressing the skin of my upper arms. Every so often the couch shakes with his laughter. Being with him like this is so effortless, so natural. I think I could sit here all night and have a great time.

I finish my second beer and belch a little too loudly. Then cover my mouth. "Excuse me. Sorry about that." My cheeks redden slightly.

"Beautiful and has manners, I like it," Taylor says.

"And spoken for," Chance says as he pulls me into him and kisses my temple. I try to ignore the little fire that lights in my belly when he does that. But I can't. And I have this horrible feeling that even if I win this bet. I'm going to lose in the end. Because I'm developing feelings for Chance Bauer, and everybody knows that she who cares the most is never the one who wins.

21

CHANCE

I'm enjoying the hell out of being with the guys again. It was pure luck that they were playing here in town tonight when I had a date with Remi. But more than just seeing them, is watching them with her. She fits right in with the crude jokes and coarse language. She may be the girliest, most high maintenance female I've ever met. But she can hang in the back of the bar trenches with the best of them. I am proud as fuck of her.

A loud knock sounds on the wall by the door. "Ten minutes, Night Moves."

"That's our cue." Carter stands up and says, "Gotta go be famous and adored."

Remi stands and walks toward the door, and I move to follow her. She pats Carter on the chest as she passes him and says, "Pretty sure you are zero for two there, son."

And right there, with one line, she gets him back for all the things he's teased her about throughout the night. The band and I all bust out laughing. Carter is the jokester of the group, and to see him speechless, with his mouth hanging open, is priceless.

I grab Remi's hand and kiss the back of it. "That's my girl," I say with a wink. She blushes ever so slightly. It's a good look on her.

I turn back to the guys and give them a small salute as a goodbye. "Gentlemen."

"Aw, what'd we tell you about calling us that," Carter says. "Not nice, man."

"She's a keeper," Trace yells.

I raise a hand over my head and keep walking. I have to smile when I hear Chad say, "She's a sassy one for sure, but did you see that ass? Dayum."

We get to the main floor and I see the guys have reserved two stools for us at the end of the bar closest to the stage. We get situated and I pull Remi's stool up close to the front of mine so she is sitting between my legs and can lean back against my chest if she wants. Hopefully, she does, because that's what I want.

"Do you want a martini or stick with beer?" I ask, my mouth close enough to her ear to nuzzle it lightly. I'm rewarded by the slight shiver that runs through her body. She puts her hand on my thigh and turns slightly in her stool to face me, our noses almost touching. Her tongue slips out of her mouth, and she licks my lips lightly.

"Mmmm," she says. "You taste good. I'll stick with beer." My cock hardens. My reactions to her are so quick and visceral.

She pulls her head back and turns toward the stage before I have a chance to kiss her. But her hand stays resting on my thigh. I order two beers as the guys take the stage.

They open with "The Fire Down Below," which always gives Taylor a chance to show off his skills on the strings. Remi sways against me in time to the beat and taps it out on my thigh. I feel good sitting like this with her.

"Rock and Roll Never Forgets" is next in the set list. When they transition from one song to the next, Remi goes a little crazy in her stool, screaming, whistling, and clapping. She's in rare form tonight. In fact, I don't think I've ever seen her so loose and unrestrained.

Except when we kissed.

She turns back to me. "Let's do shots!"

"Beautiful, I've got to drive us home."

"We'll Uber," she says. "Have fun with me."

"I am having fun with you."

"Have MORE fun with me." She places a small kiss on my lips. "Please."

I caress her cheek with the back of my fingers, enjoying when she leans into it. Then I turn back to the bartender, and when I catch his eye, tell him, "Two tequila shots, please."

Two songs later we've had two shots each and a beer chaser, and we're standing in front of our stools. I've got my arms around Remi from behind, with her pulled tight against me. She's holding my hands with hers at her waist. I can't get over how good she feels. How good she smells. How hard she makes me.

I nuzzle her neck and she leans her head to the side to give me better access. I bite her collarbone, a little harder than necessary, but instead of getting mad, she reaches back and puts her arms around my neck, pulling my mouth to hers. The kiss is brief, due to the awkward angle, but she initiated it, and that gives me hope.

Bet or no bet, I don't want to give this girl up at the end of the month. And the more I can convince her that it's good between us, the better my chances are of saving this when she finds out.

Because she will find out that she was a bet. And no matter how many times I'll try to convince her that it only started that way, it's going to take a miracle to get her to forgive me.

22

REMI

I have never felt this good.

I mean, I know I'm buzzed, but I've drunk a lot before and not felt like this. I should have set up a code word with Kat to pick me up. But even if I had, I wouldn't want to use it. I like it here. With him.

The band is finishing the song "Main Street," and yes, I brushed up on all my Bob Seger songs since finding out Chance was in a cover band. Most of the songs Chance hums or sings softly in my ear, his chin resting on my shoulder. His voice does things to my girly parts. Really good things. Kat calls them vagina butterflies, and right now I couldn't agree more.

Trace waits for the applause after the song to die down, and then he starts talking, "Any long-time fans in the audience tonight?"

I'm surprised by the amount of applause and cheering at that.

"So, y'all may remember a time when I just played bass guitar and didn't sing," Trace says. More cheering erupts.

"The Night Moves used to be a five-man band. Until our singer left us to further a career in, *gasp*, law enforcement. It doesn't get any worse than going from rock star to cop, am I right?" The roar of the crowd is near deafening.

I turn back to Chance. "He's talking about you, isn't he?"

Chance smiles and nods. "I told you I'd sing you a song, beautiful."

Holy Shit. I thought he was kidding.

A second spotlight searches the crowd and lands on Chance and me.

"So, let's say we give the cop a chance, no pun intended buddy, to relive his rock star fantasies and let him sing one. Whaddya say?"

Chance kisses my cheek and slips out from behind me. I start clapping and screaming with the rest of the crowd. Stomping my feet on the floor for good measure.

Because my date is about to get up on stage and sing a song.

To me.

Chance takes the microphone from Trace, and says, "That's detective to you, pretty boy." I put my fingers in my mouth and whistle, then stomp my feet some more because I like the sound.

Trace starts strumming the guitar softly, and the crowd quiets. The music gets a little louder.

"This one's for you, beautiful," Chance says, and the spotlight finds me again. But I'm too keyed up to be embarrassed.

Then he starts singing, and he's looking right at me.

"A gypsy wind is blowing warm tonight."

His voice is low and husky. And sexy.

Really fucking sexy.

I can see exactly why rock stars are always getting laid. He's like lady crack up there, all addictive and desirable. The lights shine on his hair, making it look even lighter, and his eyes are mesmerizing, even from this far away.

He sounds good. He looks amazing. His t-shirt tight, showing off his biceps as he holds the microphone. His foot tapping in motorcycle boots, jeans molded to his hips and legs. The slight scruff on his face, which I can still feel the scratch from on my neck, just lend to the overall sex appeal that is Chance Bauer on stage. His movements are slow and mesmerizing, I imagine that's how he would make love to me, with movements slow and mesmerizing. Oh god, did I just think that? I am getting sucked the fuck in.

Then he gets to the chorus, and I start to tear up just a little bit.

"Someday lady you'll accompany me."

I don't know if it's the beer, or the shots, or the adrenaline. Maybe I'm PMS'ing. But this shit is making me seriously emotional.

Goddamnit.

This is the sexiest song I've ever heard.

With the sexiest fucking guy singing it.

To me.

Holy shit balls. I'm all in. I don't care if I lose the bet. I don't care if he hurts me. I'm going to tell him I want to do this. I get what Kat's been saying all along about relationships. And it's going to be worth it.

I smile big at him, not sure if he can see me or not. I can tell he's nearing the end of the song.

His eyes close when he gets to a high point, he looks beautiful with his head thrown back as he loses himself in the song. I'm so caught up in the moment, I don't even notice the woman next to me.

Until she speaks.

"I remember when he used to sing this song to me," she says.

And it's like a needle scratching across an old vinyl record, everything stops.

"Excuse me?"

"Chance." She nods her chin toward the stage. "He used to sing this song to me all the time."

I look up at the stage, Chance is leaning down to shake hands and high-five some of the people near the front of the stage. The applause is crazy.

The spotlight has since left me and is back on Trace and the band as they start up another song. I watch as Chance jumps down from the stage and talks to a few people.

I turn toward the woman. "I'm sure, as the lead singer, he would sing this song a lot."

"Yes, but as his wife, I knew it was for me," she says, her tone superior.

If I thought the first time she said something to me was jarring. Then hearing the word 'wife' was like a system shut down. My ass hit the stool seat with a thud.

"Did you say, *wife?*" I don't believe what I'm hearing.

"He didn't tell you?" she smirks. "Guess it isn't that serious between you two, is it honey?"

I feel the ground drop out from under me. He's married? I look back at the woman, out at Chance, then back at her. She looks like Sylvester right after he got Tweety Bird to fly in his mouth.

Oh fuck no.

I turn back toward the bar. "Can I get another shot? Make it a double," I ask the bartender once I catch his eye.

The benefit of being friends with the band, the bartenders serve you quickly. I polish off both shots in record time, hoping this woman will leave in the meantime.

If I ignore her, she'll go away. 'Cause no way in hell is this really happening. I glance to the side.

She's still there.

Fuck.

Her attention is on Chance, who is still near the stage, so I take a minute to really look at her.

His wife.

He's fucking married?

She's exquisite looking. Not that I would expect anything less from a guy as good-looking as Chance. She has long, slightly wavy, light brown hair with blonde highlights, and big brown eyes. She looks a lot like Keira Knightley in the pirate movies. Sun-kissed, wind-blown, tan, and healthy. The opposite of my pale skin and carefully coiffed hair.

I know that I'm attractive, but it does not just come out of the box that way, I work at it. I accentuate only my best features and go with a look that I know works for me. Is it high maintenance? Yeah, probably.

I'm not one of those natural beauties that can throw on sunscreen and Chapstick and look amazing. I require spackle and a coat of paint. Or two.

But this woman, she needs nothing.

She's beautiful and she's his wife.

He's fucking married.

How could I be so stupid?

How did this not come up before? I swear Kat told me he was single. Maybe he's separated? Or divorced? Either way, he's never mentioned it.

Not that it matters, because this is a bet. And right now, I love my pride more than I love my Louboutins. So, fuck this. I slap my hand on the bar for emphasis.

I feel Chance's arm slide around me from behind and stiffen. "Shots without me, beautiful?" He nuzzles my neck, something that not five minutes ago would have made my knees buckle.

"Anything to drown out the ruckus of you singing," I say.

He straightens and pulls away from me, laughing slightly. "Wow, was I that bad?"

He spins my stool around so I'm facing him. But I refuse to look him in the eye. He tries to tilt my chin up, so I avert my eyes, but he keeps moving his head around and crouching down until his gaze catches mine.

"Hey, what happened? Are you okay?"

"Fine."

"Okay," he says, drawing the word out slightly.

"Hello, darling." My head shoots up when I hear her voice and the top of my head clips Chance in the chin.

"Ow, fuck," he says. "What the hell Remi, that…"

I can tell the minute it sinks in that someone was talking to him, and when he realizes who was talking.

His head turns slowly in her direction.

"Your hair is different," Chance says after a minute.

"Aw, you noticed," the wife says.

"Wait, what the fuck are you doing here?"

"Free country." The wife shrugs her shoulders, looking nonchalant.

"Well, leave," he says. "This is my thing, not yours."

"Clearly this is many peoples' thing, not just yours." She gestures to the crowd.

Chance takes a deep breath and lets it back out slowly, muttering something I don't understand.

It must suck to be caught red-handed.

"Look," Chance says. "We're on a date, so if you don't mind." He makes a hand motion as if to say, 'scurry along.'

"Oh, don't go on my account," I say. "I was just leaving."

"I thought you were on a date?" the wife asks with a smirk.

"We are," Chance says at the same time I say, "Not anymore." I hop off my stool and turn to leave. Chance grabs my upper arm to stop me. I turn back to him. "Let go of me."

His grip lightens. "Remi, will you just listen for a second? It's not—"

"Let go," I say again, my voice rising.

He hesitates before releasing my arm. I work my way through the crowd as best I can.

I need to get away.

I can't stand to look at him another minute.

Or it's that I can't stand to have him see me for another minute.

Either way.

The line at the women's bathroom is at least twenty deep.

Fuck.

Then I remember a small unisex bathroom backstage near the room where we'd met the band, so I head toward the back. My chest grows tight.

Holy fuck, am I going to cry?

Jesus Christ.

You're so weak, Remi.

The guy guarding the hallway remembers me from earlier and lets me by with hardly a second glance.

Again, the perks of knowing the band. I turn back, but don't see Chance behind me.

Of course.

I mean, why would he follow me when his wife is here. My gaze blurs and I can't quite catch my breath.

Fuck.

I look around, trying to find the fucking door before I lose it completely.

Ohmigod.

So. Fucking. Stupid.

Never trust anyone.

I find the door, lock myself in the bathroom, and prepare to cry for the first time in over twenty-five years.

23

CHANCE

I watch as Remi weaves her way through the crowd toward the back of the bar, and away from me.

What in the actual fuck is happening?

Helen, my ex, puts her hand on my arm from behind me and leans up against my back to whisper in my ear. "That's too bad, she was cute."

I turn around to face her. "Fuck you, Helen."

"Is that any way to talk to your wife?" Helen asks.

"Wife? Are you crazy?" My stomach tightens, I feel nauseous. "Ha. I can't believe I almost forgot. You are crazy. I could have you arrested just for being here."

"You wouldn't arrest me," Helen says. "We were practically married."

"We were never practically married. You were barely even a fiancée. A manipulative nut-job of a fiancée at that."

"I made a mistake," Helen says.

"It wasn't a mistake, Helen. It was multiple mistakes. Over months of time. And I'm not even counting your psychotic behavior afterward. You were . . . you know what, I don't fucking care." I move to walk away. Turning back again once it hits me. "Oh my God, that's why Remi's pissed. Did you tell her that we were married?" I ask.

"I might have mentioned I was your wife." She steps into me and runs her hand down my chest.

I can't believe this is happening.

Helen moves her hand farther down and tries to cup my cock.

I knock her hand away and then raise mine to her.

"You—"

"Baby—"

"Don't even, Helen, just don't."

I can't believe how volatile she makes me.

I want to fucking throttle her.

It's the closest I've ever come to hitting a woman. I'm so furious I don't even know what to say to her.

"What the . . . you're . . . FUCK." I can't even formulate a sentence.

I leave before I do something I'll regret.

I need to find Remi. She's the only thing that matters right now.

I don't see her anywhere around the stage, and the guys are still going strong, so I can't ask them. I check with the guard at the hall, he confirms that she went back about five minutes ago. I check every room back there and don't find her anywhere. I don't find her in the parking lot either. I try calling her again as I walk back toward the main floor of the bar.

Which is when I hear her phone ringing behind a closed door. I stop to listen, and hear her crying and saying, 'fuck you, phone.'

"Remi?" I knock on the door as I say her name.

"Go away."

"Can I come in?"

"No."

"Please." I rest my palm against the door and hang my head.

She doesn't answer me.

"I'm not married, Remi. Not even close." I lean against the door, trying to get closer to her.

She stays silent.

"Did she say we were married?"

Silence.

"We aren't. We never were. I'd like to explain, but I need you to open the door."

The sounds of the band echo in the hall.

"Remi. Please."

"Why does she think you were married?" she asks after a minute.

"We were engaged. I called it off. She was . . . cheating," I say, reverting back to one of my original tall tales where Helen was concerned.

She unlocks the door but doesn't open it. I turn the knob and enter slowly, not sure what to expect. She's sitting on the toilet, fully clothed, dabbing at her eyes.

"I'm not crying," she says.

"I can tell," I say with a small laugh.

"Fuck you," she says. "I'm not crying. It's just allergies or PMS. There's dust everywhere in this fucking place."

"I believe you." Even though I can clearly see she's crying. But if she says she's not, then that's what I'm going with for now.

I kneel in front of the toilet and place a hand on the outside of each of her shoulders, then wait until she looks up at me.

"Your eyes are red," I say, trying to lighten the mood.

"Like I told you—"

"I know, I'm sorry. I was just trying to tease you." I smile to show I'm serious about teasing.

"Don't tease me about crying. I don't cry."

"Ok." I run the back of my hand along her cheek and use my thumb to catch some of the tears that are clearly not there. Since she doesn't cry.

"Helen and I were engaged."

"Helen."

"Yes."

"That's an awful name," she says with a bitter laugh.

"For an awful person."

"Yeah." She blows her nose. I take the used tissue from her and throw it away, then hand her a fresh one to use. She dabs at her eyes again.

"She cheated on me. Countless times. I didn't find out until two weeks before the wedding."

Remi meets my eyes again, a horrified expression on her face. "I'm so sorry, Chance. That must have been horrible for you."

"It happens," I say. "I'm over it now, but at the time I was devastated. At the betrayal and at the loss of what I thought was going to be an idyllic life."

"There's no such thing."

"You wait until now to tell me," I say dryly.

She laughs softly, then asks, "Did you sing to her?"

"I did, a couple times."

"Did you sing that song to her?" Her voice is almost shy.

"What song? The one I sang to you?"

She nods.

"No. I've only ever dedicated that song to you."

She nods her head and seems to accept my answer.

I'm relieved.

I don't want her to be angry. And I don't want her thinking that the song I sang to her is my move or something. One step closer to salvaging the evening after Hurricane Helen blew in.

"She's really pretty," she says.

"She doesn't hold a candle to you," I say.

She scoffs. "You have to say that you're here in the bathroom with me."

"Let's get out of the bathroom, I'll say it again."

She giggles.

"I like making you laugh," I admit.

"I like it when you make me laugh." She seems to soften toward me a bit.

Thank God.

"Do you promise it's over?" she asks, looking so vulnerable I want to say anything to make her feel whole again.

"It never even began."

I take her hand in mine and we leave the bathroom. As we walk down the hall, she swings our joined hands between us. A lighthearted move that is unexpected. I like it.

We can still hear the band from back here, and I stop her and pull her into my arms. "Dance with me?"

"Here? Now? To this song?"

The guys are ending the set with "Old Time Rock-n-Roll." But I know what they plan to play next.

"No, this one," I say just as we hear the opening strains of "We've Got Tonight."

"Hey," she says with a smile. "We danced to this before."

"You remember?"

"Of course I do."

I sing softly to her as we dance. The words are eerily biographical. So much so, that I feel like I'm confessing to her, asking of her, expecting from her; all at the same time.

She looks up at me. "I think I'd like you to take me home now."

I try to swallow the disappointment that fills me when she says that. I don't want the night to end so soon. I mean, I didn't expect that she'd take me home with her tonight, but I would've liked to spend a few more hours with her. Not that I can blame her though, it's been a bit of an emotional roller coaster. If I were her, I'd want to go home too.

"Ok," I say, softly.

"With you," she adds.

My heart jumps into my chest.

"Are you sure?" I ask, hoping I heard her correctly.

She nods, then stretches up to kiss me.

Oh yeah, I'm the man!

A kiss that quickly turns heated. My mouth leaves her lips and she moans as I trail them down her collarbone. I want at those luscious tits, but I can't get her shirt to move more with just my mouth and I don't want to let go of her ass yet. If I weren't feeling so frenzied, it would be funny.

I move back up to her mouth and angle my head, so her lips are back against mine. Her tongue dives inside my mouth, dueling for control. I snake one hand under her shirt and up her side to grab her breast. She moans into my mouth. A sound that just fuels the fire inside me.

I want at all of her. I can't keep my hands still, they are at her ass, her head, in her hair, pushing up her bra, getting at her bare breast.

"My God, Remi."

I can't decide what I want my hands on most. Ass. Tit. Ass. Oh, definitely ass. I grab it and pull her up against me, kneading her cheeks through her jeans, aligning her core with my hard cock.

I back her into the dressing room for the band and kick the door shut behind us. We stumble to the couch and fall on to it, I flip us as we go down so that it's her falling on to me and not the other way around.

"That was a smooth move, Mr. Bauer," she breathes against my lips.

I want to think of something witty to say back to her, but my brain is rattled. I reach up to smooth back her hair so I can see her face.

"Cat got your tongue?" she asks with a wicked glint in her eyes. She leans in and bites my lower lip, pulling it away, then letting it snap back.

I nod in response.

I am literally stupefied by this woman. I pull her in for another kiss. She wiggles her hips in between my legs, I groan as she connects with my cock. I've got one leg bent with my foot on the ground for balance, the other I wrap around her leg to hold her in place. My hands reconnect with her ass and somehow I find my voice.

"God, Remi. I've had dreams about this ass. Fucking luscious." I squeeze it as I'm talking.

She raises her head to look at me and giggles again. Then turns serious. "What kind of dreams? What did you do to my ass?" She traces her fingernail along my lips as she says this. My dick jumps in my pants. She feels it too.

"Was that you thinking about my ass?"

All I can do is nod, back to being hypnotized by this goddess on top of me. My hands grind her hips against mine, using her ass as a handle. I'm fairly sure I could blow my load just from this.

She leans down and licks my ear. "Do you want to fuck my ass?"

Fuck me.

"Not just your ass, beautiful," I say, my voice husky and hoarse.

"I think I'd like that," she says, moaning.

"Can I touch you?"

"God, please."

I unbutton her jeans and slide down the zipper, then slide my hand down the back of her jeans to cup her from behind. Her thong is soaked.

"You're wet, Remi, you're so wet. Is that for me?"

She nods.

"Fuck, Remi." I slip a finger inside of her, she arches against me, whimpering.

"That feels so good," she says, her voice deep. "Please don't stop." Her breathing gets heavier as she fucks my fingers.

Goddamn, she can move her hips.

I bring her lips back to mine and deepen the kiss until I make myself dizzy.

"Oh God, I can't, I can't, holy shit balls, Chance," she cries into my mouth.

I slide another finger inside her and curl them slightly while pumping them in and out.

She's close, I can feel it. Her body is so fucking responsive. I crook my fingers and add pressure to her clit at the same time. She cries out into my mouth as she orgasms. Her muscles clamp down around my fingers. Her body tenses and shakes as she rides it out. Her inner muscles still tightly closed around my fingers. I keep pumping my fingers in and out while she screams through her second orgasm.

Yes!

I place my thumb back over her clit finding deep satisfaction when she comes yet again. Her entire body tightens, and I watch as the pleasure overtakes her, drowning her cries in my kiss. Her muscles relax bit by bit, and she buries her head in the crook of my neck, breathing heavily.

"Holy fucking multiples, Batman," she says. "Jesus Christ. Chance Bauer. Where have you been all my life?"

I pull my hand from her pants and hug her to me, keeping one hand outside her jeans on her ass and the other on the bare skin at the small of her back. Loving the feel of her on top of me, with her face snuggled next to mine. Loving her reaction to my touch. Loving more that I could give that to her.

We fit, her and I.

Her breathing slows, and she raises her head and laughs. "Oh my God, that was so fucking amazing," she says. "You, my friend, have magic fingers." She kisses me on the lips, then the nose, then each of my eyes, and back to my lips. "I may worship you forever for that. That was just. Wow. Thank you."

She starts to scoot down on my body.

"What are you doing?" I ask.

"I'm returning the favor," she says with a wicked smile, her hands undoing the button of my jeans.

"Come here, beautiful," I say pulling her back up toward me. "I didn't do that so you would reciprocate. I did that because I wanted to touch you. I wanted to feel you and do something just for you." I reach between us and button her pants and zip them back up.

"Well, now I want to do something just for you," she says, her tone seductive.

"Believe me, there is nothing more than I want than to see those red lips wrapped around my cock. But not here, not like this. The guys will be back any second—"

As if on cue, the door swings open and the guys barge in.

"Whoa," Carter says. "Sorry, man, didn't realize."

"It's okay," I say. "We're decent."

Remi pushes herself up, using my chest for leverage, which just serves to remind me that my dick is hard and my balls are blue.

"Dude," Trace says. "Still trying to live the rock star lifestyle I see." He winks at Remi.

Remi moves off me on the couch. I sit up next to her but pull her back on my lap. She kicks her shoes off and curls right up, like she's been doing it forever.

"Beer or water?" Chad asks.

"Water," both Remi and I say. He hands us each a bottle. And we spend the next hour talking and joking, like it hasn't been years since I'd seen these guys, and it's the most normal thing in the world. Remi excuses herself to go to the restroom.

Which is good, I need a minute to talk to the guys without her in the room.

I turn to Taylor since he knew Helen the best. "How long has Helen been coming to the gigs?"

"Dude, Helen was here?" he asks, a frown on his face.

"Yeah, and she told Remi we were married."

"Remi didn't believe her, did she?" Trace asks.

"She did believe her, we just had it out."

"Yeah, you almost had something out," Chad jokes.

I throw my empty water bottle at him.

"Sorry, dude. You know that bitch has always been crazy, man," Chad says, shaking his head.

"Seriously don't know what you saw in her," Carter says.

"True words, brother," Trace adds.

"You guys wait until now to tell me?" I ask.

They all look at each other and nod or say yes.

"It's not like we could tell you when you were about to marry her," Taylor says.

"Okay, I get that. I think. But what about after I left her?" I ask. They all look at each other. As though they aren't sure if they should say anything. Then they do.

"You went under, man. First emotionally, then, like, literally. We didn't even know where you were."

I nod in understanding. I mean, how do you explain behavior like Helen's to anyone. I can barely believe it myself half the time. But before I can say anything more, Remi comes back into the room, she looks tired. I take that as my cue.

"Gentlemen," I say.

"What'd we tell you about that word?" Chad asks.

I look at him. "If you assholes don't mind."

Chad nods as though that is the more agreeable word to use when addressing him.

I continue, "I'm going to take my lady home and tuck her in."

They all take turns hugging Remi goodbye and making her promise to come visit them on the road. It makes me wonder if Remi would do a road trip like that with me. Then I snicker, because the idea of Remi on the back of my bike for hours at a time, followed by sleeping in a tent on the ground, is laughable. She needs a plush car and a hotel with room service. And I'm okay with that.

The guys and I promise to keep in touch, and before I know it, Remi and I are in the parking lot and standing in front of my bike. I get her bundled up in her jacket and helmet, then help her on behind me.

She scoots close and wraps her arms around me, tucking both hands up under my shirt against my bare skin.

As I stand slightly to start the bike, she slips one hand into the waistband of my jeans.

"You'd better watch your hands woman, unless you're looking to create an early death by motorcycle crash for us both," I say, my voice husky.

She giggles. "I won't do anything, I'm just keeping my hands warm."

I grab her hand from my waistband and raise it to my mouth to kiss the back of it. "I'll have to get you some gloves. Which is not to say that I don't like your hands in my pants. 'Cause I do."

Which is why when she tucks her hand back in the waistband of my pants a short while later, all I can do is smile.

24

REMI

I'm getting used to the motorcycle. Granted, it's only the second time I've ever been on one, and both times have been with Chance. But it's kind of an exercise in letting go; you have to move with the bike, or with the driver of the bike. And you don't really have a choice. There's no doors or roof to insulate you, no handle to hold on to in a corner, no windows to roll up or down.

During the ride home, I remind myself just how much I trust Chance. To tell me the truth, to not be married, to not break my heart. And I obviously trust him physically, with my life, on the back of a motorcycle. I feel safe with him. And that is a stark difference from the way I've felt with any other man before. Plus, I'll get my money's worth on these jeans if I have to keep seeing him for a month.

A month.

Then we're done.

The thought of not seeing him again after the month is over makes me feel hollow and cold. As if he can sense my mood change, Chance puts his hand over mine and runs his thumb lightly over the back, then squeezes gently before returning it to the handlebar at a corner. I miss his hand when it's gone.

Miss his hand!

God, what am I thinking?

Stay strong, Remi.

This is Chance Bauer. Player extraordinaire. He wanted to sleep with Kat for fuck's sake. Although, I've wanted to sleep with Kat too, so I can't blame him there. But, if the fact that it's Chance is not bad enough, then I need to remind myself that it's a bet. A bet that I can't afford to lose.

Louboutins. Louboutins. Louboutins.

But he got me off. That's never happened by another person's hand before. And I came multiple times.

We pull up in front of my house and Chance kills the motor. He helps me off the bike, then climbs off himself. I hand him my helmet, and he offers to walk me to my front door. Which I take as a sign he's going to ask to come in. Or at the very least make a sleazy comment about it.

He takes my keys from me when we get the door and unlocks it.

"Do you want to come in?" I ask since he has yet to mention it.

"More than anything," he says. "But I'm going to pass this time." His voice filled with regret.

"Why?" I ask, more shocked than anything.

"I had a great time tonight, Remi. A much better time than I thought I would. Even with the drama with my ex. And, I don't know about you, but I'd like to explore where this could go with you and me. So, I'm just going to play my hand now and tell you that I don't want to rush into anything that might freak one or both of us out. But I want to see you again. Soon. So, for now, I'm going to say goodnight. And tell you to sleep well, beautiful." He runs his knuckles along my cheek, then leans in and gives me a soft kiss on the lips.

Is he fucking with me right now?

But one look in his eyes and I realize he's serious.

Holy shit.

"I don't do relationships, Chance," I blurt out, and then can't tell if I regret it or not.

"Me neither, beautiful. Me neither." He turns and walks back toward his bike, stopping, without turning around to say, "Don't forget to lock your door."

I walk into my house, and lock the door, feeling like my universe just got rocked a little bit. He starts his bike and I watch through the window as he drives away. I keep watching until the sound of the motor has faded to silence. Then I sit on my couch and try to figure out what I'm feeling right now.

Do I stand strong or give in? Can I stand strong and still give in? I mean, on the one hand, I had a fabulous time with him. But I'm not ready or willing to date someone outside of fulfilling this bet.

Am I?

On the other hand, the idea of not seeing him beyond a month leaves me feeling empty inside.

He's got magic fingers.

Literally.

There are solid arguments for both sides of this equation. What do I do?

You aren't going to figure it out tonight, Remi.

I wash my face and get ready for bed. As I'm climbing under the covers, I hear my phone ding with a text.

Chance: We forgot a date question.

Me: Oh the horror! What do we do now?

Chance: Well, I think we have to schedule an emergency date for first thing in the morning.

Me: Really?

Chance: I'm pretty sure in order for it to count, it has to be within 18 hours of the date when it was forgotten. And then we can do two questions.

Me: Didn't we do two questions during our lunch date?

Chance: Yes we did. I think 3, maybe 4. Which might not have been allowed. Excuse me while I consult the rule book.

Me: LOL!

Chance: Okay, multiple questions may be asked on the first date only. Subsequent dates get one question each. Only one question per date until all questions are answered.

Me: Except for the 18-hour rule.

Chance: Right. Except for that.

Me: Well, we can't break the rules. What would all your police officer friends think?

Chance: Detective, Remi. They are detective friends. Just like me. I'm a detective.

Me: Tomato, Tomahto.

Chance: You're lucky I find you attractive.

Me: Ditto, Detective.

Chance: So? Tomorrow?

Me: I need to work tomorrow.

Chance: All day?

Me: Pretty much.

Chance: Early morning coffee?

Chance: Don't do it for me. Do it for the sake of first date question lists everywhere.

Me: LOL!

Me: Can you do 8am?

Chance: I can. I'll pick you up at 8am.

Me: I can't believe we're doing this.

Chance: It's just coffee.

Me: We both know it's not just coffee.

Chance: See you in the morning, beautiful. For COFFEE. Sleep well.

Me: Goodnight.

I turn off the light and hunker down into my bed, trying to ignore the smile on my face.

I wake early the next morning so I can do some yoga before Chance picks me up. I like the muscle strength that yoga gives me, but more than that I like that it can quiet my brain for just a little bit. I shower and get ready for my day, foregoing making coffee since we're having it first thing anyway. I dress a little nicer than I ordinarily would for a Sunday in the lab since I'm seeing Chance.

Today's ensemble is a pair of dark navy-blue cigarette pants with a white V-neck wrap-around sweater and black ballet flats. I put my hair up in a ponytail and leave bangs on my forehead. Light makeup, a spritz of perfume, and I'm ready to go with fifteen minutes to spare. I should just drive myself since I have to go to work after.

Which makes me think we should just meet somewhere close to my building. I call Chance to see what he thinks.

"Good morning, beautiful." I can hear the smile in his voice. It makes me feel warm inside.

"Hey, I was thinking we could just meet at a place near my office? That way you don't have to come all the way to my house. Although I don't really know where you are coming from, so maybe that's more out of the way. Oh, but I guess not if that's where we are going anyway."

He laughs. "Not quite awake yet, huh?"

"Not quite, I suppose." I laugh.

"Text me the address and I'll meet you there."

I text him, then get in my car and head to the cafe. Anxious to get out of the house before I start thinking too much about what I'm doing.

I arrive before Chance, so I grab a table but wait for him before I order. He pulls into the parking lot a short time later. I watch as he removes his helmet and runs his hand through his hair to 'fix' it and gets off his bike.

Well, me and every other woman in the place watch him.

"Hot guy on a motorcycle, two o'clock." I hear a woman say from the table behind me to her friend.

She's right.

He's wearing low slung jeans that fit snug in all the right places, his motorcycle boots, which are sexy as hell on him, a plain white t-shirt, and his leather jacket. He's like a walking advertisement for Hot-Guys-R-Us. If such a place existed. He walks in and looks around. I give him a little wave. He smiles and heads in my direction.

"Lucky bitch," I hear the same woman say, her voice barely above a whisper.

She's right about that too.

He leans in and gives me a kiss on the cheek. "Good morning, beautiful."

He smells good, fresh like soap with a hint of something woodsy.

"Good morning yourself," I say.

"Did you order?" he asks.

"No, I was waiting for you."

"What would you like?" he asks. I tell him what I want, and he goes up to order for both of us. I watch him as he walks back to the front of the shop. He has so much confidence with everything he does: walking, talking, sitting, driving. It makes it hard not to watch him. The magnetism that comes with that confidence is dizzying.

I'm still watching him when he comes back to the table and sits down.

"Did you sleep well last night?" he asks.

"Is that my next first date question?" I tease.

"No, but I do have one for you, and it's perfect since you have to go to work anyway."

"Let me guess, what do I do, or do I like what I do."

"Ding, ding, ding," he says. "Tell the lady what she wins, Bob."

We both laugh at the corny joke.

"So, do you like your job?" he asks.

"I do. I don't necessarily like the people I work with. They can be sexist and judgmental, but I love the work that I do. I love that if I'm successful, it could make a difference in the world."

"Do you need me to beat up the sexist and judgmental ones? 'Cause I will."

I laugh.

The barista brings out our order, I see that Chance has also bought a selection of pastries. He tells me what each of them are as he cuts each one in half so we can both try them all.

"Do you like your job?" I ask.

"We're not completely through talking about your job, because I still don't totally understand what it is that you do. But yes I love my job."

"What made you go into law enforcement?" I ask, picking at my muffin.

"My dad was a detective, so was his dad before him. I grew up seeing what the two most important men in my life did, how they locked up the bad guys, and helped people in the community, and tried to right the wrongs. I wanted to do the same. I guess, like you, I wanted to make a difference. Or at least try to."

"Do you think that in *wanting to make a difference*" —I use finger quotes as I say the last part— "we are both being too idealistic?"

"I hope not. At least I don't think so. Do you?" he asks.

"I'd have to say the same."

"So, what exactly is it that you do?" he asks, leaning forward, forearms resting on the table's edge.

"My degree is in chemical engineering," I say.

"And you have a master's degree, right?" he asks.

"Yes."

"My girl is smart," he says, shoving half of a pastry in his mouth.

I ignore the flutter in my stomach when he refers to me as his girl. "Did you even taste that?"

He nods, then wipes his mouth with a napkin. "Food. Good."

He's so corny I can't help but laugh.

Then he asks, "What does a chemical engineer do, besides the obvious that I can guess from the name?"

"Well, I'm sure just that, what you can guess from the name. But I am working on developing a process that will breakdown products that were previously non-biodegradable for repurposing."

"Essentially recycling that which was not recyclable before?"

"Yeah, in a sense." I nod my head.

"That seems like a no-brainer, no offense. How come it's taken people until now to figure out how to do that?"

"Well, that's just it, I haven't figured it out yet. So, it remains non-existent. But I'm close."

"So, when you go to work today, and you sit down in your lab, what is it that you'll be doing?"

"In simple terms, I'm running trial tests on the process to see if it works."

"Keep it simple for the simpleton?" he asks with a wink.

I laugh at him.

"So, are you in danger with what you do?" I change the subject. "I mean, like, do people shoot at you?"

"Not typically. I trained, for lack of a better word, in homicide. But San Soloman is small enough that here I get a taste of everything. However, everything doesn't necessarily mean danger."

"So, people don't shoot at you?" I ask, surprised.

"I didn't say that." He chuckles. "It just isn't what normally happens every day. Why, you worried about me, beautiful?"

"I didn't say that." I throw his words back at him. He smiles at me, and I spend a minute getting lost in that smile. It's a nice feeling.

My phone dings with a text. I look down and see it's from Kat and make a mental note to look at it later. I know that she's asking about our date last night anyway. Then I glance at the time and am shocked to see that we've been here over an hour.

"Time to go?" he asks.

"Yes," I say. I'm surprised to realize how disappointed I am.

We stand, he brings our plates and cups back up to the front, then opens the cafe door for me. We get to my car and he takes my keys from my hand and opens my car door for me.

"A girl could get used to all this chivalry," I say with a grin. "Do you want to follow me around all day and open doors for me?"

"A guy could get used to the view of walking behind you all day."

I giggle at that. The sound still a foreign one to my ears. I think that Chance is the only man to ever cause me to giggle. Maybe even the only person.

Chance puts one hand on the roof of the car, and the other on the top of the open door, effectively blocking me in where I stand by the car. I put one hand on his chest and stretch up to kiss him.

"Thank you for the coffee and breakfast," I say against his lips. "That was a great way to start my morning."

"I can think of much better ways to start the morning. I'd be happy to show you." He pulls me in for a deeper kiss. I can taste the coffee and pastries with a hint of mint. I moan into his mouth. He grips my ass with one hand and lifts me up slightly, his cock already hard and hitting me in just the right place. I move to wrap my legs around his waist, but my right leg hits the car door. Which is when I remember where I'm at. I drop to my feet and slowly pull my lips from his.

"Forgot where I was for a minute," I laugh.

"You seem to have that effect on me as well," he says.

"I'll talk to you later?" I ask. Hating that my voice sounds almost needy.

"Definitely," he says. "I'll call you."

I get in the car and start it. He shuts my door and then taps one hand on the hood as I pull away. I watch him in my rearview mirror as I exit the parking lot. I'm amazed that I still enjoy his company. And, that I've not yet found a reason to stop seeing him. Well, that could change at any time.

A little less than two weeks and that'll change.

Oh Fuck.

Right.

Because this is a goddamn bet and not reality. Get your head back in the game, Remi.

Louboutins. Louboutins. Louboutins.

25

CHANCE

I have no idea what to expect with this whole movie night thing. In fact, I wasn't even sure I would be able to make it until this afternoon. Lexie had invited me last week, but I wanted the invite from Remi, and that didn't come until yesterday. I had to scramble to find someone to cover my on-call for the night.

Remi didn't let me pick her up, instead choosing to meet me at Lexie's winery, *Lovestone*, after she got off work. I get there about fifteen minutes before the movie is scheduled to start. I don't remember which movie it is. Not that I care. I'm simply happy that Remi asked me to do something.

This whole thing with her is going better than I'd ever expected. I enjoy her company, and I'm more attracted to her than I've ever been to another woman before. There's just something about her, she's different. She's a dichotomy. Girly and high-maintenance, yet easy-going and down-to-earth. She acts tough, but I think she's soft on the inside.

I still can't believe she climbed on my bike in that dress for the law enforcement gala, the woman has bigger balls than most men. But then she cried after she thought I'd sung the same song to Helen. I just want to figure out what makes her tick. Not to sound like a chick, but I want to cement something between us before having sex.

The tasting room is filled with people, but I don't see any of the three girls. I head off in search of a restroom. After which I intend to find Remi.

I hear Kat say my name as I come up on a little room down the hall, and the detective in me is good at eavesdropping.

"Okay, can I just say how much I like seeing you and Bauer together?" Kat says.

Me too, Cookie. Me too.

"It's not real, Kat, you keep forgetting that," Remi says.

What's not real? Is she saying we aren't real? Why would she think that?

We are as real as it fucking gets, beautiful.

"It's just a bet," she continues.

Wait, does she know about the bet?

If that fucker Alex told her, I will end him.

She doesn't sound that upset about it. Maybe she doesn't care I made a bet.

"It's real enough that you could lose your Louboutins if things go differently," Kat says.

I have no idea what a Louboutin is.

"Well, lucky for me, he's interested enough that I don't have to worry about losing my nine-hundred-dollar shoes, huh?" She sounds smug.

Nine-hundred-dollar shoes? Who the fuck has nine-hundred-dollar shoes? Even with three sisters, I've never heard of shoes that expensive.

"You've practically fulfilled your end of the bet already, Rem. I mean, you've been on how many dates. You only needed to last a month. One guy, once a week," Kat says. "Your shoes are safe. But I think it's time to decide where you want this to go."

Her end of the bet?

One guy once a week?

Wait, was I a bet?

A nine-hundred-dollar bet?

I am worth way more than nine hundred bills.

Of all the fucked up . . .

At least in my bet she's worth over two grand.

Clearly, I'm the more generous of us two.

"I don't know. Sometimes it's so good that it freaks me the fuck out," Remi says softly.

Okay, maybe this all isn't such a bad idea. She said we're good. So good.

"You slept with him?" Kat asks.

It does my ego proud knowing Cookie automatically associates 'so good' with me as being sexual.

"No, not yet."

Fist pump! She said *yet*.

"But I'm not going to be able to hold out much longer. It's like I lose my head with him," Remi says.

"Nothing wrong with that," Kat says.

"Easy for you to say, you're with the love of your life and he just put a ring on your finger, for the second time."

"Bauer is a good guy, Remi. What's wrong with just seeing where this goes?"

"Everything. I'm not a relationship person like you or Lexie. I don't want to have someone get to know me so well that they can anticipate my needs or finish my sentences."

"Why not?" Kat asks.

"Because that sounds like my own personal form of hell."

"Do I look like I'm in hell?"

"No," Remi sighs. "You look happier than I've ever seen you."

"Well then."

Remi whispers whatever she says next, and I can't quite make it out. But Kat whispers back, "I know." I hear rustling so I move back toward the end of the hall and make like I've just arrived. I look in the room as I pass and see that Kat is hugging Remi.

"Now that's what I like to see," I say. "Hang on, I'll shut the door and put my phone on video mode. You girls just continue with what you were doing."

Remi looks at me and rolls her eyes. I walk over and give her a kiss on the cheek and squeeze her waist lightly. Not sure if displays of affection are okay in front of Kat.

Kat gives me a hug and says, "It's nice to see that in this ever-changing world, Bauer, you've managed to stay the same." I laugh and kiss her on the cheek as well.

"Where's Romeo?" I ask Kat.

"He's on shift tonight. It's just me, myself, and I as a third wheel on your date. Yay, you."

"I'm digging the hair, Cookie. It's very bad-ass."

"Why thank you, kind sir." She bats her eyelashes at me. I smile back.

Remi clears her throat, then asks, "Did you just get here?"

"Yeah," I say. "I was looking for the restroom."

Kat points it out to me, and I leave the women alone. When I return, it's just Remi in the room. She walks toward me with a look in her eye that I can't quite identify. And it doesn't matter, because the next thing I know, she's got her arms around my neck and her lips against mine, in a real kiss. I grab her around the waist and pull her to me.

God, she feels good against me. I will never get tired of this.

Her tongue slips into my mouth, meeting mine, and I groan. I can't help it. I feel her smile against my lips. I continue the kiss until she pulls away slightly.

"Hi," she whispers.

"If I leave and come back, will you greet me like that again?"

She laughs and gives me a quick peck on the lips, then leans back to wipe what I'm assuming is her lipstick off them.

"I think I missed you," she says, still in my arms.

"That's convenient since I think I missed you too," I rest my forehead against hers.

I love the light that puts in her eyes. Such a simple thing to say, yet it seems to have an impact. Until I remember that this is a bet for her too.

"Hey, can we talk about something?" I ask. Now's the time to tell her the truth. She has her own bet going on, she will totally understand.

"Uh oh, that doesn't sound good," she says.

"It's not a big deal," I say. "I just—"

Lexie pokes her head in the door. "Starting the movie, get your butts in there."

Remi looks at me questioningly.

"We'll talk later." I take her hand in mine and lead her to the barrel room where Lexie is showing the movie.

"What movie is it, again?" I ask.

"Casablanca," Remi says.

She grabs an open bottle of wine, two glasses, and some popcorn off the end of the bar and we enter the darkened room.

26

REMI

He gets up on the barrel first, then grabs my hand and pulls me up. His leather jacket is open, so when I lean back against his chest, it's just my blouse and his tee that separate us. I use my poncho as a blanket for my chest and arms, and my blanket to cover my legs. Chance has his arms around my waist, the warmth from his body feels good.

We munch on popcorn, drink wine, and watch the movie. And for the first fifteen or twenty minutes, that's great. But the more time that passes, the harder it is to concentrate. This close to Chance, feeling him, smelling him, it's distracting.

I think about earlier in the evening, so I can avoid thinking about how much he turns me on. I'd gotten to movie night early so I could hang with Kat and Lexie a little bit beforehand.

Kat and I were talking about Chance when he popped his head in and made a joke about Kat and I hugging.

Then she flirted with him.

I mean, what the actual fuck?

It's little times like that where I think I might be jealous.

Even though I don't get jealous.

Why would I be jealous of Kat? That's crazy. She's got Brad. She's not interested in Chance. Except that I know she's fantasized about him before. And I know he wanted to fuck her.

My God, is this what vulnerability feels like? No wonder people hate being in relationships. This is an awful feeling. The constant doubting of one's self-worth and feelings. Never knowing where you stand, always having to rely on outside knowledge.

Then I remember that most people don't hate being in relationships. They like them. They gravitate toward them. How odd must it be when your goal is to illuminate your weaknesses, so someone else can exploit them, for the sole purpose of 'sharing' your life with another person.

Except Kat's not weak. If anything, she's ten times stronger with Brad back in her life.

So, which is it? Does love make you weak or strong?

Whoa, wait. Who said anything about love?

Jesus Christ, Remi.

There's the deep end and you've just gone off it.

How is it that he fits in so well with everyone else? I mean, Kat and Lexie both adore him. If I must pick someone, shouldn't it be someone that Kat and Lexie love?

I couldn't stop myself when I'd kissed him earlier. He looked sinfully good in his standard jeans, t-shirt, leather jacket, and motorcycle boots outfit. I think that outfit was created with him in mind. His ass, his cock, his pecs, his thighs. I walked up to him and kissed the fuck out of him. A real kiss, with tongue and hip grinding. I couldn't help myself. This man is going to be the death of me.

If that's not bad enough, then I told him that I missed him. Because I'm a fucking sucker. But when he said it back, I felt like I was floating on happy clouds.

Relationships make you bipolar, that's what happens.

Jesus, I need to pay attention to the movie so I can get a dose of reality from Bogie and Bergman before I lose my fucking mind.

I snuggle back against Chance as he rests his chin on my shoulder. My blouse has ridden up slightly on one side and he starts running his thumb up and down the side of my belly. It's a tiny bit ticklish, but more than that it's a straight up turn-on. The skin on skin contact makes my breath catch. My body heat rises, it feels like we are in a cloud of warmth, like when a fire first ignites and that wave hits you.

I know he feels it. I can feel his cock hardening against my ass.

Chance uses his chin to move my hair from my neck, then kisses it softly. That was pretty fucking smooth. No hands at all.

And, *oh shit*, that feels good.

His lips on my neck, his thumb at my side, his chest against my back, and his thighs surrounding mine. My heart pounds. I close my eyes. His other hand snakes up slightly and he runs his thumb along the underside of my breast. My panties soak. My nipples harden. I can smell my arousal. I shift on the barrel as he bites my earlobe softly. I put one hand on his thigh and squeeze tightly.

"Stop!" I hiss.

Kat looks over at us and tries to wink. It's a terrible look on her, but it makes me laugh and helps break up the sexual tension a little bit.

Everyone else turns around, it was not an amusing part of the movie. Which makes me laugh more. I can't help it. It's like all the sexual tension in my body from the last thirty minutes is releasing itself through laughter.

I hop down from the barrel and leave the room, so I don't interrupt the movie. I get out to the tasting room and head toward the bathroom. A hand grabs my arm before I can get there.

"You okay?" Chance asks, turning me to face him.

"Fine," I say, heading back toward the restrooms. But then change my mind. "Actually, no I'm not. You confuse me."

"I do?"

"Yes, I feel like we have all this chemistry that I don't quite know what to do with and it's frustrating. And then at the same time, you're just all normal. Why haven't we fucked? Don't you want to fuck me?"

He looks a little surprised at that. "Christ woman - yes! I do. I want to fuck you every minute of every day. But we need to talk first."

"No more talking."

"It's important," he says.

"You aren't married?"

"No."

"Fucking someone else?"

"No."

"Then I don't care."

"Are you sure?"

I nod my head.

He hesitates, as though he is trying to decide what to do. I lean into him, fisting his t-shirt to help me stretch up slightly and align our lips. He moves in closer; I can feel his breath, another inch and I'm pressing my lips to his. His tongue flicks at the seam of my mouth, demanding entrance. I open for him, and he pulls me in closer.

My entire body tingles and my head spins like I'm on one of those carnival rides where the little cages spin and turn and roll at the same time. His lips ghost across my jaw and move down my throat, the scrape from his whiskers sending goose bumps down my spine. I don't want this to end.

Ever.

This right here must be why people are in relationships. To experience this every day.

"God, Chance."

I slide my hands up his chest and cup his neck, bringing his mouth back to mine. I want to take the kiss even deeper, but he has other plans.

"Okay, let's go," he practically growls against my lips, his decision obviously made. He grabs my hand and pulls me toward the front door, and I stumble after him to keep up.

He follows me back to my place. It's all I can do to concentrate on driving there without wrecking my car. I'm so excited by the thought of getting him in my bed. I pull my car into the garage, and he pulls his bike in beside me. I push the button to shut the door and am out of the car launching myself toward him before he's off the bike.

Our mouths meet, I'm desperate to feel him. I push his jacket off his shoulders, and it falls to the floor. My hands diver under his t-shirt to feel those abs, stopping only to pull at his nipples. He pulls my face to his and takes my mouth in a kiss that is nothing like the others. This kiss is weeks of pent-up frustration and sexual energy pouring from his lips to mine.

His hands travel from my ass up my spine, he grabs the back of my blouse and rips it in half.

Literally.

It falls from my shoulders down my arms. I look up at him.

"I could have taken it off," I laugh.

"I'll buy you a new one," he says.

"It was vintage," I whisper.

"I'll buy you a new vintage."

"That's not—"

He runs his hands up my bare belly and cups my breasts. I stop thinking about my blouse. He pulls one bra cup down to release my breast, and laves the nipple with his tongue, biting lightly.

"So good," I moan.

He reaches behind me and unsnaps my bra; it falls to the ground beside my blouse.

I need to feel him against me. Nipples to chest hair.

"Shirt off," I say, tugging at his. He reaches behind his head to grab the shirt and pull it off. The motion makes his abs contract, I run my hands along them.

"Ah!" He jumps, then giggles.

Giggles!

"Don't do that, it tickles," he says.

"Don't do what?" I ask. "This?" I run my fingernails lightly up and down his sides. He lurches to the side and pushes my hands away. Nearly screeching. As someone who is not ticklish, I'm finding this to be entertaining.

"You sound like a little girl." I move toward him.

"I'm warning you," he says, backing away from me and holding his hands up, still tittering nervously.

My breasts feel heavy and full, as I advance on him; his gaze moves back and forth between my bare breasts, and my eyes, like he can't decide if he wants to stare at my tits or block my tickle.

"What's going to happen, Chance? Are you afraid I'll tickle you to death?"

"That's it," he growls as he moves forward, grabs me in a fireman's hold and heads for the connecting door into my house. Now I'm the one giggling. I'm tempted to tickle him from this angle but don't for fear he'll drop me.

"I like the feel of your tits on my back," he says, entering the house. "Now, tell me where to go." I direct him to my bedroom, and he throws me down on the bed. He starts pulling the belt from his jeans.

"I warned you," he says. "You didn't listen. Now you don't get to use your hands at all." He gets the belt off and crawls up the bed toward me, like a tiger toward his prey. I scramble back until I'm closer to the headboard, with most of my pillows bunched up behind me. But he pulls me back down by my ankles until I'm prone. My pants come off next and I'm left in only my panties. My completely soaked through panties.

My chest heaves. I'm practically panting, waiting to see what he's going to do next. He pushes my legs apart to kneel between them, then leans forward, his chest inches from my lips, as he pulls my hands together above my head and wraps the belt around my wrists. It's tight enough so I can't break free, but not so tight that it's chafing my skin.

He braces on his forearms and slides his body back down mine, settling his rock-hard cock against my core. The pressure of him, through his jeans, is almost enough to make me come.

I want that so bad. I want what he gave me the night of the concert. He's the first person to give me an orgasm besides myself. Not that I'll tell him that. It surprised me how fast it happened and how intense it was. Will it be that way every time? Can he do it again?

I moan in part at the thought of it and in part as a response to what he's doing right now. His lips are at my throat, gently dancing across the skin. His breath is hot and heavy, as delicious feeling as the warmth of his skin against mine. His hand slides down my body and cups me through my underwear. The feeling of his fingers through the flimsy material is nothing short of electrifying.

"Ohmigod, how do you do this?" I can barely get the words out. He laughs against my neck.

"Do what, beautiful?"

"Make me feel this way. This good." His fingers shift the material to the side and he sinks one inside me.

We both groan.

"This is all you, Remi. You make it feel this way." His lips meet mine, and he speaks softly against them. "It's never been this good."

His lips move from mine and along my jawline back down my neck. I whimper. "Come back."

"Nuh uh," he says as he moves his lips down my chest, nipping and kissing as he goes. Getting closer and closer to my left nipple. I thrust forward, trying to get him to take more, but he just keeps teasing. His lips hover over my skin, as though they can't decide where to land first.

"Please," I beg.

"Please what?" he asks. "This one first?" He moves his lips to my left breast and takes it into his mouth.

"Oh yes." His touch is warm and wet as he suckles, I can feel each pull from his lips down through the center of my body. My release is building quickly. It's like he's unlocked the secret orgasm hiding place and they are all going to come rushing out at once.

"Chance." It rushes over me. Wave after wave of euphoria. Stars exploding behind my eyes as my body spasms uncontrollably. My arms strain against the belt and my legs find purchase around his hips as I pull him against me to ride it out.

Holy fucking shit fuck shit balls.

I collapse back on the bed. Spent. Depleted. Stick a fork in me and all that.

But Chance is just getting started. His mouth moves to my right breast and begins the same ministrations.

"At least give me my hands back. Please."

He stops and looks up at me. "Do you plan to behave?"

I nod.

He inches back up my body, kissing as he goes, until he meets my mouth, his lips just as demanding as the rest of him. He wraps one arm underneath me and pulls me into him. The other hand moves up to the belt, which he unclasps.

One-handed.

While kissing me.

The blood rushes back into my hands, and they tingle slightly. Chance pulls away from me to look at them.

"You okay?" he asks as he inspects each wrist.

"Fine." I pull my hands from his and wrap my arms around his neck to pull him back toward me, happy to have the use of my hands. I want to touch him everywhere at the same time. My hands move from behind his neck and down his back. I encounter jeans.

"Why do you still have these on?"

"Patience, beautiful." He begins his descent back down my chest to my abdomen. Pushing my panties down as he goes. My lips and right nipple forgotten. I gasp when his mouth meets my clit as he dives right in, no pretense.

"Chance!"

I'm going to come again.

Oh God.

"Chance, I, oh jeez." I buck my hips, hard. He wraps one arm under my ass to lift me slightly, and the other over my abdomen to hold me still. His tongue takes turns plunging inside me and peppering my clit with attention. Within seconds, another orgasm washes over me. Chance moans in appreciation, licking up everything I have to offer.

This is insane.

The way my body responds to him.

My limbs fall listlessly to the bed. I thought he depleted me before. But that was nothing compared to this. My eyes drift shut. I feel a small pinch on my nipple.

"I'm not done with you yet," Chance says as he sits up, his hand moving softly over my chest and belly. I'm glad I'm not ticklish.

I open one eye. "No more. I can't," I tell him.

"You can," he says. He leans forward to give me a quick peck on the lips, then moves off the bed to remove his jeans. For this, I open my other eye. I've felt what he has to offer, but this is the first time I going to see it in its entirety, I have no intention of missing that.

He looks at me as he unbuttons his jeans, heat in his eyes. "Now I have your attention?"

"You have my full attention," I tell him, sitting up. I look him up and down again. His body is amazing. I don't know what he does to work out or stay in shape, but it works for him. Really well. He's not so bulky that I fear he'll have steroid dick, but also not so slight that I feel big next to him. I'm a tall girl with a lot of curves, it's hard to feel dainty and desirable in most situations. Especially a naked one.

He pushes his jeans and boxers down at the same time. His cock springs forward, asking for my attention. It has it. The bed dips as he moves his way back to me. A knee on each side of mine and his forearms braced around my shoulders. He slides up my body until we are touching everywhere.

The feel of skin on skin is incredible. His bare dick against my clit.

"I need you, now," I tell him, trying to find the right angle to get him inside me.

"I aim to please."

He sits back, ass to ankles, and I'm filled with disappointment. Until I realize he's grabbing a condom from the side of the bed. I don't even know how it got there. I watch as he puts it on. Even this most mundane of tasks becoming a turn-on for me.

He moves back over me and lowers his body to mine. My muscles tense. Everything else has been so amazing this far, please let this be good too.

"You okay?" he asks. I nod, then shake my head. He smiles. "Which is it?" He rubs the tip of his cock over my clit as he asks the question.

Oh, that feels good.

What if it stops feeling good?

I bite the proverbial bullet.

"I'm scared," I whisper.

He kisses me again, on my forehead, on each cheek, on my lips. Then nuzzles the side of my face, and asks with a faint voice, "Tell me, baby."

"What if it's bad?"

His body goes stiff, beads of sweat appear on his brow. "What do you mean by bad?" he asks. "Like you don't think you'll enjoy it? I think we've proven our chemistry is off the charts, beautiful. And I promise you'll enjoy every second of it."

I take a deep breath and let it all out in one big rush of words. "I know my timing isn't the best, but I've not felt anything like this with someone else before. And by that, I mean I haven't had an orgasm with another person, other than the one time with you. Only myself. And I was a little drunk with you before. And I'm not drunk now. So, this scares me.

"I've already experienced so much with you that I never had before. What if I have this with you and suddenly I know what I've been missing all these years. Then I don't have it again. Instead of being okay with nothing because I didn't know any better, I'll know exactly what I'm missing because I've had it. That's going to make it worse. Which is going to make me dependent on you and I already know better than to rely on anyone. That's just foolishness.

"And before you say anything, I know all about oxytocin and how the brain produces it with sex and that's automatically going to make me want to bond with you. I'll be honest, I thought it was total bullshit before, even as a scientist. But I get it now and we haven't even had actual sex yet. So, can you imagine how it will be once we do?"

"Whoa, beautiful." He rolls to his back, pulling me with him. "You've got a lot going on in your head right now. Let's just relax a minute, okay?"

I can still feel his hard cock against me. Thank God he's still hard. I'm sure he won't be for long if I keep talking. Which is what I wanted to avoid; I don't want this thing between us going bad. Yet here I am causing exactly that to happen.

Fuck.

Chance runs his hands up and down my back slowly. Going a bit farther toward my ass each time.

"I didn't mean to ruin the mood." My voice cracks as I say it. I clear my throat but don't continue talking.

"Remi, I'm in your bed and you're naked in my arms. Nothing could be more perfect," he says. My pulse speeds up when he says that. He keeps talking. "What do you say we try to get to a point where you're feeling comfortable and then we'll talk about things like mood?"

"I'm okay," I say, letting him continue to run his hands over me.

I pause to think about it and realize right then that I am okay, and I want nothing more than for this man to fuck me.

Hard.

27

CHANCE

She looks me in the eye. "I want you to fuck me."

I want to believe her. Trust that she's okay. But I don't want to take this somewhere that she's not ready to be. I look at her, trying to discern her state of mind.

She grabs my cock with one hand and positions it at her pussy, rubbing the tip back and forth in her wetness. Her other hand grabs my ass and tries to pull me down to her.

"Please," she moans.

I guess that's as good an invitation as any. I sink into her.

All the way in.

"Oh my God, Remi."

She gasps. Her eyes widen, her mouth forms a slight O shape.

Please be okay. Please be okay.

"You good?" I grunt.

She nods. "So. Fucking. Good."

I pull out until just the tip of my cock is inside her and thrust back in. Her hips arch up to meet mine.

So fucking good is right.

My balls start to tighten. I reach my arms around her back and pull her to me, slowing my roll. I want this to be good for her.

No, I want this to be mind-blowing for her.

If I come too soon, it won't be. I will my dick to cooperate. But sex has never been this good. Not even with Helen, who I thought I loved.

Well, shit, if I wanted to prevent myself from coming, thinking about Helen will do it.

I run my nose along Remi's jawline, breathing in her scent, bringing myself back to the present, and this goddess beneath me.

"You smell so good," I tell her.

"Harder."

I raise up onto my forearms to deepen our connection and ram back into her again. And again. Like an obsession, I can't stop. My balls slap at her ass. My muscles strain. My dick begs for release.

"Oh God. Oh God. Oh shit. Chance!" Her muscles tighten around me, pulling at my cock. She's so close.

"Come on my dick, beautiful."

It's all she needs. Her body tenses. Eyes shut. Back arching. She gives in, all the way in. I watch as the pleasure rockets through her. She screams my name again. Her body tightens like a vise around mine. I let go, coming with a roar, pumping everything I have into her. My entire body shakes and convulses like never before. I never want to leave this place. Never want to leave her. I want to stay rooted inside her forever. Locked in this moment.

"Never so good, never," I say into her neck, careful not to say anything more that might scare her away. Because in that moment, I know with absolute certainty, that I am falling head over heels in love with Remi Vargas.

I roll us over so she's on top and I'm not crushing her. She's dead weight.

My chest puffs slightly. I did that to this amazing woman. This conundrum of angst, detachment, and drive. I relaxed her, sated her; she's like a wet noodle, all bendy and limp.

I'm the fucking man.

She giggles, shaking both our bodies, then raises her head slightly to look at me.

"Did you just call yourself the man?" she asks.

"Not intentionally aloud. But I guess if the condom fits . . ."

She laughs again and slaps me lightly on the shoulder.

"Speaking of, let me up for just a minute, beautiful, so I can take care of this." I place her to the side of me on the bed, then kiss her softly on the lips before getting up and heading to the bathroom.

She's curled up on her side, facing the middle of the bed, and almost asleep when I return. I crawl in behind her and pull her back to my chest. She fits against me perfectly. It makes me smile. Which in turn causes me to laugh at how sappy I've become.

She doesn't know it yet, but I'm introducing her to my entire family this weekend. I just have to remember to tell her about the bet first. I mean, how bad can it really be when she finds out? We just had the best fucking sex of our lives. She's mine. I'm not letting her get away now.

28

REMI

Connie invites me to lunch. And I agree to go. Which doesn't happen often. We've grown close over the last few months, chatting about everything going on in our lives and such. She's one of the only other women in the company. Regardless, I still don't pal around outside work with her. But I'm feeling like a new me, one that decides to trust men, and agrees to go to lunch with women who aren't Lexie or Kat.

We decide on an Italian restaurant that is close to the office so we can walk.

She babbles on a bit about making the travel plans for our upcoming conference.

"Hey, I never asked you what kind of room you want," she says.

"What do you mean? I get a choice?"

She laughs. "Well, with me making all the travel plans, you do."

"Okay then, something far away from everyone else, King bed, soaking tub, and a view."

"Done!" she says.

I think of Chance and what we can do in a king bed. And a soaking tub. Or against a window with a view. I reach into my purse for my phone. Maybe I can talk him into coming up for a night if he doesn't have to work.

"It's right across the street here." She points to the restaurant. I slow my steps before stepping off the curb so I can start a text to Chance. I look up briefly, see nothing, then move to cross the street. Movement in my periphery causes me to pause just as Connie screams my name and pulls me back by the arm.

A blue car speeds by, barely swerving to miss me. My hands drop in shock, my phone falling from them and bouncing off the edge of the curb into the street.

I wasn't even paying attention.

I was too busy thinking about Chance to watch my surroundings. Another second or so and that car would have flattened me.

"Holy shit, Connie, did you see that? Fucking maniac almost hit me! Thank you so much. Ohmigod." My heart is racing, and I want to throw up.

"Hey asshole, watch where you're going!" I yell belatedly after the car.

"You okay?" she asks.

"I think so. I just need to catch my breath. That really scared me."

"That was a close one," she says.

I move to pick up my phone, or what's left of it, having bounced off the curb at just the right angle to shatter the entire screen.

Fuck.

"I'm going to have to hit the cell store after this, look." I hold my phone up so Connie can see the screen.

"Oh no," she cries. "That sucks. Eating always makes me feel better. Maybe pasta will make you feel better."

Somehow, I doubt that. But I don't share that aloud.

Connie had said this place was her favorite, and even though I think pasta is a little heavy for lunchtime, I agreed. Because that's the kind of thing that *new Remi* does with her friends.

Connie crosses ahead of me, but I hold back, double-checking both sides of traffic before crossing the street on still shaky legs.

The host sits us at a little table near the back of the restaurant. I grab my menu and plan on what to eat before taking in my surroundings.

Deciding on angel hair pasta tossed with olive oil, Roma tomatoes, and basil, I sit back and sip on my water, the server comes to take our order. I give her mine, but Connie asks a lot of questions before making her decision. I take the time to look around the restaurant, it's got a nice homey feel, with wood paneled wainscoting on lower half the walls and pictures of regular customers posing alongside the owners scattered across the upper half. We are sitting in a deep red high-backed booth that makes me feel like Frank Sinatra and Dean Martin are going to walk in at any time, call me *dollface*, and order a platter of pasta and gravy.

My gaze halts at a booth near the front door. A familiar head of blonde hair faces away from me.

Helen.

Of all the places.

Then, as though she senses someone watching her, she pivots, and our eyes meet. A glint of recognition lights in hers. I try to look away, but I'm caught in her gaze. The fly to the spider web. So caught up in seeing her, it takes me a moment to realize she's not looking at me. More like past me. I turn to see who is behind me.

Just Connie.

Holy Shit.

Do Connie and Helen know one another?

Fuck.

Helen rises from her booth and starts walking toward us. She reaches our booth and I brace myself for the interaction.

"Connie, how lovely it is to see you! How long has it been?" Helen exclaims as she leans down to embrace Connie.

"Ohmigod, Helen! What are you doing here? I haven't seen you since Gramma Nono's reunion dinner. How have you been?" Connie says.

"So, good," Helen says. "Couldn't be happier."

I clear my throat to try and draw Helen's attention. Because I'll be damned if I'm going to let her ignore me. She knows who I am.

"Oh, sorry Remi," Connie says. "Helen, this is my co-worker Remi, she works in the chemical engineering department. Remi, this is my second cousin on my mom's side, Helen."

"Lovely to meet you," Helen says to me, holding out her hand limply.

"We've met," I say quickly grasping her hand in a firm shake, then dropping it just as fast.

"Oh?" Helen pretends to be surprised.

"At the Night Moves show? I'm dating Chance."

"Hmmm," Helen says, giving me the once-over with her eyes.

Bitch.

"Hmmm," I say back. Then give her an identical elevator stare back. Because fuck this bitch.

She turns away from me abruptly, toward Connie. "So, I've got to get back to my friends, but it was so good to see you again, let's not make it so long between visits this time." Her eyes have a weird glint to them.

"Totally," Connie says. "Let's do happy hour or something."

"That sounds perfect," Helen says as she air kisses Connie's cheeks.

She turns toward me. "Nice to meet you, Mimi."

I narrow my eyes toward her. She knows damn well my name is Remi. But I don't bother to correct her. Because she doesn't matter in *new Remi's* life.

Helen leaves to go back to her table. I turn to Connie, one eyebrow raised in a question.

"What are the chances?" she says a bit nervously.

"Right," I say.

"So, that was my cousin, Helen," Connie says, twisting her napkin around her fingers.

"I got that," I say.

"You guys met?" Connie asks, her voice awkward and high pitched.

"Connie, she's my . . .she's Chance's ex."

"Right. Of course." She clears her throat.

"She ambushed me on my date with Chance."

"She can be a little intense sometimes," she says meekly.

"That's one word for it, I suppose," I say.

She looks like she wants to say more, but I don't really care to keep talking about Helen.

"It doesn't matter," I say waving my hand in her direction.

The server arrives with our order, preventing any further conversation. But I find it odd that Helen is pretending not to remember me.

We finish our lunch without any other interruptions and return to the office. I make an appointment for later at the cell phone store to see if they can fix my screen, then bury myself in lab tests and quickly forget about both Helen and Connie.

I leave the cell phone store, relieved they were able to fix my screen so quickly. Chance and I had texted briefly earlier in the day and set a phone/text date for tonight, so it was imperative that I get my phone fixed. We've both been working long hours and have not had a chance to see one another all week. He's working late again tonight, and I have an early morning meeting again tomorrow, so this is the only chance we'll get for a couple of days. I want to tell him about seeing Helen, but at the same time, I don't want to ruin the little time that we have together with reminding him of his ex. Especially when it's not face-to-face time and I can't see his face to tell what he's thinking.

Good God, when did you become such a wimp, Remi?

I ignore my inner thoughts and get ready for bed. My guess is Chance will be texting me soon; his shift has been ending right about the time I go to bed. Like clockwork, I get a ding from my phone signaling a new text.

I try to stop the big smile from forming on my face, but it's impossible. I like this guy and even though I hate that I do, I'm loving every minute of it.

I pick up my phone and swipe to see the text.

Chance: Hey beautiful, you still awake?

Me: I am. How did your day go?

Chance: I'd rather hear about your day.

Me: Interestingly enough, I ran into Helen at lunch today.

Chance: Helen? As in my ex, Helen?

Me: Yes.

Chance: Where were you?

Me: Out to lunch with Connie, the receptionist. A place near my office.

Chance: That's a little strange since she lives like forty-five minutes from there.

Me: Weirder still, she's cousins with Connie.

Chance: Your receptionist is her cousin?

Me: Yes. Small world.

Chance: Or psycho world. Can I call you?

Me: Of course.

I snuggle down deep into my covers in anticipation of his voice. When I talk to him on the phone, it gives me shivers. I don't try to analyze that feeling too deeply.

"Hi," I say when I answer his call.

He sighs. "God, it's good to hear your voice."

"Back at you," I say.

"Look, I don't want to spoil our conversation with bringing this up, but I want you to be very careful if you ever see Helen again."

"Why? Did something happen?" I ask.

"I don't want to bore you with the details," he says. "But suffice it to say that she did some things that would not be considered sane in most countries after we broke up."

"Oh, I'm sorry. What happened? Er, no, that's really not my business."

"It's okay, and it is your business. It's just," he takes a deep breath, then sighs. "I wasn't completely honest with you before. About Helen."

"Honest about what?"

"She can be violent and vindictive. Breaking and entering, property destruction, attempted poisoning. It's not good. I just want you to be careful. She's not right in the head and she won't get help."

"Ohmigod, Chance, that's terrible."

"I just want to make sure that none of her craziness gets fixated on you," he says. "I still don't know how it was that she was at the Night Moves show and then to have her just show up when you are out to lunch with her *cousin*, it's too convenient. It makes me uncomfortable."

"I understand," I say.

"I'm going to have someone keep an eye on you. And maybe her. Mostly to make sure she stays away from you."

"What about you?"

"I'm not worried about me. Plus, I have a restraining order, though it's more to show I've taken action than it is a protective measure."

"I get it."

"Oh yeah? I've got something you can get," Chance says.

"Is that a come on?" I laugh.

"Depends. Did it work?"

"You know, I think it did."

"Where are you right now?" he asks.

"I'm at home."

"Where in your house?"

"In bed."

"Mmm, I gotta say, beautiful, there is nothing I like more than the thought of you in your bed," he says. "Are you wearing one of those crazy little skimpy silk outfits you call pajamas?"

"If I were, what would you say?"

"Fuuucckkk."

I giggle softly. Then decide to go where no man has gone before. At least not in my house. Or at least where I've not gone before.

"How do you feel about phone sex?" I ask.

"Mmmm," he says. "Are you asking a question or making a suggestion, because my hand has been down my pants since I first heard your voice."

I giggle again. Mostly because I feel a little giddy about the power that I wield over him. Or, rather, what he lets me wield over him.

"If I were making a suggestion, what would you say?" I ask.

"I would say I'm pushing my pants down around my thighs and getting ready to rock."

"Where are you right now?" I ask, laughter in my voice.

"On my couch. Are you laughing?"

"Only a little."

"Okay, I know we are new at this together, beautiful, but laughing at a guy with his cock in hand is kind of a mood killer."

I laugh aloud. "Sorry, it's just a cute image in my head. Eager. Like a puppy."

"Cute and eager are most definitely mood killers when talking about my cock as well," he growls.

"What if I were on my knees in front of you?"

"Now, I like where your head is at," he says.

"Literally."

He laughs.

"I'm going to lick just the tip for a bit, maybe run my tongue over the slit, and circle my lips around the head until it's wet. Mmm, I'm running my lips down the side, getting the shaft with my tongue."

"Are you wearing the red lipstick?" he grunts.

"I am," I say softly as I snake my hands down my pants and start rubbing my clit.

"Are you touching yourself?" he asks, breathless.

"I've got one hand around your cock and one hand down my pants. I've got my lips around the head and I'm working them down your dick as I work my hand up. God, Chance, you taste so good."

"Fuck, Remi." He draws both words out. I can hear him jacking his cock through the phone. And, fuck me, if that isn't a sexy sound.

"I'm running my tongue down the underside and I'm licking your balls. I'm going to take one in my mouth and roll the other one with my hand. It makes your cock jump. You like it when I love on your balls."

"I do. Oh God, I do."

"My mouth is back on your dick and I'm sucking it down as deep as I can. It's hitting the back of my throat which makes me gag just a bit."

"Fuck, beautiful. You're killing me."

"It makes us both hot when you gag me with your cock." I'm close, so fucking close. Just the thought of having him in my mouth makes me almost come. I want him to finish with me.

"Fuck my mouth, Chance," I moan.

"Oh fuck, Remi. I'm gonna blow, FUCK!"

"Oh, Chance!" I cry, the warm rush running over me. Stars exploding behind my eyes. I keep light pressure on my clit and just let the flood of sensations rolling over me, again and again until I'm spent.

"Wow."

"You are a goddess." He groans.

"So fucking good," I say.

"So fucking good," he confirms. "Remi, I…"

I wait for him to finish his sentence.

"Yeah." My voice is groggy. Orgasms make me sleepy.

He clears his throat. "I hope you sleep well, beautiful."

"I will, now."

"Goodnight," he says softly.

"Night," I mumble.

I fall asleep quickly and dream, not surprisingly, of Chance. And sex with Chance. Which, in my dream, is mind-blowing. Even though we are married with kids and sneaking sex in the shower after they're asleep. And in my dream, I'm happy.

Really happy.

Go figure.

29

CHANCE

I had to jack-off again after talking to Remi, just to feel any semblance of relief. And then I did it one more time in the shower. Imagining her wet slippery body in there with me. Those tits, that ass, and those red lips.

Fuck.

On her knees, taking my cock in her mouth, looking up at me with those big eyes as she swallows everything I have to give her. That is the stuff fantasies are made of.

When I do finally sleep, I dream about her. She's the last thing I see at night and the first thing I see in the morning. Her belly swelling with my baby. And we're happy. Happy, like my parents are happy. And when she smiles at me, it's like I've been given the greatest gift of all.

And I'll treasure it forever.

I'm feeling rather good about most things in general. Until Charlie calls.

"Hey bro, how goes it?"

"Charlie, to what do I owe the pleasure?" I ask, dryly.

"Oh, come on, you know I'm your favorite sister," she says.

"Yeah, but you don't ever call me unless you want something."

"Suck it up. I don't have a lot of time. The next payment is due for the cruise for Mom and Dad. And you're up."

"Shit. Already?"

"Yup!"

"Okay, let me see what I can pull together."

"Do you need help? A loan?"

Fuck.

There is no feeling more emasculating than needing money. I can't believe I'm in this position.

"No! I've got this. And even if I didn't, I would never take a loan from you. You're my baby sister."

"That doesn't mean I can't make more money than you."

"Everyone makes more money than me," I sigh.

"Ah, the tragedy of public service."

"Okay, sassy pants, anything else?"

"Nope. Gotta go. Love you, Chancey!"

"Love you too, Charlie," I say.

We hang up and I feel a moment of panic. I don't have the money for my payment. I could almost go to Alex now and win the bet. Except I don't want to win the bet anymore. I want to win Remi. I want to tell her about the bet and have us laugh about it.

I wish I had someone I could talk to about it. But there's just Alex, who I'm not going to go to for obvious reasons, and then Matthews, who probably wouldn't help me anyway.

Fuck.

I could sell my bike.

But then I wouldn't have a means of transportation. And, Remi would question it. Shit, everyone in my life would question it. And if my parents knew that I'd sold my bike just to pay for something for them, they'd insist on paying me back.

I took a big pay cut for this job because of two things: one, it was time to leave undercover work, and two, being closer to my family. Not that I need to make a lot of money. My living expenses have never been that high to begin with. At least not outside of my Helen days where I would be buying things that made her happy. Or made her appear happy.

But having to come up with this additional money hasn't been easy. If I ask Alex for half of the bet money, since I've essentially met half the terms, it will give me what I need to make my payment.

I grab my phone and make the call.

Alex answers after the first ring. "Yo, loser. What's up?"

I adopt a fake persona and respond, "No losers here, brother. In fact, I've already won over half the bet."

"No shit?"

"No shit. I figure I'll save you the trouble of coughing up the entire two and a half G's at once and let you pay half now."

"Dude, there's no payout for half the bet."

"Hey, we both know I'm closing the deal. I'm just looking out for your wallet, man," I say.

"I can't believe you're doing it," Alex says. "Tappin' that ass."

"I told you, there's not an ice queen I can't thaw." I wince as I say it, hating myself more and more as this conversation continues. Talking about Remi like this makes me want to throw up. I'm treating her like an object or a plaything. Not like a woman I'm falling for.

"Okay, dude, half it is. Tomorrow after b-ball, at the Recovery Room. I'll bring cash. You don't close this deal though, you pay me back immediately."

"Yeah, I get it."

"And just because you're winning this, doesn't mean you aren't still a shitty b-ball player."

"Later," I say and hang up.

I'm an asshole.

Such a fucking asshole. If I lose her because of this, it will be one hundred percent my fault.

30

CHANCE

"Don't be nervous," I tell her as we walk up the front stoop. "They are going to love you."

"I'm not nervous," she says.

"Your palms are sweaty," I say, feeling the dampness from hers on my palm.

"It's just because you're holding my hand."

I drop her hand from mine. "Is that better?"

"No!" she says grabbing my hand back. "Don't you dare leave my side. Ohmigod. We need a safe word."

We are standing on my mother's front porch because I finally convinced Remi to come to Sunday dinner. I'm certain that my entire family is watching, and listening, through the window in the door. Remi wouldn't know that, however. And I want her to feel safe and not embarrassed, so I let her continue.

"A safe word?"

"Yes. Like if I can't take it anymore and I just have to get out of there, I can work a word into conversation, and you can make up an excuse that your family will believe so we can leave without hurting their feelings."

"You aren't going to hurt their feelings. My family is so low key, you could tell them that you are sick of their company and they'll all still invite you back with open arms at the next get-together."

"You aren't helping. That's not a concept that I can get my head around. What I can get my head around is that this is all going to go terribly, and I need a safe word for when I'm ready to leave since you refused to let me drive myself." Her voice trails off. "Which is fine. That's what Uber is for, right? It's not like I'm socially awkward or anything. I have a master's degree in chemical engineering for God's sake. I'm a news junkie. A girlie-girl who loves fashion. I can talk to men or women about almost anything. Except sports. And probably cooking. I'm not much of a cook. Your mom isn't going to want to talk about cooking, is she? I mean, I've seen a few episodes of Cupcake Wars, but past that, I've got nothing. Ohmigod I can't go in there. Tell them I got sick."

She drops my hand and turns back down the walkway toward the street.

I jog to catch up with her and then stop her.

"Hey," I say turning her so she's facing me. "Do you trust me?"

She nods.

"I need to hear you say it, beautiful."

"I trust you."

"Have I killed you on my bike yet?"

"No."

"Have I steered you wrong on any of our dates?"

"No."

"Have I been too invasive with our date questions?"

"Yes!" But she laughs when she says it, so I know she's not being serious.

"Why would I mislead you now? When I'm introducing you, someone who is important to me, to the other people in my life who are important to me?"

She shrugs her shoulders in response.

"Because I wouldn't. Look at me." She tilts her head back until she meets my eyes. "You are a witty and engaging conversationalist, with a great personality, and infectious smile. They can't help but love you. Okay?"

She nods. "Okay."

"And, if that fails, then just undo another button on your blouse. You'll distract everyone at the table with your boob-alicious splendor and they'll forget you can't carry on a conversation."

She laughs. "Boob-alicious splendor?"

"Hey, they distract me every time I'm trying to think clearly."

Remi leans up and kisses me on the lips, a quick peck that is over too quickly. "Thank you for talking me down off the ledge like that."

"Anytime, woman. Now let's get in there. I'm hungry." She shrieks as I slap her on the ass.

I knock on the front door instead of walking in so I can give my family a minute to disburse from the entry. But it doesn't matter because my mom and all three sisters are still there when Mom opens the door. As is my dog Hudson, who my parents pick up to stay with them a few times a week when I work overnights. Or, lately when I'm with Remi and let them think I'm working overnights.

"Hello Chancey, dear," my mom says, patting me on the cheek as she brushes past me to get to Remi. "You must be Remi. Look at you. Just beautiful." She gives her a hug that Remi returns a little less enthusiastically. I did forget to mention that my family is big on hugs. Remi looks at me over my mom's shoulder, her eyes wide and pleading.

"Ma, give her some space, we just got here."

Mom steps back slightly. "It's nice to meet you, Mrs. Bauer."

"Oh, you can call me Annalise, dear. Or Mom."

Remi's eyes grown round.

My sister, Audrey, steps in next to introduce herself and gives her a brief hug. Followed by my other two sisters, Eliza and Charlie. Hudson sits on the floor, waiting patiently, his tail thumping away at some excited beat in his head.

"Ok," I tell him as a release and he comes running to us, immediately thrusting his head between Remi's legs. At the same time, my sister Audrey asks, "So, how are the date questions working?"

I have a feeling she's setting out to embarrass me.

Remi laughs awkwardly. "That was you?" She pets Hudson on the head, trying to subtly push him from between her legs. I snap my fingers and he heels.

"They're good and make for some interesting conversations," Remi says. I pull her into my side and give her waist a squeeze. She looks up at me and smiles, I just can't tell if the smile is relaxed or panicked.

"I love your outfit," Eliza says. "Is that vintage? It's amazing!" Remi smooths her hands down her skirt and nods. All I know is there's a skirt and a shirt, both black and tight, and Remi looks amazing in them.

"Yes," Remi says. "I found it in a store down on Mission Street called *Second Chances*."

"I've been there," Charlie says. "They have amazing stuff."

"We should all go one afternoon," Audrey says. "Leave Hailey with the boys and have a girls' day."

"Yes!" Eliza says.

"You just want a day without the baby," Charlie teases Eliza.

"Duh," Eliza says.

"Okay girls, let her get in the house," my mom says. We make it through the entryway to the great room where the TV is so I can introduce her to my dad, Brian, and two brothers-in-law, Mike and Nate. My niece, Hailey, shrieks when she sees me and starts crawling toward us. I pick her up and swing her around, then blow raspberries on her belly until she squeals.

"I see you have the same wooing technique for all women, regardless of age," Remi says drily. My family quiets and glances at one another. Remi's eyes widen to an unnatural shape. She mouths something to me that I can't quite decipher but looks a little like the word *pepperoni*.

My dad starts to laugh and says, "She'll do just fine, son." He pats her on the back as he says it. Remi stumbles forward a step. Dad's a big guy and doesn't always realize his own strength. I catch her in my arms and pull her to me as my mom and sisters dissolve into giggles. Hudson barks and runs in circles.

Remi pinches my side, I look down at her, and she looks back at me, a desperate look in her eyes. I lean down and whisper, "They fucking love you." She relaxes a little against me and starts to laugh, albeit awkwardly, with everyone else.

That's pretty much all it takes for my family to immediately bring her in as their own. Exclaiming how fantastic she is and how she fits in wonderfully. So, to prove her point, I grab Remi by the waist and blow raspberries on her belly until she squeals.

My mom and sisters swarm and pull Remi toward the kitchen area and begin twenty questions times four: asking about where she works, lives, what she does for fun, and anything else they can think of.

I grab myself a beer and a glass of wine for Remi. I catch her eye when I drop it off to her on my way to the couch to catch the end of the game with my dad, Nate, and Mike, she looks at me and smiles. It's tentative, but it's not forced or overly panicked.

Yeah, she's going to be just fine.

31

REMI

I look at the beautiful blonde women who have ambushed me and pulled me into the kitchen with them. Chance's mother, Annalise, looks young enough to be his sister. I'm having a hard time keeping them all straight. I'm not sure if the wine on an empty stomach is going to help me in this situation or not. I square my shoulders and prepare myself for the worst. Bring it on Bauer ladies. I can take whatever you're going to throw at me.

I think.

Audrey, the oldest sibling, puts a hand on my shoulder and squeezes it, putting me at ease.

"Relax," she says softly. "We are a lot at first, but it's also because Chancey never brings girls home. Not since . . . well, not for a long time."

"Since Helen?" I ask.

"He told you?" Audrey asks, her bright green eyes searching mine. The only Bauer sibling with her dad's eyes. She should be a model for pregnancy magazines with her flawless skin and short pixie-cut blonde hair.

I nod.

"That was hard on all of us," Audrey says. "But it's good he told you. It means he's moved on."

"What are you two whispering about over there?" Eliza turns toward us from across the kitchen island, her blonde bob-cut hair swinging as she moves.

"The benefits of a D-cup. You wouldn't understand," Audrey says to her, gesturing toward her much smaller chest.

Eliza and her mom are built like Lexie: short, compact and petite. Whereas Audrey is tall, thin, and willowy, but with big tits. Charlie is like the perfect blend of them all but with much longer hair, and the only one who got their mom's curls. I can't even imagine how beautiful their family photos must be.

"At least mine are staying perky after having a baby," Eliza says to Audrey.

"Burn," Charlie says.

"Girls," Annalise admonishes. "Can we try to act civilized for at least the first hour that our guest is here?" She turns toward me with a smile and blows her shoulder-length curls from her face. "Is it hot in here?"

"Mom's going through *the change*," Charlie whispers loudly.

"Charlotte Ann," Annalise says, then turns toward me. "I apologize in advance for my family's behavior, Remi dear. Try not to judge us too harshly."

Me judge them? Ha! They are perfect.

"Oh, we are far from perfect," Audrey says. I look at her, my brows raised.

"You said it out loud," she says. "Don't worry, I do it all the time." I decide then that I like Audrey, and we're going to be friends, no matter what happens with Chance.

"So, Remi," Eliza says, leaning over the kitchen island, and chewing on a carrot stick. "What do you do for work?"

"I work in chemical engineering."

"Is that . . ." Annalise starts.

"It's a lot like how it sounds, yes," I tell her laughing a bit. I go on to explain what I'm working on currently and how it's going. I stop talking once I see their eyes start to gloss over.

"Oh, you're way too smart for Chancey," Charlie says. "I don't think he can even spell engineering."

I laugh, remembering that Chance said almost the same thing. He'd told me before we got here that he was closest to Audrey, but that he and Charlie had similar personalities. I can see that now after meeting them all. I'm starting to feel a lot more comfortable with these women, which is nice. Audrey refills my wine glass that I hadn't realized I'd finished. No wonder I feel more at ease.

"You're drinking for me," she says as she tops it off. "And I'm a three-glass girl. So, do me a favor, have four glasses and get loose enough for the both of us, huh?"

"I'll work on that," I say as I point a finger gun at her, then wink and make a little clicking noise with my mouth.

Oh God. I just used a finger gun.

I'm drunk.

I excuse myself to use the restroom.

Once in there, I touch up my makeup, relieve myself, wash my hands, and then return the texts that Kat and Lexie have been firing at me for the last hour.

Me: I'm a little drunk. I think. It's weird, but going okay. The visit not my drunkenness.

Kat: Of course it's going okay - you're tres fabulous!

Me: Tres?

Kat: I'm thinking of learning French. That means very.

Lexie: Oh, I'm so happy it's going well!

Kat: It's going great, I've already learned the word tres.

Lexie: I meant Remi's family time.

Me: It's not my family time. It's just meeting a family. For dinner.

Lexie: Family dinner.

Kat: Have you already had dinner?

Me: No, I think that's coming soon though. I hope. I need to eat.

Me: Fuck me. They are all such beautiful people. Like literally. The whole family.

Lexie: Just like you!

Me: Ha! Thanks Lex!

Kat: Did you tell him your safe word?

Me: I tried, but he doesn't think I need it.

Lexie: Oh, you need it.

Me: LEXIE!!

Lexie: No offense. You just aren't that good in situations like this. People have to get to know you to realize how amazing you are. And you are amazing. Tres amazing!!!

Me: FML. I used a finger gun and I winked.

Radio silence.

Kat: Well, I'm sure you got this, baby girl. Don't sweat it. You be you.

Lexie: Yeah, what she said. 'Cause your you is amaze-balls.

I nod my head at the reflection in the bathroom mirror.

I be me.

'Cause my me is amaze-balls.

Got it.

Me: Thanks guys! Love you!

I switch my phone to silent before they have a chance to respond. I've been in here too long as it is. I don't want the Bauers to think I'm weird. I open the door and run right into a wall of chest, bouncing back slightly. I look up, Chance grabs me by the waist to steady me and backs us both into the bathroom, shutting and locking the door behind him.

"Hi," he says, pushing a stubborn strand of hair back from my face.

"Hi," I say, leaning into his touch.

"You okay?"

"I think so. It's a little overwhelming. I'm a little drunk. And we never did decide on a safe word."

"Is that what you were mumbling to me when we first walked in," he asks.

I nod, embarrassed.

"What is it?"

"Pepperoni."

He laughs. "Pepperoni? And I'm supposed to work that into conversation somehow?"

"Well, only when you want to get out of something. It's not as hard as you think. And it's quick to whisper in passing."

He looks at me, his eyes dancing in amusement. "I'm going to kiss you, beautiful."

My breath catches. I love it when he tells me ahead of time. It makes my vagina butterflies come out to play.

He leans in, his lips whisper softly against mine. I moan. He hardens the kiss, grabbing my ass and grinding his hips into me and pushing me back against the vanity. I feel him harden against my stomach. My hands go up into his hair, and I pull at the strands, wishing I could pull my skirt up, spread my legs, and get him inside me now.

"I want you," he says. His hands move from my ass, down my legs, then back up, bringing my skirt with them. I break the kiss and push my skirt back down.

"We are in your mother's bathroom!"

"This is the guest bathroom. My mom's bathroom is upstairs. Guest bathroom means anyone can use it," he says as he leans in and kisses me again.

I push against his chest. "Chance, I can't do this in your parents' house, as much as I may want to."

"You're right, I'm sorry. I don't want you to feel uncomfortable," he says. He does look sorry. I run my hands through his hair trying to tame it.

"Here, let me get the wrinkles in your skirt," he says smoothing the back of it. Spending extra time and effort on the fabric covering my ass. I slap his hand away and move to the side of him to open the bathroom door.

"Wait," he says, putting his hand against it to stop me.

"What?"

He gestures to his bulging cock, which is obviously hard even with his jeans to weigh it down.

"Maybe I can give you a blow job?"

His eyes widen. "You want to give me a blow job?"

I nod, lowering myself to my knees. He pulls me back up from under my armpits.

"I don't think I can get a blow job in my mom's house," he says in a low voice.

"Wait, you can fuck me in your mom's house, but you can't get a blow job?"

"I think so. I mean, I thought I could a minute ago. But, shit, maybe not. At least not right here, when she's right out there. Maybe I could in my old room upstairs." He looks toward the ceiling, eyebrows raised, with his head tilted toward the right.

"That's. Really. Lame."

He shrugs in return.

"Okay," he says, moving to open the door.

"Wait," I say. He pauses with the door partially open. I peek out, happy to see the hall is empty of people.

"I'll go first," I say. "Then you wait thirty seconds and follow me, but go in a different direction, so it doesn't look obvious."

"Got it," he says. Then he walks with me down the hall, his hand on my lower back, directly defying what I'd just asked him to do. We run into Charlie as we turn to go into the great room. She looks at us, one eyebrow raised. The same look that Chance can do. Chance raises a finger to his lips in an 'shh' motion. Charlie pretends to zip hers shut in return, then winks at me.

My face heats up to what I'm sure is a deep red. I smack Chance in the stomach. He pinches me in the ass. I have to bite my tongue to avoid crying out.

This family is going to be the fucking death of me.

32

CHANCE

Mom calls us in to dinner and makes us sit in couples with her and dad flanking the heads of the table and Charlie between baby Hailey and my dad. Normally any one of us would help Hailey eat, but I think we are trying to keep it civilized for Remi's sake by keeping Hailey flanked by her aunt and her mom.

The civility doesn't last long.

"Yuck, Mama!" Hailey slams her hand down on her highchair tray catching the side of her bowl just right so it flips up, sending bits of mashed food sailing across the table, spraying Mike and Remi. Mostly Remi.

She gasps and jumps up.

Somehow pulling the tablecloth with her.

Down goes three glasses of wine.

My plate falls to my lap, and hers to the floor.

Mike grabs his before it falls.

"Nice catch," I say. He nods. He used to play pro baseball, his reflexes are quick.

Hailey laughs, grabbing more food in her hands and trying to throw it, albeit unsuccessfully. Eliza, holding in laughter, takes the food from Hailey and tries to scold her. We are used to the utter chaos that is family dinner. This doesn't faze us a bit. And sometimes you just have to laugh at the crazy fucking shit life throws at you.

Like this.

Hudson barks twice, then comes running, nose to the ground to find any spilled food, which he considers fair game.

Charlies covers a laugh with a cough.

Remi looks at me, eyes wild and face red, then at my mom. "Ohmigod! I'm so sorry—"

"It's okay," everyone starts to say at once. My mom rushes over with a towel to wipe the food off Remi. She pulls up her skirt slightly to dab at it, exposing Remi's garter belts and stockings to everyone on that side of the table.

"Oh, well, aren't those pretty," my mom says, her cheeks reddening.

My dad turns his head toward Charlie, his body shaking slightly.

"We should totally get you some of those," Nate says to Eliza elbowing her slightly. "They're hot."

"Because the one kid doesn't do enough damage? We don't need hot, you already can't keep your hands off me."

Dad coughs the words, "Dad in the room," in between laughs.

Charlie gives up trying to cover her laugh. I look down the table at Audrey and see that she's crying, leaning in Mike's direction. "Our kid is going to throw food, isn't it? Oh my God, I don't want a food throwing kid. Please tell me our kid won't throw food." I raise an eyebrow at Mike, he mumbles *hormones* back in my direction. I turn my attention back to Remi, who is still standing next to me while my mom continues to dab at her skirt with a towel.

"Pepperoni," she whispers. I wink at her.

"What's that, dear?" Mom says. "I can't quite hear you over the laughing." She says the last three words much louder as a hint for everyone else to quiet down. A tactic that is never as effective as she thinks it's going to be.

"I was telling Chance I'm craving pepperoni," Remi says louder.

"Oh dear, you're not pregnant too, are you? I craved sausage when I carried Chance." Which triggers Charlie's and my infantile sense of humor. Mom craving *sausage*. I start laughing, while Charlie laughs harder.

Remi coughs out, "No, God no, not pregnant."

Mom ignores us and continues talking to Remi, "Well, there's still time. We don't have any pepperoni, I'm afraid. Maybe a nice salami log?"

This time Eliza and Nate laugh with Charlie and I, full-on snorting belly laughs. Which spurns on Audrey and Mike. My dad hasn't stopped laughing since Mom commented on Remi's garter belts.

"That's enough," my dad says. But it's ineffective when he's laughing too. My mom is oblivious to sexual innuendos. God love her.

Remi's face is an unusual shade of red at this point, and I realize it's high time to save her from this.

"Ma, let me bring her into the bathroom. She can clean it off. I think Huds already took care of the floor for you." Sure enough, Hudson has licked up all the food and wine from the floor. Mom steps back and lets us pass.

"Pepperoni! Pepperoni! Pepperoni!" Remi hisses at me as we walk down the hall then up the stairs. I bring her to the bathroom upstairs, so we have a little privacy.

"How about sausage instead?" I waggle my eyebrows at her.

"Not the time!"

I get us in the bathroom and lock the door. I lay a towel over the vanity, then pull her skirt up around her waist at the same time as I hoist her on to the towel. A smooth move if I don't say so myself.

"What the fuck are you—"

I silence her with a kiss, wrapping one hand around the back of her neck to keep her still and working the other up her inner thigh. She sighs against my lips and parts her legs. I don't even think she realizes she's doing it.

"Shhh, just relax," I tell her. I push her panties to the side and get one finger inside of her. She moans. I add another.

"I thought we couldn't do this here."

"We can't," I say as I trail my lips down her jawline and along her neck. My fingers working in and out of her. Her legs fall open wider, and she arches her hips toward me. She wraps one hand around the back of my neck, her grip strong. The other clutches the edge of the sink.

"Chance, I'm going to come," she says against my lips, her voice deep and throaty.

"That's the point, beautiful." I pump faster, curling my fingers up and using my thumb on her clit. Her body tenses, I swallow her screams with my kiss as she falls apart in my arms. She's exquisite when she comes. A guy could get used to this on a daily basis. At least I could.

She slumps against me. "Jesus Christ, man. Give a girl some notice, would you?" she says into my chest.

I grab her chin and tilt her head up so her eyes meet mine. "Do you feel more relaxed?" I ask.

"So much."

"Still need pepperoni?" I nuzzle her neck as I whisper in her ear.

She giggles. "No."

"Ready to go back downstairs?"

"Ohmigod, how long have we been gone?"

I look at my watch. "Almost three minutes."

She raises her eyebrows. "Impressive timing, Mr. Bauer."

"Oh, I can beat that," I say.

She looks at me, eyes wide.

"Later," I say. "After we get home."

"You're on," she says.

I lift her down from the vanity and help her straighten her clothes. She turns to look at herself in the mirror, frowning as she pats down her hair and dabs under her eyes.

"You look beautiful," I tell her.

"You're required to say that," she says. "You just got me off with your fingers inside me."

"With impressive precision and speed," I add.

"Well, as long as not everything you do is with impressive speed, we'll be just fine."

"First you want fast, now you want slow. Make up your mind, woman."

She smiles up at me, and I'm reminded once again how lucky I am to have this lady in my life.

And how careful I need to be to keep her.

Because I am winning my bet in thawing the ice queen.

Now it's just figuring out how to keep her warm once I tell her it's a bet.

33

REMI

We go back down to finish dinner after our bathroom interlude. He's right, I am exponentially more relaxed and ready to continue to take this family on. I'm pretty sure this is the first time I've ever met a boyfriend's family.

Oh shit.

Did I just call him my boyfriend?

Fuck.

I'm getting so far ahead of myself with this. I pause my thoughts in my head to see how I feel. But, oddly, I'm okay. I know it hasn't been very long, but so far, he fits into my life really easily. My friends like him. The sex is off the charts. And, on the flip side, I seem to fit into his life as well.

I mean, I adore his family. And they seem to like me. If you had ever asked me if I would enjoy an afternoon filled with noise and chaos and socializing, I would have said fuck no. But I've had a really good time today; it's like I belong. I'm welcome; wanted even. It's an incredibly addicting feeling.

Maybe this can work. People meet in strange ways all the time. He doesn't ever have to know it started as a bet. That I *had* to keep seeing him for a month or I would lose. Maybe he'd even find it funny. I laugh slightly to myself. He squeezes my hand as we reach the dining room. The family has resumed eating without us and the conversation has turned to sports. Apparently, the entire gang is passionate about baseball. Mike, Audrey's husband, used to play professional baseball, which is how he met Audrey.

A fairy tale type story the way she told it to me. He was first to bat and got on third base. The next two guys were struck out. He saw her in the stands cheering like a fanatic, against his team, and was smitten. He had a ball-boy go ask for her number, which she refused to give because he was on the opposite team. Charlie snuck it to the ball-boy when Audrey was in the restroom.

Mike kept calling until he wore her down. They talked on the phone, texted, and emailed for close to a year before Mike got traded to Oakland, where he played for almost a year until he was injured. They dated, he went to law school, they got engaged, and are now married. Mike works as a sports injury attorney and Audrey is a freelance writer. And she's pregnant with their first baby. They are perfect.

Chance pulls my chair out for me, and we take our seats and resume eating. The baseball conversation gets heated but stays respectful.

"Remi, who is your favorite team, dear?" Annalise asks me, speaking around the debate.

"I don't think I—"

"Just say 'A's,'" Chance whispers.

"I don't even know who the teams are," I say.

Conversation at the table halts, all heads turn to look at me. Even Hailey stops chanting and cocks her little head in my direction.

I clear my throat. "Except for the 'A's'," I say.

"Damn straight," Brian thunders.

"Thank God," Audrey says at the same time that Mike says, "I thought we were going to have to oust you just when I was starting to like you."

"Nice save," Charlie says to Chance as Nate says to me, "Smart choice given this crowd."

"A's. A's. A's," Hailey yells.

"That's right, Hailey. We love the A's, good girl!" Eliza tells her.

Chance runs his hand along my thigh in what I'm sure is meant to be reassuring. I make a mental note to never bring up baseball to this family. At least not until I figure out how the game works. I mean, I know the basics, there's a bat and a ball and bases.

"Don't worry, beautiful, I will get you up to speed before the next family dinner," Chance whispers in my ear. I shiver as his lips skim my lobe. The thought of another family dinner freaks me out almost as much as it warms me from the inside out.

"There's not even body contact in baseball," Chance says to the table. "Let's talk about a real sport. Like rugby."

"Oh no he didn't," Audrey says.

Which sets everyone at the table off and running at the mouth again. I feel a nudge on my knee and look down, thinking it's Chance sneaking his hand up my skirt. I'm only slightly disappointed to see Hudson's big brown eyes looking up at me. He nudges my hand with his snout, trying to get me to pet him. I run my hand along the top of his head and scratch between his ears He, in turn, licks my skirt where the bulk of my food had fallen before.

I laugh to myself, knowing his tongue and saliva is going to kill my Dupioni silk skirt. But at the same time not really caring.

Today has been worth a hundred skirts.

34

CHANCE

Remi pulls her jeans from the saddlebag and puts them on surfer style under her skirt. Then pulls the skirt off over them and folds it into the bag. I hand Remi her leather jacket and she puts that on along with her helmet. I'm proud of her for how well she's adapted to the bike. Especially for someone who'd never ridden before. I help her on behind me and we take off. Her hands snake up under the waistband of my coat to rest on my stomach. My abs contract automatically, they like it when she touches them.

"It's a good thing you aren't ticklish in the front, huh?" she says into my ear. I chuckle then nod in response.

We make it back to her house in a short amount of time. I park in the garage, but instead of following her in the house, head down the driveway to take a look up and down the street. It's habit, looking for anything out of place.

"How long has that blue car been parked out there?" I ask, almost positive it doesn't belong to a neighbor. I feel like I've seen it before, but not because it belongs here. Because it *doesn't* belong here. It's parked in too awkward a spot, and none of the residents on this block even park their cars on the street. I shut the door and lock it behind me.

She shrugs in response to my question.

I move to the front window and look out, the car is pulling away, the driver obscured by a ball cap and sunglasses. I decide to leave it be for now and continue checking periodically over the next few days. Maybe send a cruiser or two by Remi's house. Something about the car bugs me, I just can't pinpoint it.

What I really want to do is fuck Remi so hard she can't walk. Instead I grab us both a bottle of water, sit on the couch beside her, and pull her feet up onto my lap so I can rub them. My ulterior motive being I want to see how she feels about meeting my family.

Plus, I can't fuck her again until I tell her about the bet. She leaves in a couple days for a multi-day conference, and I need to know we are all good before then.

She groans as I push my thumb into her instep. I love the sounds she makes. I never thought of myself as a foot guy until I met Remi. She has the most beautiful feet and toes. They are always soft and clean, showcased in some kind of beautiful shoe.

"So, what did you think?" I ask, not able to wait any longer. I don't know when it became important to me that Remi like my family and vice versa, but it did. And now it's all I can think about: how best to incorporate her into my life and make sure all parties involved are good with it.

"Your family is amazing," she says. "I'm going to be honest with you, I didn't think families like yours existed outside of tv shows and movies."

"How do you mean?" I switch to applying pressure to the balls of her feet, she squirms in response.

"My God, I could come just from this," she says sinking farther into the couch and closing her eyes. I stop and pull on her pinkie toe. She opens one eye and looks at me quizzically.

"You didn't answer my question," I say.

"What was the question?"

"How do you mean, you didn't think families like mine exist?"

"Oh, well, just that you all genuinely like each other. You hug and touch, you enjoy one another's company. There's love and respect there and it's obvious from how you interact."

I raise her foot and kiss the top of it lightly, trying to show her how her words make me feel without having to interrupt her. I sense she's going to say more on the subject.

She continues, "My family and I are not close. At all. My parents had me late in life. An accident. I wasn't planned or really wanted."

I run my hand up her calf and squeeze lightly.

"They weren't neglectful, I mean not in a literal way, I always had everything I could ever need," she sighs, then keeps talking. "Money, shelter, schooling. Just no communication or interaction. No holiday get-togethers, no birthday parties, no family dinners. They sent me to boarding school in first grade and left to travel. My next youngest sibling had just entered college and that's what they'd been waiting for."

I want to pull her in my arms and tell her that she has me now. But the closed off look on her face and the tension that's suddenly filled her body tells me that's a bad idea.

"My brother and sister take their cue from my parents and have never really tried to contact me. It used to bother me, a lot. But now I've accepted it for what it is. And I don't really think about it until I see families like yours, who are so different it's jarring, you know?" She looks up at me. I reach over and caress her cheek. She closes her eyes at my touch and leans into my hand. We stay that way until she pulls away.

"I'm lucky to have a family like mine," I say, leaning back and switching to her other foot.

"You are," she says. "Oh God, please never stop touching me." She gives me a look that I swear is adoring. She adores me.

Because you're the man.

Oh shit.

I can't do this.

I can't tell her about the bet. She'll leave me if I do. I especially can't tell her that I've already taken money for it. It's going to make her feel cheap when she's anything but.

"Do you know what I liked the best about today?"

"What?" I ask, loving the feel of her smooth skin in my hands.

"You are all just so real with one another. There's no bullshit between you, it's straight up honesty whether you like it or not. I've only ever seen it between me, Kat, and Lexie. Which

I thought was so rare that it didn't happen with other people. But, your family, you all do the same."

"Well, they're your family, right? Lexie and Kat?"

"They are, yes," she says softly. "Growing up, my biological family, we were so reserved about our feelings, whether they were positive or not. I hate that. I hate secrets."

Aw, fuck. If I tell her, I lose her. If I don't tell her, I lose her. How do I win here? Maybe it will be okay, and she'll understand.

Doesn't matter. It's now or never.

"There's something I need to tell you," I say. I know that this is not a good time or even the right time to bring this up. But I also know I won't have another chance before she leaves for her conference.

She straightens and pulls away from me, eyes wide.

"That's never a good way to start a sentence," she says.

"It's not a bad thing," I say. "In fact, I think you're going to find it funny and ironic. We'll laugh about it."

Her body visibly relaxes.

"So, I overheard you and Kat talking the night of the movie at Lexie's winery."

She looks off to the side slightly, as though trying to remember which conversation I might be referring to.

"About a bet, with a pair of ridiculously expensive shoes."

She gasps and bolts up straight, pulling her feet away from me.

"Look," she says looking at me, eyes wild. "It's not like—"

"It's okay," I say.

"What do you mean, it's okay?" she asks, confusion overtaking her facial features.

"I had a bet too," I say.

Her brow straightens from confusion to understanding to irritation and her eyes narrow.

"What do you mean you had a bet too?"

"I had a bet. About you and I and whether—"

"You made a bet about me?" she asks. Her voice becoming shrill and her face turning red.

"Well, yeah. But you made a bet about me."

"We aren't talking about me right now, we're talking about you."

"Really we are talking about both of us," I say.

"Don't try to change the subject," she says. "What the fuck do you mean you made a bet?" Her look getting more menacing as she talks. I back away slightly toward the other end of the couch.

"Okay, first you can't get upset about my bet when you had a bet too."

"The hell I can't." She stands up and starts pacing in front of her couch.

"I'm not upset about your bet."

"Of course you're not, you got laid."

"Yeah, but unless we count phone sex, it's only enough to win half my bet," I chuckle.

She stops.

Her head turns toward me in almost slow motion, but her body stays still. More *Terminator* than *Exorcist*, but still jolting.

"What did you say?"

Okay, clearly this is not going the way I'd expected.

Earth to Chance. Recovery mode required, stat.

"Uh..."

"Did you have to fuck me in your bet?" Her voice shrill.

I debate trying to make something up. But I'm not so good with lies on the fly.

How is she not seeing the humor in this?

"Twofucksfourdates," I say fast, hoping she won't understand.

"You bet you could take me on four dates and fuck me twice?"

I exhale slowly. I don't want to answer this. I wish fights were more like police press releases, where I can choose to neither confirm nor deny her question.

I stand up and go to her, putting my hands on her upper arms and running them up and down slightly.

"How about if we relax and sit down, we can talk about this. I'll tell you the whole story. It's kind of funny we both had bets about the other, right?"

She stands stiffly, not moving, not relaxing. I guess it's good she's not moving from my touch. But maybe not good that she's also not responding.

"What do you get if you win?" she asks. Her voice is hard and emotionless.

"What do you get if you win?" I ask back.

"I keep my shoes."

"Your nine hundred dollar shoes?"

"Yes."

I run my hands through my hair.

Who the fuck buys nine hundred dollar shoes?

"I do," she says. I can't tell if she knew what I was thinking or if I said that aloud.

"I get two-thousand-five hundred dollars," I mumble.

"Excuse me?"

"Twenty-five hundred. Well, I already got a thousand two fifty, so now it's just the other half."

"You already got . . . ? Jesus Christ. Un-fucking-believable. Who with?"

"Who with what?"

"Who is your bet with?" she asks.

"Alex."

"My Alex?"

"Yes." I wince as I say it. This looks so much worse than it is. Or else it really is that bad and I'm a complete and total asshole.

"I can't believe what an asshole you are."

I guess that answers my question. She resumes pacing, her steps getting faster with each lap.

"It's not that different. You have a bet with your girls, I have a bet with my guys," I say.

"Guys?"

"Well, not guys, per se. The bet is only with Alex."

"You said guys. Who else knows about it?"

I hang my head. "Brad Matthews and Ethan Shane."

"Brad and Ethan know?" Her voice is shrill again. "As in Kat's fiancé Brad and his partner Ethan?"

I don't even feel the slap until my head is thrust to the side.

"Remi, goddamn, that hurt, what the fuck?"

"You disgust me."

"You slapped me." My cheek stings, she can pack a punch.

"You deserve it."

"You had a fucking bet as well!"

"I didn't bet whether I could get you to fuck me."

"Well, what did you bet?"

"That doesn't matter," she says.

"If my terms matter, then your terms matter."

"I had to date someone, the same person, for a month," she says.

"How is that any different?" I ask.

"You prostituted me."

"Technically, beautiful, I prostituted myself."

A sound comes from her, not quite a scream, not quite a growl, maybe somewhere in between. She picks up a magazine off her coffee table and throws it at me.

I duck from instinct, but in reality, it comes nowhere near me and just flutters to the floor. Which just seems to make her angrier. She slumps to the floor and puts her face in her hands. I'm pretty sure she's crying.

I crouch down next to her, "Remi, baby, look at me."

"Go away," she says.

"I'm so sorry. I didn't mean to hurt you. It started as a bet, but it became real for me, fast."

"Fuck off."

"Look, can we just start over?"

"Get the fuck out of my house."

"Remi, if you think about this logically—"

"There is nothing logical about making a bet to sleep with someone. That's high school. And horrible. And pathetic. And manipulative."

"What about what you did?"

"I didn't do anything near as bad as you."

"But isn't a bet a bet? How come mine is worse?"

"Just get out, Chance. I don't want you here. I don't want to talk to you. I don't want to see you."

Does she mean just right now? Or ever?

Fuck.

I've got to fix this.

How do I fix this?

Fuck. Fuck. Fuck. Fuck. Fuck.

One step at a time. Let her calm down. Give her space.

She stands, grabs my arm, and pulls me toward the front door. I go willingly, but only because I feel like I need to give her time to calm down and become rational again. Then she'll see that we kind of did the same thing.

I hope.

"I'll call you later," I say, as she pushes me through the doorway.

"Never call me again." She slams the door behind me for emphasis.

The ground drops out from under me with about the same force as she slams the door. I sit heavily on the front stoop to try and regroup. Does she really mean to never call her? My heart feels heavy in my chest. It's hard to breathe. How did I fuck this up so monumentally?

It's my own fault for making such a dick bet to begin with. What made me think it was okay to do this? To treat another person in this manner. My God, if someone did the same to my sisters, I'd kill them. No hesitation.

Maybe it's my penance for all the one-night stands? My lack of commitment with women. Because I didn't try harder to help Helen. Or, shit, for making the bet to begin with. I don't deserve her. But fuck if I don't want her. I bury my head in my hands, then rub them roughly over my face.

I need to get out of here before I do something stupid.

Actually, maybe I need to get out of here so I can do something stupid.

35

REMI

I begin to pace the minute Chance is out the door. I need to take the edge off my anger, because right now I feel like doing something reckless. When I was younger, that something included cutting myself. But I'm old enough now to realize cuts leave scars, and I don't like scars. So now that's what drinking is for. Being reckless.

I grab a bottle of tequila and do a shot. Then another. Enjoying the warmth that begins spreading through my body. I do a third shot because the first two felt so good. But it's not enough. I resume pacing and text Kat a '911' warning her that I'm going to video-call her soon. I know Kat is home because Brad was going to make her a special dinner tonight. Just like I know that Lexie is at her winery doing things that winemakers do when the wine needs their attention.

I hate to interrupt Kat when she has quality time with Brad, but I need her. I pull up her contact on my phone and move to hit video call. Then stop and laugh at myself. I'll interrupt Kat's sexy time with no problem, but I leave Lexie to her wine. Which only serves to reinforce to me the respect that I have for work, versus the lack of respect that I have for relationships. But if tonight has proven anything, I'm right to feel that way.

Logically, part of me knows that I shouldn't be mad at Chance for having a bet when I had one too. And usually I rule by logic. But right now, my emotions are winning.

Pacing resumes.

My thoughts are spinning out of control.

Kat is going to have to talk me off the proverbial ledge and make me sane again. I feel betrayed and hurt and conflicted. I finally opened up to that asshole and this is what I get in return. Which is exactly why I should have remembered that I can trust no one.

Except for Kat and Lexie.

I pull Kat's contact back up, just as my doorbell rings.

WTF?

I storm to the door, flinging it open, not even bothering with checking the peephole.

Chance stands there looking at his feet, a flush creeping up his neck.

"I'm sorry," I say. "Was I not clear before? I don't want you anywhere around me. I don't want to see you. I don't want to talk to you. You're a pathetic excuse for a man. I hate you." I move to slam the door, but he blocks it with his hand.

He clears his throat. "My bike is in your garage."

"Excuse me?"

"I know you don't want to see me. I'm trying to abide by your wishes. But my bike is in your garage, so I can't leave."

"Walk. Call a cab. Hitchhike for all I care."

My fingernails bite into the palms of my hands as I clench my fists. I've never wanted to punch someone as badly as I want to punch him.

His head hangs low, but his eyes peek up at me. A sucker punch straight to the gut. I step back and hold the door open for him.

I follow him through the kitchen and into the garage. He pushes the wall button to open the door. Then turns back toward me. "Don't forget to lock up after I leave."

"Don't fucking tell me what to do."

He closes his eyes and takes a breath. When he opens them again, I can see they are slightly watery. "For what it's worth, I am sorry," he says. He holds one hand up, like he's going to touch me, then drops it to his side. I stand there, suddenly not sure if I would have allowed the touch or not.

He rolls his bike outside, then waits for me to close the garage.

Pieces of him disappear as the big door rolls down its tracks until there's nothing left of Chance Bauer at all. I hear the bike start up as I walk back into the house and hit the button to video call Kat.

I expect it to take her a few rings to answer. What I don't expect is for Brad to answer right away.

"Hey, gorgeous," he says.

"I'm going to need you to beat someone up for me," I tell him.

"You got it, baby girl. You just let me know who and I'm on it." He flexes his muscles and pushes out his chest, growling slightly at the screen.

"Apparently Chance had a bet with Alex that he could fuck me and date me."

His eyes widen. "He told you?"

My eyes narrow. "So you did know?" My tears dry up as my body refills with fury. There was a small part of me that was holding out hope that maybe Brad didn't really know. It seems dumb now that I think about it. Why would Chance lie about that?

"Uh . . ." Brad sets the phone down, so now all I can see is the ceiling.

"Brad?"

He doesn't answer, but I can hear him in the background, "Rem's on the phone, baby. I think you need to talk to her. Don't be mad at me."

"Is she okay? Why would I be mad at you?" Kat's head appears in the screen. "Hey sweetie, you okay?"

"No! Did you know that Chance had a bet with Alex that he could fuck me?"

"Are you kidding?"

"No. And Brad knew about it."

"What?" She turns, pointing the phone in his direction, so Brad is now on video as well. To his credit, he looks guilty as hell.

"You said you wouldn't be mad," he said.

"No, you asked me not to be mad. I never responded. You better tell us how you know, and why you didn't warn us, or I'll have your balls in a—"

"Ok! I overheard them talking. He said it wasn't as bad as it sounded. And that he liked Remi. I didn't want to get in the middle. He seemed sincere." He starts listing off excuses as to why he didn't say anything.

"Why didn't you tell me?" Kat sounds more hurt than angry.

He shrugs. "Bro code."

"Bro code? Are you fucking kidding me?" Kat asks. "He's not your bro. There's no code there. He's just a guy. You aren't even friends. Your loyalty is to me. And to my girls. For fuck's sake, Brad. What the hell is wrong with you?"

"Well, you guys had a bet—"

"You told him we had a bet?" I ask Kat. "So much for loyalty."

"That's not fair," Kat says. "I tell him everything. I have to."

"Clearly THAT doesn't go both ways in your relationship. You both piss me off," I say.

"CLEARLY," Kat says.

"I'm sorry, Remi," Brad says. "I didn't want to get in the middle of anything, and—"

"Well you're in the middle now," I tell him.

"I get it, I get it. How can I help?" he asks.

"You can go away for a few hours," Kat says.

"What?" Brad and I both ask at the same time.

"Go away. For a while. Remi and I are going to talk shit and make voodoo dolls of you and Bauer."

"Why do I have to go away? Why can't you go to Remi's?" Brad asks. I'm glad he asks because I was wondering the same thing. I kind of don't want to leave my house.

"Because I'm quite sure I'm mad at you. And I don't want to look at your face right now. But I also want to go in the hot tub, and Remi doesn't have one."

She has a good point there. A dip in the hot tub sounds awesome.

"What about date night?" Brad asks her.

"Dinner was good, but we're finished eating. So, technically the date is over."

"What about, you know . . .dessert?" he asks. I scoff. Kat scoffs right along with me.

"Oh, there will be no dessert," she says. "Not only will there be no dessert, but there is a dessert moratorium until further notice."

"What? Why?" Brad asks, his voice a little whiny. I want to tell him to grow a pair, but I also don't want to interrupt this discussion. Watching the dynamics of their relationship has always been a little bit fascinating to me. Because Kat is my best friend, and because it's a relationship that is healthy and positive. And, of course I want that for her, but I also want to analyze it and try to dissect the bits and pieces that make up the successful whole.

"Sides, babe. There are always sides and you chose the wrong one. Even if you didn't want to tell Remi, you should have told me."

"I just—" he says.

"I know," Kat says. "You didn't want to be in the middle, blah, blah, blah. Well, now you're not. You aren't even in the equation. You're going out for a while so Remi and I can have girl-talk."

"Where am I supposed to go? It's eight-thirty on a Sunday night."

"I don't know. What about your *bro* Bauer's house. Since y'all are so close and shit," Kat says.

"Try to do the right thing, and this is how they treat you," he says, but it's under his breath and in more of a teasing tone than a serious one. He gives Kat a kiss on the top of her head, then blows one toward me via the video screen and leaves the room.

"Come over," Kat says. "The hot tub is bubbling, and I've got wine and sweets." Kat and I live in the same neighborhood. But her house is on the water, whereas mine is a couple blocks from it. I can get to her house on foot in about five minutes, and the walk is an enjoyable one. So, I'm out my door before she finishes the words 'sweets.'

We sink down into the water, a floating table filled with gummy bears between us. I bite the heads off each one I grab, envisioning doing the same to Chance, then put the mangled bodies back on the table to finish off later.

"Look," Kat says. "I totally understand that you're angry. And I get why. But let's be real for a minute, you don't really have a leg to stand on with this argument."

"Of course I do. Why would you say that?"

"Because we had our own bet."

"He took money, Kat."

"Wait, he already won the bet?"

"No, he won half the bet, and he took the money."

"Hmm," she says, tapping her index finger on her lips. "Okay, that is a super dick move on his part, but maybe he really needed the money."

"Kat, he prostituted me."

"Technically, I think he prostituted himself," she says.

"Whatever," I say. I don't tell her that's the same thing Chance said.

"And," she continues. "We did have our own bet."

"But our bet didn't include sex."

"It could have. I mean our bet was for a month and in that time, most people have sex. Fuck, Rem, in that time you *did* have sex."

"Fine, but our bet wasn't dependent upon sex," I say.

"Is that the part that bothers you? That it was about sex? I find that hard to believe."

"Thanks a lot. I could get upset about sex."

"You *could*, sure. But you probably wouldn't."

I shrug my shoulders in return. She stays silent. Doing that thing to me again that only she seems able to do. I can't handle it. I start talking.

"Okay, I get logically that I shouldn't be upset about the bet. That it's hypocritical. But I can't help it. I'm hurt."

"Remi!" Kat shrieks. "That's wonderful, congratulations!"

I choke slightly on my wine, and she has to pat me on the back to help me work it down.

"I just basically told you my emotions have been stomped on and you say congratulations?"

"Yes, because you had emotions. And it hurt when they were stomped on. This is fantastic! It means you're feeling something that you've opened yourself up."

"Oh please."

"For real. This is exactly what I wanted for you. This is what you avoid in life. And I know it totally sucks right now, but trust me, it's a wonderful thing to just abandon yourself to a relationship. I promise."

"Says the girl who just kicked her fiancé out for the night."

"I know. Isn't it great? Now we have the whole place to ourselves, and we can talk total shit." She smiles big, then moves to pour us each more wine, but the bottle is empty. "Huh," she says. "That happened fast. Oh, and shit, we have to get our own wine if Brad isn't here. Dammit."

"Don't move," I tell her. "I'll get it." I stand and climb out of the hot tub. Grateful for the slight chill in the air that I'm hoping will cool my heated emotions. I get another bottle from her wine fridge and return to the hot tub.

"Rem, the beautiful thing about kicking Brad out tonight, is that he's coming back. Because we are committed, and he loves me."

"You know that kicking him out is a little extreme, right?"

"Sure. But it's not totally like that. I mean, I'll text him in a few hours and tell him to come back so he can drive your drunk ass home. And so he can fuck my drunk ass until I can't walk. Then go to sleep. He knows I'm mad. But he also knows I'm not *mad*. You know?"

"Kat, Chance made a bet!"

"Remi, we made a bet!"

"It's not the same."

"We are now talking in circles, my dear, and that gets us nowhere."

"Fine. At least let me be mad for a while."

"Oh, absofuckinglutely, beautiful girl. For the next few hours, we are pissed as fuck."

"That's what I'm talking about," I say as I take a big gulp of my wine and wash down three gummy heads. "I just, I don't want to be vulnerable, you know?"

"None of us do," she says. "It totally sucks ass."

"So, how do I avoid it?" I ask.

"You don't," she says.

"Well, what if I get hurt?"

"You will."

"Fuck, I don't want to get hurt."

"None of us do," she says. "It totally sucks ass."

"Wow, where have I heard such words of wisdom before?" I say, narrowing my eyes at her.

She shrugs in response.

"You aren't exactly selling it here, you know?"

"Selling what?" she asks. "Love? I don't have to. You're already in it."

"In what? Love? Right. Okay. Whatever. You're cut off. Clearly you're drunk."

"Not drunk yet," she says in a sing-song voice. "Just calling it like it is. And it's my wine, I can drink it if I want to."

"I'm not in love with Chance Bauer, Kat. I barely like the guy. Well, except when we're having sex, I really like him then. Or when he's getting me off. I like him then too. And on the back of his motorcycle. That's hot. Otherwise, I don't like him at all." My head spins a little bit. I'm starting to feel the effects of all the alcohol. Wine from dinner, shots at my house, and now wine again combined with the hot water.

"Exactly!" Kat says, sitting up suddenly, sloshing water all over the gummy bears.

"Hey, I was going to eat those," I say as they wash off the tray and into the tub.

"Oh shit, we have to catch them all, Remi. They'll clog the filter."

We fish all the gummy bears from the water, headless and whole, and get out of the tub. Then wrap ourselves in robes and curl up by the outdoor fireplace Brad and Ethan recently built to dry off.

"This fireplace is tits, Kat."

"We are tits, Remi."

"We are!"

"I'm drunk," she says.

"Me too."

"I do love this fireplace though," she says with a happy sigh.

"Me too."

"If I didn't love Brad, I would totally love Brad just for building me this fireplace."

"Me too."

Kat laughs.

"I'm going to be mad at Chance until after my conference," I say.

"I would be too," she says. "Conference starts tomorrow, right?"

"Yeah, I'll drive up mid-day. My presentation is the following day."

"You feel ready for it?"

I shrug. "As ready as I'll ever be, I guess."

"You've got this, Rem. I've never seen anyone prepare for anything like you've prepared for this."

"That's why you're my bestie, 'cause you think I'm awesome."

"Straight up," she says.

"Straight up," I reply.

36

CHANCE

Matthews is hands-down the last person I expect to get a text from. I look at my phone again, just to make sure.

Matthews: You home? I'm coming over.

Me: Uh, yeah. Why?

Matthews: I just said, I'm coming over.

Me: No, why are you coming over?

Matthews: You told Remi about the bet. I'm in deep shit 'cause I knew and didn't tell Kat.

Me: I had no choice.

Matthews: Uh-huh. Well, now I need somewhere to go. And you're it.

Me: I'm it?

Matthews: Yeah, open the fucking door, I'm coming up the walk with a six-pack.

I open my front door and sure enough, Matthews is coming up the front walk with a six-pack of beer.

"Hey, man," I say as a way of greeting.

"Hey, fucktard," he says.

"Nice to see you too, asshole."

He pushes past me and makes his way into the entry of my little apartment. The entry is really just a portion of the living room, my place is that small. But there's a small half-moon of tile in front of the door, and I like to think of it as an entry. Even though Matthews traverses it in less than half a step.

"I told you not to hurt her," he says. "I told you I'd end you. Instead, I'm here with a fucking six-pack pretending like we like each other's company or some shit. So, why don't you shut the fuck up and tell me what the hell happened. Why did you tell her about the bet?"

"Don't you tell Cookie—"

"It's Kat. You can call her Kat."

"Sorry. Don't you tell *Kat* everything?"

"Yes. Except I didn't tell her about *this*. So now I'm fucked. Besides, we're getting married so it's different." He makes himself at home on my couch, sitting in the right corner. It's my favorite spot, which pisses me off.

"Well, maybe I'll marry Remi," I say before I have the chance to stop myself.

I don't mean it.

At least I don't think I mean it.

I just want to get a rise out of him. I don't really want him here. I definitely don't want him in my favorite spot on my couch.

"Don't be a dick. You barely know Remi," he says.

"I know enough," I say, digging my heels into this argument.

He rolls his eyes and opens a beer. Handing me the open one then grabbing and opening one for himself.

I take a big gulp to collect my thoughts then burp softly.

"You know," I say. "You can't tell me not to hurt her, and at the same time not to be honest with her."

He pauses with the beer bottle halfway to his mouth, as though considering what I'm saying. "Fair point," he says after a long pause.

"I mean, you can't say you haven't told Kat things you did that still hurt her when you were being honest?"

He nods and takes a long pull on his beer.

"Well, then," I say.

"I'm not saying you should've lied, dude."

"What are you saying?"

"I'm saying . . . Fuck I don't know what I'm saying. All I know is my girl's best friend is upset and I shouldn't be kicked out of my house when I'm about… when it's date night. And all because you fucked up."

"Fair point," I say after taking a moment to consider what he's saying. Pretty sure I'd feel the same way in his shoes.

He laughs, a bit sardonically, then raises his bottle toward me.

I keep talking. "I'm out of my element here, man. I'm not a relationship guy."

"All the more reason why you shouldn't have started this," Matthews says.

"Well, I did. So . . ."

"I'd like to say she's going to come around, but it's Remi."

"Tell me about it," I agree.

"She and Kat are like two peas in the same fucking stubborn-ass pod."

I raise my beer in a show of solidarity.

He keeps talking. "You just got to ride out the storm, man. Ride out the storm, then apologize."

"I did fucking apologize," I say.

"My guess? Too soon. Don't jump on the apology until she's ready for it. But, definitely not before."

"How do I fucking know when she's ready for it?"

"Beats the fuck outta me," Matthews says. "I barely have a handle on Kat, I can't figure Remi out too."

"That advice is useless, man."

"I don't have to give you advice at all, asshole. I mean, at least you didn't take the money, right."

I think a minute, not really knowing what to say or if I even want to continue this conversation with him. I feel like anything going down between Remi and me is just that. Between Remi and me.

"Well," I start.

"You fucking took the money?"

I nod while taking another swig of my beer.

"Are you a moron? My God, man, where is your head at?"

"I needed it," I say.

"The fuck you need that much money for, that bad, you'd do this?"

I shrug my shoulders. "Personal."

"Little late for that, don't cha think?"

"It's for my parents," I mumble into the mouth of my bottle before I gulp the rest down.

"What?" he asks.

"The money," I say more clearly. "My sisters and I are sending my parents on a cruise for their fortieth wedding anniversary. I needed the money for the rest of my share."

"Well, fuck, that's almost decent of you, brother."

"It is decent of me. My parents are amazing, and they deserve this."

"At Remi's expense?" he asks.

My face reddens with shame, I look down at my feet. "No."

"It's solid, though. You doing this for your folks. I feel the same about my dad. Totally do it for him."

I nod my chin at him in acknowledgment and stand to get us both a fresh beer. I open and hand him his. We sit in silence for a minute.

Matthews chugs his beer, then asks, "Hey, wasn't there a game tonight?"

I grab the remote and turn on the TV. We settle back to watch sports highlights, him in my favorite corner, and me at the opposite end.

Our truce sits between us, unspoken, but still there.

Almost like we're friends or something.

37

REMI

I spend the morning hydrating and packing for the conference. I flip on CNN because I'm a bit of a news junkie and can't handle when I don't know what's going on in the world around me. I'm surprised to hear the local station break into my national news program to announce an out of control wildfire that has sprung up a few counties away due to the *Diablo* winds in that area. I'm thankful that fires like that aren't common in San Soloman.

But then I realize Brad will probably get called away and grab my phone and shoot a quick text to Kat to let her know I'm thinking of them and sending hugs. I know she frets every time Brad is called out to a fire. Not that I blame her. In fact, I don't think I could do it. Be romantically involved with someone who constantly put their life in danger as a career.

Ha!

Dangerous like a detective, Remi?

Except, the Chance Bauer express is no longer a ride I'm interested in. I still laugh to myself at how ironic it is. Or would that be coincidental? Kat confused me once on the difference and I've not got it straight since it drives me crazy.

Regardless, I don't think being a detective is as dangerous as fighting fires. Not that it matters since Chance and I are over. I look back over to the tv screen and see the aerial view of the area affected; the fire looks huge. The tickler at the bottom of the TV screen reads that the fire has spread to just over four thousand acres and zero percent contained.

As selfish as the thought may be, I'm thankful I live near the ocean and that hundreds of miles separate my home from the devastation I'm seeing on TV. My phone dings with a text, it's Kat telling me that Brad hasn't been called out to the fire yet, but they are all on call and anticipating having to move in to assist in the next few hours.

I grab my phone to text Connie.

Me: Hey, I don't need a double occ room anymore, if that helps with the scheduling and stuff. Going solo.

Connie: Probably doesn't matter anymore. Everything okay?

Me: Yep.

Connie: Chance have to work or something?

Me: Don't know. Don't care. We broke up.

Connie: Oh no! Remi! Are you okay? Do you want me to call you? Do you need anything?

Me: That's sweet. No. I'm fine. Getting ready to head out the door. I'll talk to you later.

Connie: I'm serious. Call me if you need to talk.

Me: Will do.

The local newscaster breaks back into my program to alert the fire has reached one of the northern freeways that I need to take to get to my conference today. Most of my co-workers, including my boss, went up last night, even though nothing starts until later today. I chose to wait since I don't understand the draw of sleeping in a strange bed any longer than is necessary. Now I wish I'd joined them. If what she's saying about the delays is accurate, I should have left over twenty minutes ago to make it on time.

I'm meeting my boss to discuss my presentation. I'm in the mid-morning slot tomorrow, which I prefer. Unlike the first morning slot, it gives people time to wake up a bit, and they aren't too restless because we will have just had a coffee break. Which means they won't be hungry and watching the clock for lunch.

The clothes that I pack are a lot more conservative than the clothes that I wear to work every day. Mostly because this is people in my industry on a global level and not just the sexist piss-ants that I enjoy distracting on a day-to-day basis. What I'm packing still maintains a bit of my own fashion sense, I just try to rein it in a bit. So, today is a mid-calf, navy blue pencil skirt with a matching short waisted jacket and a pillbox hat. I call it my flight attendant outfit because it reminds me of what they would wear back in the day.

For the presentation, however, I'm packing a black suit, similar to what I will wear today, minus the hat and decorative buttons. But I'll pair it with sheer, black seamed stockings, and a pair of killer black heels. My feet will hurt all day, but these heels make me feel fierce, so it will be worth it.

I know my presentation is good, and my data is solid. My boss even said so when I submitted it for final review. But that does nothing to calm the nerves I feel, even this far in advance.

No matter how prepared I am, there is always a small part of me that is convinced I'm going to fail. That same small part of me, lays in wait, like a snake, waiting until I am most vulnerable to strike.

Shake it off, Remi. You've got this!

Traffic is insanely heavy, and it takes me twice as long to get to the venue. I listen to a book on tape as I drive, it's about reaching your fullest potential in life and love. Self-help books are my guilty pleasure. Even Kat and Lexie don't know I read them. One of my therapists when I was a teenager, gave me a book on co-dependency in regard to my relationship with my parents. That was all it took. From then on, I've been convinced that each new book, or the next book I read, will be the one that will have the magic solution to fix my life.

Believe me, I know the lunacy in that. I'm a scientist. Not only is there no magic solution, but I sure as fuck am not going to find it in a book. But it doesn't stop me from trying. Hoping. Reading. Listening.

I pull into self-parking and am at the front desk checking in by four fifty-two in the afternoon. Twenty-two minutes late to meet my boss in the hotel bar. I send him a quick text to let him know I've arrived, and then ask the bellhop to bring my luggage to my room. I know it's pretentious, but I tip them well. And I really, really hate pulling a suitcase on wheels behind me. I make a quick trip to the restroom to touch up my hair and makeup and send a quick text to Kat and Lexie to let them know I arrived okay. Kat texts me back immediately.

Kat: Did you see the fire? Was it really bad?

Me: I couldn't see flames or anything, but the smoke was heavy.

Kat: Brad got called out a little bit ago. It's huge, Rem.

Me: You okay?

Kat: I think so. Thanks for asking.

Kat: I'm glad you got there safely.

Me: It was a mess and took twice as long, but I'm here.

Kat: Hey - did you talk to Bauer?

Me: No. Why?

Kat: Well, just based on everything we talked about last night.

Me: Nope.

Kat: I think he's sad.

Me: Did you talk to him?

Kat: No - but Brad did.

Me: Really? That doesn't seem normal.

Kat: Get this, Brad actually went to his house last night after I kicked him out.

Kat: They hung out and drank beer.

Me: Did they talk about me?

Me: Wait. Don't tell me.

Me: I don't want to know.

Kat: For real?

Me: No.

Me: Yes.

Me: I don't know. Fuck.

Kat: They did talk about you. That's why I think he's sad.

Me: Well, too fucking bad. I'm not calling him.

Kat: Ok.

Me: What do you mean, ok?

Kat: Ok, you're not going to call him.

Me: Don't play this game with me.

Kat: What game? I'm not playing anything.

Me: Oh yes you are. This is just like where you stay quiet until I talk. Except you're saying ok until I change my mind.

Kat: That's all on you, sweets. I've done no such thing.

Me: Bitch.

Kat: Aw, you do love me.

Me: Whatevs.

Me: I'll talk to him when I get home.

Kat: Ok.

Me: Stop it!

Kat:??

Me: You know.

Me: I gotta go. I was supposed to meet my boss at the bar like half an hour ago to go over my presentation.

Kat: Have fun!

Me: I'll try.

It's just turning five minutes after five o'clock as I walk into the bar to join my boss, Stephen with a *ph*, as he's sure to tell everyone he meets. I scan the room for his balding head and see him at a small table near the back. Talking to a woman with beautiful blondish brown hair. Hair that reminds me of Helen's, Chance's ex. Which just goes to show how badly I need to get him off my mind. A stiff drink ought to help that. Good thing I'm in a bar. The woman leaves as I approach. All I see is her thick hair and tiny ass walking away.

Stephen looks up at me. "Remi, good to see you finally made it. Have a seat."

"Sorry. The fire is causing all kinds of problems with traffic," I say.

"I just would have expected you earlier, is all."

I hate it when he speaks in conditional verbs. Which he does often. I bite my tongue to avoid asking him if he did expect me earlier or he just would have expected me earlier.

Idiot.

"Again, sorry. I didn't anticipate the delays. The fire is huge and causing major gridlock on the roads. Besides, I thought this was more of a casual meeting, you know, in a bar and all."

"Well, no matter. I wanted to talk to you about your presentation tomorrow."

"I'm ready. My presentation is solid."

"Good. Good. I'm going to have you run second chair on it. Donaldson is going to run point."

"Excuse me? Donaldson as in Jeffrey Donaldson? The twerp?"

"Yes. And there's no need for name calling."

"Everyone calls him a twerp. He's barely—"

"Is there a problem, Remi?"

"Yes, there's a problem! This is my presentation. My work. My research. I know this data inside out. I can't have some little man with a short guy complex using his overinflated ego to—"

"I'd rather you not get emotional about it," Stephen says.

"I'm not emotional. I'm pissed. You can't do this, Stephen. I've worked hard on this. For over a year. It's my idea, my theorems, my tests, and my results."

"All true. But, I can. And I did."

"Okay. Well. My name is already in the program."

"As second chair," he says.

"What?"

"Remi, please understand that information such as this, important data, is better received when delivered by someone more... commanding when on stage."

"Commanding? You think the twerp is commanding? He's five feet tall. He breathes too heavy through his nose. He can't even make it through an entire sentence without exhaling noisily. He's not commanding. He doesn't inspire confidence in what he's saying. If anything, he's going to make people doubt my finding. What do you even mean by commanding? My God, I can't believe this. You've never seen me on stage, Stephen, you have no idea what kind of presence I have when I speak."

"I can see that you are quite upset now, however. And we can't have that. You are exactly right; I don't know what kind of presence you have when you speak in public. Whereas Donaldson has a lot of experience with presentations. I know exactly what to expect. His name is respected in this industry."

"His father's name you mean. He hasn't done anything on his own to warrant respect."

"Remi, please—"

"He doesn't even know my study. Or my findings. He knows nothing about what I plan to present."

"I've provided him with a copy."

"Of my study? My presentation? The copies that I gave to you?"

He nods, I'm assuming his answer to all questions, then takes a drink of his white wine. Which I'm guessing is Pinot Grigio or something equally emasculating. I look down at the napkin I'm shredding on the table and move to cover the pieces under my palm. I don't want him to see that I'm this undone. I'm having a hard time wrapping my head around the fact that he's doing this.

The server appears. "Can I get you something to drink?" she asks looking at me as she lays down a fresh napkin.

"Vodka martini. Dirty. Three olives. Please."

Stephen declines anything more, so she leaves to put in my order. I can't believe that in the time it took to sit down in the bar before I even ordered my cocktail, he obliterated my world. And there's not much I can do about it.

"What do I have to do to change your mind? I'll do anything. Just say it. I need this." I say, as I slowly move shredded napkin pieces under my fresh one.

He chokes slightly, then clears his throat. "Is that a . . . Are you . . . Is that a proposition, Ms. Vargas? Because I'm sure I don't have to—"

"What? Are you kidding me? Ew, gross. No. I meant work wise? My God. What is it with you guys?"

"I'm not sure—"

"Would you have asked that same question to Donaldson?" I ask.

"I don't see where that is—"

"Sexist?"

"I was going to say relevant," he says.

"Un-fucking-believable."

"Remi, please calm down. You are a good engineer, you just aren't—"

"Taken seriously apparently."

"Well, since you brought it up, it can be hard to take you seriously at times."

"Why? My results are always above par, I am in the lab crazy long hours checking and double checking everything. I mean, I work my ass off, Stephen."

"I agree, you put in long hours and your work is good. Solid even. But we have a certain image to project outside the office and you don't always fit that image."

"Because I'm a woman?"

"Because of how you dress. Remi, your wardrobe can be, shall we say, a bit risqué at times."

"To prove a point! The office is completely sexist. It's a good ole boys club in there. Everyone treats me like a pretty face who doesn't know anything. So, I dress the part and kick ass at the same time. To prove a point and show you all you're wrong."

He raises his eyebrows at me and does a little shoulder shrug, head cock at the same time.

"I brought a very conservative suit to wear tomorrow," I tell him.

"So did Donaldson," he smirks.

What a dick.

"I may as well go back home then, no reason to stay here." The server sets my drink down, I pick it up and down it in a few large gulps. The fire of the vodka coursing through my system, leaving a comfortably numb feeling in its absence. I take a deep breath and look at Stephen, whose mouth is hanging open. And then up at the server, who has yet to leave. Her eyes have widened to an almost comical size.

"I'll have another please, and put them both on his tab." The server looks to Stephen for confirmation. He nods.

"What is it with people not taking my word for anything?" I ask.

Neither answer. The server scurries away.

"Remi, it is important that you attend as second chair. In case Donaldson has questions on the research—"

"My research."

"Or the audience has questions that he may not be able to answer."

"Because it's not his work."

"I would appreciate you not having an attitude in regard to this," Stephen says.

A short bark-like laugh comes from my mouth.

"Your cooperation is expected and, of course, appreciated," he says.

The server appears with my second drink. God bless her for sensing this is a tense situation and getting drink number two back to me in a speedy manner. I tip my empty glass to my mouth and tap the base to let the olives roll into my mouth before exchanging glasses with her.

A fresh drink in hand, I take a big gulp, feeling better and nauseous at the same time. "Okay, well, if that's all you needed me for, I'll just take my cocktail and be out of your hair." Then I laugh since he barely has enough for his comb-over.

"I will see you tomorrow, Remi."

"Yep, see ya."

I'm well on my way to drunk, a martini and a half on an empty stomach will do that to a girl. I don't think I've eaten since dinner at Chance's parents' last night. If I don't count all the gummy bear heads at Kat's.

My God, was that just last night? It seems like forever ago. I head out of the bar toward a small lounge area in front of a fake fireplace and take a seat in the middle of one of the couches facing it; just to make sure no one sits next to me. I don't want company, I have no desire to interact with anybody, and I'm beyond pissed off.

How dare he do this. I am so fucking tired of men.

Men in authority.

Men named Chance Bauer.

Really, just one man named Chance Bauer.

And then all other men named everything else.

Like Stephen.

I'm just tired of men.

I down the rest of my drink, then pull out my phone checking for new text messages. I've got nothing from the girls. Nothing from Chance. It's barely six o'clock and I'm ready to either cry—which I don't do—or go to bed. Which sounds awesome.

I head to the elevators exhausted, not even wanting to be here anymore. I don't really care about the keynote speakers in the morning. I didn't have many in-sessions or table talks that I wanted to see, and thanks to my boss I'm no longer speaking, which is the main reason I'm here.

What's the point? So I can save Donaldson the twerp.

Fuck that.

I could be at home and not working.

Instead I'm here.

And we all know I'll stay here. Because that's what I've been told to do. And good girls always do what they are told.

I get into the elevator really wanting to just kick my shoes off now, but I wait. Knowing that if I do, the walk from the elevator to my room will be torture when I have to put them back on. The elevator doors open, and I awkwardly make my way down the hall toward my room.

Because after the day I've had, a strange bed has never sounded so sweet.

CHANCE

I wake after only having slept for a couple of restless hours. Hudson lounges lazily at the foot of the bed. I wait a few minutes to see if I can go back to sleep.

Nope.

I get up, hit the bathroom, then back in my room to dress for a pre-dawn run. I peek out the window, knowing it's early, even for me, when the sun hasn't even thought about approaching the horizon yet.

Huds perks up the minute I grab my running shoes. His cue that something exciting, at least in his world, is about to happen. We head outside, the chill in the early morning air waking us both. I clip his leash to my waist belt and take off toward our normal five-mile round-trip route.

As we run, I think about what Matthews said last night. About women, and apologies, and waiting until they are ready to hear it. I know enough about women, having grown up with my mom and my sisters, to know that what he says is true.

Total rookie mistake.

One that I won't make again.

You've got this, I remind myself.

You're the man.

No one is better prepared, with a mom, two older sisters, one younger sister, and a bat-shit crazy ex-fiancée. I've experienced all sides of the female psyche. Or at least most of them. I just need to apply what I know to what's happening with Remi.

Huds and I hit the end of mile three and turn back toward home. Past our normal turn around point, but worth it for what I've been able to sort out in my brain. If my sisters were upset over a guy, what would they want?

A gesture.

A grand gesture. To show her that she's important to me.

That's it.

I'll go to the conference, maybe even in time for her presentation. Show her I support her work, that I think it's important. I make a note to text Kat to see where it is, once it's a more reasonable hour, then pick up the pace so I can get back home faster.

Not only does Kat tell me where the conference is, but she offers to go with me. Before I know it, I've rented a car, picked up both Kat and Lexie, and we are on our way to San Francisco to see Remi.

I feel nervous but excited. Now that I'm actually on my way to see Remi, the adrenaline of having made such a spontaneous decision has started to wear off.

Am I doing the right thing?

I gut check, but all I feel is nerves.

Traffic is heavy but not as bad as I'd anticipated given the wildfires in the next county over, where my parents live and where I grew up. Luckily my parents are on the opposite side as the fires, so they aren't in any danger. We'll drive past their freeway exit on our way to Remi's conference.

As much as I try to remain positive, I break about three minutes into our trip.

"Ok ladies, I need your help. I don't know how much you know about what went down with Remi and me, but I'm going to admit that I was wrong."

"Thank God," Kat says.

"Hey!" I object.

"Chance," Lexie says. "You bet you could have sex with Remi. For money. That's going to make any girl mad."

"I also bet that I could date her. The whole point was to get her to loosen . . . you know, she had a bet with you guys too," I say.

"Maybe," Kat says. "But—"

"There's no maybe about it," I counter. "You ladies had a bet."

"Okay, suppose we did," Kat says.

"'Cause you did." I glance at her.

"Are you going to let me talk?" Kat asks.

"Yes. Sorry," I say. I do a 'zip my lips' gesture so she knows I'm serious.

"We bet shoes and some dates," Kat says. "You bet sex and money."

"I bet dates too. Look, is that the big problem?" I ask. "That it was sex that I bet on?"

Kat just looks at me, her eyes narrow and expression fierce.

I sigh. "I know I did something shitty. I hurt Remi in the process. I didn't mean to. I mean, it was a bet at first, but I didn't even know who I was betting on. It was just a girl that Alex was talking shit about. Once I realized it was Remi and we spent some real time together, it became so much more than that. I mean, I really like her. I think I always have. Ever since the rugby championship party in college, I've been, you know, pining."

"Barf," Kat says, pretending to stick her finger down her throat.

Lexie bounces in the back seat, barely containing her excitement over my revelations. "I love a good pining, as long as there's a happily ever after," she says.

I smile at her in the rear-view mirror. "The question remains," I say. "How do I fix this? I mean, you guys are closest to her, so you know her best."

"A grand gesture!" Lexie says.

"Isn't that what I'm doing?" I ask.

"Yes!" Lexie says. "Which is how we know it's going to work."

"Slow your roll, tootsie pop," Kat says to Lexie. "Just because it might work for you, doesn't mean it will work for Remi."

"Grand gestures work for everyone," Lexie says, tilting her chin up.

"Okay," I say. "Clearly, I'm doing the grand gesture. So, past that, how do I fix this? I mean, fuck." I run my hand over my face. Not sure if I want to go where I seem to be about to go. But it's the best way to get them on my side. "I think I'm in love with her," I whisper loudly.

"Ohmigod! Ohmigod!" Lexie bounces in her seat and claps her hands simultaneously. "I'm so excited. You guys will be so amazing together!"

"I have to say, Bauer," Kat says. "At the risk of negating my earlier barfing reference, I agree with Lex, it's a good match."

"Thanks, Cookie," I say.

"So, what are your intentions toward our girl, Bauer?" Kat asks.

"You want to know what I intend to do to her once she forgives me? Dirty talk. I like it. First, I'm going to get her alone—"

"I meant the honorable kind of intentions," Kat says.

"Do you want to get married?" Lexie asks.

Her question stops me.

After Helen, I swore I would never get engaged again, let alone married. I had no desire to lay myself out on the line like that again. It's too risky. You never know what you're going to get.

But then I think of my parents and how strong their relationship is. And my sisters and how much their spouses bring to their lives. How much easier their lives are with someone to share the journey with.

Is that what I want?

The answer washes over me like a cold shower over hot skin.

I take a deep breath before I answer. "If you'd asked me last week, I would've said no. But today, I'm not sure. I know I don't want to lose Remi."

"That's so sweet!" Lexie cries. "I love this so much. Remi needs someone who will keep her in line. Otherwise, she just walks all over guys. Chews them up and spits them out."

I laugh, even though I can picture Remi doing just that.

Figuratively, of course.

"And you love her, despite that." Lexie sighs.

"Let's slow it down a little bit. I said I *think* I'm in love with her."

"Oh, I just know she feels the same. She loves—"

"Hey, don't go putting words in Remi's mouth," Kat interrupts. "You don't know how she feels."

"Is that some kind of warning?" I ask, frowning.

"Not necessarily," she says. "I just don't think we should assume anything. That's all."

"Ok," I say. "I get that. It makes me nervous, but I get it."

"How much longer 'til we get there?" Lexie asks.

"Considering we've been on the road about twenty minutes and it's a two-hour drive without traffic delays..." Kat says.

"I'm just so excited to get there," Lexie says. "Remi will be so happy to see us. I love surprises."

"Not all surprises are good ones," Kat says.

"Okay, cranky pants. No need to be so negative," Lexie says.

"I'm not negative, I'm—"

"A realist, I know," Lexie interrupts Kat with a sigh.

I break into the conversation. "Ladies, I have to ask, why did you guys have a bet anyway?"

"Does it matter?" Kat asks.

"Because," Lexie says. "Remi has a hard time with relationships, and we wanted her to see that they aren't so bad."

"Not that a month would have been a full-blown relationship," Kat says. "But it would give her an idea of consistency. No, that's not the right word. Gah! Lex, what's the word I'm trying to think of?"

"Stability?" Lexie suggests.

"No, but that will work," Kat says to Lexie. Then turns to me and says, "Besides, Bauer, you know what I mean."

I nod because I think I do know what she means.

"And we decided on a month because that's practically the longest that Remi has dated someone who lived in the same city as her. She needed to see that it's not so bad to do."

"Right, and that relationships can be okay. Good even. And they don't need to last forever to have a positive impact on your life," Kat says.

"Since her Louboutins are her favorite thing, and are crazy expensive, we figured she would take it most serious if they were at stake," Lexie says. "The bet was that she had to date someone for a month, seeing them at least twice a week, or she had to give her shoes to a homeless woman on the street."

"Longevity!" Kat says, referring back to her earlier point. "It gives her an idea of longevity with a person. No, that's not right either. Maybe I just meant commitment."

"Jesus Christ," I say. "You mean to tell me she can commit to a nine hundred dollar pair of shoes, but not to a few dates with the same guy?"

Both girls stay oddly silent when I ask this question.

I keep talking. "Let's be real, I have three sisters and I still don't understand the draw to a nine hundred dollar pair of shoes."

"Maybe your sisters aren't very fashion oriented," Kat says.

"My sisters are fashionable."

"Maybe they are just more frugal in their choices for footwear," Lexie says.

"What makes them worth that much money?" I ask.

"I've never had a pair, I don't know," Lexie says.

"Picture this," Kat says. "Your foot is your dick, and the shoe is the most beautiful, wet pussy you've ever seen."

"Kat!" Lexie says.

"What? Bauer has had sex, with Remi even. I'm not saying anything he hasn't already heard, Lexie."

For some reason, now that I have been with Remi, talking about sex with Kat makes me feel uncomfortable, guilty even. My face reddens.

"Ha! Bauer, are you embarrassed?" Kat asks.

"Pfft. No. Yes. Why does this feel weird now?"

"Because, you're in love with Remi," Lexie says.

"How do you get that from that?" Kat asks.

"Easy, he used to hit on all of us all the time with no problem. Now he's embarrassed when you bring up S-E-X," Lexie says.

"You're spelling it why?" Kat asks.

Lexie shrugs in return.

"Oh, to live in your head, Lex," Kat says.

"No better place to be!"

I turn to them both. "Can you explain about the shoe without comparing it to sex?"

"Nope," Kat says with a smirk. "Your foot is the cock, and that shoe is the best motherfucking pussy in the world. And you'll pay just about anything to get in it."

"Apparently," I say dryly.

"And, they are sexy as hell on," Kat says. "They make your legs look a mile long. And when you strut, that beautiful red sole flashes and everyone knows that you are wearing—"

"A vagina shoe," Lexie interrupts.

We all laugh at that.

"Good one, Lex," Kat says, still smiling.

"Thanks!" Lexie preens.

I decide to change the subject. "Matthews get called out for the fires?" I ask Kat.

"Yep. It's outta control, they need all the help they can get."

"That's got to be difficult to deal with," I say.

"I'd like to say I'm used to it, you know. But you never get used to it. So I have to remind myself that people die, every day. From all sorts of crazy, mundane things. And just because his job is more high-risk, doesn't necessarily make it more deadly. Even though that sounds like an oxymoronic statement," she says.

"Not really," I say. "I get what you're saying."

"Plus, I have cancer," Kat says. "So it evens the score."

"Fuck cancer," Lexie shouts from the back seat.

"Oh, I love this song." Kat leans over and turns the radio station up.

"Ain't No Mountain High Enough," blares from the speakers, she and Lexie sing the entire song at the top of their lungs. And every song thereafter until we reach the city limits. For some reason, it doesn't bother me a bit.

39

REMI

The fucking presentation couldn't get over fast enough. For over two hours I was subject to Donaldson butchering my hard work from the last twenty-eight months. It's not that he's stupid. He holds his own. But it's not his data. He didn't run the trials. The results aren't his babies. He doesn't know them like I do. When he tried to portray it otherwise, it showed.

Being slightly hungover doesn't help my mood either. And, despite how much I drank last night, I didn't sleep well at all.

So, it's with relief that I finally head back to my hotel room at the end of the day. I'm exhausted after watching the desecration of my work by Donaldson. Not to mention staying awake during the other presentations, trying to follow along with the panel discussions, and fending off the wandering hands of the lecherous keynote speaker.

What is it with men that make them think that just because you are in their general vicinity, they own the right to have you? To touch you? Just because you engage in conversation, they can then watch your tits the entire time you are talking. Or casually slide a hand across your ass 'by accident.' Fucking assholes.

The elevator dings at my floor and I exit, anxious to kick my shoes off, grab vodka from the mini bar, and watch some shitty TV. I get to my room and run my keycard through the lock. It beeps and flashes red.

I try it again.

Same thing happens.

What the fuck? I double check to make sure I'm at the right door.

Six one five.

Okay, one more time.

Beep. Red flash.

Fuck.

I head back down the hall toward the elevator so I can get a new key from the front desk.

"I show we just issued a new one a few hours ago, Ms. Vargas," the desk clerk says.

"No, that's impossible. I've been in panels all day at the engineering conference, I didn't ask for a new key."

"Maybe the notes got put in the wrong record. But I will run a new key for you now. Give me just one moment."

I wait as she runs the keycard through the magnetizer, drumming my fingers on the countertop just to make sure she knows I'm not happy with having to do this.

"Here you are, Ms. Vargas. Again, I'm sorry for the inconvenience."

I fake smile back at her and trudge to the elevator.

"Remi!" I stop when I hear my name and look around, not immediately seeing anyone I recognize. Until he slows his jog and stops in front of me.

Trevor. Lexie's ex. The one she's still hung up on.

"Trevor? What are you doing here?" I ask as I move in to hug him, albeit awkwardly. "Wow. It's been, what? Three months?"

"That sounds about right." He looks down at his feet and shuffles them a bit.

"You aren't the most popular guy amongst me and my girls you know."

"That's kinda why I'm here," he says sheepishly. "I was hoping to run into you."

"Me? How . . . why?" I ask. The elevator dings open, but I ignore it.

"I saw there was a chemical engineering conference, two hours from San Soloman, I figured you'd attend."

"No," I say. "I mean why did you want to find me?"

"Can we talk? Somewhere that's not in front of the elevator bay. Maybe get some coffee?"

"Make it a drink and you got it. Let me just run up and change my clothes. I'll meet you in the bar in like fifteen minutes. Does that work?"

"Yes," he smiles, relief on his face. "Thank you, Remi. I really appreciate it."

I take the next elevator up to the sixth floor, marveling over running into Trevor. I'm kind of anxious to hear about what he's been up to. And he'd better fucking be back to grovel at Lexie's feet if he knows what's good for him. God, I hope he's back for Lexie. That he wants to talk about her. That would be amazing. I find myself suddenly feeling better about things.

Then my phone rings. I look down. It's Stephen.

I hang my head, take a deep breath, and answer the phone.

"Hello, Stephen."

"Remi, I'm glad I caught you. I'd like to discuss how you think the presentation went today."

I stop walking, having now reached my door.

"How I think it went?"

"Yes, will you be at the mixer?"

"No, I'm meeting a friend for drinks."

"This is a company trip, Remi. Not a vacation. It is strongly recommended you attend all of the events."

"I'll be there after, then."

"I think you misunderstand—"

"I don't, Stephen. I don't misunderstand. I just don't agree. I'm off the clock. I'm on my own time, I can do what I want."

"Remi, tsk tsk. There is no off the clock as a salaried career professional. Your time is my time."

This guy, I swear!

"You know what, Stephen? I think you should take your time and shove it up your ass. I quit."

I disconnect the call but can't tell if I feel relief or regret. I swipe my card in the door lock, pissed that I can't hold my temper better. This time, my keycard swipes green and I move into the room, kicking my shoes off as I go. Groaning at how wonderful it feels to be out of heels. I can't wait for yoga pants, flip-flops, and a stiff drink with an old friend.

I turn and put out the 'Do Not Disturb' placard from habit and deadbolt the door. Then toss my purse, and phone, on the floor and walk into the room from the entryway, unzipping my skirt as I go.

It isn't until she clears her throat, that I notice the woman sitting in the chair at the writing desk.

Helen.

"Why don't you just zip that back up and have a seat on the bed. No one wants to see your skanky panties anyway," she says.

What the fuck is she doing here?

"No one?" I look around, feigning nonchalance.

Think fast.

"Is there someone else here besides you and me?" I sound braver than I feel.

How did she get in my room?

Oh shit, that explains the other key that was given out. Don't they ask for ID with that shit? Of course not, they didn't ask for mine just now.

I watch, in horror, as she pulls a gun from under the hand on her lap and levels it on the desk, pointed at me.

Oh fuck.

"Sit."

I comply, zipping my skirt back up as I do.

"Why are you here?" I ask.

"Isn't it obvious?" she asks, waving the gun in my direction.

"You plan to kill me?"

"Kill. Seriously fuck up. Put a bunch of holes into. Maim for life. Yes."

"Why?" I ask.

"Because, Mimi, I can."

"That's not really a reason, Helen."

She shrugs her shoulders.

"I can't be worth going to jail over."

"Oh, I'm not going to jail."

"What makes you think you can shoot, maim, or kill me and not go to jail?" I ask.

She stands up and starts walking toward me, the gun flailing a bit in her hand, her wrist limp. I don't like how her hand keeps changing direction while her finger stays on the trigger.

"I'm not worried about that. Chance will make sure the charges don't stick."

"Is that what you think? That Chance will get you out of this? Are you sure about that?"

She looks at me, her eyes defiant, but her countenance unsure. She doesn't answer. I use that to my advantage.

"There is no way that is happening, Helen. He'll be the first one to lock your crazy ass up."

She smirks. "He won't care. You broke up."

I choose not to confirm or deny that. And instead, continue to try and stare her down.

She continues, "You broke up because of the bet."

"How'd you—"

"Know about the bet? Maybe Chance told me."

I feel like the wind has been knocked out of me. Why would Chance tell her about the bet?

And which bet did he tell her about? His or mine? I didn't think they were even speaking to one another. Are they talking now? It's been two fucking days! Why would he go to her? Tell her? What happened is personal. It's embarrassing. Well, for me. How dare he?

Asshole.

Not that he is my concern any longer, because he's not. She's right, we broke up because of the fucking bet. His fucking bet. So, what he does on his time is his business. And who he talks to or spends time with is his business. If he wants to go back to a crazy whore-bag that's his problem.

Except when it becomes my business because that same crazy whore-bag is holding me hostage in my own hotel room. She starts pacing in the small space between the end of the bed and the writing desk.

"Or," she continues. "Maybe I found out from your good friend Connie."

Connie?

My Connie? From work?

Fucking hell. The first time I venture out and get a friend, she turns out to be a backstabbing bitch. See, this is why you never trust anyone. I look back at Helen, trying to gauge which is the more accurate of the two statements.

"Blood is always thicker than water, Mimi. Connie and I grew up together. She tells me everything."

I really don't like how this is sounding.

"Or, maybe after I saw you with Chance at the concert I started following you around and watching your every move. How else would I have found out that my favorite cousin is also your friend. It was like kismet."

Everything she's saying is not only possible but plausible. Why didn't I notice anything? Why did I tell Connie so much? How the hell am I going to get myself out of this?

Think, Remi!

I glance around the room, looking for inspiration. My gaze lands on the mini-bar.

"Helen, I think I'm going to have a drink. Would you like a drink?"

Bad idea, Remi. Don't give her alcohol. It makes people volatile. Especially crazy people.

Shit.

Luckily, she doesn't hear me. Or else she's ignoring me.

"And then, to know in advance exactly where you were going to be and for how long. A girl just doesn't get any luckier than that, now does she?" She continues to pace, filling up the space in the small room.

I count the number of steps she takes each way and try to calculate how much space I would need to attack her from behind. Until I realize I have nothing to use as a weapon against her.

I'm at the foot of the bed, any lamp, phone, or radio is on a nightstand at the head of the bed. The dresser is in front of me, but all that's on that is the coffee maker and the TV. Neither of which will do much damage when wielded by me. I stand and look toward the mini-bar.

"Don't move!" she yells. She stops pacing to look at me. Her eyes flitting around the room but still on me the entire time.

"I'm not moving," I say. "I was going to see if you wanted a drink. Some water. I was going to get some water."

"No!"

"Okay," I say, sitting back down.

I need to call for help. I see my phone on the floor by the wall. Just not within reach. Even if I try to stretch my legs and grab it with my toes. I'd have to stand and walk over there to get it. If I stand again, she'll notice. Why didn't I just keep my phone in my hand?

What to do? What to do?

If she wants to shoot me, why hasn't she done it yet?

I need more answers. Is Chance involved in this? Does he know she's here? Is Connie here? Is she involved? What does Helen want to do? Maybe I just need to keep her talking.

"How do you want to play this, Helen?" I ask.

"Play this?" she says. "Do you think this is a game, Mimi?"

"You know it's Remi," I say.

She waves her hand in the air, dismissing what I say.

"This is life and death. My life and your death." She laughs at herself. "Besides, with you out of the picture, Chance and I are free to spend the rest of our lives together."

"And I have to be dead to be out of the picture?" I ask.

"Of course you do," she says.

"But I'm not in the picture now, right? Because Chance and I broke up. So, I'm not in the way of the two of you being together."

She stops and looks at me, tapping the barrel of the gun on her lips, as though pondering my statement.

I want it to go off, sending a bullet straight through her brain.

"Yeah, that's not good enough," she says, resuming her pacing and shaking her head. "He's going to feel bad about the bet. He always feels bad. It's his nature. He's going to want to make it up to you. And we can't have that. No making up. So, no, you need to be gone, Mimi. Completely. Gone. Only gone. Dead. Gone. Only dead. Completely."

I let the Mimi thing go, under the circumstances, it's clearly the least of my worries. I'm not even sure why it continues to bother me.

"What if I move?" I ask, hoping that will appease her.

"No, I want you to sit over in this chair, actually." She points to the desk chair that she's pulled to the side of the room.

"I meant from San Soloman," I say.

"Sit!"

I move to sit in the other chair.

"I like your obedience, Mimi. It will help with what I have planned." She resumes pacing and talking to herself. "This is going to work well. Chance will be so excited. Won't he? Yes. I'm sure of it. Once he gets over it. No. No. Nothing to get over. You're gone. Dead. And we're together and happy."

She grabs something from the floor and throws it at me. "Here, fasten your ankles to the legs of the chair," she says. I bend down and grab the industrial polypropylene twine she tossed over. Which I only recognize because I often receive boxes of lab equipment wrapped in it. It's strong and hard to cut or get loose.

I start to tie the rope around my ankles and circling the twine on the legs of the chair.

"Above the footrest," she says. "So you can't slide it off the bottom of the chair leg."

She's smarter than I give her credit for.

"Tighter!"

I pull the strings tightly, then double knot them. She tries to move my legs with her foot, they don't budge.

"Perfect. That's perfect," she says. "Now clasp your hands behind the chair."

I wrap my arms behind me and join my hands around the back of the chair. Not a comfortable position.

She ties my wrists together, so tight I fear the twine is cutting into the skin. She secures my tied wrists to the slats in the chair back. I try to pull my wrists apart when she's through, they don't budge.

She goes into the bathroom, and I hear rustling around, then the clink of metal dropping to the floor. Light metal, not heavy like another gun. I don't want to know what she's got, but I fear I'm about to find out. I see the gun lying on the bed and hope that means my life is spared for a bit longer.

She appears back in my line of vision, something thin in her hand.

"Do you know what this is, Mimi?" She holds up a scalpel, her eyes wild.

I nod.

"Did you guess that it's your worst nightmare?" she asks in a sing-song voice. "If so, you'd be right. Oh, but poo, there's no prize. Not for Mimi. No prize except this."

I watch in horror as she drags the tip of the knife along my left thigh, cutting through the fabric of my pencil skirt. It falls open and I see little droplets of blood pepper my thigh. I didn't even feel her nick my skin.

"Oh, garter belts, well aren't those pretty." She slices the elastic strap on the belt, hard, piercing my skin in the process. This time I feel it. The pain is intense. I blink back tears.

"Oops, I'm not being very careful with this, am I? What a pity, you're bleeding on your little skirt. Maybe if we do the other side, no one will notice." She runs the tip of the knife down my right thigh and repeats the entire process. My legs burn where she's cut them. Making me wonder if there was something toxic on the blade. I know the feel of a regular cut and this is much worse.

My breath catches as she marks me again. The cuts aren't deep, and maybe only a few inches long, but they hurt.

A lot.

I think about Kat, Lexie, and even Chance, and wonder if I will see them again. Will Helen really kill me or just hurt me? My head throbs. I try to mentally transport myself to another place. A happy place where I can ignore where I am now.

My leg muscles tighten as she cuts them again. My ankles pull against the bindings trying to break free. The blood tickles as it slithers down either side of my thighs. I scrutinize Helen's eyes, hoping to find a hint of contrition. But all I see is pride as she watches the blood trails her cuts created. And then glee as she opens my blouse and cuts some more.

40

CHANCE

We hit the city limits right at afternoon rush-hour traffic, which puts us at a standstill. I change the radio station to classic rock. Needing something other than 80s and Motown to get me through this.

"Hey!" Kat cries.

"Don't bother me, woman, I'm fightin' traffic," I say to her, with just the hint of a smile.

ZZ Top's "La Grange" comes on and it's all I can do to not pull off to the shoulder and blow by all these cars. This song begs to be driven to. But it's near the end and I'd probably only get thirty seconds of solid balls to the wall speed before it ends.

I'm still tempted when the next one comes on.

You'll accomp'ny me.

The song I sang to Remi.

It's a sign.

I pull off to the shoulder and speed to the next exit.

"This is the song, isn't it?" Kat asks, her eyes twinkling.

"It is," I say with a smile.

"I love it! It's a sign for sure!" Lexie says, bobbing her head softly to the beat.

I sing along to the radio, feeling free for the first time in days. The song ends, and Kat changes the station. I glare at her.

"I know, no 80s and no Motown. I'm compromising with hit singles of today," she says.

"The Man" by The Killers comes on.

"Oh, I love this song!" Lexie says. I smile at her in the rearview mirror. She says everything with an exclamation point.

I know the song. I hate to admit, but I love it. Like, it's my theme song. I sit up taller and mouth the words softly to myself. Getting myself pumped.

"I would so fuck Brandon Flowers just because of this song," Kat says.

"Me too," Lexie says with a sigh, in between singing.

"Ohmigod, Bauer." Kat looks at me. "This is your theme song."

I laugh at her because I'll never admit it's true.

"I'm serious!" she says. "We're going to get your girl, and you've got to convince her that you're the man, right. You're *the man*. I mean, Lex and I can only help so much, the rest is up to you. You gotta ball up, take your girl, fuck her against the wall, let her see who's boss. Remind her that she can't live without you."

"Now who's putting words in Remi's mouth?" Lexie asks.

"I'm not putting words in Remi's mouth, I'm putting actions in Bauer's head. The guy in that song is exactly what Remi needs," Kat says.

"I agree," Lexie says. Kat turns around and beams at her.

I just try to hold it together as we get closer to the hotel. A song can't really do much when you've fucked up so far beyond belief that your girl says never to call her again.

We pull into self-parking and I find a spot surprisingly quickly. The girls scramble to collect their things. They were smart, each bringing a small overnight bag with them. Me? I didn't even remember a toothbrush. I pat my sides only to realize I don't have my gun either. I panic until I feel the telltale bulge of my wallet and badge.

At least there's that.

"Where's your bag?" Lexie asks.

"I don't even have my gun, apparently. Why would I have a bag?" I ask.

"Well, clearly you didn't think this was going to work out well if you weren't planning to spend the night," Kat says.

"Well, clearly it doesn't matter since you two would be here anyway," I say.

"We're getting our own room," Lexie says.

"Really?" I ask. "You're getting your own room at the same hotel as the largest chemical engineering convention in the nation?"

"Oh," Lexie says. "I didn't think about that."

"Sucks to be you, Bauer," Kat says. "Dibs on sleeping with Remi!"

"Wait, where am I going to sleep?" Lexie asks.

"In the other bed," Kat says.

"Then where's Bauer gonna sleep?" she asks.

"In a chair," Kat says as though she has it all figured out.

"Or," I say. "I can sleep with Remi and you two can have the other bed."

"That could work too," Kat says with a wink, that makes her look like she's having a face spasm.

The girl can't wink.

"I got this, Kat," Lexie says. Then she turns to me and winks, a perfectly adorable and sassy wink.

"It's why you're my bestie, Lex," Kat says as she hugs her around the shoulders. "The yin to my other yang."

We make our way through the parking garage, I offer to carry the girls' bags, but they refuse. So I fidget with the keys, not really knowing what else to do with my hands. But that seems to make me more anxious, so I shove them in my pocket.

We get to the elevator bay and wait for the car's descent. The doors open right about the time I'm tempted to just take the stairs.

"Settle down, sparky," Kat says. "Getting there faster isn't going to make any difference."

"You never know," Lexie says.

"Maybe not," I say. "But it would make me feel better."

"Did you bring a peace offering?" Kat asks.

"What do you mean?"

"You know," Lexie says. "Like flowers or something."

"I'm already doing the grand gesture. I have to have flowers too?"

"Or something, yes," Lexie says.

Kat glares at me.

"I didn't know," I say.

"I thought you had three sisters?" Kat asks.

"I do," I say. "But they didn't help me with this."

"You came up with it on your own?" Kat asks.

"Yes," I say frustrated.

"That's so romantic," Lexie gushes.

"I hope you're able to pull this off, buddy," Kat says.

The elevator doors open to a crowded lobby. I scan the room for Remi, but it's hard to see anyone clearly.

"I'll get us a key to her room," Kat says.

"How are you going to do that?" I ask.

"Just watch," she says.

Kat struts to the front desk with Lexie and I following a short distance behind. Even though I no longer watch her ass, I notice she garners looks from most of the men in the room.

"Remi Vargas, I lost my key and need a new one," she says to the desk clerk. The clerk narrows her eyes at Kat.

"That's funny," the clerk says. "Since you just asked for your key about an hour ago and you didn't look anything like you."

"Okay, you got me," Kat says. "Remi is my best friend and we're here to surprise her."

"We?" the clerk asks.

"The three of us," Kat says, gesturing to Lexie and me.

"Ms. Vargas is in a single room, not a double," the clerk says. "Her room can't accommodate four."

"And which room might that be?" Kat asks.

"I can't give out guest information like that."

"It's important," Lexie interjects, pushing herself toward the desk. "She and Bauer, here, are in love and they got into a fight and he's here to apologize."

The clerk looks around the girls at me. "Young man, what did you do wrong?"

"A lot," I say.

"Where's your peace offering?" the clerk asks.

"I'm doing the grand gesture by coming here," I say.

The clerk rolls her eyes at us. "You still need a peace offering."

"See?" Kat says.

"Is this some kind of joke?" I ask. "Are you all in on it together? This is ridiculous."

"Come on." Lexie pulls at my arm. "We'll get flowers in the gift shop."

"She's gonna know they are gift shop flowers," the clerk says.

"Oh, good point," Lexie says.

"You're a nice looking boy, so I'm going to give you some advice."

"Can we just get the room number, please?" I'm exasperated and annoyed.

"No. Now, you go down the block about five buildings, on the right you'll see a flower shop. You tell Marianne, she's the owner, you tell her that Wanda sent you. She'll get you sorted out."

"Wait here," I tell the girls. I hit the street running, making it to the flower shop in record time, get Remi a bouquet of lilies, then sprint back.

The girls are still standing at the counter talking to Wanda.

I hold up the flowers. "Good?"

"You know I'm not supposed to give room information out," Wanda says.

I pull out my police badge and show it to her. "How about now?"

"Oh, now, don't you fuss. I was just teasing." She clicks a few buttons on her keyboard and looks back at me. "Your girl is in room six one five."

"Thank you," I say and sprint back toward the elevators.

"Wait for us," Lexie says, grabbing Kat's hand and running after me.

The elevator doors open on the sixth floor and I practically sprint down the hall.

"Bauer," Kat hisses. "Wait for us, dick head."

I stop.

She's right. I can't go running up to Remi's door. I barely even know what I'm going to say. I'm gripping the flowers so hard I've crushed most of the stems.

I walk back toward them.

"Fuck, what do I say when she opens the door?" I ask.

"Well, first say you're sorry, then hand her the flowers," Lexie says.

"Then we'll push our way in," Kat says. "She'll let us, 'cause it's us."

"That works," Lexie says.

"Lex and I will convince her that she needs to hear you out," Kat says.

"Yep," Lexie agrees.

"Then Lex and I will go down to the bar while you and Remi do the horizontal bop apology style."

I'm not sure if she meant to reference a Bob Seger song or not, so I ignore it.

"Dude, you gonna ignore my Seger reference?" Kat asks.

"Of course not," I say. "That was good."

"Your praise means nothing when I have to ask for it," she says, flipping her hand in the air.

"Fuck. Here it is." We arrive at door six fifteen. I raise my hand to knock, but Kat beats me to it.

"Open up, Rem," she says as she bangs on the door. "Lex and I are here to cheer you up."

I stand back behind the two girls and hold my breath. Waiting to see her face when she opens the door.

God, I hope this works.

41

REMI

I got past the point of not crying long ago.

Because apparently I cry now.

All the fucking time.

Tears stream steadily down my face, my teeth grinding against the pain. Helen has made cuts on my thighs, chest, calves, and stomach. Now she's going for my arms.

"Oh, looky here, are these little scars? Mimi, were you a cutter as a girl? Oh my, isn't that fitting? We're using your past coping mechanisms to hurt you now."

She laughs, wildly. "Do you think you'll go back to cutting to deal with the fact that I've been cutting you?" She's laughing so much she can hardly get the words out. "Oh wait, no, you'll be dead!"

I am beyond answering her questions or responding at all. Most of what she says doesn't even make sense. It's all I can do to try and block out my current reality.

"Oh Mimi, if I just let you live there could be so many scars."

It doesn't matter. Even if she doesn't kill me, I'm never showing my skin again.

"Just do it, Helen," I say.

I'm exhausted. I have no fight left. The pain is immense, yet for some reason, I haven't passed out. All that's holding me up right now are the ties on my wrists. The rest of me has slumped over.

"Okay!" she says, grabbing the gun off the bed and pointing it at me.

I jump when I hear the noise, except it's not a gunshot, it's a loud knock on the door.

"Open up, Rem," I hear Kat say as she bangs on the door. "Lex and I are here to cheer you up."

"Kat!" I try to yell, but my voice comes out as more of a croak.

"Shut up!" Helen says. I'm not sure if she's talking to me or to Kat.

Until she backhands me across the cheek. Which is enough to shut me up. Truth be told, I don't want Helen getting her hands on Lexie or Kat anyway.

Helen resumes pacing and talking to herself. Then, seeming to decide, moves to open the door.

"You must have the wrong room," I hear Helen say. I try to yell for Kat again, but I can't get my voice to work. My throat is so dry.

"Helen... what the fuck... if you hurt her—"

I hear Chance's voice right before I hear the door slam open and hit the wall.

"By all means, come in and join the party," Helen says.

I raise my head slowly and watch as the three most important people in my life file in with Helen and her gun bringing up the rear.

"Remi!" Chance cries and is at my side in a second. "My God, beautiful. Oh my God." His voice breaks, his eyes fill. "I'm so sorry, baby. HELEN, what did you do? I'm going to get you out of here, beautiful. Oh God. We've got to get her to a doctor! Help me untie her!" His voice is frantic as he pulls uselessly at my bindings.

Helen cocks the gun. It's not a loud noise, yet somehow the click is one we all hear clearly.

"Get away from Mimi, or this one loses her head," Helen says laughing, I raise my head and see she has the gun pointed at Lexie's head.

Chance stands up slowly and turns toward Helen, his hands raised in front of him.

"Helen…" he warns.

"Oh no you don't," she says. "You don't call the shots here. I do. The one with the gun wins, right?"

"Okay, why don't we all just calm down a little bit," Chance says in a low, even tone.

"I'm calm," Helen says. She turns to me. "You calm, Mimi?"

I nod my head.

"Speak!" Helen yells.

"I'm calm." My voice barely a croak.

"See?" Helen says. "We're all calm."

"What are you doing here, Helen?" Chance asks.

"I'm getting rid of Mimi so we can be together."

Chance stiffens. I turn to look at Lexie, she's crying silently, not that I blame her. Helen has the gun at her head. I look to Kat, who is the exact opposite. Kat looks ready to kill. I silently beg her to calm down. She must see something in my eyes, because her body visibly relaxes a small amount.

"I've been waiting for this opportunity," Helen says. "I just had to watch and wait. I've been watching for a while. Listening. Taking notes. For instance." She glances toward Chance. "Did you have a nice time with cancer girl's boy toy last night?"

"Helen," Chance says. "Why don't you give me the gun?"

"Did you know that Connie tells me everything about you and Mimi?"

"Helen, give me the gun." Chance holds his hand out toward her.

"Did you know that I've been following you and your girl?"

To his credit, Chance's expression stays neutral.

"I've seen everything, Chancey. And I do mean everything. Mimi's ass is kind of big, don't you think?"

"Listen, bitch," Kat starts. Chance holds out a hand in her direction and she stops talking.

"The gun," Chance grits out, still holding his other hand out to Helen.

"Now, why would I do that? If I give you the gun, you have control. That doesn't work for me. I'm in control here."

"Fine," Chance says. "How about if you just lower the gun a bit, so you aren't upsetting Lexie."

"Lexie?" Helen asks. "Like I give a fuck about Lexie." She swings the gun away from Lexie, we all breathe a small sigh of relief. But then she points it right back at me. Chance's body is taut, poised, and ready to strike.

"Don't do it," Helen says to him. "I know you better than you know yourself. You try to help her, she dies." She walks closer toward me. I flinch as the cold metal of the gun kisses my temple.

"Helen, you said you want us to be together," Chance says.

"I do, Chancey," she says.

"Don't call me that," he growls.

"I can call you whatever I want," she says in a sing-song voice. "Just like I can shoot whomever I want."

"Well, shooting someone isn't going to get us back together," Chance says. "It's going to get you sent to jail."

"If she dies, you can get the charges dropped for me," Helen says, shrugging her shoulders.

"Helen, a murder charge isn't exactly like a parking ticket. The charges aren't up to me. The District Attorney does that. I can't just get them dropped."

"So, I'll kill all three of them," Helen says. "That way there are no witnesses."

"But I'll still . . . look . . . killing all three isn't . . . maybe we should take a minute and talk. What do you think?"

"Talk about what?" she asks.

"About us. We need to talk about us if you want us to be together again, don't you think?" Chance asks Helen.

"Hmmm. Maybe." She sounds flippant.

"Why maybe?"

"I don't think I trust you yet, Chancey," she says. "You seem upset about Mimi, and that's not how this story goes."

"How does this story go?" he asks.

"You know," Helen says. "You know exactly how it goes."

"Okay. Why don't we go somewhere and talk about it, just me and you."

"Just me and you?" she asks.

"Yeah. We'll go somewhere quiet, just the two of us. Like we used to do. Before."

"Before," she says, continuing to parrot what he says. Her face changes as she looks at him, her eyes wide. "You mean it?"

"I do." His voice softens. "I want us to go away, just me and you. Please. We can talk. I've missed you."

Chance is convincing. So much so that I start to doubt why he's here. What if this is all real and he wants her?

Fuck!

I can't think. My thoughts are too jumbled.

"We were so good together," Helen says. "That's why I'm here, so Mimi can go, and we can be together again."

"Mimi doesn't matter to you and me," Chance tells her.

"She doesn't?" Helen asks.

"No," Chance says, inching his way closer to us. "She's not even a blip on our radar."

"You're lying! I always know when you're lying!" Helen swings the gun in Chance's direction. He stops.

I try to catch his eye, but he won't look at me. He only has eyes for Helen.

"Helen," Chance soothes. "Have I ever lied to you?"

"No," she says softly, her mood rapidly changing again. "You were always good about that, Chancey. Can we go to the park?"

"The park?" Chance asks.

"Where we had our first date. You remember? You made me a picnic."

"How could I forget?" he asks. "But, Helen, Rai—"

"Uh uh uh, Chancey, no reason to tell anyone where we're going."

"Okay, we won't tell anyone," he says. "But I think there's a fire *somewhere over* there right now."

"There won't be a fire. Not in our special place. Besides, if we're going to talk, it has to be somewhere special. And our first date was special." She lowers the gun to her side. "It was special, right, Chancey?"

"It was, Helen," he agrees.

"Okay, then, it's settled."

"Perfect. That's where we'll go, even if it is *somewhere over on the* other side of Brighton County, where there's no *rain* with the fire."

"Yay!" she claps her hands together, the gun still clenched in one of them.

I'm convinced it's going to go off and one of us is going to die. And it probably won't be me.

"You!" Helen turns the gun toward Kat. "Tie my handsome husband's hands behind his back with the rope." She hands Kat two pieces of the same twine she used on me earlier, a shorter piece and a longer one.

"What?" Kat asks looking sharply at Chance. He shakes his head slightly at her.

"Don't look at her!" Helen screams at Chance, her face contorted with anger.

"I'm only looking at you," he says to Helen.

Her face softens just as quickly. "Tell them, Chancey. Tell them we're married."

"I thought we were going to leave," he says.

"Right! Okay." She turns to Kat. "Put the small piece between his palms and have him hold them together," Helen instructs Kat. Kat follows the instructions, then takes the longer piece and wraps it around his wrists.

"Tighter," Helen says. Kat looks at Chance, he nods.

"Don't look at him! You get your direction from me," Helen says to Kat. "Now tighten."

Kat pulls it tighter until it's almost cutting into his skin, then ties it in a double knot. It looks painful. Helen looks pleased.

"Now, take the other piece and tie his hands to his belt loop."

Kat curls the shorter piece through his belt loop and secures it.

I try to catch Chance's eye, but he won't look at me. His face stays impassive.

Helen turns to Chance. "Ready to go, darling?"

"After you." He motions to the door with his clasped hands.

"Oh no," she says, waving the gun at him. "After you. I insist."

"You," Helen says, pointing the gun at Lexie. "Be a dear and open the door for him, will you?" She asks it as though it's the most normal question in the world. "He's a little tied up right now." Helen laughs crazily at her own pun.

Lexie hurries forward and opens the door for them.

"Chance," she starts to talk to him, but he leaves through the door without even a glance back.

I watch, tears streaking down my face, as the door closes after them.

Kat comes rushing over to me. "Oh my God, Remi, are you okay? Holy shit. What the fuck happened? Lexie, help me find something to cut these ties."

"Here." Lexie hands Kat the scalpel. I can't help but flinch as she comes toward me.

"It's okay, beautiful girl. We're just going to cut these loose, okay?" she says softly. I nod my head, still unable to really speak. Relief floods through me with just as much fervor as dread. Relief to be free and alive. Dread over Chance leaving with Helen.

Kat cuts the ties and I cry out as the blood rushes back into my hands and feet. "We need to get you to the hospital," Lexie says as she dabs at my cuts with a warm washcloth.

"No," I croak. "We need to go after them. I need water."

"Oh goodness, of course." Lexie runs and grabs a bottle of water, opening it for me and helping me bring it to my mouth. My throat instantly feels better as the water coats it.

"We need to help Chance." I stand. "If we leave now we might be able to catch them."

Kat pushes me back down in my chair. "We aren't going anywhere, except to a hospital."

"I don't need a hospital," I say. "We need to go. We need to call the police and let them know that Helen took Chance."

"Bauer is the police," Kat says.

"Why are you being so stubborn?" I cry. "We need to help him. I can't lose him."

Kat just looks at me.

"I think I love him," I whisper.

"Okay, that's all I needed to hear," Kat says. "Lex, call 911. And, Remi, let's get you cleaned up and we'll go after your guy."

"The lines are busy," Lexie says a moment later.

"It's the fire," Kat says. "Try calling from the hotel landline."

She does, but with the same results. "I hate to be the voice of reason, but if we can't get through to 911, how exactly are we going to save Bauer?" Lexie asks.

"We need a plan," Kat says. "We'll think of one while we're bandaging Remi up, grab the first aid kit from the bathroom, Lexie. Then keep trying to call."

Kat makes me drink two mini-bar sized bottles of tequila as I wait for her to clean my cuts, dab them in ointment, and cover everything in bandages. All the while, trying to concoct a plan to rescue Bauer.

"Hey, Lexie, maybe it's a better idea to call Alex and ask him what to do." I hand her my phone. "His number is in my contacts."

"I didn't think he was a cop," Kat says.

"He's not. But he works for precincts. Maybe he'll know someone or something we can do."

Kat finishes bandaging me up as Lexie disconnects her call.

"That was fast," I say to Lexie.

"I know! That's 'cause it's good news, Alex can trace the GPS on Bauer's phone and give us directions on how to find him."

"Oh, thank God," I say as I gingerly pull some yoga pants over my bandaged legs, then do the same with a long sleeve shirt over my arms. "How do we get the directions from Alex?"

"He'll do his search and then call me back." Lexie touches my shoulder lightly. "Are you sure you're up for this?"

"I'm fine, Lex. For real. I just need to go. I can't sit here not knowing if Chance is okay."

"I get it," she says.

"Okay, then," I say. "Let's go." I toss Kat my car keys and tell her she's driving, then gingerly make my way out the door and down the hall.

We reach the parking garage and exit on the floor where I'm fairly certain I parked my car. I just don't remember exactly where, Kat keeps clicking the panic button on the key fob until we find it.

We get in, Kat starts the car and then begins to move her seat and adjust the mirrors.

"Kat, can we get a move on, please?" I ask.

She puts it in reverse and pushes down on the accelerator. The car moves at a very slow pace.

"Let's go, Gramma," I say.

"Remi, there's something wrong with the car, it's not moving right," Kat says.

"Fuck."

We get out of the car to inspect it, belatedly noticing that two tires have been slashed, front passenger and rear driver.

"No, no, no!" I cry. "Fuck, I can't believe this." I think I'm going to cry. Again.

Kat rushes to give me a hug. "It's okay. We'll just call an Uber or something." She gets her phone out of her purse to make the call. "No service. Lex, you got service?"

Lexie shakes her head. "And neither does Remi," she says holding up my phone as well.

Tears sneak out of my eyes and begin their descent down my cheeks. I don't even have the energy to wipe them away.

"We got this, Rem," Kat says. "We'll just head back to the lobby where we have a signal and make the call. Easy peasy."

I nod.

We make our way back to the elevator and make the ascent back up to the lobby. Lexie gets a signal back shortly before we reach the lobby floor.

"Texting Alex now," she says. The elevator doors open, Lexie heads out first, head down, fingers moving. Kat takes a moment to wipe my tears away before we exit.

I hear Lexie grunt before she bounces back into us. Large hands grip her on the waist to steady her.

"I'm so sorry," Lexie starts "I wasn't watching… ohmigod."

Kat and I both look up to see what's happening, and at the same time Kat says, "Trevor?"

42

CHANCE

Helen and I leave the room and head toward the elevators.

"Oh, Chancey, I'm so happy we're back together," she says.

I feel sick to my stomach when she says that. I can only hope that Remi understands what I'm doing. And, more importantly, understands that I only left with Helen to keep Remi and the girls out of danger.

"Do you think, maybe we can put the gun away? I would feel more comfortable if it weren't still pointed at me," I say.

"No," she says. "Not until I'm certain you've really come back to me."

"You just said we were back together," I say.

She looks at me, eyes questioning.

"How can I prove it to you when you have me tied up and at gunpoint?" I ask.

"You can prove it at the park," she says. "I'll untie you when we get there."

"How are we going to get to the park?" I ask, holding out hope that I will be driving us somewhere.

"I'm going to drive us, silly."

I realize, too late, that I've foolishly put myself in a situation where I have no control. Helen has me tied up, at gunpoint, and about to be a passenger in her car. The rental car keys in my pocket now totally useless. The girls are stranded and I'm a hostage.

Fuck.

We reach the parking structure. Her car is parked near the elevator bay, which puts us in the car much faster than I'd anticipated. I still don't have a plan. How do I get Helen under control? How do I get out of this situation? How do I get back to Remi?

I can only hope that Remi and the girls picked up on my clues to where we had our first date and are going to send help. Fuck, unless they follow us.

But maybe I want that. Which has more to do with discovering how Remi feels about me over having her rescue me. If I can't get myself away from Helen, there's not much the girls will be able to do about it.

We get in the car. Helen buckles her seatbelt and starts the car. I'm not able to buckle mine with my hands bound to my waist as they are. The car dings in protest as soon as she reaches the road.

She looks at me, an odd noise rising from her throat.

"Put your seatbelt on, Chancey."

"I can't reach it." I fan my fingers as proof.

She slows the car slightly and looks over. Her eyes flit back and forth as she decides whether or not to fasten it for me and risk getting too close. I'm not sure I could come up with a way to disable her this quickly anyway.

Seeming to decide, she speeds up and drives toward Brighton County and Rainbow Park. I wonder what's going through Helen's mind. I mean, I haven't seen her in years, outside of the concert. And suddenly she has resurfaced and she's still acting out of control. Or at the very least, completely off-balance. Maybe I need to try another tactic with her to either keep her off balance or get her on a new level.

"Helen," I say. "What do you think is happening here?"

She looks at me, head cocked, a slight frown on her face. "Uh, we're going back to when everything was magical." Her fingers are tapping on the steering wheel.

"Which is Rainbow Park?"

"Yes."

"Well then what happens once we get there?"

"We go on our first date and then we fall in love. Just like before," she says with a long sigh. "And it will be perfect."

"We don't have any picnic things with us," I say, not knowing how else to try and deflate this plan of hers.

"That's okay," she says. "I'm not hungry anyway."

It doesn't surprise me that she fails to wonder if I am. She's always been more narcissistic than anything else. When we were together, I mistook that for independence. But after meeting Remi, I now recognize the difference.

The smoke on the horizon looms larger the closer we get to the Brighton County line.

"Helen, do you see the smoke up ahead?"

"Yep."

"Okay, so don't you think we should go in a different direction from the fire?"

"No."

"Why not?"

"Because," she says. "The fire won't get us."

"Okay," I say. "But do you see all the cars on the other side of the freeway who are leaving the area?"

Traffic is bumper to bumper and at a stand-still on the other side of the divider.

"Yep."

"Don't you think that maybe we should be going in the same direction as everyone else?"

"We are not sheep, Chancey. We don't follow. We blaze our own trail. Ha! Blaze. And there's fire. Oh, I'm funny."

I can tell by her responses that I'm not going to get anywhere with her as far as this conversation regarding the fire is concerned.

"Chancey," she says. "It doesn't matter. True love conquers all."

"Yes, it does." I think of Remi as I say it.

Fuck it.

If I'm going to die anyway or end up having something horrible happen at the hands of my crazy-ass ex, it's going to be on my terms with her knowing my truth.

"Helen… you know that I'm in love with Remi, right?"

"No! No! That doesn't work, Chancey. The only way the plan works is when we are together. You and me. That's the plan. Nothing else. Just you and me. We are in love," she says, her brow furrowed. The car accelerates with a jerk. She switches lanes rapidly back and forth, as though she's dodging traffic, even though there are few cars on the road with us.

"I'm not in love with you, Helen." I soften my voice. "I haven't been for a long time. I'm not sure I ever really was. I'm sorry. But I can't pretend to have feelings that aren't there."

"You said at the hotel that we were getting back together," she says, her voice rising.

"Helen, I don't want to hurt you. I care about you. But, I can't have you thinking we are getting back together. Even if I'm not with Remi, it's not going to happen."

"Mimi, Mimi, Mimi! It's always her. I hate her. God, why didn't I kill her? Stupid! Stupid!" She bangs the heel of her hand on the steering wheel, causing the car to jerk sharply to the left. I try to grab for something to hang on to but am flung against Helen anyway.

Which makes me wonder if I can somehow fling her out of the driver's seat. But I'd still have no real way to steer the car. I've been trying to loosen the twine around my wrists, but it just cuts into my skin farther. The resulting blood does nothing to lubricate the bindings. If anything, it's more sticky.

Fuck.

I try to move my hands toward the door handle, but I'll never reach it without pushing my whole body in that direction. And I'll never manage that maneuver without alerting Helen.

"She can't find us, you know," Helen says.

"Remi?"

"I flattened the tires on her car. She won't be going anywhere."

My stomach drops like a lead ball. Even though part of me didn't want Remi to follow, I still hoped she was. I wanted the big climax after my grand gesture.

Helen looks at me. "Aren't you proud of me, Chancey?"

"Why would I be proud, Helen?"

"Because. I flattened her tires just in case I didn't kill her. And look? I didn't kill her after all."

"Helen, Remi needs medical attention, how is that supposed to happen when she doesn't have a car."

Fuck. Why didn't I leave the rental keys with the girls?

"Mmm, not my problem," she says. "But you're still proud, right?"

"I . . . am . . . happy that you didn't kill anyone."

She exits the freeway at the offramp for the park. The place where we had our first date is actually just on the outskirts of Rainbow Park, a huge two-hundred-and-fifty-acre plot of wild hills, flat land, and hiking trails, interspersed with picnic areas and playgrounds. When I brought her here for our date, we took an old fire road to get to the top of the largest hill, mountain really, and had a picnic. We were on my bike, so trespassing was much easier than if we'd been in a car.

Helen drives past the entrance to the park. The fire is close enough to see flames. I know she's headed for that same fire road. If she takes it, we'll be driving straight into the fire. She turns left and heads up the fire road. Her little blue car bouncing and sliding along the uneven dirt surface.

How can I be such a terrible detective? I saw this car, I knew it didn't belong. Why the fuck didn't I do something?

I look over at Helen. Beads of sweat break out on my forehead and upper lip. I don't know how to get us out of this safely. And where are the fire crews? I was counting on this area being flooded by officials.

Why isn't anybody on this road?

She seems intent on getting us to the top of the small mountain. Her car slides backward almost as much as it climbs. She's having a hard time controlling the car with one hand still holding the gun. The flames are a few hundred yards away.

"Helen, stop the car. This isn't funny."

"No, Chancey, we need our date."

"Helen, this is dangerous, you are heading right for the flames."

"I know what I'm doing."

"Helen, goddamit, stop the fucking car!"

"Everything is going to be perfect, Chancey. We just need to get to the top."

She tries to accelerate; the wheels spin then catch throwing the car forward then side to side.

I use the motion of the car to try throwing myself against either her or the door, whichever will give me the most traction. It doesn't help. We just continue to get closer to the fire. I pivot my body and try for the door handle.

She's going to kill us both if she doesn't stop the car. I think I can get the door open and throw myself out. I can't worry about Helen right now.

The car starts to fishtail to the left, giving me enough momentum to finagle my door open. The heat is immense, the roar of the fire near deafening.

I barely hear Helen scream, "No, Chancey!"

What I do hear clearly is the shot, seconds before I feel the bullet enter my thigh. Or it just feels like it takes that long to hit me. I curl into a fetal position and roll myself out the door. I hit the ground hard and roll from the car. Looking back up just in time to watch as she careens straight into the wall of fire at the crest of the hill. It's like the flames opened its massive mouth giving her access, then closed and swallowed her back up.

How could she just drive into the fire? I wait for the car to back up and reverse down the hill, not believing what I've seen.

But it doesn't. And the fire is approaching fast. I try to stand, but with my leg shot, and no use of my hands, I can't. With no other choice, I shut my eyes and start to barrel roll down the big hill.

43

REMI

"What the—" Lexie exclaims.

"Lexie." Trevor practically breathes her name in reverence and has yet to let go of her arms.

"Of all the elevators, in all the hotels..." Kat murmurs to me.

"Trevor, thank God. I forgot you were here. Do you have a car?" I ask.

He finally looks away from Lexie at Kat and I. Shock registering on his face. "My God, Remi. What happened to you? You were just fine a bit ago."

"You forgot he was here?" Kat asks.

"What . . ." Lexie starts.

"Trevor!" I say sternly. "Focus, do you have a car?"

"Yeah, I have a rental. I was going to have my car shipped, but I sold it figuring I'd buy a new one when I got—"

"Don't mean to be rude, but no one cares about your plans. Where's your car?"

"In the parking garage," he says hazily, still looking at Lexie.

"What are we waiting for?" Kat says, pulling Lexie and Trevor by the hands back into the elevator.

The motion snaps Trevor out of his Lexie induced fog. "Is that why you didn't meet me at the bar, Remi? Because you were hurt? My god, what happened?"

"Remi's boyfriend, Chance, has this crazy ex-girlfriend, Helen, who held Remi hostage and tortured her. And now she's kidnapped Chance at gunpoint and we need to rescue him because I can't get through to 9-1-1. Wait, you were meeting Remi at the bar?"

Trevor ducks his head shyly and I punch the button for the parking garage repeatedly. Willing the elevator car to go faster.

The elevator doors open. "Great," I say. "Let's go." I grab Kat's hand and head toward the rows of cars. I turn back toward Lexie and Trevor, who haven't moved from the elevator. "Hey! Let's go." I snap my fingers to get their attention.

I don't like this feeling of being so on edge. I just need to know that Chance is okay. That he doesn't really want Helen. That he still wants to give us a try. That's all I ask for, a try.

And that he's okay.

Please be okay.

We reach Trevor's car, a large SUV. Kat and I get in the back, leaving the front passenger seat for Lexie. She looks at us questioningly.

"You have to navigate, remember?"

"I'm on it," she says.

She gives Trevor the starting directions and we head out.

Right into bumper-to-bumper traffic at a stand-still.

"Fuck! Kat, I can't do this. I can't. I'm not meant for this. This is exactly why I don't do relationships," I whisper.

"Because of traffic?" Kat asks.

I laugh.

"Yes, and because traffic prevents a girl from saving her guy from his ex-psychopath-girlfriend."

"Good point," she says.

We finally reach a breaking point in the traffic and are able to move at about forty mph. Which feels amazing compared to the stop and go. Lexie continues giving Trevor directions.

"We're almost there, Remi!" she says.

My heart stops. Literally. I have no idea what we'll find when we get there. Did she kill him? Did he kill her? Are they both alive and back together? Am I stupid for even going after him?

Stop it, Remi!

Trevor stops the car in front of a vacant lot.

"Why are we stopping?" I ask.

"We're here," Lexie says. "This is where he is."

"There's nothing here, Lex," I say, a feeling of dread weighing me down.

"Call him," she says.

I dial his number hesitantly. We roll down the windows and wait. Kat opens her door and gets out, returning a moment later with Chance's phone.

Tears escape my eyes again.

"He's not here," I whisper, a sob catching in my throat. "Oh my God, Kat. He's not here."

"It's okay, Rem. He's a big, tough, alpha asshole. Some off-her-rocker wackadoo isn't going to get the best of him."

Her words reassure me.

A little.

Chance is big and tough, and probably an alpha asshole as well. But he was tied up, and Helen had a gun. And he went with her willingly.

Wait, he has a gun.

"Does he have his gun?" I ask Kat.

She shakes her head.

"He just wanted to get to you, Remi. We never thought something like this would happen," Lexie says.

"We're never going to find him." I feel weighed down.

"Okay, you said he was going to the place where his first date with this girl was right?" Trevor says.

I nod my head.

"But you don't know where that is?"

I shake my head.

"And he didn't tell you?" he continues.

"No, Trevor. He didn't tell us. He tried to, but crazy-ex stopped him before he could say it."

"Maybe he gave you some kind of clue?" Trevor urges. "Something he said?"

"Of course he did. Chance is smart. We can figure this out," Lexie says.

"Figure what out? How?" I ask.

"When he almost said the name and Helen stopped him, what was it he said? We just need to figure out what the whole word would have been had he said it." Lexie has a way of making even the most challenging of things seem easy.

Like now.

I have to admit, it's kind of inspiring.

"Well, they said something about a park, right?" I ask.

"And a picnic," Lexie adds.

"Didn't Chance also say something about Brighton County?" Kat asks.

"His parents live in Brighton County," I say.

"Do you think she took him to his parents'?" Lexie asks.

"No, they don't like her. She wouldn't go there. That's not where they would have had a date?" I ask.

"Right." Lexie nods her head absently.

"If he almost said the name," Trevor says. "He must have said something else he thought you would take as a clue. Was there anything that seemed odd or unusual?" Trevor asks.

"Everything, all the time," Kat says.

I backhand her on the shoulder.

"He did!" Lexie says. "He said something kind of weird that reminded me of something else that I thought was weird."

"That clears it up, Lex. Thanks," Kat says.

"What did it remind you of, Lex?" Trevor asks. He takes her hand and runs his thumbs over it in what I imagine to be a soothing motion.

Lexie closes her eyes for a moment. "I think it was a movie, maybe. It triggered something odd at the time. I remember thinking it was out of character for him."

"You're right," Kat says. "He did say something weird. That he was over something? Or going over something?"

"Getting over something?" I'm ashamed I don't remember more of what he said.

"No, it was more like somewhere," Lexie says.

"Somewhere ovah dare," Kat says in an unidentifiable accent that I'm sure thinks is spot on. "Actually, I think he said somewhere over the."

"What is somewhere over *the*?" I ask, my voice rising. I'm getting increasingly frustrated the longer we sit here.

"I don't know," Kat says. "But he also said there was no rain. Wow, I am just pulling shit out of my ass here. It's like chemo-brain in reverse."

"Somewhere over the, and no rain," Trevor says.

"Rainbow." Lexie shrugs her shoulders. "Somewhere over the rainbow?"

"There is a park on the other side of Brighton County called Rainbow Park," Trevor says.

"Do you think that's what he meant?" I ask.

Don't get your hopes up.

"It's as good a clue as any," Trevor says.

Don't get your hopes up.

"Crikey," Kat says. "I think we just solved the mother fucking mystery, Scooby."

"Let's go, Trevor," I say.

He speeds off in the direction of the park. And my anxiety ramps up once again.

Will he be okay that we came after him? Did he really mean the *somewhere* comment to be a clue? He doesn't want Helen. He couldn't. That would be stupid. Right?

"Are we doing the right thing?" I ask.

Lexie turns around to face us. "You said you love him."

I nod.

"Then there's no question," she says. "He needs us, we help him."

"What if he doesn't want our help?" I ask.

"If he didn't want our help, he wouldn't have given us the clue," Lexie says.

"I have to agree with Lexie," Trevor says. "He wouldn't have a reason to hint at where he was going unless he wanted you to be there."

I feel my resolve kick back in. Trevor is right.

"Sorry I'm such a fucking pussy," I say.

"Happens to the best of us," Kat says, pulling me in for a one-armed hug.

"Kat," Lexie says. "Have you heard from Brad?'

"No," Kat sighs. "But that's normal in situations like this. It could be as long as forty-eight hours before he's able to take a break or reach out to let me know he's okay."

"That's got to be tough," Trevor says.

"It is," Kat says. "I mean, I'm kind of used to it, but it doesn't make it any easier."

"Not to be an asshole," I say.

"Asshole," Kat says.

"*But*, can we get back to how we're going to rescue Chance once we get to Rainbow Park? *If* he's even there."

"We've got about four minutes to figure it out," Trevor says right before traffic comes to a total stand-still. Again. "Or longer."

"What's going on?" I ask.

"I think it's the fires," Trevor says. "They aren't letting anyone through."

"So, maybe Chance and Helen are stuck in traffic too?" I ask.

"It's possible," Trevor says. "But if I remember correctly, Rainbow Park is just to the east of us."

"Like right now?" I ask.

"I think so, yes," he says.

"How far?" I ask.

"Maybe half a mile—"

I've got the car door open and am climbing out before he can even finish his sentence.

"Remi, wait!" Kat yells.

"I'm coming too!" Lexie cries.

"Well, shit, I'm not letting you out of my sight now," I hear Trevor say. I turn in his direction in time to see him pull his car off the road, passenger doors still open and climb out.

I head out toward the direction of the park. I can see the smoke in the distance, closer than I feel comfortable with. But I've got my entourage with me.

Somehow, that makes me invincible.

44

REMI

I break into a run. Well, as much of a run as I can in my Ugg boots with a million tiny cuts all over my body. Relief floods through me once I reach the clearing of the park.

Except it's empty.

There's no one here.

I cry out and sink to my knees. I was right the first time I thought it. I can't do this. I'm not cut out for it. The ups and downs emotionally. Knowing and not knowing.

Kat appears beside me. "Remi, are you okay? Did you fall?"

"They aren't here, Kat. Look, no one is here. This is hopeless. We have nothing to go on. We don't even know if we're in the right place. We don't even know if he wants us here."

"Look," Kat says, kneeling down next to me. "That man drove all the way here for a grand gesture. That grand gesture being to prove to you that he wants you. And I gotta tell you, beautiful girl, I may love you to death, but you are no peach when it comes to relationships. So, if that guy has seen what you have to offer, and *still* wants you, you better hop on that train before it leaves the station."

Somehow, that makes me feel better. I smile at her gratefully.

Trevor and Lexie arrive, slightly out of breath.

"Do you see them?" Lexie asks.

I shake my head.

"Don't worry. There's a road that runs along the perimeter of the park," Trevor says. "Maybe they went that way." He leads us in the direction of the road and we walk at a brisk pace.

The quiet of the park freaks me out. We can hear the crackling of the fire and see the embers and smoke in the air, but no cars, no kids playing, no music, no sports; nothing else to convey that this area is a popular family entertainment spot. My feet hurt from running on the uneven ground and my pants keep snagging on my bandages.

I want to cry.

Again.

"This is ridiculous," I say. "Why are we even doing this? I can't anymore. I hurt. I'm bleeding. I'm tired. They clearly aren't here; we got the clues wrong. They probably weren't even clues at all. Maybe he wanted to go with her."

Lexie stops and grabs me by the shoulders, forcing me to face her. "Look, you admitted not even an hour ago that you are in love with this man. He came up here to tell you the same. He was taken away from you, at gunpoint, with his hands tied. But before he left he gave us clues. Multiple clues. So don't you dare stand here and ask why we are doing this or whether he wanted to go with her—"

An explosion sounds from atop the hill to the east of us, drawing our attention.

"Fires don't just blow up," Trevor says. "Something just happened over there."

"Do you think it's Chance?" I look at my friends.

Lexie returns my gaze. "Well, what are you waiting for? Let's go find out!"

We head in the direction of the explosion.

And the fire.

The closer we get, the more anxious I feel.

I just want to find Chance.

He has to be here.

He just has to be.

I break into a run, rocks digging into the soles of my shoes. The uneven terrain causing my ankles to twist about. My gaze sweeps back and forth across the road. I feel like I'm in a nightmare, where the road just stretches longer and longer, the destination getting farther and farther away. I'm going nowhere, finding nothing. I can't breathe. My eyes hurt from the smoke. My muscles are screaming, and I can feel the blood running down my legs.

It serves me right. This is what I get for opening myself up and trying to find love. It doesn't work. Not for me. I was better off before.

So stupid, Remi.

Something rolls into the road.

A tree? Is that an animal?

"Oh God," Kat says. "Is that—"

"That's a body," Trevor says.

It's Chance.

Somehow I just know.

I run faster, but it still takes forever to reach him. My lungs burn, my eyes are watering. The fire is so close. I just want to get to Chance. I need to get to Chance.

He's not moving.

Oh God, please don't be dead.

Please.

I'm so sorry.

I just want to try this with him one more time.

I stumble, nearly falling to my knees, I crawl the last few feet toward him.

"Chance, baby, are you okay?" I palm his face, trying to get him to respond. He's covered in dirt and blood. His beautiful face cut and starting to bruise. His eyes shut.

"Oh God, Kat, he's not responding. He's hurt! We have to help him."

Trevor uses a pocket knife to cut the twine binding Chance's wrists and then looks him over. "He's been shot. We need to stop the bleeding."

"I'm trying to get through to 9-1-1," Lexie says.

Chance's wrist wounds are covered in blood, dirt, and rocks. Trevor takes off his dress shirt and cuts off the sleeves, wrapping one around each of Chance's wrists. Then he uses the rest of his shirt to tie around the gunshot wound in his thigh.

"Chance, please wake up, baby, please. I need you. Don't leave me. Please. Oh God. I'm so sorry. I'm such an asshole." Tears pour down my face. Real tears that make me sob.

Chance opens his eyes slightly. "This you not crying, beautiful?"

I half laugh, half sob and throw myself over him. He flops an arm over my back and attempts to hug me.

"Don't go, baby, please. Don't go. We have so much to do together, still."

I hear him whisper, "Date questions," but I can see in his face when he slips back out of consciousness.

"I got through!" Lexie cries. "An ambulance is on the way."

"We've got to get out of here and closer to the edge of the park," Trevor says. "Ladies, do you think we can carry him?"

"I can help," Kat says.

"That's good, Kat, 'cause sorry to say but you and I are closest in height, so you're going to get the brunt of it with me. Lexie, Remi, let's get him up and drape his arms around Kat and my shoulders. Then you two can assist in supporting him by helping to hold him in place."

It's a struggle to get him up and draped around Kat and Trevor's shoulders. I know it has to hurt. Each time we grab his wrists for traction, we dig into the wounds even more. Dragging him down the road is near impossible. With each passing second, I feel him drifting farther and farther away.

The sound of sirens in the distance is a welcome relief. I just wish I knew if they were fire trucks on their way to the fires, or an ambulance on its way to save him.

Relief floods through me as I see a vehicle approaching.

The ambulance arrives in a blur, followed by two police cruisers. We give the officers an abbreviated version of what happened and a description of Helen. I feel so inadequate, not knowing much more than that about her.

Next thing I know, Chance is getting strapped to a stretcher and loaded in the back of the rig. They won't let me in the ambulance with Chance, so we run back to the car with renewed adrenaline and head to the hospital. One of the cruisers escorts us past the traffic, I have to wonder if we would get this kind of attention if he wasn't in law enforcement.

"Fuck, Trevor," Kat says. "I don't know where the hell you popped out of, but you pretty much saved the day, my friend."

"Thank you, Trevor," I say. "Even if…" I choke on my words. "Regardless of what happens, you got us here and we found him. I will be grateful to you forever for that."

"Anyone would have done the same," Trevor says.

"I doubt that," Lexie says with pride.

Oh yeah, she's still so gone for him.

I hear a phone ding with a text. We all check ours to see whose it is. Kat holds a phone out to me.

"It's Bauer's," she says.

I take the phone, unsure as to whether I want to check his text messages. There's no lock on his phone so as soon as I swipe, the screen comes to life. The text is from his sister, Charlie. I open it.

Charlie: I sure as hell hope you went after her and groveled your little ass off.

I half laugh/half cry at the text.

Kat reads it over my shoulder.

"Oh God," she says. "They don't know any of this has happened. You need to call them, Rem."

"I don't think I can," I whisper. "This is all my fault. God, Kat, if he dies, they will all hate me. It will ruin his family."

She grabs my hand and squeezes it. "None of this is your fault. Helen is the one who did this, not you. His family will understand that. He's not going to die. He's a tough motherfucker. I mean, no doubt he's going to be messed up. You can't prevent that. But you can help to prepare them by letting them know what's going on before the hospital does."

She has a point.

I hit the button to call Charlie.

She answers after the first ring. "Shit, if you're calling me this quickly it means you totally pussed out, didn't you?"

"Charlie?" I ask, my voice barely a croak.

"Remi? Is that you?" she asks. "What's wrong? Where's Chance? Is everything okay?"

"No," I say, then burst into tears. I can't breathe. I can't talk. All I can do is cry. Kat takes the phone from me and explains everything to Charlie. She says she'll alert her family and they will meet us at the hospital.

I bury my face in my hands to hide my tears.

Please don't die, Chance.

Please.

We get to the hospital, Trevor drops me and Kat off at the entrance while he and Lexie find a place to park.

We find the front desk and ask about Chance.

"Only immediate family is allowed any information. You are?" the nurse asks.

I freeze.

What am I?

"She's his wife," Kat says.

I stand up straight and try to look wifely. The nurse looks at us, eyes narrowed. But anyone can see how distraught I am. That has to count for something.

Deciding to believe us, she says, "They are taking him in to surgery. If you want to wait down the hall, the doctor will be in to give you an update as soon as he can."

Kat grabs my hand and holds it tightly as we head down the hall toward the waiting area.

"Maybe we can get someone to look at your cuts while we're here," Kat suggests. I give her a look in return that I hope convinces her of how little I care about her idea.

"Remi, what good are you to Chance if your cuts get infected or you get sick?"

She has a point. We flag a nurse down, who has me fill out some paperwork, then takes me into an exam room to check everything out.

"My God, what happened to you," she asks once I've stripped out of my clothes.

"My uh, boy… husband's ex held me hostage and cut me up with a scalpel."

She laughs. Then looks up, realizing I'm serious. "Oh my God."

"He's the one in surgery right now with a gunshot to the leg. She shot him."

"Jeez," she says. "You're definitely winning first prize for whacked out emergency room story of the day."

I grunt in reply.

"Sorry," the nurse continues. "That was incredibly insensitive."

"It's okay. Really. The story is seriously fucked up. And the worst part is, I don't know where she went after she shot him."

"Have you told the police?" she asks.

"Oh, yeah," I say. "We told them everything that happened and stuff, but I wanted to get to the hospital to check on him more than I wanted to stick around and file the report."

She nods her head. "I understand."

She finishes checking the bandaged cuts and tells me that Kat and Lexie did an excellent job of cleaning and bandaging everything. And that the ointment she put on will prevent infection and minimize scarring. She leaves the room, and I re-dress, grateful she didn't try to continue a conversation.

I'm barely back in the waiting room to let Kat know I'm okay as Chance's parents rush into the room. Or at least, that's how fast it seems.

"Oh, Remi, dear girl, how are you? Have they told you anything? Is he okay? Of course he is, he's a strong boy. What happened?" Annalise and Brian both speak at the same time. Annalise has been crying.

We sit down, and I tell the two everything that I know, with Kat interjecting every so often to clarify. Lexie and Trevor arrive soon after, with Eliza and Audrey right behind them and Charlie bringing up the rear. We fill them all in on what we know, and then we settle in to wait. I think I doze off because I wake to someone saying the words I've been waiting to hear for hours. "Mrs. Bauer?"

I jump up at the same time as Chance's mom. "Yes?" we both say. She looks at me, eyebrows raised. My face reddens with embarrassment.

Kat jumps to my defense. "This is his *wife* and his mother, doctor. Both have the same title." She looks around at the Bauer family. No one says a word to the contrary.

Annalise, Brian, and I approach the doctor. He tells us that the bullet had lodged in Chance's thigh and he'd lost a lot of blood. But that Trevor tying off the wound when he did, saved his life. They were able to remove the bullet in surgery, but it did hit his femur at just the right angle to shatter it. Once he recovers from the gunshot wound, he'll still require physical therapy for the femur injury. They will try to get him up and walking as soon as possible, but he will still require someone to help him with everyday activities for the first week or so. In addition to a wheelchair and then crutches.

"Oh my, he's going to just hate that, isn't he Remi, dear?" Annalise says.

I nod dumbly.

"When can we see him?" Brian asks.

"He's coming out of surgery now and can have limited visitation once he wakes. Immediate family only. Wife, parents, maybe a sibling or two. But I can't stress enough the importance of rest right now."

"We understand." Brian nods.

"I'll have the nurse get you once he's awake," the doctor tells Brian.

Annalise clutches my arm as we return to our seats.

"Now, don't you worry, Remi, dear. Chancey is a strong boy. It's not his time yet. He still has to give me Bauer-named grandbabies." She pats me on the back as she says that. It's all I can do to halt my sputter at the idea. I'm barely used to the idea of a relationship. Babies are nowhere on my radar.

Kat comes to sit on the other side of me. She pulls my head down to her shoulder and smooths my hair back.

"Have you heard from Brad?" I ask.

She nods. "He and Ethan are good. And the Rainbow Park fire is eighty-five percent contained."

"That's fantastic," I say. She nods.

"Wow. You okay?" I ask her.

She nods again. "Just blows my mind sometimes when I think about what Brad does for a living."

"He would never put himself in harm's way," I say.

"I know," she says. "But sometimes harm has a mysterious way of finding you."

"Kat," I say. "I didn't come all this way in my little love journey, that you practically forced me into I might add, just to have you be single again. Not happening. We're going to be in this relationship shit together. For a long time. I need you to help me navigate. How else will I survive?"

"You always know how to straighten a girl right up, Rem," she says. "You just make it all about you instead of her." She smiles. I smile back.

The nurse approaches. "Chance Bauer family?"

"Yes," I say, at the same time Brian says, "We're right here."

"I can take you back now," she says to the three of us. "He's asking for Remi, I'm guessing that's you?" she says just to me.

I nod. Relieved to hear that he's asking for me. That's got to be a good sign. Right?

Still, we reach his room, and I pause. Why the hell am I here with his parents? His sisters should be here. Or someone else. Hell, even Kat deserves to be here more than I do.

"He asked for you, dear," Annalise says quietly, as if recognizing my hesitation.

I steel my shoulders and walk in.

Nothing could have prepared me for Chance in a hospital bed. Somehow, this big hulk of a man looks frail. With the IV in his arm, bandages and an oxygen mask covering his face, machines beeping all around him, and his wounded leg elevated slightly.

I make my way to his side, slowly, not sure if I should touch him. I lean down and kiss his hand. His eyes flutter open and he slowly pulls the oxygen mask from his face.

"You're here," he sighs. "You okay?" His voice is all gravel and rough.

Tears stream down my cheeks at a rapid rate. "I'm good, great," I sob.

"Not crying," he rasps with a hint of a smile.

"I'm not crying," I say, wiping at my eyes.

"Beautiful," he whispers. I lean down and kiss him softly. His lips one of the only areas on his face that don't appear cut up and scraped. He looks beyond me, seeing his parents.

"Ma."

"Don't talk, Chancey," Annalise says, choking back a sob. "Just rest. You just rest and know that we love you. We'll be here when you wake up." She leans down and kisses him on the cheek. Brian does the same. And even though I know they are close, it amazes me to see affection from parent to child. Especially parent to adult child. They leave me alone with Chance after a few minutes.

I pull a chair up next to his bedside, and lay down with my head on his chest, my hands clutching his.

I need more.

I don't feel safe.

I need his arms around me.

"Come here," he rasps. As if he knows my thoughts. I crawl into the hospital bed next to him and make myself as small as possible. He scoots over with a groan. I hate that he's in such pain. But then he puts his arm around me and pulls me into his chest.

"Thank you for coming after me," he says, his voice barely above a whisper.

"I'm pretty sure I would do anything for you," I breathe.

"Look at me," he says.

I want to. But I'm afraid. This moment that I feel we are about to have. It's too much. I'm feeling too much.

Then why are you here in his hospital bed, Remi?

I take everything in around me: the antiseptic smells, the heat of his body, the firmness of the mattress, the cool push of the bed's handrail at my back. Then I let my eyes travel up his body toward his. His chest, rising and falling steadily beneath his hospital gown. His neck, tanned from the sun and still slightly dirty from his roll down the hill. His lips which are so soft when they are on me, yet so commanding when they speak. And finally his eyes, so piercing and blue, and shining with love. It takes my breath away.

45

CHANCE

I muster all the strength I can to talk. I have to tell Remi, I can't wait any longer.

"I'm gonna take a chance here. I get that it might scare you, but it's got to be said, Remi." I inhale deeply and let it out slowly, the effort causes me to cough. I don't want her to run. But if going through Helen abducting and hurting us both has shown me anything, it's how much I love her. I want her in my life. For the rest of my life. Of that I'm certain. I want to protect her, shelter her, make her laugh, make her coffee. Make her mine.

"I love you, Chance."

I want to hear it so badly, I'm certain I've imagined it. I look at her, her eyes bright and clear. Her expression filled with love. Even though I see it on her face, I want to hear it.

"Say it again."

"I love you." She says it with more conviction this time. But even if she didn't, her eyes shine with it. Plain as day. My beautiful closed-off girl is letting all the emotions shine through.

I use my free hand to cup her cheek. The IV hindering my movement a bit. She nuzzles my palm, her eyes closed. I wait until she opens them again. "I love you. More than anything in this world. You are it for me. I'm so sorry this happened. So sorry about Helen. I swear I will never let anyone hurt you ever again, Remi. I will spend the rest of my life making this up to you."

"There's nothing to make up for," she says. "All I wanted is for you to be okay."

We lay there for a minute. She shifts on the bed, wincing slightly.

"Did you have someone look at your cuts?" I ask.

She nods, then asks, "What happened out there? Why did she shoot you? Where did she go?"

"She was driving straight into the fire, it was like she didn't even see it. Or she didn't care. I tried to get her to stop, to turn around, but she just kept accelerating, trying to get her car up the hill."

"The top of the hill was where your date was?" Remi asks.

I nod. "She never stopped, Remi. I still don't know how I managed to get the car door open and that's when she shot me. I managed to roll out, but she still didn't stop the car. Helen drove straight into the fire."

"I'm so sorry, Chance," Remi says, turning to kiss my chest.

"Oh, beautiful, you have nothing to be sorry for. I'm the one who is sorry."

"I'm fine," she says. "You, on the other hand, have been shot, your leg is all broken up, and your ex apparently just committed suicide by fire."

A small part of me wishes we'd been able to get Helen the help she so obviously needed. As much as I hate her for what she did, I know that it wasn't her doing it. It was her illness and she just needed help. Help that we couldn't give her. I pull Remi tighter into me, so grateful to have her here.

A light knock on the door, then it opens. "Just wanted to make sure one of you hasn't killed the other yet," Kat says.

"Not funny," Remi says.

"We've got a bet going at the station, Bauer. I give you two weeks before she kills you in your sleep. And I'm being generous."

I smile at Kat, then turn my head to kiss my girl on the forehead.

My girl.

I'm still amazed she's here.

"Still not funny," Remi says to Kat. "You haven't had a chance to go to the station to make a bet. And you aren't even a real cop. So, shut the fuck up."

"Someone's a little touchy," Kat says.

"He almost died today, Kat," Remi whispers harshly.

"He's fine," Kat says. "Look at him, he's a fucking tank."

"See?" I look up at Remi and nod my head in agreement. "Fucking tank." But then I start coughing and quickly lose my breath. Remi moves the oxygen mask back over my mouth. It's hard to be a bad ass when you can't breathe.

The girls move to leave soon after and I take a minute to tell Lexie how much I appreciate her and Trevor. Remi's eyes start to tear up, so I stop and let them leave.

"Love you guys," Remi says after them.

"Love you more," Lexie says. Kat turns back and blows us a kiss. They close the door softly behind them, only to have it open right back up.

My sisters come into the room. Remi tries to push away from me to get out of the bed, but I don't let her. She relaxes her body and lays back down.

It's clear that Audrey and Eliza have been crying. Charlie, not so much. But she's a lot like Remi in that way. Won't show her emotions to others.

"Always have to grandstand for attention, don't you, Chancey?" Charlie says.

I shrug my free shoulder and pull the mask away again. "It worked. I got the girl," I say with a smile.

Audrey comes toward us. "Remi, how are you? I heard, well, Helen..."

"I'm fine, Audrey, thank you for asking," Remi says.

I turn and kiss her forehead. My girl is tough.

"I just wanted to tell you both I love you, and I'm so happy you are okay," Eliza says. Remi stiffens in my arms.

Eliza notices. "Are you okay?" she asks Remi.

"Remi is going to have to get used to affection and attention," I tell my sister. Guessing as to Remi's sudden discomfort. When she relaxes back against me, I know I was right. "We have to go slow with her at first, Eliza. Ease into the endearments."

Remi slaps me lightly on the chest. "I'm not that bad."

Charlie and I both laugh. "Two peas, one pod," Charlie says to Remi. "I've got your number, like recognizes like. They're my freaking family and I still have a hard time with it. You'll get used to it. They are all a bunch of gummy sweetness inside. Especially Mom, watch out for her."

I laugh even as a wave of exhaustion washes over me. And I know that I've been talking too much. Doing too much. Audrey must see it on my face. "We're gonna go. I'll let everyone else know that you're doing okay."

"Thank you, Audrey," Remi says with a yawn. I have a feeling the day is catching up to her as well.

My sisters leave the room, closing the door softly behind them.

"I should go too," Remi says trying to push herself up.

"You aren't going anywhere, woman. I've finally got you back in my arms, I'm not letting go now. Stay with me. Please."

She snuggles farther into my side and swings one leg over mine. I'm happy she's on the side that wasn't shot.

"I love you, Remi."

"I love you, Chance."

I put the mask back over my face, close my eyes, and listen as Remi's breathing evens, until I'm certain she's fallen asleep.

Then, feeling at peace for the first time in days, I do the same.

EPILOGUE

Chance – Six Weeks Later

My family has a barbecue planned for today to celebrate my 'graduation' from the wheelchair to crutches. My leg has been healing nicely, and faster than the doctor predicted. I've followed all of his instructions, for the most part. We did start having sex sooner than I should have. But when you are in love with a woman like Remi, you can't help yourself. Or at least, I can't help myself.

She practically forced me to move in with her after I was released from the hospital. I'll admit, it didn't take a lot of convincing. One, because I am head over heels gone for this girl. And two, because my apartment is upstairs, with no elevator. So getting to it was near impossible. Her house is a one-story mid-century rambler on a large lot with a fenced yard, and Hudson loves it. I deprived him of a decent yard for too long.

Plus, her house feels like home. I mean, I think anywhere I was living with Remi would feel like home, but it's also just comfortable here. It's not too knick-knacky or refined and the furniture is big and cushy, made for sitting in. For as particular, and dare I say uptight, as she is about everything else, her house is all relaxation. I can even put my feet on the coffee table. Well, as long as I don't have shoes on. And not just because I can't bend one of my legs and it has to remain slightly elevated. She puts her feet up on it too.

Remi comes down the hallway to the living room, connecting a back to one of her earrings. She looks incredible, as usual. Today she's 'casual' in a tank style jumpsuit that is fitted on the top and cuts in at the waist, then a little loose at the hips and legs. My girl knows how to dress for her curves, that's for sure.

"You look amazing, beautiful," I say. She looks up, eyes wide, then her face breaks into a smile. Even after a few months, she's still not used to a compliment.

She comes toward me, wrapping her arms around my neck, I balance on my crutches and place my hands on her hips. Which makes me think of earlier when she was riding me. Head thrown back, eyes closed, mouth open, tits bouncing, screaming my name through her third orgasm. Turns out she likes to be on top.

I still can't do much pummeling with my leg in a cast, so it works great for me. Though I can't wait until I can be in control of the fucking again. Taking her from behind. That luscious round ass tilted up in the air, her head hung low, tits swaying back and forth, pounding into her until she cries out my name and can't remember her own.

"Well, someone is at attention," she says referring to my hardening cock, then kissing me lightly on the lips.

"I was thinking about this morning," I say. Her gaze turns hot and her face flushes slightly.

"This morning was amazing," she says slightly breathless.

I nuzzle her neck. "Then I was thinking about when I finally get to fuck you from behind again."

"You were behind me the other day," she says, referring to when we laid on our sides.

"I want you on your knees." I bite down lightly on her earlobe.

"Oh," she says, her body shivering.

God, this woman. I can't believe she's mine.

"Only me?" I ask. Still not able to fully comprehend that such an incredible creature, such a sexual being, didn't orgasm at the hands of another before me.

"Only you," she says.

I capture her lips with mine and quickly deepen the kiss. Not caring that I'll probably mess up her lipstick and end up with a faint red stain around my lips. She slows the kiss, then pulls away, slowly opening her eyes.

"What was that for?" she asks.

"Because I love you," I say, kissing her on the tip of her nose.

"You know, I thought it would annoy me, you saying that all the time. But it doesn't. I kind of like it."

I laugh. "I'm glad."

"Hey, it works," she says, running her thumb under my bottom lip.

"What works?"

"New lipstick. Long last, smudge proof. There's nothing on you. Is it smeared on me?"

I inspect her lips. "Still intact, you look flawless."

She smiles big. "You ready to go?"

"Lead the way," I say, motioning with my crutch toward the door.

"You just want to watch my ass when I walk away," she says.

"Every day, baby. Every fucking day."

∽

We arrive at the BBQ a little late. Remi is still getting used to driving the rental car and takes it slow. It's a little crossover SUV we had to rent since I can't fit my casted leg into her little vintage Porsche. Truth be told, I'd much rather have her driving something larger, with more metal protection around her. But she loves her car.

I had a service driving me around for a while when I was in the wheelchair, but they don't provide it any longer now that I've transitioned to crutches. I hate that Remi has to drive me everywhere. Which makes getting to drive myself again another thing I can't wait for.

I'm living at her house, waiting for her to drive me places, and only making sixty percent of my previous pay, thanks to disability. It doesn't get more emasculating than that. I try to make up for it by giving her as many orgasms as possible. Even if she doesn't appreciate it, which I'm pretty sure she does. It helps to make me still feel like a man. I never would have thought losing the use of a limb, temporary though it may be, would have such an impact on my self-confidence. But it does.

We pull up outside my parents' house. Remi shuts off the car and turns to me. "Do you need help getting out?"

"Pfft, no. I got this," I say.

"Good," she says. She gets out of the car and turns back to me before shutting the door. "Because I think I'm pregnant. And I'm freaking the fuck out. Audrey brought a pregnancy test with her today, I'm going to take it here at your parents' house."

She shuts the car door and strolls up the front walk toward the door. Audrey and Eliza were obviously waiting by the front door because it opens before she even reaches the stoop, and they quickly usher her in.

What the fuck?

I knocked my girl up?

She's pregnant?

Fuck, yes!

I'm the man!

My leg may be weak, but my swimmers are strong.

Remi is mine. All mine. And soon she'll be swelling with my baby and everyone will see my mark on her.

I punch my right fist in the air in victory, hitting the ceiling of the car. Which would hurt, except I'm way too pumped about Remi's news.

Pregnant.

I bungle my way out of the car with my crutches and head toward the house. Feeling full of manly testosterone and all sorts of other anti-emasculating things.

Yeah. I'm the fucking man.

Remi

Audrey, Eliza, and I squeeze into the upstairs guest bathroom. The same one that Chance got me off in one of the first times I was here. I remember it feeling so strange that day. Trying to fit into this family and understand their close dynamic. Now it's natural, because they feel like they are my family too.

"Okay," Audrey says. "We each got a different one so we can be sure. Use as many as you need." Audrey and Eliza both hand me their boxes. I sit down on the closed toilet seat and open each with trembling hands. I never would have thought the day would come that I would be taking a pregnancy test.

"You know," I say. "I'm not even sure I want kids. I mean, I've never thought about it before. I didn't even really want a relationship a few months ago. Now I've got this guy living with me and I might be pregnant with his baby. Don't you think that's a little fast?"

"Nope," both Audrey and Eliza say simultaneously.

"We Bauers have always moved fast in love," Eliza says. "I knew Nate was the one after our first date."

"It wasn't that fast for me with Mike," Audrey says. "And I'll tell you, Remi, you may feel like you have doubts, but there is no doubt in anyone else's mind how much you love my brother. It's all over your face when you're with him."

"But, that doesn't mean we should have a baby," I say.

"Doesn't mean you shouldn't," Eliza says.

"Fine," I say. I open a test from each box and set them out on the bathroom counter. I stand and lift the toilet seat, then turn, gesturing for one of them to unzip my jumpsuit in the back.

"It's a good thing nudity doesn't make me uncomfortable," I say to them as I peel my underwear down with the jumpsuit and sit back down on the toilet.

"Okay," Audrey says. "With each one, you have to hold it under the stream for a few seconds, so make sure you stop going in the middle then start again with the second test."

I nod my head and grab the first test, and wait.

"God, your breasts are fantastic," Eliza says. "Breastfeeding is going to ruin them."

My hands go up to my breasts instinctively and cup them. The first test still in my right hand.

"Shit, I didn't even think about what it's going to do to my body. I can't do this. I have a hard enough time with my weight as it is!" I say.

"Are you kidding me? You have such an amazing body," Audrey says.

"Says the tall, willowy model with no muffin top," I say sourly.

"Right?" Eliza says in my defense.

Audrey waves her hand at us in dismissal. "Can you pee?" she asks.

I nod and concentrate, do my thing with each test stick, redress, wash my hands and wait the requisite three minutes.

"Where do your parents think we are?" I ask.

"Dad won't notice we're gone," Eliza says.

"And Mom thinks we're getting your opinion on maternity fashion," Audrey says.

"Charlie wasn't here yet, so she doesn't matter," Eliza says.

The timer Audrey set on her phone goes off. We all look at each other.

"I think I'm going to be sick," I say, bending over to put my head between my knees.

"Oh, that's definitely a sign," Audrey says clapping her hands.

"What do they say?" I ask, still bent over. Part of me wishes I was doing this with Kat and Lexie. But I've grown close to Audrey and Eliza over the last couple months, and I definitely appreciate them being here. I don't think I could do this alone. I'm not sure what I want. I'm hoping the results will tell me what I want.

Like, if I'm pregnant and I'm happy about it, then I'll know having a baby is the right choice. Although I guess if I'm not pregnant and I'm sad about it, that is the same thing.

So, what if I'm pregnant and I'm sad about it? Do I abort? Does Chance get a say either way? Does his family?

Fuck.

I wish I knew what I wanted.

"Ready?" Eliza asks.

"Ah! Yes. No. Yes," I say.

"Pregnant!" Audrey and Eliza both say at the same time.

∽

Chance

My dad and Mike have to help me bounce on one leg up the stairs to get to Remi. According to Audrey, she fainted in the guest bathroom and hit her head on the sink.

"What were you all doing in the same bathroom anyway?" my dad asks once we enter Audrey's old bedroom.

"Girl talk," Eliza says.

Remi is laying on the bed with an ice pack on her forehead.

"Baby, are you okay?" I ask as I perch myself on the side of the bed.

"I'm fine," she says. "It was just stupid."

I peel the ice pack away. "You're going to have quite a goose egg," I tell her.

"I know," she says. "Eliza warned me already."

My mom enters the room with Hailey in her arms. "Remi, dear, do you need anything? Would you like some soup?"

"No. Thank you, Mrs. Bauer," she says.

"Memi, Memi, Memi!" Hailey cries, having developed quite the attachment to Remi over the last few weeks. I'm just glad that for Hailey, Remi comes out as Memi, and not Mimi. My mom sets Hailey down and she waddles to the bed, pulling herself up by my pant leg.

"Memi. Booboo," Hailey says. Then she hits me on the thigh. "Kiss it."

I lean over and lightly kiss the goose egg forming on Remi's forehead.

"All bettah, yay," Hailey says, clapping her hands.

"Well, you come back down when, or if, you feel better, Remi dear," my mom says as she hustles everyone else out of the room. "Let's go, people," she says. "I've got enough to feed an army and I don't want leftovers."

They leave the room and shut the door behind them.

"We were taking the test," Remi whispers.

"The test?" I ask, with a smile.

"Yes," she says. "And, I'm—"

"Don't tell me," I say quickly.

She looks at me, head cocked, brow furrowed.

"Marry me," I say. "Marry me and then tell me."

"Chance, weddings take forever to plan. I think in the next few months you'd be able to figure it out either way." She smiles.

"We'll go tomorrow," I say. The idea growing on me the more that I think about it. "We'll call Kat and Lexie, we'll go to the courthouse tomorrow, and we'll make it official. Then you can tell me."

"What difference does it make?" she asks.

"Because," I say. "I want you to know that I love you for you. And I've wanted to marry you almost since the moment I met you. I never want you to think I'd want to marry you because you were, or weren't, pregnant. So if we do it before I know any better, you'll always know I wanted you. Just you."

She blanches when I say that.

"And our future kids. Just you and our future kids. Don't mistake what I'm saying," I say. "I just want to make sure you understand that I want to marry you because of you. And not because you're carrying my baby. If you are, that is."

She looks at me, her eyes squinting slightly.

I think she's actually considering it.

"Would it help if I gave you a ring?" I ask.

"You have a ring?" she asks.

"Well, no," I say. "But I am wondering if it would help if I did."

"No." She laughs as she says it.

I look at her, eyebrows raised in question. She looks at me, brow furrowed in concentration.

"Oh, what the hell?" she says. "Let's do it."

"That's my girl!" I say, pulling her into a hug. "Nothing like a *what the hell* to make a guy feel deserving of a proposal."

~

Remi – Five Months Later

"Ready, wife?" Chance asks me, reaching over to squeeze my hand.

"Just help me get out of the car," I say. He's been calling me wife for like five months. I can't tell if it annoys me or not. I mean, it still blows my mind that we are married. And that we are having twins. I never, not once, thought this would be my life. But I'm settling into it okay.

I think.

We bought an SUV a few months ago. Which is good because I can't get my fucking stomach behind the wheel of my beautiful Porsche. God, I miss her. She's under a tarp in the garage. It's not fair, because Chance still gets to ride his motorcycle, but I'm forever stuck in this monstrosity of an ozone layer killer.

Today we get to find out the sex of the babies. Chance runs around to my side of the car and helps me get out.

"Have I told you today that I love you?" he asks. A question he asks almost every day, even though he does tell me he loves me. Multiple times, every day.

I smile. "I don't think so," I say, playing along.

"I love you," he says. We get to the elevator bay and he moves to stand behind me as we wait. "You know, you get more beautiful every day." He reaches around and rubs my belly as we wait for the elevator. "More desirable." He nuzzles my neck and nips at my collarbone.

"If by beautiful and desirable, you mean fat with cankles, then I believe you."

"Feel that?" he asks as he presses up against my ass, and whispers in my ear, "I think about you, I touch you, I smell you, I'm near you, and I'm hard."

My body shivers, and I'm not cold. The worst thing about pregnancy? The drastic hormonal mood swings. I'm pissed and self-conscious one second, and a horny out of control sex monster the next. I lean back against him.

"Chance," I breathe. He moves his hands lower, under my belly, beneath the waistband of my pants and between my legs. Two fingers sink inside me.

"Oh," I cry.

"Mmm," he says into my neck. "Wet already. You fucking wreck me, woman."

He uses his thumb to caress my clit, while his fingers pump in and out of me. I'm going to come in a matter of seconds.

"Oh my God, Chance, I'm going to—" I fall apart in his arms as my orgasm roars through me. A spectacular rush of white lights exploding behind my eyes, my body shudders and my limbs turn to something akin to Jell-O. He pulls his hand out of my pants and pulls me back against him. The elevator dings, and the doors open. An older gentleman is inside.

I can smell myself. I'm sure the man can too. Chance positions himself behind me in the elevator.

"Three, please," Chance says. The man presses the appropriate button for us.

Chance leans his chin on my shoulder, then brings his fingers to his mouth, the same fingers that were just inside me, and licks them.

"Mmmm," he moans softly. "My favorite taste in the world."

A shiver runs through me. Again.

The elevator stops, the man gets out. I turn to slap Chance on the chest.

"That was fucking hot, but someone could have seen!" I say.

"My beautiful wife," he says. "Do you really think I would finger fuck you if someone else could see?"

He has a point.

"No," I say.

"No," he says, leaning in and kissing me on the forehead.

We reach our floor and head into the doctor's office.

Chance checks us in, and I try to find a decent magazine to read, vacillating between news and fashion.

I want a magazine in front of my face because I never want to get caught talking to any of the other moms. They all have such stars in their eyes over being pregnant. Like it's the most wonderful thing in the world. I hate it. I have mood swings, none of my shoes fit, I have to wear maternity clothes, and I'm fat. None of which seems to upset these other women. So, either I'm cold and unfeeling, or they are vapid and idiotic. I don't care to examine that too much to figure out which holds the most truth.

I look back to the magazine selections, but we get called back to the room before I can make my decision.

The nurse checks my vitals, then preps the ultrasound machine. Chance pulls out his phone and video conferences Kat and Lexie before the appointment officially starts. Just like he does with every appointment. Because he knows, and understands, that it's important to me to have my entire family with me at these appointments.

"Ohmigod, I'm so excited!" Lexie squeals. "I can't wait to hear what we are having!"

"It's going to be girls," Kat says. "It has to be. Boys would be a nightmare. Can you imagine two little Bauers running around? Shoot me now."

I laugh at them. So grateful for their support.

Chance pulls his chair closer, resting his forearms on the edge of the exam table. His eyes already shining before she even pulls up the image. If he were remotely vapid or idiotic, he would be the male version of those women in the waiting room.

She squirts the lubrication on my stomach then moves the wand around. We hear the heartbeats, sounding like a herd of thundering hooves, racing to see whose will be heard first.

"Oh, look at that," the tech says pointing out something that looks just like every other piece of baby blob on the screen.

"What?" Chance asks.

"Congratulations, Chance, Remi, Kat, Lexie. The Bauer babies are boys. Twin boys," the tech says.

"Oh God, not boys!" Kat says.

"I think boys will be fun," Lexie counters.

"Oh wait..." the tech pauses.

Chance and I both lean toward her, waiting.

"What?" Lexie asks.

"Did I miss something?" Kat asks.

"Is everything okay?" Chance asks.

"I think," the tech says. "Yep... there's another little guy in there. You've got yourselves a set of triplets!"

The world starts to spin around me. I feel faint.

"Woohoo, one for each of us!" Lexie cries, at the same time Kat says, "Oh, shit, you're gonna be outnumbered."

Chance fist pumps the air and says, "Yes! I'm the man!" As he starts dancing to his own tune in his head.

My husband preening around the room is the last thing I see before I faint.

~

Chance – Two Months Later

The babies came early, which the doctor warned us might happen. Remi handled their birth like a fucking champ. Eleven hours of hard labor before they brought her in for a C-section. And if that wasn't the most horrifying and beautiful thing all at once…

Seeing your wife on the operating table being cut open. Some guy pushing his hands inside her. And then, just like that, there's a baby. Or, in our case three babies. Kat, Lexie, and I have spent the last few hours in the NICU, taking turns cooing at each of them.

Brian. Braden. Brianna.

Yep, number three is a girl. I'm scared to death about that. But it made Remi happy, she said it evened the score and she wouldn't feel so outnumbered. I didn't have the heart to remind her that the kids outnumber us anyway.

We should get to take them home in a couple of days. I'm excited and nervous. I feel like Remi and I barely have a handle on being with one another and now three more people will be with us. Which reminds me I want to check on her.

I leave Kat and Lexie with the babies and head back to Remi's room to check on her. My mom is still sitting in the chair next to her bed, knitting booties and stocking caps, like when I left her hours ago.

"Ma, go home, we're fine," I whisper.

"I know you are, Chancey. She was in some pain and I just wanted to make sure she got something for it and got to sleep," she whispers back.

"Thank you," I say softly. "Now go, you've got some packing to do."

My parents leave for the big trip in less than a week. Ma was frantic when she realized the timing might coincide with the babies' birth. She was the only one who was excited when they came early. Well, she and Lexie.

I get her out the door and then pull a chair up next to Remi's bed and watch her. She's sound asleep, which is good considering she'd gotten almost no sleep in the weeks leading up to the birth.

My beautiful angel who blew back into my life after ten years and rocked my world all over again. It's crazy to think it's been barely over a year. Now I can't imagine my life without her.

The door opens softly, and Kat peeks her head in.

"They kicked us out so we're going to take off. She doing okay?"

"Yeah," I say, walking to the door. "She's sleeping."

I give both Lexie and Kat a hug and kiss on the cheek. These women who have become as important to me as they are to Remi. This extended family that brings so much joy to our lives and who are going to love my kids like their own.

I watch them walk down the hall a bit before turning back to my wife.

My wife.

I still can't get over that she picked me.

Then married me.

And had my babies.

I sit back down in the chair and pick up her hand to kiss it.

"I'm so lucky to have you," I whisper. "I love you so much. Thank you for being in my life. For being my wife."

"Hey," she mumbles, opening her eyes slightly.

"Hey, beautiful. Everything is okay, go back to sleep."

"Babies okay?"

"The babies are perfect."

"Lay with me?"

I slip onto the bed behind her, careful not to jostle her or the IV coming out of her.

She takes my hand and tucks it under her cheek with her own.

"Love you," she says, sleepily.

"I love you more," I say.

"Thank you," she sighs.

"For?"

"Giving me the life I never knew I wanted," she says.

"I'll give you anything in the world, beautiful."

"Mmmm," she replies.

Her breathing slows, and I close my eyes and try to sleep. I'm too keyed up by everything that has happened today.

"Chance," she says a few minutes later.

"Yeah, baby?"

"You're humming that fucking song again."

"I can't help it, beautiful. It's my jam. And it's never fit more than today."

"Mmmhmm," she says.

"Remi?"

"Yes."

"Will you do it? Just once? Please."

She sighs.

"Who's the man?" she asks.

Fuck yes. I am SO the man.

BAUER'S BAD-ASS JAMS

"Stranglehold" by Ted Nugent

"Burnin' For You" by Blue Oyster Cult

"Sunshine Of Your Love" by Eric Clapton

"You'll Accomp'ny Me" by Bob Seger

"Cinnamon Girl" by Neil Young and Crazy Horse

"Fortunate Son" by Credence Clearwater Revival

"Can't You See" by The Marshall Tucker Band

"Sweet Home Alabama" by Lynyrd Skynyrd

"Blinded By The Light" by Manfred Mann's Earth Band

"La Grange" by ZZ Top

"Feels Like The First Time" by Foreigner

"Roadhouse Blues" by The Doors

"You Can't Always Get What You Want" by The Rolling Stones

"Live And Let Die" by Paul McCartney and The Wings

"Feel Like Makin' Love" by Bad Company

"Simple Man" by Lynyrd Skynyrd

"Philadelphia Freedom" by Elton John

"Reelin' In The Years" by Steely Dan

"Stone In Love" by Journey

"Free Ride" by The Edgar Winter Group

"Jet" by Paul McCartney and The Wings

"Band On The Run" by Paul McCartney and The Wings

"Emotional Rescue" by The Rolling Stones

"Baby I Love Your Way" by Peter Frampton

"Ain't Talkin' 'Bout Love" by Van Halen

"Thunderstruck" by AC/DC

"Lick It Up" by Kiss

"Ready For Love" by Bad Company

And, of course,

"The Man" by The Killers

THANK YOU FOR READING!

If you enjoyed this book, please consider leaving a review. Hell, even if you didn't enjoy it please consider leaving one. That way I'll know what to change for next time.

If you want to know more about my books and new releases, join my newsletter!

~

Positive mental health is important at every stage of life for our psychological, emotional, and social well-being. If you or someone you know suffers from mental illness, please get help. Resources like MentalHealth.gov provide valuable information on how to help yourself and others.

~

Much thanks to such organizations as:

The American Cancer Society

METAVIVOR

Breast Cancer Research Foundation

For their tireless efforts in fighting a horrible disease. And providing support to my loved ones during their times of need. We appreciate you.

IF YOU ENJOYED . . .

Did you enjoy reading about Remi and Chance? You can get more of them, along with Charlie Bauer's story in: OVERDRIVE (A KB Driven World Novel)

How do you send a fake relationship into overdrive?

Turn it into something real.

With your best friend's ex.

Who hates you.

My life is about risk - racing cars for a living. So, a fake girlfriend should have been no more dangerous than anything else.

It was supposed to be temporary, just a few fake meet-ups, nothing too serious.

A small white lie to help fix my so-called "bad" reputation.

Who would have thought I'd want more than a few dates?

Not me.

Or that the girl who was supposed to be my fake something would turn into my very real everything?

Also not me.

The question is, do I let her believe it's all still pretend?

Or tell her how I feel and wait to see what happens?

ABOUT THE AUTHOR

Denise has been reading since before she could talk. And to this day, escaping into a book is her go-to activity before anything else.

She likes to write about sassy women and semi-flawed alpha-esque men (hard on the outside and just a little soft on the inside.) Denise's female characters always have strong friendships, potty mouths, and like to drink—a lot.

Denise is loyal to a fault, a bit too sarcastic, blindingly optimistic, and pretty freakin' happy with life overall. If she couldn't be a writer, she'd be a singer in a classic rock band. Right after she learned to carry a tune. She has more purses than days in the month, an obsession with colored ink pens, and a slightly unhealthy bracelet habit.

Home is in the Pacific Northwest where she lives with five Siberian Huskies and a husband (BW) who has the patience and tolerance of a saint. And, lest she forget, Denise also lives with too many to count characters inside her head, who will eventually have their stories told.

For more about Denise visit her website at: www.DeniseWells.com

Or follow her on any of the social media sites below.

ALSO BY DENISE WELLS

AGENTS AND ASSASSINS TRILOGY

Fearless - Book One, a steamy romantic thriller

Careless - Book Two, a steamy romantic thriller

Ruthless - Book Three, a steamy romantic thriller

SAN SOLOMAN

Keeping Kat, a steamy second-chance firefighter romance

Romancing Remi, a steamy enemies to lovers romance

Loving Lexie, a steamy cowboy enemies to lovers romance

Seducing Sadie, a steamy firefighter romance

Trusting Tenley, a dark second-chance romance

STANDALONES

Summer Shivers, a romantic thriller in the **Summers in Seaside Collection**

Overdrive, a steamy enemies to lovers romance **in KB WORLDS - DRIVEN COLLECTION**

Love Off The Rocks, a romantic comedy short

Pour Decisions, a romantic comedy novella in the **Girl Power Collection**

How to Ruin Your Ex's Wedding, a romantic comedy

I Heart Mason Cartwright, a romantic comedy

Rebel without a Claus, a M/M romance novella

Breaking Dylan, dark coming of age story

ANTHOLOGIES

GIRLS JUST WANNA HAVE FUNDAMENTAL RIGHTS - A Charity Anthology. Pre-order now. Releasing 9/8/22.

SEEDS OF LOVE A Romance Anthology to benefit Ukraine - Don't Break The Chain, a steamy romantic short

CAUGHT UNDER THE MISTLETOE - A Holiday Affair to Remember, a romantic comedy holiday short

STORYBOOK PUB CHRISTMAS WISHES - Mistle Oh-No, a romantic comedy holiday short

STORYBOOK PUB - Breezy Like Sunday Morning, a romantic comedy short

HOT AS F$#K SUMMER ROMANCE ANTHOLOGY - SULTRY SUMMER NIGHTS - Limited Release

LOCKED AND LOVED: An Isolated Romance Collection - Limited Release

SUMMER WITH YOU: Summer Shorts - Limited Release

JUST A LICK - Limited Release

LOVE LETTERS - Limited Release

STOCKING STUFFERS - Limited Release

SNEAK PEEK - LOVING LEXIE

LEXIE

Trevor freakin' Vaughn.

Here.

In the flesh.

The last person I ever thought I'd see again. Period. Let alone at this random hotel, thousands of miles from where he lives, AND when my besties and I are in the middle of a crisis.

Remi, my best friend, was just held hostage by her boyfriend Chance's ex, Helen.

Kat, my other best friend, and I had barely rescued Remi, with Chance's help, before Helen kidnapped him at gunpoint. So now we've got to try and save him.

Except we just bumped into Trevor.

Literally.

He's my ex. Twice over. And he's at this same hotel.

Of all the hotels in all the world, why this one? And at the same time that I'm here with Kat and Remi?

Crazy, right? I mean, the chances have got to be at least a million to one. Maybe more.

I look around, wondering if it's a joke. But my eyes can barely see beyond the broad chest in front of me. The one I just bounced off. I pat the pecs at eye level and nod appreciatively. He's filled out really well in the last few months. The shirt he's wearing does nothing to hide that fact, or the muscles in his arms, for that matter.

Was he this built before? Is he lifting farm animals for exercise instead of healing them?

Trevor's hands haven't left my shoulders from when he prevented me from falling backward after we ran into each other. The heat from his palms sear through my shirt, warming my skin from the outside in.

The hubbub of the elevator bay continues around us. Remi is talking at a high-pitched level and gesturing her arms around. Kat tugs at my phone, which I still have grasped in both my hands. Hotel guests jostle about.

But all I see is Trevor. He's had this effect on me since the first time we had sex, where I get all stupefied when he's near.

"Lexie," he breathes, his voice low and his expression soft. I sway toward him, wanting to feel him against me. I've missed him. I don't care that he disappeared without a word. I don't care about the crowds around us. Just one full body connection. One more time where every bit of me touches every bit of him—

"Trevor, thank God. Do you have a car?" Remi yells, yanking me out of Trevor's grasp, forcing me to hear her.

Shit!

I forgot about Remi.

And Chance!

We are in an emergency. I don't have time to deal with Trevor Vaughn right now.

Plus, I'm mad at him.

I forgot that too.

I move to Remi's side as Trevor turns toward her, his eyes widen, and his mouth falls open.

"My God, Remi. What happened to you? You were just fine earlier."

Wait? What?

"How would you know how she was earlier?" Kat asks.

"Trevor!" Remi yells, her voice shrill and panicked. "Focus! Do you have a car?"

"Yes," Trevor says. "I have a rental. I was going to have my car shipped, but then I gave it to a friend figuring I'd buy a new one when I got—"

"Don't mean to be rude," Remi says holding up her hand in front of his face. "But nobody cares about your plans. Where's the car?"

"In the parking garage," he says waving his arm in that general direction.

"Okay. What are we waiting for?" Kat says, grabbing both mine and Trevor's hands and pulling us back into a waiting elevator.

"Remi, is that why you didn't meet me at the bar?" Trevor asks. "Because you got hurt? What happened to you?"

Kat and Remi both ignore the question, so I answer.

"Remi's boyfriend's crazy ex-girlfriend, Helen, held Remi hostage and tortured her," I explain, finally finding my voice.

"And now she's kidnapped Chance, that's Remi's boyfriend, and . . . wait, you were meeting Remi at the bar?" I ask, surprised.

Remi punches the elevator button for the floor of the parking garage repeatedly. As if her finger connecting with the buttons will somehow make the elevator car lower us faster.

"Yeah. It was crazy that I ran into her," he says.

"I'm sure." I nod in understanding.

"I had some issues to handle back east, but that's all squared away." He puts his hands in his pockets and looks down at his feet. "It's why I left before. But, hey . . . I'm moving back to San Soloman. For good." He says this like it's the most natural thing in the world. Instead of something that is shaking me to the core.

For a second time.

Because the last time he was in town he did the same thing. Clearly that didn't last, because he left again.

"Moving back, huh?" Kat nods and makes a face that is part frown and part agreement.

"Great, one big happy fucking reunion . . . once again." Remi turns to look at us. "I know that this is probably rocking your world, Lex. And Trev, I'm sure your intentions are solid. At least they'd better be. But we can't do this right now. It's just . . . we need to focus on what's really important here." Her voice breaks, she clears her throat softly. "We need to go. Now. He could be lying somewhere in a ditch, hurt and bleeding. And I can't . . . I need . . . Can we just go? Please." The elevator doors open; she grabs Kat's hand and pulls her toward the rows of cars.

Trevor motions toward them, letting me exit the elevator first.

I can't move.

I want to move. I want to help Remi. I want to find Chance. I just can't move.

Trevor's coming back to San Soloman. Which is all I've wanted since the last time he left. Which makes me sound like a glutton for punishment. And maybe I am.

Shit.

The first time he left, I waited for years for him to finish his veterinary program and remember that he loves me and come home.

Which he did just over eight months ago.

And it was perfect. Everything I'd ever dreamed it would be. And I've got an active imagination, I can come up with some crazy romantic things. For close to two months, it was pure bliss.

Until he left again.

Without a word.

And now, after months with no contact he's back again and saying it's for good. No explanation, just back. I mean, I don't want to put too much hope in what it might mean for he and I as a couple. But I can't help myself.

It also doesn't help that I can rarely stay in the present. Give me a scenario and I'll push it years into the future in my imagination. I have to know, or at least be able to realistically envision, how something ends before I can accept it.

Which is why I can't move.

As long as I stay in the elevator, this is open ended. Anything could happen. Trevor could be here for me, again; I could be the reason he's moving back. We could get back together, and everything could be perfect once more.

But after I step out of the elevator, life goes on, and I must face reality. I don't know how this is going to play out. He's shocked me before. He can do it again.

"Come on, Lex. Pick up the fucking pace," Remi yells back at us, snapping her fingers. "Trevor, let's go! Which car is yours? Beep your lights."

Trevor unlocks his car remotely with one hand and grabs mine with the other as we head toward his car. His skin feels so smooth against mine. I wonder if he can feel the callouses on my palm.

He clears his throat. "I'm here for you, Lexie. All the way. One hundred percent. Here on the West Coast, here in this fancy hotel."

Well, that answers one question. But raises quite a few more. "How did you know I'd be here?" I ask, confused.

"I didn't. I'm here in the city for a night or so to tie up some loose ends. As luck would have it, I ran into Remi after I arrived this afternoon. We made plans to meet up at the hotel bar, only she never showed."

"So, you made plans with Remi, but you came *here* for me?"

"No . . . Yes . . . I didn't have a plan, Lexie. I guess I still don't. I saw Remi. I thought of you. I knew I wanted to get to you, I just didn't know how. I thought I could talk it out with Remi to find out where I stand with you. Then by the time I saw you, I'd have a plan. It just didn't work out that way. Don't get me wrong, I'm so happy to see you, plan or no plan. Especially, with how you and I left things."

"Wait. With how *you and I* left things? Are you kidding me?" I hiss. "You mean when you came back, and stayed with me for months, re-kindled our entire relationship, made promises about the future, then disappeared without a word? Is that the 'how you and I left things' you're referring to? Your memory is seriously selective, mister."

He nods in agreement.

"You have to explain, you know that, right? And that explanation needs to be really fucking good. But even then, I don't know if I can do this with you again. You hurt me, Trevor." My voice lowers to a hoarse whisper and my eyes flood with tears. "Goddammit!" I punch my thigh, tempted to also stomp my foot. I can be a crier. But I also hate it when I cry.

"I'm so sorry, Lexie," he says softly.

We reach Trevor's rental car, a large SUV. Kat and Remi are already situated in the back, leaving the front passenger seat for me. I look at them both, questioningly, not sure I want that degree of separation from them. Plus, I'm nervous to be this close to Trevor again.

"You have to navigate, remember?" Remi says, pointing to my phone. That's right.

Shit! I lost sight of what's important here AGAIN!

Worst. Friend. Ever.

The only reason we are even in Trevor's car is so that we can go find Chance. And the only way we'll find Chance is with the help of his friend, Alex—who does IT work for the police department—by tracing the tracker on Chance's police-issued phone. Alex is who I was texting when I ran into Trevor to begin with.

Get it together, Lex.

"I'm on it," I say, renewing my focus and sending my text to Alex. There is no way I am letting Remi down with this. She has finally found love and I'm not going to let her lose it just because her man has a psycho ex who kidnapped him.

And I have the attention span of a dog when it sees a squirrel.

Alex responds quickly with the address and wondering what's going on. I promise to fill him in later and input the address in the GPS to start navigation. It's going to take us fifteen minutes or so to get there. I give Trevor the starting directions and we head out of the structure and north on the main thoroughfare. This route will take us from the heart of the city, across the bridge, to a more suburban and spread out area with wider streets, and tree filled medians. Trevor takes the onramp for the bridge, leading us right into bumper to bumper traffic.

I hear Remi start to lose it in the backseat, crying softly and whispering furiously at Kat. It makes me wish I was back there with them.

"Sending you hugs, Remi," I say, not certain if she can hear me.

Trevor reaches over to grab my hand and squeezes it lightly. Then leaves it there, resting softly on mine. He glances over at me every few seconds until I finally glance back. "I came here, Lexie," he says, softly, "to remind you that we belong together."

I pull my hand back to my lap. "Trevor, it's been months, you left without a word after promising so much. You can't just come waltzing in and expect everything to be hunky dory," I hiss.

You tell him, Lexie. Be strong.

GIRL POWER.

"I don't expect anything of the kind." He looks sincere. "If anything, I know I need to work hard to prove I'm worthy of you, to win back your heart. I know what happened was my fault. And I know that I am more than a fair share to blame for . . . what happened."

"Trevor, you are one hundred percent to blame for *what happened*. You—" We make it off the bridge and the phone buzzes, alerting me to the next direction. "Turn right at the next light."

He nods.

The car quiets for a moment. I don't feel like picking up the argument again. At least not verbally. I'd rather fuel my fire for why I'm so angry at Trevor.

I have plenty of reasons to spurn him, ranging from today to five years ago. Trevor and I first met during the last year of undergrad. We were partnered in a BioChem class. What began as a platonic friendship, turned into crazy, frantic sex late one night in a library study room. One day we were friends, the next day we were a couple. Just like that. We got an apartment together, made plans to attend the same grad school, and pretty much planned out our entire lives.

And it was fan-fucking-tastic.

Until it wasn't.

Because he didn't get into the grad program at San Soloman University (SSU), where we'd planned on attending together. It still pisses me off even though logically I know it's not *fair* to be mad about something like grad school admissions. Especially since the vet program at SSU is a highly competitive program. Doesn't matter. We had a plan and he screwed it all up. By not being smart enough to get accepted. And when he fucked that up, he fucked up everything else as well.

So, we agreed to table our relationship until after he finished his vet program. Between the distance and our studies, continuing to try and see one another would have been next to impossible. We broke up. He left.

Soon after, both Kat and Remi left as well. Remi to graduate school down south, Kat to law school up north, but that was okay, I was expecting the two of them to leave. And I still had my family and other friends. I made do.

Until I couldn't.

Because just over a year after that I lost both my parents and my twin brother in a plane crash during winter break.

They were coming to visit me for the holidays.

And they died.

The plane went down, there were no survivors.

I went from having everything to having nothing. Everyone I loved was gone, one way or another. I managed. I pretended to move on. At least that's what I told everyone I was doing.

Except I didn't move on. I didn't date. I didn't go out. I let no one get close. I barely talked to people outside of classes and my studies. I figured it would get better once I graduated and started my winery.

But it didn't.

Even still, I limit most social interaction to events at my winery, the occasional meal with Mavis, and meeting Kat and Remi for dinner and/or drinks.

Then Trevor showed up earlier this year out of the blue and pieced me back together again. After that, I was good, solid, whole even.

Right up until he vanished without a word and broke me all over again.

But he's here now.

Again.

And I don't know what the fuck to do with him.

Get your copy of Loving Lexie here

ACKNOWLEDGMENTS

(FROM THE ORIGINAL PUBLISHING OF THIS BOOK AS LOVE UNDISCOVERED - ROMANCING REMI IS A NEW VERSION OF THAT BOOK)

I really love Remi and her story, I hope you do too. I miss her now that she's finished. Maybe she needs a follow-up novella...

She never would have happened without the assistance and support from a whole freakin' team of people.

My amazingly talented critique partners:

-**Rachel Radner** – Seriously, girl. Thank you seems so inadequate for the impact that you have on my stories and my writing. You always understand where I want to go, and then you get me there. You're a strength to my weaknesses and a light to my darkness. And at the risk of sounding even more emo, I don't know what I'd do without you. For real.

-**Lauren Campbell** – I know we are still in our honeymoon phase, but I'm going to say thank you nonetheless for giving it to me straight, right out the gate.

-**Victoria Bright** – Okay, so we never trade shit anymore. But you are still a PM away whenever I need you. For that, I am grateful.

Ellie McLove, Gray Ink – I know I'm an asshole. Thank you for sticking with me. I do so very much adore you.

Linda Russell, Foreword PR – I can't believe it's already our second book together. No matter what my question or concern is, you answer it/handle it/fix it/make it better, and all the while with smileys and hearts and a positive attitude. Even when I do stupid stuff right before release. You are a gem among gems. And your heart emojis are never annoying.

Shari Ryan, Madhat Books – You are one talented woman. Like, crazy good talent. Thank you for sharing that talent with me.

My Beta Girls – **Sue Henn**, **Jamie Gray**, and **Lora Hasse** – I gave you each an insanely long list of requirements and you delivered. I appreciate you. Thank you.

To my ARC Readers – I'm sorry you had to slog through a messy draft. Thank you for seeing the story through my mistakes.

Gabriela Scavella-Bell – It's only recently that I realized how fun your entire name is to say. Now I can't refer to you in my head, or otherwise, without saying the whole thing. I'm fortunate we've reconnected; your support and critiques are invaluable.

Scott Hoxie - your insight on rugby players and all their dirty deeds was not only helpful, but fascinating. Your time is very much appreciated. Any mistakes are mine and not his.

Stephie Walls – You just kick ass, bestie! I will never stop singing your praises forevermore. Thank you for imparting your wisdom and so freely sharing your time.

To **Carter** and **Taylor** – You're so awesome that I had to name characters after you.

My **Remi IRL** – If you weren't you, I wouldn't have Remi. Or you. I love you.

NOTE: Every male MC I write is comprised of various aspects of BW. Whether they be physical traits, personality quirks, or verbiage used. One thing stays true amongst them all, and that is they know how to treat a woman right. How to help her feel unique, loved, and supported; all the while keeping life light and fun. So…

BW – Thank you, babe, not only for the inspiration, but for this insanely incredible life of ours. I love you.

PS - I kid you not, our wedding song just came on in the playlist I'm listening to while writing BW's portion of my acknowledgements today. (Someone Like You by Van Morrison.) That is some crazy fucking kismet right there.